PRAISE FOR *THE OTHER MOCTEZUMA GIRLS*

"Robleda is quickly becoming a historical fiction powerhouse. *The Other Moctezuma Girls* is a superb reclamation of history rarely seen through the lens of women who endured, researched intelligently and written with heart. A deeply moving portrait of sisterhood, family, power, and legacy, full of love and defiance. Robleda has a true gift for centering voices history often overlooks. I adored every page."

—Mariely Lares, international bestselling author of *Sun of Blood and Ruin*

"An epic of inheritance, resilience, and discovery, this novel carries readers from the heart of Tenochtitlan to the farthest edges of the Valley of Mexico with breathtaking beauty and peril. A luminous blend of history, legend, and adventure, it captures the pulse of a world remade by conquest and the fierce spirit of those who refused to be erased. Robleda delivers a tale so absorbing it claimed me completely—I loved this book."

—Carolina Flórez-Cerchiaro, author of *Bochica*

"Overflowing with suspense and heart-wrenching emotions, Robleda's novel weaves a riveting drama that's a love letter to the beauty and depth of Mexican history."

—Liana De la Rosa, *USA Today* bestselling author

"A rare glimpse into the little-known history of Tecuichpoch, thoughtfully and vividly brought to life through her daughter Isabel and the adventure she embarks on to piece together her family legacy."

—Eve J. Chung, *USA Today* bestselling author of *Daughters of Shandong*

"Gorgeously written and intricately woven with Aztec heritage, *The Other Moctezuma Girls* provides a thrilling adventure full of self-discovery and familial healing. A powerful portrait of the hardship yet beauty that is survival."

—O.O. Sangoyomi, author of *Masquerade*

THE OTHER MOCTEZUMA GIRLS

OTHER TITLES BY SOFIA ROBLEDA

Daughter of Fire

THE OTHER MOCTEZUMA GIRLS

A NOVEL

SOFIA ROBLEDA

Published by Amazon Crossing, Seattle
www.apub.com

EU product safety contact:
Amazon Media EU S. à r.l.
38, avenue John F. Kennedy, L-1855 Luxembourg
amazonpublishing-gpsr@amazon.com

ISBN-13: 9781662532504 (paperback)
ISBN-13: 9781662532498 (digital)

Cover design by Emily Mahar
Cover image: © Andrii-Oliinyk, © Anzhela Shakriyeva, © Elena Smirnova, © Maria Tolkacheva, © Toltemara / Getty; © Arthur Balitskii, © Shonyjade / Shutterstock

Printed in the United States of America

This book is dedicated to three Lucías: my mother and sister, who loved my stories from the beginning, and to my baby niece, Lucía Manzano Gutierrez . . . who was taken from our family too soon.

Valley of
Mexico
1551
Lake Zumpango
Lake Xaltocan
Coatepec Hill
Cuauhtitlan
Teotihuacan
Chiconautla
Alcoman
Sierra de Guadalupe
Ecatepec
Texcoco
Huexotla
Tenayuca
Atzacoalco
Shrine of Guadalupe
Tepeyac
Azcapotzalco
Tlacopan
Tacuba
Lake Texcoco
Tenochtitlan
Viceroy's Palace
Chapultepec
Chimalhuacan
Mixcoac
Coyoacan
Iztapalapa
Tizapan
Strait of Culhuacan
Iztapalpa Peninsula
Ixtapaluca
Lake Xochimilco
Lake Chalco
Three Skull Island
Iztaccihuatl
Sierra de las Cruces
Xochimilco
Chalco
Popocatepetl

THE ENEMY OF MY ENEMY IS MY FRIEND

Before the arrival of the Spanish, the valley that was known by its Nahuatl-speaking inhabitants as Anahuac was divided into several nations. The most powerful of all were the Mexica, more commonly known in the present day as the Aztec people.

They, along with the people of Texcoco and Tlacopan, had formed an incredibly successful alliance, an empire that stretched from the Pacific Ocean to the Gulf of Mexico, governed from the famed island city of Tenochtitlan, a city made abundantly rich by the constant tribute flowing into it from other nations across the land.

In February 1519, the Spanish conquistador Hernán Cortés sailed from the colony of Cuba to the coast of Yucatán and, through the help of his Indigenous interpreter Malinalli, quickly grasped and took advantage of the fraught political landscape and the deep resentment toward Tenochtitlan and the Mexica. Despite initial resistance, he began to amass the support of thousands of Indigenous people who desired nothing more than to overthrow the Mexica Empire, whose ruler at the time was Moctezuma Xocoyotzin.

Cortés was welcomed into Tenochtitlan in November 1519 with his small army of almost five hundred conquistadores and over a thousand Tlaxcalteca warriors, the Mexica's worst enemies.

Moctezuma Xocoyotzin was playing a game of stealth, a game he lost along with his life, and the lives of most of his children, estimated to have numbered between twenty and over a hundred. His daughter Tecuichpoch, baptized Isabel Moctezuma, was one of four who survived.

A BRIEF AND NONEXHAUSTIVE NOTE ON NAHUATL PRONUNCIATION

This is not meant to be a lesson; it is simply a note for those readers who are genuinely curious about how to pronounce the Nahuatl words sprinkled in this text. I hope these very basic principles will help as you read along.

First, the stress or accent in Nahuatl words nearly always falls on the second-to-last syllable, so you would say "Tenoch*ti*tlan," not "Tenochti*tlan*."

The *x* is pronounced as *sh* for *sugar*. Thus, you would pronounce Mexica as "Me*shi*ca."

The double *ll* is pronounced as a single *l*, held for slightly longer.

The *tl* sound exists in English, such as in the word *kettle*. But when it falls at the end of a word, it is much softer: You pronounce the *l* while gently holding the tip of your tongue against your teeth. For example, a name like Axayacatl is pronounced "Asha*ya*cal."

At times, the ending of names may change, such as Axayacatl to Axayacatzin or Tecuichpoch to Tecuichpochtzin. The *-tzin* suffix is simply an honorific, denoting fondness, respect, reverence, or submission on behalf of the speaker, which I have kept because it is culturally relevant and achingly poetic to me.

I have also kept many of the original Nahuatl names for English words, such as tomatl (tomato), ahuacatl (avocado), chocolatl (chocolate), and tamalli (tamales), because it is important to me that people today realize where these words and products come from.

Finally, I have also kept the more familiar Moctezuma instead of the Nahuatl Moteucsoma, because it is the family name that his descendants carry today.

ISABEL MOCTEZUMA FAMILY TREE

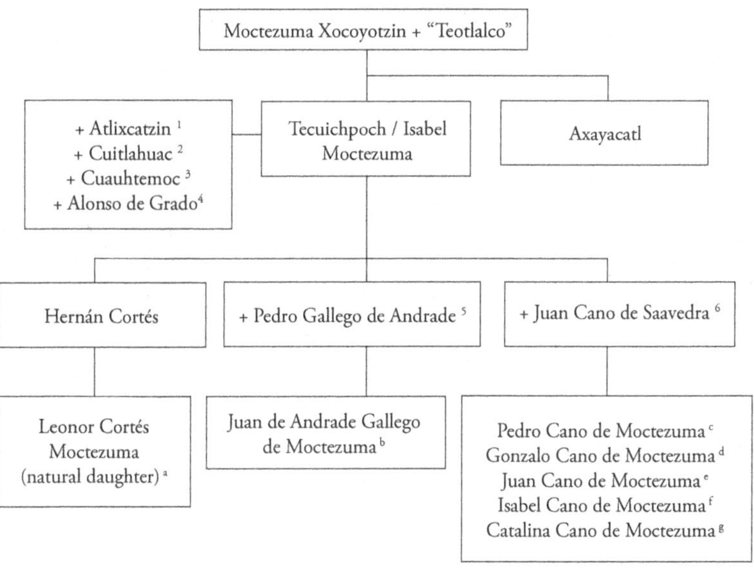

+ Isabel's husbands
1–6 Order of Isabel's husbands
a–g Birth order of Isabel's children

You died among the mesquite plants of the Seven Caves.
The eagle was calling, the jaguar cried.
And you, a red flamingo, went flying onwards,
from the midst of a field to a place unknown.

—Adapted from *Cantares Mexicanos*, Song XXXIII, translated by John Bierhorst

CHAPTER 1

Isabel Cano

19 February 1551

Four groups of black-clad mourners lingered in the bleak antechamber of the courthouse, silent except for the soft rustling of slippers and capes; a dozen uneven, impatient breaths; and the occasional clearing of a throat. The type of heavy silence that spoke of nervous anticipation, of barely repressed tension mingled with the pressure of decorum. The respectful way one was expected to act while waiting to hear the contents of one of the most important wills of this generation. My mother's will.

Our mother's will, for there were seven of us, all in attendance. Not that we gave any indication of those good, amiable feelings one might associate with being near your closest kin. No comforting gestures, no holding of hands, no sharing of handkerchiefs. There were no tears anyway. Not for us, *never* for us Moctezumas.

We all stood, rigid as players in a ball game, waiting for the beat of the deadly drum to spur us into our final fight. My stomach coiled, and a pang of sorrow rang through my hollow chest at the realization that Nantzin had been the only one who could temper us with her presence and bring us together. The threads between most of us had loosened and thinned over time, but they had been there. Now, the only things that marked us as siblings were the identical rings on our fingers with Nantzin's eagle-and-snake crest, gleaming under the flickering candlelight.

The jarring sound of multiple door hinges thirsting for oil made us all turn and immediately line up in a bustle of rippling skirts and a quick smoothing of veils and straightening of feathered hats. Wordlessly, we arranged ourselves by order of status and birth, the way we had rehearsed and performed in hundreds of dinners and banquets and daily at Mass. Except now we were missing our most important and beloved member, Nantzin, the name for *mother* in Nahuatl. What we had always called her.

My father, Juan Cano, Nantzin's widower, headed the procession at a steady pace. He strode past the guards flanking the elaborate, heavy doors and into the dim courtroom beside his heir, my full brother Pedro, the third of Nantzin's seven children. Between them and us youngest girls marched Gonzalo and Nano, heads held in a high, gallant gesture, which I tried to imitate. Beside me, my little sister, Catina, lowered her own head and grabbed my slick, cold palm with trembling fingers.

Behind us, and grinding his teeth so loudly I could hear it, walked my half brother, Andrade, with his wife. For though he was older than Pedro and married, my father and our family, the Canos, took precedence over his. And I needed not turn to know that behind him trailed my half sister, Leonor Cortés, all by herself.

She was the firstborn child, and recently married, but her status as a natural-born daughter, the only one of us conceived out of wedlock, sealed her position. It did not matter that her father was the most famous man in the world, or that his title outranked my father's, or that she was legitimized by the pope himself. In relation to this family, she had to walk in last. I had felt pity for her once, but she was so awful I no longer cared.

My father, Juan Cano, made straight for the seats of honor opposite the judge's broad writing desk. My four full siblings and I took the seats surrounding him, leaning toward him like chicks longing for the underside of their mother's wing. In many ways he seemed more lost than us children, though he held up his balding head proudly. Beside him, my two older brothers Pedro and Gonzalo glared at the small crowd flocking through the doorway.

I arranged my skirts behind them, in between Catina and Nano, the only two people I had any true affection for, aside from my father. Our knees touched the backs of their three chairs. Everyone else spread about the room, standing a few steps away, looking either respectful or wary of the invisible plume of sorrow we emanated.

Towering behind us like a set of grim, stained gargoyles were Nantzin's witnesses: important, respected men from the highest ranks of New Spain society. Men I had not realized Nantzin held more than a passing acquaintance with.

Andrade positioned himself to our right, near the two narrow windows. His first name was also Juan, but we had always called him by his father's last name. His back was straight and his round face impassive. He held hands with his beautiful young wife, and never once looked in our direction, which hurt, for he was my second-favorite brother.

My absolute favorite was my full brother Nano, older than me by nearly two years. His real name, to be truthful, was also Juan. Indeed, it seemed that our family, and society as a whole, did not believe creativity was a virtue when naming children. A name ought to be biblical, preferably apostolic, or you might as well have no children at all. Now, if I ever felt the absurd desire to have children, and I thought I never would, I'd give them a memorable name. Something like Scheherazade, or Cipac, meaning *alligator* in Nahuatl. I'd like my children's very names to make the rotten people of this city squirm in their gilded seats.

Almost as if he sensed my dark mood, Nano shifted beside me. His chair creaked as I stole a glance at him. He was studying the large portrait hanging on the elaborately carved oak-paneled wall behind the judge's desk, of our heavy-jawed emperor, Carlos V, wearing the outfit his male subjects aspired to replicate each day—a somber black doublet and breeches with white stockings and pointed slippers, matching ruff collars and frilly cuffs on his wrists. Nano's frilled wrists were crossed, and the bored expression on his face was all too familiar, but his leg was bobbing up and down, a sign of anxiety, which filtered into me.

My breath quickened as I remembered that soon, everyone would know Nantzin's wishes for my future. My knee bounced in tempo with Nano's, and I fought the urge to pull at the pearl necklace choking my neck. I flicked my black veil behind my shoulders. How much longer would we need to sit in this stifling cave of a room? We had already waited for hours in that antechamber, and my patience was frayed.

The men's murmurs set my teeth on edge. I looked to our left, slightly behind us, toward the door, wishing I could just leave. Next to it and standing alone in the shadows was Leonor. We rarely saw her, and hadn't seen her once since Nantzin's passing over a month ago. Whenever we did, she had a tendency to look down her perfectly straight nose at us. It wasn't hard to. She was statuesque, majestic, a monolith of a woman, and we Canos were . . . well, we were all rather short.

Leonor caught my eye and sneered.

I scoffed, rolled my eyes, and turned away. In truth, however, a tinge of sadness pulled in my chest. It would've been nice to have grown up with an elegant older sister instead of four reckless, stupid older brothers who loved nothing more than to swear and wrestle and hunt. Perhaps I would've turned out better—sweeter, gentler, more like Nantzin. I had Catina, of course, but she was the youngest and painfully shy, sometimes even with me.

Finally, one of the guards announced the judge, who came trotting inside the room, begging pardon. We stood to curtsy and bow and sat back down after two young clerks carrying thick leather sleeves containing wads of papers followed him in. They stood on either side of him after he sat down on the ornate, high-backed chair behind the desk.

He nodded at all of us and stretched out his palm, and one of the clerks handed him one of the sleeves. He set it down on the desk, opened it, and began. "Hereby I read the last will and testament of Isabel Moctezuma, daughter and heir to the late deposed Emperor Moctezuma Xocoyotzin, signed tenth December 1550."

He crossed himself and everyone in the room followed suit. "In the name of the Holiest Trinity, Father, Son, and Holy Spirit, three beings and one single true God, who lives and reigns forever. I, Isabel Moctezuma, legitimate wife of Juan Cano, neighbor of Tenochtitlan, the city of Mexico, being ill of body but sound of mind and judgment and natural understanding, with license and faculty and with express consent, demand and order my extensive testament and will to be actioned by . . ."

Nano and I rolled our eyes at each other. It was going to be a long morning.

The judge took a sip of water, and I tried to focus again, but his plump lips droned on, and I simply could not reconcile the convoluted string of words entering my ears with Nantzin's soft feminine voice and modest vernacular. She'd had a light accent too, whenever she spoke Castilian, which she almost never did to us. Where was she in this mess of a document? What was the point of all this preamble? Why did we have to come here at all?

It was not until my brothers in front of me hissed that I came back to my senses and caught the last part of the judge's statement: "All my men and women, born from this land. I order them to be free of all servitude and captivity. As free people they shall do as they will. I command them, if they are slaves, to be free."

"But . . . all of them?" asked Gonzalo. Papa nodded and shushed him.

The judge continued as though there had been no interruption. "A fifth of my goods must be disposed of and the proceeds spent on masses, almsgiving, and charitable works for the salvation of my soul and conscience."

"A fifth!" whispered Nano into my ear. "What a waste."

"I hereby swear that I revoke, annul, and deny any other testaments, codices, clauses, legalities, or statements that I have made or opened in any other prior manner, whether written or spoken, and I hereby give my executors power to revoke and nullify these false and worthless legacies."

By the window, my brother Andrade made a gesture to his wife, who shook her head.

"My merchant goods, canvases, and linens from this country and Castile, upholsteries, tapestries, and rugs, cushions, embossed leathers, personal dresses, and all other textiles and cloths must not be sold but instead given to my legitimate daughters, Isabel and Catalina Cano de Moctezuma, who must also receive one-third of proceeds from any and all other goods sold at auction."

"Not bad, sis. Not bad," murmured Nano. I shushed him and squeezed Catina's hand twice. She took out a tiny notebook and a fine charcoal stick from her purse, and I wrote, *We get tapestries.* She gave me a small frown, which made sense when the next part was read.

"These proceeds must be used to pay for their entry fees into El Convento de la Concepción de la Madre de Dios and in support of their express wishes to dedicate their lives to upholding their virtue in the name of our most Holy Lord and Savior, Jesus Christ."

In other words, we had agreed to become nuns and live the remainder of our lives in a convent. So what was the point of beautiful rugs, cushions, and tapestries if we'd be living in a place that forbade them? From the corner of my eye, Nano gave me a puzzled look.

I hadn't told him. I hadn't told anyone. Only Papa and Catina knew.

A cold sweat broke over my brow. I hadn't even donned the habit yet and already I felt it constricting my body. Why had Nantzin ever entertained this ridiculous notion? Why had *I*? I could not believe she had decided this for me—did she not know me at all? Or maybe she did. Most girls my age avoided me, not that I wished for their company. But they seemed to know what an almighty mess I was, an utter catastrophe, the complete opposite of what a lady ought to be, no matter how hard I tried. Perhaps this was the best thing she could think to do for me. But who were we fooling? Certainly not my brother, who was practically bending forward now, determined to catch my eye.

We were both distracted, however, when the judge read the following statement: "I order that my encomienda, the town of Tacuba, be given to my eldest legitimate son, Juan de Andrade Gallego de Moctezuma, son of my deceased husband, Pedro Gallego de Andrade. It is my express volition that Juan de Andrade Gallego de Moctezuma possess it, and afterward his heirs and successors, in perpetuity, forevermore."

Even the judge fell silent. We'd all expected Andrade to take the lion's share of Nantzin's encomiendas, the land and labor grants given to her by the Crown. But there it was. Tacuba, the largest encomienda in the Valley of Mexico. Everyone living there, including us, would pay tribute to him now. He lifted his head and smiled for the first time, then kissed his wife's hand. She was glowing, which was not surprising. They were rich beyond measure.

Then the judge went on, struggling with forming the Nahuatl words on his Castilian tongue, but nevertheless trying. "My towns of . . . of Ocoyoacac, Chapulmaloyan, Coatepec, and Tepexoyuca, I give and inherit to my legitimate son Gonzalo Cano, and afterward—"

"Hold on—that's not right." Andrade's smile was gone.

Nano elbowed me, his face alert and alight with interest now. I elbowed him back, hard, a warning to keep himself in check, and because it pleased me to watch him wince.

"Do not interrupt, Señor Andrade," said one of the clerks.

My brother was not cowed. "I was assured those towns would be left under my name."

In front of me, Pedro bristled and barked back, "Clearly that's not what her will says."

"Any matters arising will need to be taken up to the court separately," said the other clerk. There was more grumbling and muttering, but the judge simply went on. "To my eldest, my natural daughter Leonor Cortés de Moctezuma, recognized and legitimized by His Holiness the Pope as the rightful child of Hernán Cortés, I leave six hundred pesos de oro—"

"Mother of Christ!" Andrade and Pedro swore at the same time.

Pedro stood up. Father pulled on his sleeve and begged him to settle down, but he kept on shouting. "That's an outrage!"

I understood their confusion. Six hundred gold pesos was an incredible sum. Why was Nantzin leaving a fortune to a daughter she'd hardly ever seen? An illegitimate daughter who was already wealthier than any of us would ever be?

For her part, Leonor simply nodded at the judge and one of the executors, her face devoid of feeling. She opened the door and stepped out. Right before it shut, she turned and looked straight at me, raised a brow, then walked away.

It was Catina's turn to give me an odd look. She'd seen Leonor's gesture too. I shrugged in confusion, then gawked as all the other men in my family sprung to their feet and started shouting. That was something we did quite well, in fact.

We were useless at crying, but by God, could we roar.

My father and brothers began swearing at Andrade, who placed himself in front of his wife and bellowed back, along with the clerks. The judge and a few of the executors were stunned into silence. Some chimed in, though I couldn't make out what they were saying. Two of them, both priests, shook their heads. The others smirked, clearly enjoying the spectacle.

No doubt by this evening it would be the juiciest piece of gossip in the viceroyal court, the way the Moctezumas had turned on each other like vagrants brawling over crumbs. For a brief moment I envied Catina's deafness, for she couldn't hear the ugly things being shouted: cabrón, pendejo, cobarde, bellaco—*cuckold*, *moron*, *coward*, *knave*.

I stole a glance at her, and realized she didn't need to. All their hurt, their resentment, their rage was plain on their faces. Our family had finally shattered, and there was no way of hiding it, of knowing where we'd gone wrong, where and how we'd begun to drift so far apart.

And now, there was no way of turning back. The only person standing beside me now was Catina, whose tears had begun to stream down her freckled cheeks. My gut twisted, because there was nothing I hated more than seeing my sister cry.

Worse still, I was afraid that soon enough I might not be able to hold back either my tears or my temper, which would be disastrous. The tears would dishonor Nantzin, the temper my father, no matter that he was screaming too. I had to get us away from this mess.

Without waiting for permission, I grabbed Catina's hand again and, just as I'd seen Leonor do, nodded in the direction of the judge and the executors, then turned and left the rest of them behind.

CHAPTER 2

Isabel Cano

19 February 1551

We emerged from the dark town hall onto the steps facing the Plaza Mayor, the grand, bustling center of our great island city, Tenochtitlan. She was proud and thorny, like me. A city used to violent change, built atop an unwanted, briny swamp within a valley surrounded by volcanoes. She had overcome floods, earthquakes, and fiery eruptions. But there was a current of uncertainty, perhaps, of loss, of who exactly she was since the Spanish had taken a sword to her succulent flesh and rebuilt her in their image, since they'd replaced her colorful pyramids with fortlike palaces, her conchs with bells, her canoes with horses.

It was not a friendly time, nor a friendly place to be. People walked in huddles and pairs straight to their destinations, hardly sparing a second glance to those they did not know. The seeping wound of conquest and the swift crushing of a dozen desperate rebellions was ever present, ever raw. This year would mark the thirtieth anniversary of the city's surrender. The last viceroy had spoken of monthlong festivities, but now he was gone, replaced only in the last year, and it was anyone's guess what the new one would be like.

Catina dabbed her eyes and snuggled against me as a chill, humid gust battered our skirts. Darkening clouds threatened a cold shower. I scanned the busy square for our carriage, but I couldn't see it. I stood on my tiptoes to see if it had been moved to the viceroy's palace to our immediate right, a long, tall, rectangular building meant to have been Cortés's home. He'd not lived to see it completed, and then the government had taken it from his family.

This, of course, gave me great satisfaction, because those perfectly cut quarry stones and auburn tezontle, a volcanic rock, had once been ours. Or Grandfather's, at least. Nantzin had always made a point to touch them, whenever we passed by. She said they were her silent witnesses. She had been born under their protection. When the Spanish attacked, they'd kept her alive. After Grandfather's empire crumbled, they'd survived and reshaped themselves into something new, just like she had.

I could almost see her there, in the palace corner, placing her tanned, slender fingertips against the towering wall. I swallowed the knot tightening around my throat, rubbed my prickling nose, looked up, and forced back the burgeoning tears. I longed for a release from this awful feeling, like I'd been set adrift in a deep, dark sea, with no paddle, no anchor, no sail, and not a single guiding star.

What was I going to do? How would I survive without her?

Catina tugged on my sleeve and whispered, "I can't see the carriage anywhere."

I shook my head and let out a long breath, and my gaze fell on the line of horses tied to the wooden hitching posts next to the entrance, four of which were my family's. The promise of trouble was a balm, a rush. The knot in my throat loosened, and my stomach leapt. I tapped her shoulder and pointed at them, a sly, dangerous smile tugging my lips.

"No, Isabel, we shouldn't," she said.

I held back the urge to call her a coward, clicked my tongue, and gestured for her to move. Our heels clattered and echoed down the stone steps.

"At least take Nano's mare," she pleaded.

"Where's the fun in that?" I gestured using Hand Talk, another gift of Nantzin's.

After both Catina and I had recovered from a terrible fever and we realized she had been left permanently deaf, Nantzin had found an Indigenous man from the far north, who'd tried to teach us all how to communicate using our bodies.

I say *tried* because only Nantzin, Nano, Catina, and I managed to learn. Papa was never home, and our oldest brothers didn't care enough to master even the basics. In the years since, my sister, Nano, and I had added our own signs and expanded our secret language until it seemed as though no one outside our circle would ever truly understand us.

"Father's ordered us to go home," I lied to one of the lackeys guarding the horses. He apologized and explained the carriage had been taken away for a wheel repair, as he'd thought we wouldn't be needing it for another few hours.

"Never mind, we'll take that one." I pointed at Pedro's stallion, and although Catina shook her head at me, she didn't argue anymore.

The lackey helped us onto the saddle. We both knew Pedro would be livid, but very few things made me happier than seeing his ugly face flushed with rage. Catina would never admit it, but deep down I knew his ridiculous fits amused her too.

My sister held on to my waist from behind, and we began the trot home, trailed by another one of Father's armed men, past the grand houses of commerce and Cortés's second palace on the east side of the main square. We followed the straight cobbled streets out of the traza, the designated area at the heart of the city where only full-blooded, highborn Spaniards were allowed to live. We had to slow down to a walk as we joined the long, congested avenue dividing the districts of San Juan and Santa Maria, where the more prominent Mexica families resided. Other Nahua people lived here too, now, like the Tlaxcalteca and Otomí, who'd been my grandfather's deadliest enemies.

This was all water under the causeway now. Or at least that's what we had to pretend.

I concentrated on maneuvering the horse over the busy dirt road. There were people everywhere, vendors selling crayfish and green nohpalli cactus paddles, woven baskets, colorful cotton cloth, and animal pelts. The multitude of smells and sounds were dizzying, overpowering. Tradespeople wheeled carts, tiny stray dogs barked, and parrots squawked. By the side of the road, next to a ceramics stall, an old Mexica woman balancing a basket with two chickens dropped to her knees.

"Tlahtocacihuapilli!" *Great ladies,* she shouted in a clear voice, keeping her eyes firmly on the ground as a mark of respect. The chicken basket barely wobbled.

"Bless your heart, grandmother," I replied in Nahuatl. We kept moving, but I could tell she heard me, because she smiled. Many others recognized us, both Spaniards and Indígenas alike. Some pointed and whispered. A few even shouted their condolences, their prayers for Nantzin. They called out her many names and titles—Doña Isabel, the Lady of Tacuba, Tecuichpochtzin, princess, empress. They blessed her soul in heaven.

Catina buried her face into my shoulder blades, and I forced myself to nod and wave back in gratitude, though it felt like a farce. As certainly as I knew that my sister would never hear again, I knew that I would never measure up to Nantzin. But this was the least I could do for the people she had loved.

I breathed a sigh of relief when we crossed through to the quieter chinampas of the west side of the city, the lush, perfectly square artificial islands where the common people lived and worked, in and among endless crisscrossing canals. Finally, the view of the lake opened up in front of us and we reached the causeway, one of the four long road-like structures stretching over the great body of water and connecting the city to the surrounding mainland.

There were fewer people now, only a couple of fishermen trying out their luck with wide nets and long poles. I pushed the horse to a canter now. The animal's steps synced with the glistening brown-green waves lapping on the reeds and water lilies bordering both sides of the densely packed dirt bridge. The clouds parted for a moment, and a fresh breeze circled down from the volcanoes surrounding the valley, filling my nostrils with the scent of pine and liquidambar resin, and flapping my veil behind my ears.

The hills and forests of the mainland drew near. We passed by poorer thatched-house compounds built on land reclaimed from the shallow lake, and followed the mainland road for a quarter of an hour or so, until we reached Tacuba, Nantzin's town.

No, not Nantzin's anymore, Andrade's.

For a moment I wondered whether our half brother would force us out of our own home, but then I remembered that bit of land was in Papa's name. More likely that Andrade would never set foot through our doors ever again, not without a bloody fight. The thought made my shoulders drop. The weight of sadness lay heavy on my chest, as though I could feel the physical gorge between all of us, the canyon separating us for good, from each other and from Nantzin.

How was it possible that I would never see her again? That we would never walk through the gardens together, that she would never tell Catina and me stories of the old gods using only her hands? With my left hand, still holding the reins, I made the sign of the hummingbird. The sign we had made up for Huitzilopochtli, the sun god of war who had guided Nantzin's people to our city of Tenochtitlan. Perhaps he would guide me too.

"I can't wait for a warm bath," said Catina, breaking me out of my dark, blasphemous thoughts. High in the near distance, our home had come into view. Next to the lake, surrounded by trees, our two-story palace had been built out of quarry stone on top of a huge rocky outcrop. It was a Spanish-style building, with intricately carved arched windows and wrought iron balconies draped by plants and ferns. The heads of armed sentries bobbed along the rooftop parapet, looking out onto the busy, canoe-filled lake and the road, though there had never once been an attack on our home, even at the height of the rebellions.

We turned into the side road leading to our father's property. Once we were let through the huge main gate, we began the climb up a cobbled path framed by a multitude of trees and flowers. Every season we had a different variety, magnolias in spring, dahlias in summer, cempohualxochitl in autumn, and now, bright-red-and-white cuetlaxochitl, the Christmas Eve flower, which Nantzin had said was Grandfather's favorite.

Two gardeners took off their straw hats and greeted us with warm, reverent smiles. I returned one with a nod of my head, but inside, I felt a twist of unease. They had been enslaved for decades. I wondered what they would do once they found out they were free. Would they want to stay? They were not poorly treated, and seemed happy enough, but was true happiness possible if one never had a choice, a say in one's life?

A thick, towering convent door shut in my mind's eye. Bile rose and clogged my throat. I was ashamed of my selfishness, for never truly considering it before. Only now, when I was faced with a choice I could not escape.

Indeed, if they all left us, I would understand.

I pushed the horse forward. I couldn't wait a moment longer. Marta, our governess, and one of the stable hands ran out to greet us by the main door.

The boy helped us off as Marta fussed and fretted all over us. She was a distant relation of Papa's, an older spinster from a poorer family who'd thought to try her luck at finding a husband in the New World, as many other ill-starred Spanish women had done. She'd finally married the love of her life, almost two months after her arrival. But he'd died four years later, from some plague or another. Even now she wore black, though grief hadn't marred her good heart. Papa had taken her in so she could teach us proper Spanish manners, so she said. I wouldn't say she'd succeeded with me.

"You rode all the way? Astride too? In broad daylight! What about your ankles! Your—your shins, even! Santa Maria, what a disgrace. It's a miracle your skirt isn't ripped."

"Catina rode sidesaddle," I mumbled at her. At the same time, I signed to my sister, "I need to be alone."

She looked into my eyes for a brief moment and nodded.

Marta kept bombarding me. "What are you saying to your poor sister—you better not be leading her astray again. Why didn't you take the carriage? And where are your father and brothers? What will poor Pedro do without his horse? He'll be in a right state!"

I took my veil off and handed it to her. "Marta, please—Catina wants a bath."

I gave both of them a kiss and walked off, away from the house, toward a second set of stairs leading down the slope of the hill and straight into our private walled garden.

"Young lady, you better come back in one piece before your father gets home!"

Hidden behind the trunk of a dying ahuacatl tree was a small, thick wooden door. It was meant to be locked at all times, but the key had been lost years ago, and no one had replaced it. The door led to more steps, which had been carved into the outline of the cliff, winding back toward the lake. I climbed down the familiar route and reached the bank, a sloping layer of pebbles and grass expanding over a bed of silt.

I took off my heels and counted a thousand steps to an old gnarled oak, knowing Marta would have a fit over the state of my hem and stockings. I'd probably need to bury the latter. When I reached the tree, I took a left turn, back into the forest.

In another quarter of an hour, I'd reached my destination, the abandoned dovecote. It had been built to breed turkeys instead of doves, but it had burned down ten years ago, and Papa had not bothered to rebuild it. The roof had caved in, but most of the circular brick wall remained, covered with vines and bushes. A perfect sanctuary.

I squeezed in through the gap of the open wooden door, which was hanging off its hinges. Inside was a wide, open space with rows of open cubicles built into the round inner wall, where the birds would've roosted. The ground was wet and muddy, but my cold feet were already soaked. I took off my stockings and easily climbed up the cubicles to the top level, where some of my most prized possessions were hidden. I unwrapped the woolen blanket used to keep them dry.

My fingers trembled as I decided between them: an old steel rapier sheathed inside its leather scabbard, an atlatl—a handheld spear thrower—and my ultimate favorite, the bow, along with a round target and a long quiver full of arrows and darts.

I threw the straw target down, where it landed with a soft thud. I carefully strapped the quiver over my shoulder and grabbed the atlatl and the bow. Then, feeling a little like a spider monkey, I jumped off the ledge, grinning at the air rushing over me, lighting me up with a bolt of life. Unfortunately, I lost my footing and landed on my knees with a squelch, soiling the front of my skirt. I sighed, knowing Marta would be beside herself. And yet, it was worth it. All my troubles—the heavy pit of sadness and loss, the constant flutter of uncertainty in my stomach—were fading to the background, and I hadn't even started target practice.

I untied and removed the bulky, puffed-up sleeves constricting my arms, although I had no choice but to leave on the stiff bodice around my torso, as it was tied from behind. It was uncomfortable, but there was nothing I could do. I set up the target and walked to the other end of the dovecote, then shot a few arrows on target, well at ease.

Papa had taken great pains to teach all his children how to shoot, even us girls. He told us we might need to defend ourselves one day, although he never said from whom. It was probably the most time he had ever spent with any of us. I think perhaps he couldn't help himself: he had to see which of his offspring had inherited his greatest talent.

All of us, even Catina, who was hopeless, had desired the honor of being named best shot by our father. As children, we had held an annual family tournament and competed against each other, and I had nearly won, trailing behind Nano each year, until I turned fourteen and finally overtook him. That was the year Papa declared that we girls could no longer participate. He had been trying to discourage me ever since, to make me act more like a lady. The unfairness of it all made my hands shake with rage.

Again and again, I drew and aimed and shot, until I was drenched in sweat, until I'd hit the bull's-eye seven times in a row, and then seven more for luck, until the periphery of the world was a blur, and I'd forgotten anything else existed except that narrow middle circle.

Until I heard soft footsteps close by. Too close.

I ran at the target and pulled the arrowheads out as fast as I could, but I wasn't fast enough. I hadn't even loosened three when a face appeared in the gap by the door. I gasped and froze.

"Relax, it's just me," said Nano. "You'd be dead otherwise."

I huffed and pointed at the target. "I beg to differ."

Nano followed the line of my finger and pinched the bridge of his nose. "I thought you'd stopped this nonsense. Papa asked you to after—you know."

A surge of hot rage shot up high, from my stomach onto my cheeks. "I never broke Pedro's bow! That wasn't me!"

Nano squeezed himself into the dovecote and nodded, but I could tell it was only to pacify me, and perhaps to not have to think of the whole incident, one of the worst fights our family had ever had. Around the same time we were told we could not compete, Pedro had wrongly accused me of breaking his favorite bow, and Papa and Gonzalo had believed him. Nantzin and Andrade had defended me, and it had all ended in a terrible shouting match between the men. Pedro and I had never recovered.

The silence stretched on, until I snapped. "I don't care if you don't believe me, I know I didn't. And anyway, why would Papa teach me something he didn't wish me to be good at? Plus, Nantzin never asked me to stop, because she knew how much I loved it."

Nano's gaze was measured. I returned to pulling the arrows out of the target, but after a moment, I stopped and glared back. "Are you going to tell Papa?"

A smile tugged at the corner of his lips. "How do I know you didn't just stick those in the middle by hand? Let's see you do it."

I paused for a moment, eyes narrowed. Then I ran to the other end of the dovecote, quick as a deer. Before he'd even had time to take two steps back, I'd shot the arrow in his direction and struck the center of the target.

His mouth hung wide open. Then he turned and dashed at me with a furious look in his face. "You could've missed, pendeja! I was standing right there!"

I let out a mad, delighted cackle. He tried to grip me around my waist, but I was too fast and the ground too slippery. He fell face forward into the mud, which only made me laugh harder. My head was hanging back, so I didn't realize he'd grabbed a fistful of mud until it hit me square in the neck, splattering into my open mouth. I broke into a coughing fit.

Now he was the one howling. "You're filthy! Your hair, undone and uncovered. Face dripping with mud. Out in the birdhouse, half naked, hurtling banned weapons." He could hardly get a word out. "And *you're*—going—to a—convent?" He let out another manic laugh and pounded the ground with his fist.

I, on the other hand, suddenly felt a dreadful chill, as if the ghost of a triple noose had once again tightened around my neck. The future vows I'd be forced to take: poverty, chastity and worst of all, obedience. How could Nantzin do this to me?

Nano saw the look on my face and fell silent. "Agh, sister—what have you done? Come on, you can tell me on the walk home."

Sunset was approaching as we made our way through the forest.

I spoke low and fast, trying not to feel the mess of emotions from those awful moments in time, trying not to see Nantzin's wasted body in my mind's eye. She'd covered herself in her favorite furs and jewels and perfumes, but the truth was plain to see in her sunken cheeks, her shrunken body, and her sallow skin. Death had not been kind. She had been dealt a slow and cruel end—the last thing she deserved.

"Nantzin summoned Catina and me to her chamber one night and said she had important truths to share with us. Truths she'd wished her own mother had told her, when she'd been alive. 'Although,' she said, 'your grandmother could've never pictured my life, not in a hundred thousand years.' Most of what she told us had to do with her six husbands." Heat warmed my cheeks, and Nano averted his eyes.

I hesitated, then I thought maybe it would help him to hear it. "She said she had enough experience to know it was rare the man who thought of a woman's pleasure in the marital bed, let alone her willingness to lie in it."

He spluttered and grabbed my arm. "She never!"

"She spoke those exact words, I swear upon my soul!" I crossed myself. "She said both Spanish and Mexica men were the same in this regard. She said she would never rest in peace knowing we'd be left at the mercy of men whose characters she'd never know."

The memory of the look on her face, of fierce concern, of determination, made my voice crack and waver. "She asked us if we were set on marriage and children, if our hearts desired those blessings."

"Of course *you* said no." He snorted.

"Indeed. I couldn't say no fast enough. I thought Catina would've said yes, but she also shook her head."

"I suppose she prefers the company of books to men. Much like you prefer blades."

"And food too, don't forget. Anyway, she promised she'd make arrangements to befit our status, and sent us off. I never thought for an instant she'd consider a convent. I thought maybe she'd have us trained as governesses, perhaps."

Nano looked at me as though I were a half-wit. "Of course she wouldn't, you dolt. Both Father and she would've rather been fed to wolves than have you become servants."

"Marta is not a servant!"

"Yes, she is. She serves us, and she's at the mercy of Father's whims. He can cast her off at any time. She has no say. I see why Mama chose a convent, if she was worried about you being beholden to a man. You'd have no man to serve at the nunnery, except our Lord Jesus, and you'd soon have all those other poor sisters under your thumb." He laughed. "You'd be abbess in no time, free to do as you like, within the confines of those walls."

My lips parted at the echo of truth in his words, and at the quick ease by which he'd understood Nantzin's intentions, when I'd been struggling with her reasoning for weeks.

"Anyway, when I found out we'd been accepted to the Convento, I went to speak to her, but it was the week before she passed. She was in so much pain. Her face was pinched—she was as pale as Papa, she could hardly breathe." I swallowed the pressure tightening around my larynx, and my lower lip wobbled.

Nano groaned, then wrapped an arm around my shoulders.

"She asked if something was bothering me," I whispered. "But the look on her face . . . I lost my nerve and said no. She asked again, she asked me *specifically* if I was happy about the convent." I made an exasperated sound. "I ought to have taken my chance then! But I did not. Instead I—I said I was, and she made me swear. So, I swore I was glad to go to the convent. She seemed so peaceful after that, and in a way, I don't regret it."

"And yet . . ."

Tears began to threaten me in earnest, so I pounded the ground with my foot to make them stay back. "Nano, I cannot possibly live like those women! Always covered, always praying in whispers, always cloistered behind those impossibly high walls, never speaking to anybody but each other. But now it's too late! It's out there, in my promise, in her will. Everyone knows about it now. My name is down at the convent, payment is on its way. I've got less than two months. I don't know what to do."

I beseeched him with a look. "What must I do?"

He'd always known how to get us out of trouble. Surely he'd come up with something brilliant. But after a moment's pause, he simply shook his head and looked down.

"I wish I could help, but I think you're right. It would be . . . dishonorable to fall back on your word now." Once again, his voice was like a bell, dooming me with its candor. "It's . . . it's too late. I'm sorry. You'll have to go."

The triple noose tightened.

CHAPTER 3

Isabel Cano

19 February 1551

We were supposed to sneak through the kitchen quickly and quietly, but the mouthwatering smell of pozolli, tamalli, and chunky black beans cast its spell on my lower limbs, and dragged them to a halt.

"I should've known," said Nano with an eye roll. The kitchen hands didn't even blink. They were used to my relentless appetite, and I'd run in through their doors with frizzled hair and my dress covered in mud enough times that it caused no concern. They waded through the thick steam and handed me a large ceramic bowl and a ladle. I strode up to the large pot of simmering broth and served myself, making sure to scoop a double portion of hominy and pork. I turned to the large table where other similar bowls of condiments sat ready for use, tomatl and red-chilli salsas, translucent diced onions, dried oregano, and succulent lime crescents from Papa's orchard, and dressed my soup with extra spice.

Nantzin's old cook, Toño, a large Nahua man with a square face and hairless boulders for arms, brought me some fresh tortillas wrapped in a linen cloth to keep them warm. He pointed at the mountain of ahuacatl at the center of the table, some cut to reveal the creamy green flesh and large round seed at their core.

"I can mash them and make ahuacamolli too, if it pleases the señorita."

I'd already stuffed my mouth, so I shook my head and conveyed my gratitude with a look. He gave me an approving nod and left me to continue devouring his delicious work, but not before huffing and shaking his head irritably in Nano's direction.

Nano winked back. He was leaning on the table, picking out mud from underneath his fingernails. The complete opposite of me, he only ever ate bread rolls and the occasional grilled chicken. He was so fussy with his food it was a miracle he'd grown at all, let alone become the tallest of us Canos. Nantzin and Toño had tried their best, but Nano was hopeless.

"Hurry up, will you," he said. "These fumes are overpowering, and I'm late."

I swallowed hard and asked, "Late for what?" before taking another bite.

"Ana Velasco's dinner party."

I gave him a stern look. We were meant to be in mourning. That meant no parties, no promenades, and definitely no balls. But perhaps I needed to be kinder, like he had been with me. I hadn't struggled with those particular rules, but maybe dancing and flirting was his own way of coping with Nantzin's death, his own target practice.

He shrugged. "I'll also be going to the viceroy's welcome ball in eleven days, if you're interested. Though I hear he's unhappy about it."

I gave him a quizzical glance, and Nano answered with a whisper. "Apparently it was all the bishop's idea, and the viceroy thinks it's a waste of gold. Perhaps that means he will be different, better. For the people."

When my mouth was free again, I gestured at the door and said, "I hope so. Well, go on. Don't leave all your pretty women waiting on my behalf."

He chuckled. "Believe me, you'll want me around in case Pedro finds you. I'll just take you up to Marta and go."

I clicked my tongue, thinking he was giving Pedro too much credit.

When I finished my meal, we sneaked out into the hallway. At the end, we poked our heads around the corner leading to the gray stone arches of the huge inner courtyard, which seemed clear. We tiptoed out into the light streaming down from the open ceiling, but before we had taken four steps, our older brothers leapt from behind the thick, tall pillars of an arch.

Gonzalo rammed his elbow into Nano's stomach, winding him. He fell to his knees on the tiled floor, sending a jolt of blind rage, a rush of blood to my head that was made worse when Pedro grabbed my ear alongside a fistful of hair and bellowed into my face, "Perra maldita—how dare you take my horse! Don't you know how to mind your elders?" His booming voice echoed through the tall patio.

"Let go of her!" Nano wheezed.

"Get off me, pig!" I swiped at his face with my fingernails, and he jumped back.

He touched his grazed cheekbone. I hadn't managed to draw blood, but his shaking hands went to the hilt of his sword. He glared at me with a look of utter disgust on his face.

"You're a nasty, unnatural piece of no-good work. The sooner we get you locked up in that convent, the better for this entire family!"

"Go drown yourself, cabrón!" I spat. "*That* would be best for this family."

After a moment of stunned silence, he sneered. "Oh, you might've been Nantzin's pet. She might've turned a blind eye to your obscenities, but she's gone now. Father will be off to Spain soon, and I'll be in charge. And then we'll see who drowns. Vamos, hermano."

Gonzalo gave Nano one last push, and they walked off toward the wing leading to the stables. I rubbed my hot, pulsating ear and glared after them until they were gone, then rounded on Nano. "Papa is leaving?"

He was still doubled over and trying to catch his breath, but he nodded.

"When? Why?"

"Do you mind?" He groaned. "I think that bastard broke a rib."

"Don't be such a baby," I replied, though my tone softened and my hands were gentle, just like Nantzin's had been whenever we were hurt or sick, as I helped him straighten up.

He hitched in a breath and said, "I guess you're safe now he's thrown his little fit."

"Yes, I'll escort myself to my chambers now, brother, and you can go to your party." I winked at him to try cheer him. "Your assistance was no use anyway."

His face darkened. "Don't be so sure. I'm worried about them. We must be careful."

I spluttered with derision. "Con esos pendejos?"

He flinched. "Isabel, would you watch that mouth of yours for once? No, listen—I hear how they talk at night. It's all gunpowder, pulque drinking, fighting, and women." He shook his head. "Since Nantzin passed, it's like a dam has broken."

Surely he was exaggerating. Those two didn't seem much different to me. Sure, Pedro had never actually *touched* me during any of our fights before. He'd always yelled, or chased, or put his fists up as a threat. I guess today he'd crossed the line for the first time. But it was only my ear, although it was throbbing. I touched it with my fingers, and it was still hot.

Nano's eyes were still watering too.

My eyebrows knotted with doubt. I couldn't remember Gonzalo ever hitting him so hard he'd been unable to move to help me.

I couldn't remember Pedro ever reaching for his sword.

Nano was studying my face. My shifting thoughts must've been plain to see, because he nodded again. "Like I said, we must be careful."

◆ ◆ ◆

That night, I dreamt of old wounds. The girls crowded around me in the tiled patio; they pushed and whispered the poorly written song they'd made up that week. The monks were too far away, or didn't care. But the girls pushed and sang, pushed and sang . . .

Your mother is a cannibal.
Your mother is a whore.
She killed two of her husbands.
She prays to heathen gods.
She still gives up her blood for them.
She gives them sacrifice.
And when she dies to Hell she'll go,
Along with all her lice.

I pushed back and screeched, but in the dream, my voice spluttered to a pathetic little caw. My limbs felt heavy, and no matter how hard I struck, my fists landed as soft as feathers. The girls roared with laughter. They slapped me so hard across the face that my vision sparked.

I saw the truth behind their words, the fear of what would happen if I could be myself, the eagle of my lineage.

They trembled because they knew they were but country mice.

The next morning, I woke up to a shriek.

"What? What?" I bolted upright and reached behind to where I kept a dagger lodged between the mattress and headboard, but my hand froze when the outline of Marta became clearer. She was standing in front of the bright open windows, waving something like a large dark sheet in the air. Fragments of dust spiraled around her glowing, haloed head like tiny buzzing fireflies, granting her the look of an overlarge saint.

Until her angry face came into focus and she shouted, "What have you done to this dress!"

I groaned. Marta groaned back, twice as loud. "This is *raven's wing*, Isabel Cano de Moctezuma! The emperor himself pays a premium to have his breeches dyed as black as this gown! Look at what you've done to this gold embroidery—look!"

She shoved the sullied cloth right under my nose. It stank of horsehair and damp mud. I pushed it away and looked around our chamber, at the elaborate fireplace and the huge window opening into a small balcony overlooking the forest, hoping for a way out of this situation. But we were alone, except for my sleeping sister. I had no way of hiding from Marta's barrage of threats.

"Outrageous, disgraceful! Your father will hear about this, let me tell you! The little care you show for these priceless gifts from him and your mother—"

"It was an accident," I interrupted in a small voice.

"Not a chance! This is the last time, young lady. You'll never again—"

There was a knock on the door. "Enter!" I yelled before she could continue.

The oval, amber-brown face of our chambermaid poked from behind the door. "Good morning, señorita. Some large parcels have arrived for you and your sister." She looked over to the bed across from mine near the opposite wall, where Catina was sleeping peacefully next to a pile of books, having heard none of Marta's commotion.

"Thank you, Jacinta. You may bring them in."

Marta tut-tutted as Jacinta nodded and opened the two doors wide. Then, like an experienced orchestra conductor, she signaled to the other maids outside to carry in the differently sized parcels, one by one. After a while, their movements must've disturbed Catina, for she stretched and yawned, and sat up.

"What are they doing?" she gestured to me.

"Someone has sent us gifts, apparently," I signed back.

The maids placed the parcels on top of the four cushioned armchairs and small carved table arranged between my sister's bed and mine. Then, together, four of the girls carried in a very long, heavy circular object, wrapped in a linen canvas like the others.

"What on earth is it, do you think?" I signed.

She responded with a look of confusion. "A rug?"

Jacinta bowed. "Señorita, if you please, we have received instructions to hang this new tapestry on this wall here. The men are waiting downstairs already, but I can tell them to come back in the afternoon?"

My curiosity was piqued. "Who ordered all this?"

"Why, it seems the artist recently received a commission from your lady mother." She looked taken aback. Perhaps she thought we were expecting it.

I blinked. For some reason I sensed it was best to play along. I smacked my forehead. "Of course, yes, the tapestry from Nantzin. I forgot it was due this week."

"What are you saying, Isabel?" shouted Catina, and I flinched. Because she couldn't hear, her voice emerged too loud sometimes. It was one of the many reasons she hardly spoke anymore. "What about Nantzin?"

She must've read my lips. "Pretend you know. It's a tapestry from Nantzin," I signed.

Catina had never been great at pretending. Her eyebrows shot up. But perhaps she would've looked even more surprised if I hadn't said anything.

"Come, let's go to the drawing room so they can put it up," I both spoke and signed. "Jacinta, tell them they must come up right away—do not delay."

"No, but empty the chamber pots first please, Jacinta! I'll stay and make sure they hang it on straight. And you girls—put a robe on, por el amor de Dios," said a mollified Marta, who loved when beautiful new things arrived at the house. We quickly did as we were told and shuffled to the next room, but not before grabbing a couple of the other parcels.

They were light and easy to carry, and all were wrapped in beautiful white cotton cloths and silk ribbons in shimmering bright colors.

"Open the curtain, Isabel," said Catina, who had unwrapped one of her parcels the moment we'd entered the drawing room. "Oh, oh! It's a lovely cushion!"

Light flooded the room, and we saw that, indeed, it was a cushion, a large one with an elaborate hand-stitched scene of a crowned eagle hovering above the summit of a long snowcapped volcano. The men began hammering next door as we unwrapped the other parcels. All were exquisite cushions with Mexican eagles flying or perched over various landscapes: a beautiful leafy hill with flying grasshoppers and a waterfall, a mist-covered island with three skulls, and a green pyramid under a half moon.

"Are those . . . numbers?" Catina pointed at the eagles' crowns.

I took a closer look and nodded. Each crown had a tiny single digit.

"How odd," said Catina. "Why would Nantzin order these?"

I shook my head and signed, "I think some of these are places, like the hill with the grasshoppers. Could it be Chapultepec?" Nantzin had never mentioned anything special about that place, except to point out the marvelous clay aqueducts her ancestors had built, which supplied Tenochtitlan with fresh water from its springs. The Spanish had recently rebuilt them, after first destroying them during their siege.

Catina glanced at our chamber. "Have they stopped? I can't feel the vibrations from the hammers anymore."

She was right—the racket had died down. A few moments later, Marta poked her head through the gap of the door. The look of consternation on her face made me stand up.

"What's wrong?"

Her voice was odd and hoarse. "You better come and see."

We rushed back to our chamber. The first thing I saw was Jacinta, staring with limp arms and an open mouth at the wall. I turned too, and gasped.

The image before us was huge, astounding, and . . . disturbing. The Valley of Mexico, with its surrounding white-tipped mountains and lush green cliffs, with its enormous lakes and island city at its center. Except the city had only one pyramid, a massive white one. Upon its tallest step stood Nantzin with arms wide open, dressed in a simple white tunic, though it was sprinkled with red dots.

Blood. From the open, empty gash where her heart should've been.

With a rising ache in my chest, I took a step closer and reached up, but I couldn't touch her. She was too high. I studied her tawny-brown face; her beautiful, sad doe eyes; thin, dark lips; and long, thick black hair, undone and parted to the side. So real it hurt.

Yet beneath that initial pain, my gut was tightening. My frown was deepening with a sense of disquiet, and unease, and intuition. As if another world, a hidden world, were trying to reveal itself to me. With hungry eyes, I studied the picture further. The red dots flowing down her tunic were not shaped like droplets, but letters. I tasted their sounds on the tip of my tongue.

T-H-U-R-T.

Thurt? That made no sense. I inspected the image some more. In one hand, Nantzin grasped a large black knife. In the other hand she held a dangling golden cage. Inside the cage floated a brown heart—or it appeared to be a heart at first glance, but on closer inspection was clearly a sleeping eagle, with its talons gripping the swinging perch.

Catina had also stepped closer. She whispered, "Is that . . . us?"

I followed her gaze to the bottom of the tapestry and counted. There were thirteen people standing on two separate canoes. One of them was full of men, looking outward, like Nantzin was. They stood in strange positions, their hands and mouths in odd angles. Papa was at the front.

The other boat was indeed us, all her seven children. We also appeared to be gesticulating at something. Andrade, Pedro, and Gonzalo were all looking out of the frame, like the men. Leonor's eyes were pinched in pain, and the profiles of Nano, Catina, and I were gazing at Nantzin, and by the looks on our faces, it was clear we were weeping.

Catina pressed her arm next to mine. I drew her close and clenched my jaw. I could not let anyone see me cry, though my lip wobbled and my nose felt like I'd inhaled smoke from charred chilli, and my chest squeezed so tight that I thought I would never draw in another full breath again.

Our struggle must've shown somehow, because Marta exclaimed, "Oh, my poor lambs!" and pulled us both into her bosom. The world was blocked out for a moment, and I was enveloped by her warm, rose-clean scent. This was one thing Nantzin had hardly ever done—held us, touched us. Only when we were sick or injured. And soon, we would leave Marta's side as well, for the convent. A curl of fear mingled with the rest of my feelings, and I eased into Marta's warm embrace, secretly praying it would not be my last.

"May I get you something to drink?" Jacinta peeped. "Or eat, Señorita Isabel?"

My head popped out from Marta's arms. Jacinta smiled kindly at me, although there was a note of pity in her look too, which made me feel even more awful. Here I was, standing in front of my soft down mattress, warm in my plush velvet robe, high- and freeborn, which, until yesterday when she'd been freed by Nantzin, was the complete opposite of her own life.

I shuttered my grief away, reminding myself that Nantzin had never cried, ever. Even in her last agonizing moments, when her breathing had become ragged, when the doctors had been called in to drug her in an attempt to spare her some pain, not a single tear had slipped down her cheek. I would be strong like her, for her, and for my sister too.

I cleared my throat. "Thank you, Jacinta. We'll have whatever Toño's made for breakfast today, please."

She nodded and slipped out the door. All of us turned again to look at the tapestry.

"Sweet babe," said Marta, still holding Catina, petting her head. "Whatever was your mother thinking?"

I'd been asking myself the same thing. Nantzin never seemed to do anything without careful consideration, unlike me. But I shook my head. Even if I could've guessed at her meaning, I wouldn't tell Marta. She was good, and loving, but she was Papa's kin. Her disapproving tone told me all I needed to know about how I should respond. "She was very sick when she commissioned this. Perhaps the artist misunderstood what she wanted."

Marta nodded. "I'd say. We ought to tell your father to send it back. This—it's not suitable for a young lady's room."

I laughed and pointed at the oil painting of a bloody, half-naked, and crucified Jesus in the midst of unbearable agony, hanging right above Catina's bed. "It's no less appropriate than that." I signed Marta's words to Catina, then added, "I like it. It's different, and it's from her."

Maybe it was the wavering note in my voice, or the way Catina was nodding her head, but Marta pursed her lips and sighed, resigned. "All right. We'll leave it up for now."

She turned and grabbed my dress. "Anyway, I must take this *wreck* to the seamstress."

I ducked my head, grimacing in apology. She huffed and walked off.

Once again, Catina and I turned to stare at the tapestry.

We stared and stared. I looked at the tiny blood-like letters, and pondered what Nantzin could've meant. Was *thurt* a word I didn't know? I'd have to ask Papa before his trip to Spain. Or maybe she meant *hurt*, and the artist had weaved an extra *T* by accident.

Who was the artist anyway? I questioned Jacinta when she came back with our breakfast, but she didn't know. The men had gone, and she knew not who they were or where they'd come from. She laid the tray on the table.

Even the bright, runny fried eggs and steaming soft tortillas failed to distract me for long. We ate our breakfast in silence, mesmerized. I noticed seven well-known locations were marked on the tapestry, which seemed more like a map the longer I looked. The locations had a type of Greek cross—golden, with arms of equal lengths. The artist had stitched their names in beautiful, flowing calligraphy . . . Chapultepec, Teotihuacan, Iztaccihuatl, Guadalupe, Tacuba, and two more, Palacio and Xochimilco.

Later, Jacinta came back to clear our table, and still we sat and stared, until the light from outside the window shifted and mellowed.

Until Catina sucked in a breath and jumped to her feet. I jumped too, startled by the intensity of her sudden movements. She ran to the front of the tapestry.

"Look!" She pointed at the two boats and began to do a strange dance.

"What are you doing?" I signed, shaking my head. She groaned, and I blinked, completely taken aback by her unusual expression of frustration.

"The boats have a message. The men, us—we are speaking in Hand Talk! Read my hands, my face." She did her strange little dance again, and I saw it too.

Together, the men were signing two words: "Lordly Daughter," the meaning of Tecuichpoch, the Nahuatl name Nantzin was given by her royal parents at birth.

And we, her children, spelled yet another word: *Testament.*

A chill ran down my arms, my legs, and then another, and another. My lips parted, and my heart sped to a painful frenzy. My sister's face was wild too, flushed and fevered. She ran to the drawing room and came back with the cushions, ran to the two unopened ones and pulled them out, then spread them all over her bed.

The two new cushions had images with crowned eagles again. One sat on the shoulder of the Virgin of Guadalupe. Another eagle was flying over a palace.

The one built with Grandfather's stones.

"Are they all places?" Catina asked. "Chapultepec, the shrine of the Virgin of Guadalupe, the viceroy's palace . . . some pyramid? I'm not sure, but each one has an eagle with a number from one to seven." She leaned down and studied the others, then reordered them by number. "Isabel? Isabel—what do you think she meant by all this?"

She beckoned me closer, but I stood there, frozen, immobile. A single word kept beating through my brain, bouncing off my skull like a rubber ball.

Thurt, thurt, thurt, thurt.

"Not *thurt*, idiota," I whispered to myself, and turned to look at Nantzin's open breast.

Not *thurt.*

Truth.

CHAPTER 4

Isabel Cano

20 February 1551

"Truth. Testament. Tecuichpoch." I gasped. "The true testament of Tecuichpoch!"

"What?" said Catina, looking annoyed.

"Sorry, forgot to sign," I gestured. "Listen, I think Nantzin wrote another will, another testament. Look." I pointed at the drops of blood, then spelled out the word *truth*.

"Maybe—maybe these cushions are clues! Places or people we must seek to find it." I ran and picked the first one up, but the eagle flying over a man holding a fork and knife, standing near some type of fireplace, made no sense. The next one did, however, and I threw it to her. "Look, they match! The seven crosses on the map match the locations on the seven cushions. Number two is definitely the viceroy's palace, see? It looks just like it. Nano says he's having a party later in the week! We should go—we should go find it!"

Catina caught the cushion, but that sudden wild look in her face was gone, replaced by a pallor of crippling uncertainty. Her forehead glistened, her voice dimmed. She took a step back and said, "I don't know. I mean, Nantzin couldn't even read or write."

"Well, maybe it's a treasure map!" I signed. "All the eagles are wearing gold. The Spanish never found Grandfather's treasure. Maybe she knew where it was all along!"

Catina shook her head. "Even so, what would we gain from it? We don't need it."

My brow creased. I tried to keep the roughness from my face and gestures, but I failed. "Listen. Nantzin left us something precious. I don't know what it is, but why would she use Hand Talk? Why would she go to all this trouble to ensure we were the only ones left with her cushions and tapestries? She clearly wanted us to seek this thing, whatever it is. She wanted us, her daughters, to find it. And you're going to turn your back on her? Because you're afraid of a little party?"

I regretted my last words immediately. Catina's knuckles around the cushion turned white, and she hung her head.

"That's not what I mea—"

"Not everyone is born a warrior, Isabel," she whispered. Before I could say anything else, she dropped the cushion and ran out of the room.

"Carajo!" I yelled. I threw one last glance at the tapestry, then chased after her, but she was quicker than me and had disappeared. She had several hiding spots: the library, the garden. Our parents' chambers were closest, so I went there first.

The intricate, colorful murals on the walls blurred as I stomped at the most ladylike pace I could muster. But as I neared the boys' chambers, I heard a murmur of voices, male and female. I halted midstep and sneaked a look through the door, which had been left ajar.

Pedro was leaning on one of his bedposts, looming over an uncomfortable-looking Jacinta, who was carrying a basket of dirty linen. His two enormous wolfhounds, Nero and Caligula, were by the fireplace, tugging noisily at a rope and sprinkling ugly gray hairs over the carpet, but I could still hear his voice.

"All these years, chasing you . . . you can't leave without giving me a proper goodbye."

Something about the awful way Jacinta grimaced, her stone-dead eyes and hardened shoulders unsettled a deep pool of anger inside me. I kicked the door open, and it crashed against the wall. Both Pedro and Jacinta jumped, and the dogs yelped.

"What is this?" I growled.

Tears welled in Jacinta's eyes. "Señorita, it's not what it see—"

"Not you. I'm talking to that swine. You may go," I said more gently to Jacinta, who didn't wait to be told twice. Eyes on the floor, she scuttled past me and out the door.

I glared at Pedro, who had recovered from the initial embarrassment that had turned his tanned skin a shade darker. He straightened his doublet and dusted his breeches, found his feathered cap, and put it on. Nero and Caligula whined excitedly, probably thinking he was taking them out. One of them jumped on his leg, and he gently caressed its ears.

"You know, you remind me of those shrill Toltec lapdogs," he whispered. "Always picking fights with bigger hounds, not realizing you're one bite away from losing your head."

I snorted. "At least those little dogs have spirit, unlike you. No wonder Jacinta's skin was crawling! You're ugly, stupid, and have the personality of a soiled mattress!"

His dogs barked as he scrambled forward, face flushed and nostrils flared, but I'd been expecting it. I was too far away, and too quick. I cackled and ran down the hall, feeling a twisted sense of triumph as he chased after me, shouting obscenities, but my joy was short-lived. Papa and Nano stepped out from his chambers across the balcony.

"I'll not allow it! Not a cent! Her father is a rogue and a disgra—" Papa stopped mid-sentence when he spotted me. His brow set, and I stopped running. Pedro must not have seen him, because he caught up with me, grabbed me by the shoulders, and spun me around.

"I'll show you ugly," he huffed. I flinched as his palm went up to strike me.

"Pedro!" Papa's voice boomed through the courtyard, along with Nano's strangled shout. My brother's eyes went round with terror. His hand froze midair.

"What in the world!" Papa marched toward us, mustache flickering the way it did when he was particularly irate. The sight sent a tremor of fear through my ribs. He might've been a slight man, he might've never laid an angry hand on any of us, but there was an edge to him we all sensed. The arrowhead, small but sharp and deadly—the lethal conquistador everyone knew him to be.

That look on his face never failed to put every single one of us in our place.

Pedro let go of me and backed away. "She—she came into my room."

"And so bloody what!" He tipped my chin up with tender fingertips and inspected my face. When he saw I was unharmed, he nodded. I bowed and looked down at the floor.

"How dare you," Papa hissed. The sound sent a chill down my back.

Pedro's face was as pale as it had ever been, but he must've been feeling especially hateful toward me, because for the first time ever, he spoke back. "She's been spoiled and—and stubborn and—she needs a good whipping!"

A couple of footmen walked through the bottom courtyard and looked up at us.

"Leave us!" he said to the footmen and my brother Nano, whose eyes were red rimmed and angry. I had no time to wonder about this, because Papa barged past us, beckoning Pedro and me into the boys' chambers. Pedro shot me a murderous glare before following him. With a dry throat and thrumming heart, I trailed behind them.

Papa pointed at the dogs in disgust. Nero jumped up, nearly reaching Pedro's shoulder, and Caligula growled low before my brother ordered them to the corner. They obeyed with a whine.

"I said no dogs inside the house!" Papa shouted, making us both flinch. "Whatever is the matter with you? How can I leave you in charge when you pay me no heed? When you raise your hand against your own flesh and blood? A sister is a precious gift from God! A flower to care for, to water and shield from the worst of storms."

"Flowers need pruning too, Father, especially ones covered in thorns!"

I blinked, not quite believing Pedro capable of such depth of thought. But when he opened his mouth again, I realized it had been but a lapse.

"If you were ever home, you'd see how she storms around the house like a bull, how she speaks to me as though I'm nothing but a fly!" Papa's eyes narrowed, and he shook his head in disbelief. Pedro went on, ranting, "She shows no proper deference or obedience to me, her older brother. She never gives me my due. *And* she called me ugly and soiled!"

"A soiled mattress, actually," I whispered in spite of myself. I knew that I should keep quiet, that I had the advantage of Papa's ignorance, but I was no saint like my sister and Nantzin. I had none of their restraint. Perhaps a part of me wanted him to see *me* for once.

He looked to the heavens as though praying for strength, then turned to me and spoke through his teeth. "Isabel, that is unseemly. What would your mother say?"

That liquid monster inside me reared its ugly head, daring me to let him see who all of us were and be damned. I opened my mouth to tell, to say out loud that I'd seen Pedro harassing Jacinta, but then held back. What if Pedro blamed her? Would Papa believe him over her? Most likely. Would she lose her freedom over it? Maybe not, but would her reputation be ruined? The slightest blemish on a maid's good name could mean the difference between employment and starvation. I knew this from the way Marta talked about them, and I was sure she was one of the kinder mistresses in town.

I hung my head. "Forgive me."

He sighed softly, then reached out for my hand, then Pedro's. "This won't do. We've all been desperately sad since . . ." His voice went hoarse, his eyes swam.

Pedro looked away, whether to hide his own grief or because he could not stand to see our father's, only he knew. But I put my hand over Papa's and squeezed it, my rage spent like a puff of smoke smothered by falling rain. It was always like this with him. A few kind words, a gentle touch, and all was forgiven.

He cleared his throat and gave us a weak, shaky smile. "Well, we know why we're sad. We've lost the soul of this house, and Andrade too, whom we all loved." Pedro huffed, but Papa continued. "We mustn't let our heartache divide us, we must find solace in each other. I wish it weren't so, but I must seek support from my brethren in Spain."

"Papa, don't go . . ." I tried to keep the pleading from my tone, but couldn't. First Nantzin, now him. True, he was a busy man, always embroiled in some lawsuit or another at court, usually in Nantzin's name. We girls only ever really saw him on Sundays, but who knew how long he would be gone now? It could be years, and that was if he survived the treacherous seas. My throat latched up, and I fought the urge to fling myself onto his chest.

"I must, my dear, otherwise Gonzalo may never see his rightful inheritance." He did not say the words, but I thought I heard the underlying meaning—that all his work on behalf of my mother would be for nothing. All her lands would go to another man's son.

He let go of my hand and turned to my brother, giving him a thud on the arm. "Son, you must care for our family, keep them safe until I return. You must behave like a grown man, and a grown man is not afraid of a little girl with a sharp tongue. Swear you will protect your brothers and sisters, that you will let no harm come to them, that you will be temperate and kind in my stead."

Pedro, now serious, glanced at me, then down at our father, who was slightly shorter than my brother. He nodded solemnly and answered in a sober voice, "I swear to you, upon my honor, I shall do as you command."

Father seemed satisfied, unlike me. He turned to me and put his hands on my shoulders. I looked up into the sad green eyes only my brother Nano had inherited, and resisted the urge to cry.

"My girl, you share a name with your mother, so please, do not tarnish her reputation in fits of temper, but be mindful of how lovely she was, how modest and charitable, how noble and stoic." My lower lip wobbled, and his grip tightened. "She was a princess, an empress, the queen of all our hearts. It is a heavy burden to carry, but you are sixteen years old now, and I know you are up to the task."

"Yes, Papa," I whispered. His loving words did nothing but plunge me into a cold pool of tension and regret, for I knew one day he would realize that I was the complete opposite of Nantzin, a failure of a girl, a failure of a daughter. One day, I would break his heart.

He smiled sadly. "You will be a wonderful nun. In a few weeks, Pedro will see to it that you're safely and comfortably installed in the convent, and I will come visit you and Catina upon my return. I am sure you will be happy there."

The only thing I could do was prolong the illusion, not cause him more pain than he already felt, not leave him with cause to fret over me during his journey. So I swallowed and nodded.

"Now, I have much to do, for most of our servants have decided to take their papers and enjoy their newfound freedom elsewhere. I'll need to pay them all and replace our cook before I leave. Otherwise, Lord knows what you'll do for food."

"Toño's leaving?" I asked.

He sighed. "Yes. Now, I best be off. Be good to each other."

He walked out and left us there, standing and looking everywhere but at each other. The dogs came over and sniffed us. I patted one of them on the head. Pedro cleared his throat.

"I shouldn't have raised my hand against you," he mumbled.

I narrowed my eyes, not truly believing this sudden change, and unsure of how to respond to it. He knelt and began to scratch Caligula's belly. The dog kicked its leg in a reflex, coaxing a rare smile out of my brother. Whatever else was true about him, I couldn't deny he'd always been good to his dogs. Maybe he could, in fact, be good to us too? If I stopped goading him? If he stopped behaving like an ass?

"I shouldn't have called you those mean things, or taken your horse," I said.

He nodded once. I made my excuses and made to leave. At the door, he called out, "And thank you, for not telling on me."

I froze for a moment, grappling with the sudden nauseating sense that I'd made a terrible mistake, that I'd once again lost my chance to speak out and tell the truth, that I'd let him get away with something he obviously knew was wrong.

I gripped the doorframe and turned. He seemed to shrink from the look on my face. I made my voice turn to ice, just like Papa's could, and responded, "It won't happen again."

I couldn't find Catina anywhere, so I made my way to the kitchens, thinking I would say goodbye to Toño in person.

The place felt different. Still an assault on the senses, with two dozen quick hands plucking birds, grinding corn, mopping floors, scrubbing tabletops. But the atmosphere felt lighter, happier than even before Nantzin had fallen ill. The kitchen boys immediately rounded on me and recited the menu for this evening. They insisted I try the steamed crayfish, with sizzling peppers, juicy tomatl, and grilled squash, and the side of frijoles flavored with savory romerito, a type of seepweed that grew along the marshes. I inhaled the comforting aromas and took a bite. The mix of flavors, sour, sweet, and biting, burst against my tongue, and for a moment, I forgot the reason for my visit.

Then Toño came back in from wherever he'd been and strode up to me. "I think it's missing heat, but the boys tell me it's good as it is."

I put up a finger and considered the matter. Once I'd swallowed, I said, "I think they're right. Catina and Gonzalo will struggle if you add any more, but bring out a bowl of chilli for those of us who like a sharper bite."

He huffed and barked the order. He turned back, and his eyes fell on me, and a chink seemingly appeared in his hardened veneer. I didn't know what to do, so I offered my hand, meaning to shake his. Instead, he took it and kissed it, very lightly, very fast, then said in a gruff tone in Nahuatl, "I will miss our debates, but it is time I left."

I nodded and smiled, though my throat squeezed at the thought of another loss. "Of course. Thank you for everything, for all these years."

The kitchen suddenly went very still, and a strange sense enveloped me, of being an intruder, an outsider in my own home. Heat flowered behind my cheeks and my gut tightened, and I thought perhaps I'd said the wrong thing, that there was no way you could, or should, convey gratitude to someone who'd been enslaved into serving you for the entirety of your life. Looking around, and yet without making eye contact with anyone in particular, I gave a sharp nod and said, "Please take care. You all shall be missed," then briskly walked out of the room.

Before I could take two steps away from the door, however, Toño called me again.

"Isabel, wait," he said, and I whirled in surprise. The man had never called me by my first name. Not that it bothered me, but it was quite puzzling. The look on my face must've amused him, because he nearly smiled.

"I thought perhaps you had come for this book. The men who brought your parcels this morning left it with me to give to you." He handed me a thin leather diary.

I opened a random page and saw that someone had written in tiny, squeezed calligraphy, in Nahuatl, though with Latin script. A painful tremor ran through my body; my throat squeezed tight. Tears sprung to my eyes. I looked up at Toño.

"I cannot read it," he said, "but I hope for all of us that you will."

He offered me his hand, and I shook it, then ran to the dovecote as fast as I could.

CHAPTER 5

Tecuichpoch

1509–1519

When you are born, as I have been born, the favored daughter of the huey tlatoani—una princesa, as they say in Castellano—you have but two fates: to die, or to be married. And what is the latter but a long, drawn-out version of the first? I would know, for I had already been married three times by the age of twelve.

Oh, how it will stun you to hear me speak so. To hear me speak at all, in this last great act of defiance. I say last, for there have been many, although I could never stake my claim to them. I did not wish to add suffering to my life.

But this is Tecuichpoch indeed, daughter of Moctezuma Xocoyotzin and his principal wife, Chimalexochitl, "Shield-Bearer Flower." The Spanish called her Teotlalco, but that was the place she was from. Writing that sets me more at ease, for how can I leave a world that does not know my mother's true name?

Oh, but I know . . . men would leave us nameless, if they could.

Who shall suffer the consequences of my indiscretion? When no one believes you can read, write, or strategize, these musings may well be explained as the ramblings of a frail old woman, a ruse, or a lie. It will be up to you to decide, but one thing is certain: I will not die silent. Now that I must die, I will speak my truth.

I *must* speak my truth, for I cannot be free while this great turmoil lives inside me. I must expel it, lest I be damned to wander throughout the earth as a restless wind spirit. I do not wish to wander the world any longer. I wish to be at ease. Oh, how I have earned it.

Indeed, death has threatened me many times, though my survival was foretold. It was written in star and blood, that I would not perish. The soothsayers said, upon my birth, that I would live until I had borne all my seven children and seen my first son's wife carrying my line forth, a line that would never end. Then, and only then, would death come for my soul, my yolia, and take me to Mictlan, where Xolotl the salamander dog would carry me swiftly on his back to paradise in the ninth level.

I know I shall be spared the trials of the underworld, for there are no jagged winds and crashing mountains, no rivers of blood that I have not already swum through in life tenfold and over. And if it is indeed true that there is no underworld, but only a golden heavenly sky with a great bearded god who is my one true father . . .

Well, I already know what it is to be the favorite child of a man who is revered as a thing divine, who holds the power of life and death at his hands. The love of gods and kings is a double-pointed lance, black and sharp, glimmering and deadly.

Indeed, I was his silken feather, his spring hummingbird, his heart of jade. Yet it did not stop my father from giving me as a prize to his enemy. It was he who taught me not to trust in the pretty words of men. But I will say this of my father: He was no coward.

Oh, he was beautiful, and powerful. Even the priests of the Flayed Lord, Xipe Totec, feared him. Yes, even the ones who dressed themselves with the skins of captured slaves. Not even us, his own children, were allowed to look at the huey tlatoani's face.

But I always did, and he never once scolded me as he did my brother and sisters. His eyes, large and black and piercing, would twinkle in amusement at my daring. For a blink, he'd break his grave, majestic veneer, and twitch the emerald piercings above his nostrils up and down, to watch me struggle not to laugh. I never did, for he was much too imposing and I was not fool enough to push my luck.

But it is that image of him that I wish to take with me, that I wish you to have. My father, standing in all his glory in front of the carved stone throne covered for his comfort in jaguar and deer pelts, his copper brow adorned with a panache of a thousand quetzal feathers, his earlobes weighed down with jade and emeralds, his neck shining with light reflected from the plaque of gold and macaw feathers resting on his chest. His luxurious mantle, dyed a brilliant shade of turquoise, embroidered with perfect geometric patterns.

My father, doting on his prized daughter. The mighty warrior, an emperor who wished to spare his people a war he knew he could not win. Not from prophecy or misplaced belief, and never from lack of nerve, but because he was a perfect scholar. He was used to studying his enemy like a jaguar tracking his prey through the underbrush, and he'd scarcely ever failed. Only the Tlaxcalteca had ever outwitted him before.

Yet he was a veteran, a conqueror himself, precise and ruthless. Before they even set foot in our city, my father knew everything about the weaponry the Spanish men carried, unlike anything we'd ever seen. He knew they were only men—not teteoh, not gods. He knew that even if we won the battle against this company, more were coming from across the seas. He saw the truth as clearly as the sun shining on a cloudless day.

The Spaniards were greed incarnate, insatiable, a swarm of chapulin grasshoppers that would wreak destruction on his empire. And still, he tried bribing, diplomacy, subterfuge, everything except warfare. When they eventually marched into our city, he welcomed them as honored guests, as though he had expected them all along, and gave his entire nation a sublime performance. Their huey tlatoani, entirely in charge of an unfathomable situation. In the end, he fulfilled his ultimate duty as a ruler. He gave up everything he loved to protect his people. Even though he failed, I believe—I must believe—that when he gave me to the Spanish, he thought there was some hope.

But this is not *his* story, it is mine. Though I must admit, it is truly difficult for me to disentangle myself from the people who claimed to love me, whose schemes and battles, victories and defeats engulfed my life in such a way that I look back sometimes and blink in astonishment that I am here when they are not.

Moctezuma, Cuauhtemoc, Cortés, Malintzin . . . they reshaped the order of the entire world. They may be dead, but by God, they are known.

Yet no one but you will know me. I may be mentioned in passing as the child, the wife, the mistress. People shall assume all things about my courtly life and training, which was rigorous and relentless. They'll guess how my mother schooled me on palace manners and the endless rules of protocol, religion, ceremony, self-sacrifice, cleanliness, order, and virtue. They might imagine the way she taught me how to moderate my voice and keep my face serene. How to show no fear, no hesitation.

They'll believe, because I have said naught until now, that I learned my place, to bite my tongue and obey my mother and father and my six husbands.

They will swear I was the perfect woman.

Indeed, these were my lessons, and I was expected, as the daughter of the huey tlatoani's principal wife, to excel at them. It was demanded of me, and I met those demands without complaint, for I wished more than anything to make my father proud.

Yet no one but you will know about my stone tank full of axolotl, the two dogs, and the seven monkeys that I kept in Father's zoo, near the family of tapirs.

No one but you will know that, whenever I could, usually at dawn after the priests sounded the enormous drum to wake the city and greet our lord Quetzalcoatl, I'd give our guards the slip, and take my beloved brother Axayacatzin with me to the palace gardens to swim in the freshwater pools and catch lizards. We'd sneak them into the other wives' chambers and wait outside their windows to hear their shrieks. Oh, how we used to laugh! Indeed, that was me!

No one but you will know how my mother became so frustrated at my tricks that she pricked my arm with a sharp maguey thorn and threatened to take me to the Great Temple to bathe me with the clotting blood of the newly sacrificed. She knew I hated the sight and the clouds of flies. When this warning didn't work, she swore she'd tell my father.

I never got caught again.

Listen to me, rambling on. Trying to carve out a pinprick of light in the darkness these people have cast over my life. It is very difficult, for I was also taught, as all Nahua are, not to exalt myself, not to seek attention, lest I be judged or mocked, or worse, publicly shamed. As my mother would say, *Tlacoqualli in monequi*—moderation is a must.

Her counsel served me well. Modesty and moderation and silence helped me survive, but I no longer need to. I no longer can. I feel instead, in my dying bones, in this well of pressure in my throat, that I must speak. I must share everything I have held back all these years.

And perhaps speaking about motherly threats and monkeys and lizards doesn't matter. But Axayacatzin loved them, delighted in them, and I delighted in him.

He is worth remembering. His cheeks stuffed to bursting with tamalli. His long brown hair fluttering above him as he leapt off a boulder into the clear pools blanketed in a rainbow of fragrant flowers. His eyebrows furrowed in concentration as he pulled the string of his bow. The look of wonder on his face when he struck his first kill, a turkey.

He loved birds and rocks, which he used to collect in a little wooden box. Obsidian, crystals, amber, volcanic rocks—he would find them and pick them up and say, "Look, sister, is this not a wonder? I shall save it in my box."

He was the only one of my family who shed tears when I was taken away. I wish my mother had cried too, for then I might not have felt ashamed of my own soaking cheeks. Although I found out much later that she begged my father to spare me, and never spoke a word to him after that day. When my captivity began.

Though that is a tale for another day.

My hope is that you will find it.

CHAPTER 6

Isabel Cano

20 February 1551

I emerged from reading Nantzin's account dizzy and disorientated, as if Pedro had dunked my head in the lake and held it there, as he'd once done years before. My eyes blurred with tears; my throat and chest pulsated with a mixture of grief and awe and pity.

I read it again and again. Ten, twenty times, marveling each time at the command, the bitterness, the *rage* oozing from every line, when I had no recollection of ever seeing Nantzin angry. She'd never had a bad word to say about anyone, especially not her father. She'd hardly ever mentioned her mother, or Axayacatzin, her brother. I felt a twist of guilt and bit my lip. I'd never spared him, my uncle, a second thought. I'd never met him.

And then there was the outright heresy, when every outward sign pointed at her being a true, devoted convert. The Spanish even called her the darling of the Augustinians, for mercy's sake! I read that line again: *And if it is indeed true that there is no underworld, but only a golden heavenly sky with a great bearded god who is my one true father . . .*

I shuddered and crossed myself by instinct. She must've deeply trusted Toño, to give him this journal. I knew the right thing would be to build a fire and burn it, keep the memories I had of Nantzin as they were, as she had been—pristine, pure.

Perfect, as she said everyone would think her to be.

Indeed, I thought, I ought to burn this and never give it another thought.

But . . . here was proof that there were parts of me that were more like her than I had ever realized. That she trusted me to know this side of her. Her true side, perhaps. And there was more—my heart thrummed with the realization that Toño had been that first clue, the man in front of the fire, holding a knife and fork. The first clue matched one of the seven locations marked with a cross on the tapestry map, Tacuba. She had left us six more of these treasures to find. The keys to her heart . . . and perhaps the key to mine.

I swore then and there, I would do her bidding and find them.

A week later, Papa left for Spain in the midst of chaos, both inside and outside our home. I'd only been out to the forest, and for my daily horse rides and trips to Mass, but I could tell by the intensified looks and whispers that gossip about our family feud was rampant. One of my old enemies from catechism had even strode up to me to ask if it was true that Nantzin had freed all her slaves. I'd given her a look of disgust and turned away. But it was true, of course, and most of them had indeed decided to leave our household, including Jacinta.

Marta was beside herself, incensed at having to manage with so little help, though I did not think we were so much trouble. She had at least managed to hire a new cook, whose creations so far, I was reluctant and surprised to say, were vastly superior to Toño's. I wanted to meet him, for everyone said he was only a young moreno, a dark-skinned boy. They said he was the son of a freed Moor, which intrigued me because we'd never had one work for us before. But I'd not had the time.

I'd been too busy spending my nights at the library, carefully copying each and every single one of the images stitched on Nantzin's cushions onto a scroll, ensuring that no detail was missed, and preparing for my escape.

I would do it after the ball, when everyone was either too drunk or asleep. I'd asked Nano to take me with him, and he'd agreed. Even Pedro had given us permission. Both he and Gonzalo would be going too. My plan was to give them the slip and find Nantzin's next journal, come back home and change, go to the dovecote and grab my weapons and the satchel I'd stuffed with a spare set of traveling clothes and other supplies, and run off to find the rest. I highly doubted it would be too difficult.

The six remaining locations on the cushions and map were commonly known by everyone across the valley, and not too far, except Teotihuacan and Iztaccihuatl. It might take me two or three days to travel to each of those places by foot.

I wouldn't take a horse again. Horses were still a rarity in this side of the world, easily recognized and very expensive. I'd only be making myself a target for thieves and anyone looking for me. I felt sure my brothers would try to find me, or Nano at least.

My only problem was Catina. She'd accepted my apology, but things hadn't been quite the same since our argument. She seemed to be watching me a lot more than usual too, and I guessed she suspected my plans, though she never said anything.

Thus, it came as a huge surprise for me, for all of us, when she spoke out loud during dinner that evening. We were all sitting around the long wooden table. Above us, an iron chandelier lit with many candles faintly illuminated the room around us, the paintings of leafy vines and wild birds: hummingbirds, egrets, and woodpeckers. Pedro had taken Papa's seat at the head, my brothers to his right and left. I sat next to Nano, with Catina opposite me, beside Gonzalo.

Pudding had just been served: a bowl of creamy dulce de mamey, a striking red fruit that was sweet and heavy on the tongue. Nano and I were fighting over the last serving when Catina cleared her throat. We all froze mid-gesture and turned to look at her like a clump of broken marionettes. She closed her eyes, as though shutting out our attentions even though she'd invited them, then took a breath.

"I'd like to go to the viceroy's ball with all of you," she said, too loud.

There were several heartbeats' worth of silence. I don't think Pedro and Gonzalo had realized she could still speak. She opened her eyes, and the corner of her lip tugged upward at our expressions. We must've all looked ridiculous, like owls caught by torchlight.

Without being asked, she offered an explanation. "I think it would be nice to show a united front, as a family. Put a stop to all these awful rumors. And I'd like to see why everyone makes such a fuss about these dance parties before . . . before we join the convent."

Pedro and Gonzalo looked at each other. Nano frowned, then said and signed at the same time, "Really? Are you sure?"

Catina nodded. She locked eyes with me. "I'm sure."

I understood her meaning. She wanted to find Nantzin's treasure too. She was coming with me.

The next morning, I showed Catina the diary that Toño had given me, told her my plans and where everything was kept. To her credit, she only looked half terrified, and proceeded to assemble her own traveling clothes and other supplies with minimally trembling hands. She only dropped a wineskin and a blanket once, when we heard Marta walking past our chambers, huffing and complaining about being unable to chaperone us to a ball of such distinction—she'd recently discovered that all her best gowns had been devoured by moths, which may or may not have been recently collected and deposited in her wardrobe by me for that singular purpose.

Right before the maids came in to help us get dressed for the ball, we studied the cushions and my copy of them, and agreed I'd not missed anything. We took note of several symbolic images: a roaring lion on the door of the palace, a pile of books under a large tree, and the two-headed eagle of the Habsburgs on a flag waving over one of the palace columns to the right. We agreed the clearest symbol was the pile of books, and that we would first look in the palace library, wherever that was.

I was so thrilled about the prospect of this adventure, I barely noticed the time passing. I didn't even glance once at my reflection. Catina, too, was even more pensive than usual, and simply gazed out the window as the maids braided her hair and pinned it beneath a black veil, squeezed her into a beautifully beaded bodice, and powdered her nose.

The sun was setting by the time the maids bowed out. We thanked them and stood. I grabbed my purse and folded the scroll with the drawings of the first cushion into it, feeling a little like I was waking for a second time that day, rousing from a daydream.

Catina turned and gasped. I whirled around, thinking she was looking at someone behind me. My wide farthingale and skirts swayed and brushed the floor.

"No, it's you! You're—pretty!" She squeaked. A myriad of emotions flickered across her face: surprise, confusion, envy, joy.

"Am not!" I narrowed my eyes and ran to the looking glass. My brows shot up. "Oh."

Catina laughed and knotted her arm around mine, scrutinizing our reflections. I wondered if she compared herself to me as much as I did to her. We usually dressed much the same, like today. Both of us wore matching high-necked silk gowns the color of the midnight sky, embellished with silver brocade adorned with sparkling pearls. Our hair was pulled back into looping braids and veiled in Spanish lace, as becoming of our virtue and age.

We were almost the same height, the tips of our noses drooped slightly, and her eyes were just as brown as mine, shaped like two perfect almonds. Nantzin's eyes. There was no doubt we were sisters, even though Catina's skin was several shades lighter, her cheeks adorably freckled, oozing sweetness in a way I never could.

A tinge of jealousy stirred within me, thinking how she had always been considered the more beautiful one. Women at court had praised and doted on her, petted and pampered her, until she had fallen ill and deaf. Then, it was as if they'd forgotten she existed. I'd even overheard one of them loudly exclaiming that it must've been a sign that God was displeased with my father, for tainting his blood with that of an *India*. Father had overheard the insult and, to my everlasting pride, boomed that there were none so deaf as those who refused to listen to the word of God. The woman had turned scarlet and nearly fainted. Nevertheless, people rarely looked at Catina nowadays, unless it was to pity her. I would rather have died than be looked upon like that. The awful thought struck me, and I saw my reflection blanch.

Luckily, Catina was staring at her luxurious skirt and failed to notice. I tapped her with my elbow and mouthed, "You look beautiful too," hoping she would understand. Hoping it would somehow make up for my terrible mind, my luck in being the one to keep my hearing, though I was the least deserving of us both.

She smiled again, shy and lovely. This time I felt no jealousy, just a loving warmth pulling at my cheeks. I signed without thinking, "You're going to break all the boys' hearts tonight."

She shut her eyes and shook her head. A look of pain crossed her features, and too late I remembered how much this outing was costing her, how much she hated being away from home, around gawking strangers and unforgiving crowds, who thought being deaf meant she had no language, no capacity to think or understand. I took her into my arms.

"Promise me," she whispered into my chest, "we'll leave as soon as we find what we're looking for."

I nodded. She let go and looked into my eyes. I signed, "Of course. I promise."

"And also swear, swear to the Lord, that you won't let *anyone* dance with me."

I rolled my eyes, but swore again.

CHAPTER 7

Isabel Cano

1 March 1551

The six of us stood at the top of the enormous staircase, facing the mingling, jovial crowd milling around the sparkling rectangular patio. The polished stone floors reflected the lights of hundreds of torches set around the surrounding inner arches, which had been draped with flowers. Their delicate perfume lingered in the air, and the sounds of laughter and chatter filled our ears, although there was no music or dancing, for we'd arrived between songs. The musicians, who were perched on a cloth-covered circular stage around the grand central fountain, were tuning their instruments, preparing for the next round.

It was not surprising, therefore, when everyone heard the doorman shouting our introductions: "The Lords Pedro Cano de Moctezuma, Gonzalo Cano de Moctezuma, Juan Cano de Moctezuma, and the Ladies Isabel and Catalina Cano de Moctezuma!"

There was a hush and lull as every creamy, prim, powdered face turned to look up at us, mostly in shock and bewilderment. I was not surprised by their attention, for they were always staring in some form or another. I didn't mind it so much when it came from the Mexica, when they gawked and pointed in the streets. I could understand why they cared about the people they had once revered as living gods. But in this crowd, it was a different level of scrutiny. A thousand pairs of eyes waiting for the tiniest misstep, a thousand tongues waiting to trill about it for weeks on end, to confirm their worst beliefs about you for being half blooded, for having darker skin.

Having an empress for a mother had only made it worse.

What is the point of being an empress, the catechism girls had said to me, *if you rule over savages? That only makes you the greatest savage of them all.*

In fact, most of the people who shared my skin tone were rushing around dressed in the gray palace livery, bowing and serving. Those who weren't stood out by the glorious panaches on their heads, the haughty looks on their faces. They had either formed an alliance with the conquistadores from the beginning, or fought and lost, then agreed to bend the knee, keep their heads and some of their privileges. If it tasted sour to me, I could only just imagine how it did to them.

I matched their expressions with an upward tilt to my chin and brow, but Catina shook beside me and took a step back. Pedro was standing behind her, however, and she couldn't escape. To my surprise, he put a steadying, gentle hand on her shoulder. He offered his arm, and she took it.

We descended the staircase in unison, Pedro and Catina in front of us. Nano, Gonzalo, and I followed behind them. When we reached the ground, we nodded at several important people, and bowed low when Viceroy de Velasco came into view. Even though he was new, he was the representative of Emperor Carlos V, and therefore the most powerful man in New Spain. To not pay him homage would've been akin to treason. Otherwise, we walked around, ignoring any and all whispers about us, looking bored and unimpressed. Or at least, Nano and I did.

It was an unspoken agreement between us, something that had always bound us together: our mutual, tangible disdain for these people, which had grown every time they had humiliated me or Nantzin, every time they'd called her *Empress* in a mocking tone and forced her to correct them. Every time they'd looked at her with pity or spoken about her in hushed voices.

Nano and I had always felt it, the feigned, snakelike . . . rancid tint of this court. It lived in the bend of their eyes, in the tautness of their nostrils, the gilded brightness of their smiles. It made me despise coming to these events. Even the daily trip to Mass gave me a pounding headache. This crowd made that monster inside me screech, transform into a fierce golden eagle, that ancient symbol of my ancestors—Huitzilopochtli, the resurrected warrior, god of war and fire. It wanted to fly; it wanted to hunt.

It wanted to tear their heads off.

"Are you all right?" Nano whispered in Nahuatl.

"If there's any reason to shut myself in a convent for the rest of my life, it's to never have to see these people again."

He burst out laughing.

To my surprise, a collective giggle and sigh echoed around us, and I noticed, for the first time, that we were being trailed by at least a dozen beautiful, bejeweled young women, blinking profusely, fanning themselves, pouting and grinning. The white ostrich feathers adorning their velvet toque hats trembled as they gazed at my brother and me with a strange mixture of adoration and jealous passion, and for a moment I thought they would willingly cut out their own hearts if he gave the word.

Nano appeared to be completely oblivious, so I cleared my throat and gave him a pointed look. Unfortunately, Pedro and Gonzalo turned too. Their faces darkened.

Gonzalo put his arm around Nano's shoulders and raised his oily voice. "It's an heiress for him or nothing, ladies, so most of you are wasting your time. Our poor brother has received a pittance from our mother—he must marry well! Now me, on the other hand . . ." He winked and patted the sword at his hip. "I've been left well endowed."

Luckily, the music had started and only the immediate circle around us heard my brother's crude words and the ensuing gasps of outrage. The ladies dispersed like lemon drops on grease, and Gonzalo and Pedro howled with laughter.

"You two are filth," I said, and grabbed Catina. "Let's get a drink."

"I'll escort you," Nano said, and we walked away.

As we crossed the courtyard, my sister glanced at the musicians with a look of desperate yearning, and my heart wrung into itself. As a little girl, she'd loved music, even more so than books. Sometimes she hummed her favorite melodies in a voice that was no longer in tune. A pair of young men stepped forward, eyeing us with interest, probably mistaking her expression as a desire to dance, but my scowl and her terrified look quickly turned them away. We made our way to the refreshments behind the musicians.

A long table was covered in the finest white cloth embossed with golden double-headed eagles, decked with silver candelabras that cast a flickering light over dozens of glistening honey-roasted quails, several succulent venison shanks, and a magnificent suckling pig sitting on a bed of apples. There were gold platters heaped with freshly baked breads, salads, and local nuts and fruits that most of the court could hardly pronounce—guayaba, mamey, tejocote, zapote.

I threw a cube of papaya in my mouth, turned to Nano, and said, "You don't have to stay. I'll mind Catina."

"She's fourteen, Isabel, she's nearly a grown woman."

"Yes, but you know she's scared witless. I'll stay with her so you can dance."

I thought he would jump at the chance to get away, and we would be able to sneak off quietly to look for the library, but he laughed again and shook his head. "Well, that's mighty thoughtful of you. But I'd prefer to stay and chat about your secret plans."

"Hmm?" I'd been so certain he'd be well on his way that I'd already begun to look around and wasn't really listening. I'd spotted my half sister, Leonor, with another woman at the other end of the party. Leonor had lived here before the last viceroy had taken residence. I could probably ask her where the library was and save us time.

"Isabel!" Nano's voice was hard. I tweaked my neck as I spun back to look at him. "Tell me the truth. You hate these events as much as Catina, so what are you doing here?"

My stomach dropped, but I think I managed, somehow, to convey a look of mild, benign perplexity before responding, "Sorry? I don't know what you mean . . ."

With narrowed eyes, he turned to our sister. "Catina," he signed. "Tell me what you're up to. Why did you really want to come tonight? And don't you dare lie."

Her eyes went as round as the gold platters behind us. After a painfully long moment, in which Nano's smile twisted into a more menacing, knowing shape, she glanced between him and me, and finally shook her head.

I stifled a groan. It was so obvious we were hiding something, and I wanted to tell him, but I knew he'd try to stop us. His first instinct was always to protect, to shelter, so I shrugged and said, "We just wanted to come laugh at these fools and eat their food, that's all."

He nodded, though his eyes seemed to shimmer with a drop of hurt. "I see . . . well you might not want to share your secret with me, but if you think for one moment I'll be leaving you alone . . ." His hands dropped mid-sign, slowly, down to his sides. Catina and I both followed his wandering gaze and turned around.

A young lady was humming as a server piled food on her plate. She kept pointing at each choice with a look bordering on reverence, and sneaking a taste with her fingers, letting out quick, chirping sounds of delight. A drop of sauce fell on the richly embellished bodice covering her ample bosom, and she wiped it away with a napkin.

She had a pretty face, not as striking as the other girls, but lovely. She was almost as short as we were, but with generous curves, flawless alabaster skin, and full, heavy lips. She was so immersed in the food, she didn't even notice us staring. I immediately approved. After one particularly delicious-looking bite, she sighed and sucked her index finger.

Nano groaned. I looked back at him. He appeared to be in physical pain.

"What's the matter with you?" I thought perhaps his stomach ailed him.

"Juan!" The girl had finally noticed us, and her face brightened even more. "Oh my goodness, are these your sisters? Is this Catina? Wait, wait!"

She cleared her throat, then signed, "Nice to meet you."

I smiled, but Catina's face burned carmine. She looked at the floor, too ashamed to greet her back. I clenched my jaw, fighting a burst of hot irritation at her inability to return even the smallest greeting.

"Oh no, did I do it wrong?" The girl looked at me with concern.

"No, she's just shy," I said. There was no point elaborating on the hundreds of reasons why—they were dancing and laughing and drinking all around us. And from the way the girl nodded with her lips pressed together, it was clear she had enough experience of it herself to understand, or perhaps my brother had filled her in on the many incidents Catina had suffered. Not that it made it any easier for me to make friends, having to constantly defend both my sister and Nantzin from the vixens of this court.

The girl's voice was airy and light. "Well, Juan's been teaching me, and I hope to learn much more from him." She flickered a shy, hopeful glance in his direction.

Nano returned a strangled nod. He had such an odd look on his face, and his body was so stiff, as though stuck between wanting to rush to her and run away. I stared pointedly at him as we all waited for him to say anything. I would've jammed my heel onto his foot, but it would've been too obvious.

Finally, I turned to the girl with my most cordial smile, then said and signed at the same time, "Any friend of our brother's is a friend of ours. Pray, what is your name?"

"Oh, silly me! I'm Elvira. Elvira de Toledo." She offered her hand to both of us. I glared at Catina, who forced herself to shake it after me.

To her credit, Elvira did not make any fuss of the stilted interaction and said, "How are you finding the party?"

"It's quite . . . fine." I shrugged.

"Oh yes, it can be a little boring, especially if you're not keen on dancing. I love dancing, but . . ." Her voice wavered. "Anyway, the food is magnificent, have you tried these tiny baked fish wrapped in corn husks? Mextlapique, I believe the dish is called. Does Catina like fish? Tell her it's delicious, please, I don't want her to be left out!"

I interpreted what she'd said. Catina nodded, still looking at the floor, and whispered, "I love fish." My feelings for her mellowed, for I knew she was trying her hardest. I squeezed her hand and said, "Yes, we love fish infinitely more than dancing, which is the opposite of Nano. Alas, our older brothers have chased all his admirers away!"

Elvira's smile faltered. "He is ever so popular at court."

"Ah, but we prefer quality over quantity, don't we?" I nudged him, and he returned a threatening smile. I fluttered my eyelashes back at him. "In fact, I was just telling him how much happier he'd be on the dance floor. Why don't you indulge us all, brother. Take Elvira with you! You can't possibly deny her, not after all the effort she's made for Catina!"

His jaw set. A myriad of emotions flickered across his features. He pinned me with a look that conveyed his deep desire to strangle me, but when his gaze landed on Elvira's glowing, expectant face, he warmed and slowly extended his palm.

"May I please have the pleasure of this dance, Señorita de Toledo?"

Her shoulders dropped infinitesimally. Likely she would've preferred for him to call her by her first name, like she had done with him, and the return to formality was disappointing. Regardless, she didn't wait long before nodding and taking his hand.

"Don't you dare move," he said under his breath as they left.

I bent low as I bowed so he wouldn't see the victorious smile on my face.

"Come on, we don't have much time," I signed at Catina, then grabbed her hand and pushed our way to the other side of the patio, where Leonor and her friend were still immersed in discussion.

There was a reverent gap between them and the rest of the crowd, who kept glancing at them in awe. Perhaps it was their way of carrying themselves, as though they were more than queens, goddesses, for whom no one else existed. Perhaps it was that Leonor was a child of Cortés, that she had his height, his olive skin, and his bearing.

But even if she hadn't, and many of his other children who were born out of wedlock didn't, their name was still currency in this land. They were the new royalty, second only to the viceroy and his family. Then, of course, there was the fact that Leonor had gold coming out her ears, and gold was valued by the gentry above everything else. Twice an heiress and newly married to one of the richest men this side of the Atlantic, she had enough wealth to buy herself an altar to be worshipped over.

Fortunately, I was no devotee. I didn't care, and I certainly wasn't cowed.

I strode up to them with a determined smile, gave them a clipped nod, and said, "Evening, ladies. Pardon the interruption." I looked at my half sister. "Leonor, I'm wondering if you'd be so kind as to give us directions to the library, please."

Leonor's friend's eyebrows shot up. Her lips parted with a mixture of amusement and surprise. My half sister, however, was unimpressed. She stared at me as though I were a fat, buzzing fly she'd like nothing more than to swat, then turned to her friend.

"Maria, these are my late mother's daughters, Isabel and Catalina. Pray excuse their manners." She blinked slowly back at me again and said, "This is my friend, Maria Jaramillo, and I do not, indeed, appreciate the interruption to the precious time I have left with her."

"Fine, then *quickly* tell us where the library is and we'll be on our way."

Maria snickered. "Goodness, she's a feisty one."

Leonor shook her head as though my behavior pained her. "Dreadful," she said, and turned her shoulder to shut us out. "Anyway, you were saying, the nausea has been awful?"

"A nightmare," Maria said, without giving us a second glance. "No one seems to be able to come up with a good remedy for it. I think I'll ask one of the Mexica midwives."

"That's *such* a good idea. Please, do write and tell me what they say . . ."

I cleared my throat.

Leonor took an exaggerated breath and turned to me. "There are a multitude of servants who can answer your tiresome questions. I am busy. Goodbye."

Maria had the decency to cover her smile at the outraged look on my face.

I huffed, and we walked off.

"What happened?" asked Catina.

I shook my head and took us to a more private space. When we got there, I shot a glance at the dance floor to make sure Nano was still busy with Elvira, which he was.

"She's such a snob," I signed. "We're going to have to find the library without help."

I was about to hand her the scroll when two of the girls from catechism stopped to look at us and then at each other with wide, amused eyes.

"What do you want?" I said.

The girls began to mime with their hands at each other, giggling stupidly. "What are we saying?"

"That you have air for brains!" I spat, trembling with rage.

They burst into a fit of laughter and sauntered off, and I had to stop myself from running after them and tearing their toques off their scalps. I turned around and growled. Catina's eyes were downcast again. A terrible guilt and helplessness pulled on my heart, for this had been my idea. She had not wished to come and place herself at the mercy of some of the cruelest people on God's forsaken earth.

He had already given her the harder path. Even though both of us had been afflicted with that terrible fever, she'd been the one deafened by it. The least I could've done was protect her from human viciousness, and I had failed once again.

"I'm sorry," I mouthed with tears in my eyes.

"Forget them," said Catina in a soft, hollow voice. "May I please see the scroll?"

I swallowed my pain, gave her the scroll, and pointed at the symbols. "Can you see this flag somewhere? Or this door?"

"It's such a huge place, we'll get lost." She looked up. "Wait, there!" She pointed at the sky, and I followed her line of vision. There was the flag, identical to the cushion's, hanging off a diagonal flagpole off the second floor of the palace.

"Let's go."

The halls quietened and darkened, and we came across fewer people as we surreptitiously made our way to the southeastern wing of the palace. We passed several canvases painted with hunting and fishing motifs, sneaked around pillars, and stuck to the shadows. Luckily, no one spotted us, but unfortunately, all the doors we tried on the ground floor were locked. We shook all of them, despite the fact that none had a tree nor a roaring lion carved onto them. Only the door at the end of the hallway was ajar. It led to a winding staircase, which we took to the upper level.

My heart began to race as we opened another door a sliver to peek through, then shut it again as a palace sentry walked past at the end of the passage. A moment later, we tried again and were relieved to find the place deserted. Better yet, a few meters away, in the middle of the passage, there was a set of double doors. The iron handles were wrought into two identical roaring lions. We pulled the doors and found they were unlocked.

My breath hitched as we walked inside.

"Where do we look first?" said Catina.

It was a large room, handsomely decorated, with polished wooden bookshelves stacked against the wall, lined with dozens of books and scrolls and embossed leather parchments. A fire burned in front of an enormous, unusually tall desk. The light glimmered and bent as it struck two half-drunk glasses of wine sitting on the corner.

My eyes widened nervously. I tapped Catina's shoulder so she would look at me, and signed, "Let's hurry. The last clue was a tree." I began to search the titles. "Are there books about trees anywhere?"

"No, but there's a big painting right there with a tree on it," said Catina.

We ran to look at it. The tree was loaded with fruits and surrounded by a golden frame, which contained the words *Serit arbores quae alteri saeclo prosint.*

"That's a quote from Cicero! I think?" Catina said brightly.

I signed, "What does it mean? Something 'trees' . . ." My Latin was beyond abysmal.

"Um, I believe it translates to 'One plants trees for future generations.' I think it's about being generous." She went back to searching through the shelves. "Doing something you might not necessarily benefit from, but because someone down the line will."

She hummed tunelessly. I groaned and looked around, feeling a growing sense of irritation. These were the kind of fanciful, scholarly discussions I'd always hated but which Catina reveled in. What was the point of them anyway? To prove how clever you were? How many books you had read, how well you could quote, and how deeply you could think? I did not remember Nantzin caring much for these discussions either. But then again, what did I really know about her. I glanced at the two half-empty drinks and a gnawing sense of worry built inside me. I was just about to say we should give up and leave when Catina gasped.

"Here, here! Cicero's treatise! *Cato Maior de Senectute.*" She pulled out an old tome. "The book is called *Concerning Old Age*. Oh my word . . . it's made out of wood!"

I ran to her side, my heart thrumming painfully in my ears. It wasn't a real book. It was a box painted exactly like a book. She opened it, and out into her palm fell a thin leather diary just like the one Toño had given to me. We dashed over to sit on the floor beside the fire and opened it. Catina, to my surprise, was almost turning the first page before I'd even started.

I stopped her hand with my own quivering one, knowing I was about to be near my mother once more. Fighting back tears, I began to read.

CHAPTER 8

Tecuichpoch

1519–1520

I know not how others keep track of the passage of time. When you look back, do you mark festivities? Natural disasters? The death of your beloved pet or grandmother?

I no longer remember the days of the sacred calendar or their meanings. I simply recall the years of my life by the husbands I've had and the moment they died.

My first, Atlixcatzin, had grandchildren older than me. He was tlatoani in the east, a relative of my mother's. My father wished to renew their alliance and reinforce our borders from a nebulous threat which was only whispered about at court: of small hills moving on the surface of the water, men riding enormous deer with no antlers—men who had captured the sound of thunder in long sticks. They spoke of an alliance formed between these inexplicable beings and our bitter enemies, the Tlaxcalteca. They spoke of ancient prophecies and terrible omens, temples burning with unquenchable flames, tongues of fire lighting up the night sky, foaming lakes, and war. Above all, they spoke of war.

I listened to palace gossip as a treasured child of nine years who had never faced a day of true hardship in her life. Just as I'd listened to countless other frightful, astonishing tales of gods and battles and mystifying power—with an excitable curiosity my mother reminded me I ought to keep to myself. Which I did, except with my brother.

With Axayacatzin, I would play fight in the garden. We would charge these shadow strangers from the backs of our own monstrous beings, our winged serpents and fire-breathing eagles, and vanquish them back to the sea whence they came. For our father was huey tlatoani, blessed by Tezcatlipoca and Huitzilopochtli, the brilliant lords of death and war, and we had nothing to fear. Especially if we did our duty, we would keep chaos at bay.

That is what we strove for, from my father to my brother to the lowest slave: we all helped maintain cosmic and civil order by doing what was expected of us. And what was expected of me was to marry or die, so I was married to Lord Atlixcatzin. This was done in ritual only, and I never met him, or his children or grandchildren who were older than me. It was agreed that I would be sent to the east only after my education was complete, for I was not old enough to attend temple school even, and could not yet weave or spin well enough or say the proper prayers for my marriage ceremony and the rest of my wedded life.

This is all I knew was possible for me, the only choices I was presented with. I had no say in my life, no wishes of my own that I could articulate, except to breathe in fresh air, and run with my brother through the gardens, and swim in the lake with salamanders. That is all I cared about—that and pleasing my parents.

In the end, the alliance did nothing to spare us. I never got to attend school.

My first husband was defeated by the Spaniards and the Tlaxcalteca, and I was widowed a few weeks before turning eleven. A pity, for I might've been spared my year of capture, a whole year of missing my mother and brother.

But my father thought perhaps Cortés could be brought into an alliance by marriage. When the Spanish finally made their way into our city, followed by thousands upon thousands of our ancestral enemies, my father offered a mighty gift: his four most beautiful daughters.

I was the youngest of the four by several years, though the most important. Even Cortés's interpreter, Malintzin, took pains to explain to him my lineage, my significance as the firstborn child of the huey tlatoani's primary wife. And though she spoke no lies, for better or worse, Malintzin marked me to the Spaniards forever.

Cortés, of course, accepted Father's offer, even though he was already married. We did not understand, you see, that in the Christian tradition, he could only have one wife.

I was not there when Father found out, if he ever did, that his prized daughters had been accepted as mere concubines. Our last parting, the last time we saw each other in person, was brief and formal, surrounded by my three half sisters, Citlalin, Metztonalli, and Yolloxochitl, my full brother, Axayacatzin, and our mothers.

Citlalin and Metztonalli were full sisters, and their mother was distraught. Her loud sobs were a shameful breach of propriety, an expression only appropriate for funerals. Yet it was a mark of the seriousness of the situation that not one of the other women so much as spared her a glance. Nor did they pinch or reprimand my little brother for his feminine weakness when silent tears streamed down his cheeks. We were all trying our best to hold on to our noble bearing, and show our father that we were worthy of serving him and our people, the way we'd been raised to serve them. For we all, myself included, knew what it meant to marry. Or at least, we thought we did.

We'd been taught to keep our chastity, we knew what it took to lose it—the act between man and woman that led to children—and we knew the cost. It was not so long ago that Tlatoani Nezahualpilli of Texcoco had had his daughter executed for simply speaking to a man she was not married to. We also knew of the pains of childbirth. Father had plenty of wives and concubines who loved to swap stories of winning their battles with birth. It was how they were elevated, how they became as good as warriors. I felt myself a warrior then, though I was but a foolish girl who'd not yet bled.

Only a slight waver in his throat told me what it cost my father to give us up. It may seem like nothing, but believe me when I say I'd never before heard a flawed note in his voice, which I would never hear again. But of course, I knew nothing of what would come. Of the monstrous journey that would begin with just a few steps.

It was only a short walk between my father's palace and my grandfather's, where the Spanish army and their allies were being housed. My legs had never felt so heavy. The din of the great market of Tlatelolco had been silenced by the beating of the evening drum, signaling the end of trade and the start of night curfew. Later, young men studying to be priests in the calmecac would come out blowing flutes and banging drums and trumpeting the great sea conchs, announcing the time of the night sacrifices, but for now, the pristinely swept streets were eerily silent. Only the light clatter of the Huey Tzompantli was present, the rattle of bones from the great rack where tens of thousands of perforated skulls were displayed as a sign of our might as a nation . . . and of our frailty as human beings.

The smell of maize and wood fire was pungent in the air, and I was suddenly seized by the most powerful urge to run back, run home to my mother. To be wrapped in one of her rare embraces. Too rare, but enough that I knew myself to be endlessly loved. My step faltered, and I was bumped slightly forward by one of the men escorting me, Pedro de Alvarado, the man who would later trap and massacre half my family, hundreds of them, while they danced and prayed for rains during the festival of Toxcatl.

He showed no malice to me then, and only opened his palms in a gesture of apology, but I did not wish to look at him, at any of them: these tall, bearded men who smelled nothing of home, of clean, of safe. Cortés's most trusted captains walked in a ring around us, along with the slave Malintzin, a woman who hailed from Olutla, near the eastern sea, from a people not allied to us. She could not have been much older than Citlalin, who at sixteen was the oldest among us. I wondered if she, too, felt as threatened by these men as we did.

Malintzin caught my glance, smiled in a friendly way, and whispered, "Fear not. Until your breasts are formed, you shall be as tempting to Cortés as a bowl of broth without salt." To my two oldest sisters, however, she offered no such comfort.

I will admit, we all cried when we were led to our new chambers. Though we knew these spotless halls, though we were still in our own city, though we could see our father's palace from the high window, it felt as though we were four flightless eaglets in a den of coyotes.

We had servants, of course, for our status as princesses had not changed, but they were Tlaxcalteca women and we could not trust them. Every creak, every step, every echo of laughter made my muscles tighten and jump. We huddled together on one mat by the window, holding our knees to our chests, and took turns staying awake. Not that it would've made any difference if someone came for us. We were not warriors in any true sense of the word. We were little more than cattle waiting for the butcher's knife.

The next morning, before we were summoned, a cheerful Malintzin explained that we were to receive the Spanish God from their priest. A tall, bearded man, who stank of sweat and dung as all the others did, came to say some words and sprinkle us with water.

Of course I had no idea what he was saying at the time. I remember wishing, as the droplets fell over my face and hair, that he had washed himself as thoroughly as he was trying to wash us. Nevertheless, Malintzin tried her best to explain what holy baptism was, and the new God we must pray to. She said we had received new names, Christian names, and that we must use these from now on. And so it was that Citlalin became Ana, Metztonalli became Maria, Yolloxochitl became Mariana Leonor.

And I, Tecuichpoch, was baptized with the name of Isabel.

In honor of their beloved late Catholic queen.

That very same night, Cortés called his newly purified wards, my oldest sisters, Citlalin-Ana and Metztonalli-Maria, one first and then the other, to his chambers.

We did not speak of it. We didn't know how to. Even though marriage and childbirth were our purposes in life, what we had been raised for, what our married sisters had already been through, it was not the same. At the time, I could not understand what made it seem so very wrong. I was childish enough, innocent enough, to think that perhaps it was because our ceremonies had not been performed, that we had not said the proper rites and prayers to our gods, that the men smelled so bad. My sisters' wishes never occurred to me, but I could see they were desperately sad.

Mariana and I took it upon ourselves to serve them as best we could. We tried to cheer them with sweet words, with offers to wash and brush and braid their hair. We ordered pine resin and flowers to scent the rooms, and tried to encourage them to spin and weave and sew and embroider. But unless they were sleeping, they only wished to sit in the boiling steam bath. They did not join us during our Castilian lessons with Malintzin and Don Bernal Díaz del Castillo, who was the only one of Cortés's men apart from the priest who was allowed to speak to us. They ate sparingly, and said it tasted of ash.

I wondered, too, why my sisters wept when Malintzin never did, though she was called to Cortés's bed twice as often as they were. And I do not think for one moment that she enjoyed his attentions. She did not love him, as he later claimed she did. I know this because the muscles of her jaw would tense whenever I saw him touch her, though her smile never wavered. I know this because I studied her at every opportunity.

Whenever she brought us news and greetings from our mothers or the palace beyond our reach, or when the priest called her to translate for him, I observed her closely. There was not much else for me to do, nowhere for me to go. She was one of the only people allowed near us, and she was kinder to me than even my sister Mariana was. And truly, I could not help myself, especially once I knew her story.

Born a noblewoman but sold into slavery by her own family, sold to pay tribute to us, the Mexica. She spoke more languages than I can recall. She'd seen more of my father's empire than even he had, and witnessed more battles than most men on either side.

I had never seen anything like her. She was unnatural, spectacular, bright like volcanic fire, and she was Cortés's right hand.

He needed her: not her body—he had dozens of those—but her mind. Her skills in language, courtesy, and the political bearings of an empire he did not understand. That is what she truly loved, I believe—being allowed to wield her talents with impunity. She was audacious in her wit, charming, coy, and playful, flitting about the palace like a merry little hummingbird. But oh, how she reveled in hearing the sound of authority in her voice, of looking at mountainous men straight in the eye and seeing them awestruck and cowed. They admired her so much they even titled her doña, a great honor, especially for a sixteen- or seventeen-year-old girl who'd been sold three times over and was not yet free.

I tried to judge her, as I'd been taught to, as Mariana did when we were alone.

Malintzin is shameless, she said. She ought to keep her eyes low, her head down, and her voice soft. But in truth, a female had never held a position of real importance by my father's side. I did not think it was possible for a noblewoman to do anything more than be a wife and mother. Yes, my own mother had been a mighty queen, but Malintzin, despite being a slave, had the bearing of a god.

I will admit, now that I am near death, that despite being enemies in war . . . I could not help but like her. It may be difficult to understand, how one may learn to like a flame that burns them. But I defy you, I defy anyone, to prove me wrong, to spurn the only light shining in a world of darkness.

She came to say goodbye one morning. She told us that a second fleet of Spaniards had arrived from La Hispaniola, that she needed to follow Cortés and meet them. Cortés journeyed away from Tenochtitlan with her and a few other men, and left my sisters and me behind with Pedro de Alvarado.

Now, those last few days of captivity are a blur. It seemed to me that the fury of our city, built up after nearly a year of living alongside these god-awful strangers and our deadliest enemies, suddenly spilled over, as quickly as if the top of the Popocatepetl had erupted in a cloud of ash and liquid flame.

Everyone suddenly started to scream. From my window, I saw my people scattering in all directions, running and shouting, and arming themselves. Mariana pulled me away right before a burning arrow flew inside.

I did not know at the time that Alvarado had massacred all the nobles in the temple and strangled my father. I did not know why my grandfather's palace was suddenly under attack, under siege. Why Cortés was back after only a week, why half the city was in flames, or why we were being made to run over the dismantled causeways, over piles of bodies turned into bridges.

I can tell you, however, that I knew where Malintzin was at all times, because of the Mexica darts and arrows showering on her and Cortés like droplets falling from a moving rain cloud, piercing every inch of the shields of the men protecting them. I remember praying for her safety. Let Malintzin be spared, I thought, to whichever god would listen.

Kill only Cortés and his men.

That is what I thought, right before one of our own wayward arrows struck my sister Citlalin in the gut and she fell in the water. All three of us wrestled away from our guards and jumped in after her, but we could not save her.

I can still hear Metztonalli's screams echoing in my head.

I can see clearly, as if it were a painting in my mind, how she held Citlalin and splashed and kicked the water as though it was her mortal enemy, as though the lake itself had been keeping her locked in a room for a year, keeping her body prisoner to a godforsaken man who reeked of horseshit. Even when Cuauhtemoc, our cousin, found us and pulled us out of the depths, she ripped out her hair and scratched her face and screamed and screamed that her one true friend was gone.

I, for one, cannot claim to have had many true friends.

Axayacatzin, my brother, was one. Mariana, for a brief time, was another. And though she was, in large part, the person who brought down my father's empire, Malintzin holds a place of warmth in my heart.

It would be a year before I would see her again, after I was crowned the last empress of the Mexica. Though that is a tale for another day.

My hope is that you will find it.

CHAPTER 9

Isabel Cano

1 March 1551

The library door banged open, and in swirled two people who appeared to be dancing with their faces melted together. It was a miracle that I didn't scream, that we were on the floor, and that they were too preoccupied with each other to notice us at all.

I grabbed Catina, and we scrambled backward underneath the desk. I put an arm around her and a hand over my nose and tightly sealed lips. It was partly to stop any breath escaping, but also partly because I was in a state of wild astonishment.

I was thunderstruck at our discovery, at Nantzin's second account, at the image of her curled up by her sisters, waiting to hear if she would be called to her enemy's bed. My skin crawled with disgust. It was evil, pure evil, to put a child through that, whatever that nebulous thing was that men and women did whenever they were alone together, which no one had ever really explained in enough detail for me to understand fully.

Sure, I'd heard the catechism girls gossiping about which doña was having an affair with which don, or the priests endlessly denouncing the sin of fornication, and the sin of lust, and the sin of adultery, and so on.

Once I'd even walked into the stables as Pedro's stallion was beginning to mount Nano's mare, but Nano quickly turned me away before I could get a good look, saying it was not a sight for girls. And I knew by the way my brothers were constantly insulting each other's manhood that the words *prick*, *cock*, *shaft*, *pistol*, and *rod* were related somehow.

Nantzin *had* promised to explain matters once I turned sixteen and was at a suitable age to marry, but she had become too ill, and then I had sworn to become a nun.

Indeed, most of my knowledge came from Papa, of all people, who had warned us that men had swords between their legs while women only had sheaths filled with virtue and honor. Not just *our* honor, but our entire family's as well. He'd said that we would need to be watchful. That we ought to defend and protect our sheaths with our purity and chastity, for men were forever trying to steal them, an act which would bring shame and ruin to us all. This, of course, sounded terribly dangerous and awful and unfair. Could men simply try *not* to steal our sheaths instead? Perhaps that is why Papa taught us how to shoot.

I wished someone had taught Nantzin how to as well.

I pictured her as she would've looked, a little like Catina did now, younger than her, shyly studying the formidable woman everyone knew as La Malinche, running behind her through the burning, embattled streets of our city. The terror she would've felt to see an arrow sticking out of her sister's body. I clutched Catina closer and smelled her hair, said a prayer for her safekeeping, and closed my eyes, trying to picture something else, anything else that was good and happy and just.

But I only got so far as to imagine a strong, tall woman, someone like my sister Leonor, transforming into a deadly panther intent on tearing those Spanish soldiers' throats out, before I was distracted by the nauseating sounds emerging from the couple's mouths.

I'd never heard anything like it. The gasps and moans and slurps. I wanted to gag, because whatever they were doing sounded utterly revolting. At the same time, I had a blazing curiosity to look and find out what was happening, but when they began to talk, my revulsion increased tenfold and made me freeze.

Because I realized the man's voice belonged to my own brother Pedro.

"Ana, wait, wait. I must tell you something," he said in a gruff tone.

"Oh, truly?" Her chest sounded like mine when I'd been shooting arrows for hours—her voice was husky and alluring. Like she had been enjoying whatever they'd been doing. "I'd rather you did that thing again, with your tongue."

"No, you must know." He paused for several breathy moments, and his voice trembled when he continued. "I love you. I wish . . . I wish to marry you."

Ana laughed. Really laughed, from the bottom of her belly. It shook the whole desk, which they seemed to be lying on top of. Then she suddenly stopped.

"Oh dear. Oh no, don't look at me like that."

"Why do you laugh?"

"Oh, darling, surely you don't mean it? You know I could never marry *you*."

A long pause. Then, "Why?"

"Uh, my father?" Her voice took on an impatient edge.

"What about him?" He sounded so thickheaded, it was no wonder she lost her temper.

"He's the bloody viceroy, Pedro. I am fated to marry someone of *real* consequence. Not the second son of a vanquished India queen and a lesser noble. Now, you can either take what you're offered, or I can leave."

Another long pause, in which I felt a surge of violent rage so powerful I would've jumped up onto the desk and strangled her, had my sister not been pinning me down with her petrified, trembling body. The heaviest of silences rang in my ears.

Until Pedro spoke again. "Never speak of my mother again, you upstart, stupid, filthy . . . whore!" His voice was shaking with fury.

Ana jumped off the table. Her heels landed an inch from my skirts.

"Maybe I am, and so what?"

"I'll tell everyone what we've done."

She laughed again, cold and sharp. "Who'll believe you? There is no corner in their minds in which I'd let *you*, Pedro the hound, get anywhere near *this*. You have no friends, unlike me. Only your brother, and not even the handsome one people like."

More silence, then Ana sighed. "Too bad. We could've had fun."

And before my brother could respond, she turned on her heel and clattered away.

Meanwhile, my sister and I stayed hidden underneath the table, although only I could hear my brother as he slowly began to cry, then sob his heart away.

It felt like a whole season passed before Pedro collected himself and left the library. I made us wait even longer before emerging from under the desk. The first thing I noticed was that the wineglasses had been drained, my bottom was numb, and my shoulders were so tightly knotted I could barely move my arms. Catina put Nantzin's diary away in her purse as I gave her a quick, and extensively censored, summary of what had happened.

"Oh, poor Pedro!" Catina said.

I shrugged. Part of me did feel sorry for him, but part of me still thought he deserved it after the way he had treated Jacinta. However, the way that cow Ana had spoken about our mother was unforgivable, and if I ever met her alone, I vowed she would pay.

We sneaked back down the way we'd come, rushing through the dark corridors. At the last arch, before we could mingle back into the courtyard where the party was still in full swing, Nano stepped out into the light.

The grim expression on his face made us halt. Catina squeaked.

"I'm taking you home. Right now," he said, and gestured back toward the staircase.

It was only when we were facing the line of horses and carriages that I dared to ask, very gently, "How was your dance with Elvira?"

"None of your business. Where the devil is our coachman?" He went down the steps to investigate. While he was away, our oldest brother, Juan Andrade, emerged from the party, arm in arm with his wife, Mari. I squeezed Catina's arm, and she turned.

As soon as they spotted us, their steps slowed down. We stared at each other in discomfort for a painfully long moment, unsure of what to do. I didn't know whether to even greet him, when usually we would've bounced up with glee and hurtled into his strong arms.

Even that thought, that further loss, filled my eyes with tears.

Andrade noticed. "Agh, Isabel, no tears for us Moctezumas. Come here, come here, both of you." He stepped forward and opened his arms, and we fell into them. He was so solid, so warm, and he smelled so good, like a mixture of copal incense and leather, that I couldn't help but let out a small sigh.

"It's not been an easy time, has it?" he whispered into our veil-covered hair.

"The worst. Plus, we miss you," I mumbled. "Both of you."

"We miss you too." He let go and looked us over as we kissed Mari's rouged cheeks. She smelled lovely too, like a fresh bushel of carnations. Andrade took her hand again and gave it a kiss. They made a striking couple, dressed in all their Spanish finery. But there was real tenderness between them, which stirred something in me. A longing, perhaps, for something I was certain I would never have.

"Why are you two out here alone?" Andrade said.

"Same as you, I guess. We're going home. Nano is trying to find our coach."

Right on cue, Nano came back, looking so incensed he didn't notice Andrade and Mari straight away. "Those pendejos left without us! How the hell will we get ho—oh."

Andrade nodded a greeting at him. "Juan."

Nano cocked his head and then mock bowed. "Tlatoani."

Andrade's jaw tightened at the loaded word. Commander, ruler, speaker, king. Everything he could've been. Leonor might've been Nantzin's firstborn, but Andrade was her successor. *Tlatoani* was what she'd called him each time she'd kissed his forehead and caressed his curls. Each time she'd made it clear that no one else shone quite like him. It could've made us hate him, and Pedro and Gonzalo certainly did. But Andrade had always been so loving to us, so sweet and gentle, that it was impossible to.

I stabbed Nano with a look. "Don't start, please."

"Fine, well, nice seeing you." He grabbed our arms. "Let's go back inside and find a ride with someone else."

Mari piped up, "Oh, don't be silly. We'll take you."

"Absolutely not," said Nano.

"Why not? I *want* to go with them!" I said and signed.

Catina nodded and whispered, "Nano, please. I'm cold and tired. Please, can we go?"

Nano ground his teeth.

"Let us take you home, brother," murmured Andrade.

After a long pause, Nano nodded. Andrade called his carriage, and we all squeezed inside with me in the middle, facing the back, where Andrade and Mari were sitting. For a quarter of an hour, as the coach lurched and jerked and tossed us in our seats through the cobbled streets, no one spoke. Andrade spent most of the time looking out the window, while Nano glared at him. Mari and I kept shooting them furtive glances and awkward half smiles at each other. Catina couldn't handle the tension. She closed her eyes and somehow fell asleep on my juddering shoulder.

When we reached the smoother road of the causeway, Mari cleared her throat and whispered, "I don't know if you've heard, by the way, but we're . . . expecting." Even with little to no light, I could tell her pale cheeks had blossomed red.

"That's wonderful news!" I said, nudging Nano in the ribs.

"Wonderful indeed," he said, "a little heir to take up your vendetta against our father when you're gone."

"Nano!" I exclaimed over the crunch of the wheels crushing dirt.

Andrade pinched the bridge of his nose. "This has nothing to do with your father."

"He raised you as his own and you thank him with a court battle!"

"As soon as Pedro was born, your father made it clear that I meant nothing to him."

"Just because he didn't pamper and pet you like Nantzin, you think you meant nothing? He loved you, loves you still! He treated you exactly like he did all of us!"

"I do what I must to protect my birthright as her legitimate firstborn. I fight the same way she did," Andrade said, voice low. Mari tried to intervene, but Nano was quicker.

"No—you're just a greedy pig," he spat back.

Nano glowered at Andrade, who met his deadly stare with an impassive, inscrutable one of his own. After a moment, Nano shook his head in utter disappointment and looked away. The carriage turned off from the causeway toward our gate.

No one said another word until we had arrived and Nano had smacked the door open and leapt off the coach. I shook Catina awake, and we whispered our gratitude, and I reiterated once more how happy I was for them, though it seemed as though my voice was incapable of piercing the painful, unpleasant wall that once again towered between us.

Catina stepped off the carriage, and I was halfway out when Andrade placed his hand on my arm. "Remember," he murmured, "I am always here for you two if you need me."

I nodded, gave him a quick peck on the cheek, and hopped off.

One of the guards opened the door for us, and we made our way through the dark, echoing house, up the stairs, and into our brightly lit room. Marta was sleeping on top of Catina's bed, curled up with only a light blanket covering her.

"We need to get rid of her and make sure Nano's asleep before we can go," I signed.

"Do we have to leave tonight?" Catina signed back, throwing a wistful glance at her mattress. "What is the hurry, really?"

I gawked at her. "Pedro and Gonzalo are out. They'll be nursing their heads tomorrow, too sick to come after us. Nano will probably sulk in his room all day too, after the argument he's just had. Marta's going to Mass early and won't notice we're gone till she returns in the afternoon. It's the perfect time."

"The perfect time for what," Nano spoke loudly, shattering the silence in the room. I whirled around. He was standing there, arms crossed over his chest, leaning on the doorframe. His brows were jutted and so close together, they seemed to have become one.

Marta snored and rolled over but, to my relief, continued sleeping.

"You're not allowed in here," I gestured.

"I'll give you one last chance to come clean," he signed back. "Or I'll see to it that you don't leave this room until it's time to escort you to the convent, which I will do myself."

I strode forward, fully intent on launching myself at his face, but Catina grabbed my arm and stepped between us, signing, "Stop it! We need to tell him. Nantzin would've wanted him to know too."

"What are you on about?" Nano signed.

Catina began to take the diary out from her purse, but I stopped her. "All right, but we can't let Marta see it. Nano—hide for just a moment."

He hesitated but seemed to decide from the look on my face that it was best to do as he was told, and crawled under my bed.

We gently shook Marta's shoulder. It took a few tries, but eventually she stretched and sat up. "You're home! How was it?"

"Atrocious," I answered. "I'm pleased we never have to do it again."

Marta's shoulders dropped. "Did you dance at all?"

I shuddered a no, and she shook her head sadly. "I suppose it's best—what with you going into the convent and all. Don't want any young men ruining your plans."

It was a constant source of dissatisfaction for her, our complete indifference for all things courtly and romantic. The news of our decision to become nuns had crushed any vestige of hope she'd fostered for us. I nodded and gave an exaggerated, loud yawn, then rubbed my eyes. I didn't want to speak of the convent, and I needed her to be gone.

She stood up. "I'll help you untie your bodices."

"Oh don't bother, you're tired. Catina and I can help each other."

She gave us an appreciative smile. "I *am* glad I got to see you both dressed so finely, at least one last time. My lovely girls."

Catina read her lips and understood. They hugged. I smiled back and pretended to yawn again. "Yes, thank you. Good night, Marta."

She bobbed out of the room, and I closed the door tight behind her.

"You can come out now," I whispered. Nano emerged from under the bed. He was turning his head to look at us when his gaze caught the tapestry on the wall.

His jaw slackened. "What the devil is that."

I proceeded to explain everything in a rapid, hushed tone as I let my sister out of her bodice and collected our things. He didn't even glance once in our direction, but continued to stare up at the image. I was too busy changing to see his face, though it was in shadows anyway. I imagined it would've looked very much like ours when we'd first beheld the tapestry: a mixture of bereavement, astonishment, and fear.

"We thought the treasure might be gold, but Toño had the first journal, and when we followed the clues, we found the second in the palace library," I concluded. "We plan to find the rest. We're leaving now."

"What?" He turned, and his eyes widened. Catina and I were standing side by side, dressed in our traveling clothes. Boots; light-brown cotton tunics; long, warm hooded cloaks; and a pair of leather satchels. I'd donned a leather belt too, and strapped my dagger onto it.

"Absolutely not." He moved and opened his arms as if to block the door.

"Read it to him," I signed at Catina. "Quickly." Catina shot me a reproachful look, but took the diary back out from her satchel and moved to sit in front of the fireplace.

As she began to read in Nahuatl, a shiver spread down my back. Her voice sounded just like Nantzin's. I turned to face the tapestry and looked at my mother's face, and felt for a moment that she was in the room again. And I was suspended in warmth. I floated in comfort, held in a way only she had been able to hold me during those times when I'd been truly unwell, as if her arms and gentle kisses could make it all better again—because she willed it so, she could take away all my suffering and pain.

No one else—not Marta, not even my own father—had shown me love like that.

Then it struck me again, like a bolt of lightning cleaving me in half, hollowing me out. She was gone. Her arms were gone, her lips were gone, buried under the earth along with the rest of her, and I would never see her again. This was not her real voice. I clutched my stomach and nearly howled, but I did not wish for Nano and Catina to see me like this. I bit my trembling lip and tried to breathe, listened to Nantzin's story again.

After several heartbeats I began to calm down again, and my resolve renewed. Because it may not have been her real voice, but it was her real story.

I knew it with every fiber in my body, even if it was raw and terrifying and painful. Even if I did not understand why she'd kept it hidden until now, perhaps to shield us until she thought we were ready, old enough. Only she knew. But it was real. And if it was the only thing left of her, I would search for it and have it.

I would have every single part.

CHAPTER 10

Isabel Cano

2 March 1551

Nano grabbed his head and sunk to his knees with a groan. "This can't be real."

"It is." I grabbed my satchel and pulled Catina from her chair. "Now get up, let's go. We've wasted too much time."

"Whoa—wait up now, one moment, you can't—"

Whatever he was going to say was interrupted by shouts and cheers from what seemed like a small, advancing party.

Nano froze and turned his head. "The boys are back."

"Then why do they sound like women?" I sneaked a look through a gap in the door.

My brothers were climbing the stairs, tottering with each drunken step, though they were well supported by a pack of giggling girls who were half pushing them up.

There were six girls at least, scantily dressed in a poor imitation of Spanish ladies, with wide hooped gowns but frilled low necklines, and wearing no veils or caps. Indeed, two of them seemed Spanish enough from their light skin, but the other four were a few shades darker: one was doubtless a Moor. Her skin tone didn't faze me. It was seeing my brother Gonzalo sticking his tongue down her throat which made me turn away in disgust.

"What's happening?" said Catina.

"Get into the bed," I signed. "Nano, hide just in case."

Nano crawled back under the mattress. Catina and I had just tucked ourselves in when another scream ripped through the air. "How dare you bring such filth into your father's home!" Marta's voice boomed. "Out with you! Out! Guards!"

"Shut up, woman! This is my home now and I'll do as I like!" Pedro slurred back.

"Guards! Guards!" Marta screeched.

"I said shut it!"

The girls screamed. I jumped out of the bed and Nano stood. We ran out of the room.

The girls had spread out. Some of them had run back down the steps, and three guards were waiting to escort them out. Pedro and Gonzalo had kept hold of two of the others and were trying to push past Marta, who stood at the top of the stairs in her robe and slippers, her hair disheveled, her arms open in an attempt to block them.

Marta made a sudden grab for Gonzalo and pulled him away from the Moorish girl, but she thrust too hard. Gonzalo reached for the girl's hand, but it slipped away from him and she fell backward. Her beautiful long curly hair flew back in an arch through the air.

Then her elbow hit the step with a sickening crunch. She let out a howl of pure agony that echoed through the house. Her body slid down, but her arm twisted at an odd angle. The other girls joined in the screaming, though the sound was strangely muted. It was only when Pedro turned, and I saw his eyes, unfocused and wild with fury, that the noise became deafening.

"We paid a fortune for that one!"

My breath hitched as he drew his sword.

I ran toward Marta, who was staring at the girl, sobbing in horror and regret, and tackled her a mere blink before Pedro could plunge his blade into her belly.

But he wasn't done. He let out a roar and fell on her, strangling her neck. I was a frenzied beast, trying to claw him away from her, but he was too strong. She let out a choked gasp and looked at me, her brows near her hairline in surprise, her pupils wide and black as night and filled with terror. I struggled to breathe, to think, to comprehend. Everything in my periphery blurred. Nothing made sense. I was only dimly aware of Gonzalo running down the steps, shouting for help, carrying the other girl away.

Marta's eyes bulged, her face turned purple.

Then Nano punched Pedro across the jaw, and he let go. I don't know what I said, or even if I said anything to Marta. I just cradled her, even as her eyes closed, as her wheezing breath became more and more shallow. It was only when a hysterical Catina threw herself around Marta's bosom and I was shoved aside that I came back to my senses. As if I were emerging from near drowning, I heard a cry of pain and turned. My stomach dropped.

Pedro had overpowered Nano, who was curled into a ball, trying to preserve his body from the heel of our brother's boot. Before he could land another kick, I jumped and ran at Pedro's torso, trying to tackle him, but he threw me off with ease.

"Help! Guards! Gonzalo!"

Gonzalo stood by the foot of the stairs, dazed and swaying. All the other girls were gone, as were the guards. I ran down and slapped Gonzalo across the face.

He blinked at me, and I pointed up. "He's going to kill Nano!"

We ran back up the stairs just as Pedro landed a particularly hard kick to Nano's gut.

Catina screamed, "Stop him, Gonzalo!" and her voice was so eerily like Nantzin's, and she so rarely used it, that it roused our brother in a way my slap could not. Before Pedro could land another kick, Gonzalo threw him on the ground.

"I'm going to teach you all some respect! Get off me!" Pedro kept shouting. I looked between my favorite brother and the woman who had partly raised me, knowing I could only save one of them tonight. I roared in frustration and helplessness as I ran over to Nano and helped him to his feet.

"Marta! Marta!" Catina sobbed, but I had no spare hands to explain.

"Help me!" I mouthed. We half carried Nano down the steps. Two guards in the garden ran toward us.

"Help the lady Marta! Call a doctor, quick!" I shouted.

We tumbled out of the empty courtyard and into the walled garden and out the unlocked door, slowly making our way down the dark cliffside steps. The furious growls of our brothers faded until only the sound of our sobbing, ragged breaths disturbed the peaceful forest ground. It did not last. We had barely reached the edge of the mist-covered lake when Pedro's frenzied shouts reached us again, sending a jolt of fear through my spine.

"Come back! Come back or I'll set my hounds on you!"

Nano groaned.

"Why have we stopped?" Catina asked.

Because I'd spotted someone. A boy leaning over a canoe loaded with crayfish nets. He was poised and ready to launch it into the mist, away from here.

"Wait!" I hissed.

The boy snapped back to look at us. His eyes widened as we emerged from the shadows, and I couldn't blame him. We were two hooded girls half carrying their pulp of a brother.

"Dios mío, que ha pasado?" He pulled the canoe back to the shore and ran toward us. "Is that Señor Cano?"

A pair of deep, gruff barks and a long piercing howl made him jump.

"Please," I said, "help us! We need to get away from here!"

He looked at my face, dark underneath the shadow of my hood. We'd never met, but whatever he saw in my expression moved him quickly to pity. "Come with me," he said.

I pulled my brother and sister forward. The boy threw out the nets and helped us to load Nano onto the middle of the canoe.

"What about our supplies?" Catina panted. "Shouldn't we go to the dovecote first?"

She couldn't hear Nero's and Caligula's barks growing louder, the sound of our brother's murderous screams piercing the night.

"Get in" was all I managed to sign. She scrambled behind Nano and placed his head on her lap. The boy and I pushed the canoe to the edge of the water, and we splashed our way inside, nearly tipping it over in our haste.

The boy made a clicking sound with his tongue, and I turned my head back to look at the rear, where he sat. He slid a paddle through the water toward me, at the front.

"I'm Juan Juanes, by the way," he whispered.

In any other circumstance, I might've laughed. But I merely grabbed the paddle and rowed for my life.

The scent of vanilla roused me. For a brief, wonderful moment, I forgot where I was and what had happened, and simply breathed. Then I opened my eyes.

I had fallen asleep holding my dagger, in a chair that I could not remember climbing into. I sat facing a door made from several rough wooden planks nailed haphazardly together, letting in glimmers of light into the small room. It smelled pleasantly of clay and straw, probably from the thatched roof and walls comprising hundreds of marsh reeds and long sticks strung tightly together. Pots and jars, baskets, and dried gourds hung from the rafters. I shifted upright and groaned at the pain in my forearms, at the ache in my head. Still groggy and confused, I glanced around me and spotted my brother lying on his side beside my sister on a tiny straw mat. The dark bruises on Nano's face brought it all back.

The Moorish girl's beautiful wavy hair arching slowly through the air. The earsplitting crack from her elbow landing on the steps. Pedro's hands squeezing the breath out of Marta. I bit my fist to stop myself from screaming and ran out the door.

The sun was quickly sinking behind the mountains in the distance. Their jagged profiles, dark against streaks of red and orange, were mirrored on the glassy, still lake. We had slept almost the entire day inside a hut built on top of a grassy outcrop, a small chinampa. In front of me was a small makeshift dock amid a crop of water lilies with a canoe tied to it.

Clouds of insects buzzed and chickens clucked by my feet, but I was distracted by the unbearable pressure building up inside me, a kind of demonic wrath threatening to consume me. Something terrible would happen if I didn't let it out, possibly to the chickens. I might snap their necks, or set the grass on fire, or grab an oar and beat the canoe until it sank.

So, I did the least awful thing I could think of. I ran to the dock, sending two hens flying back inland, knelt, dunked my head into the cool water, and howled.

Once, twice, four times. I don't know how long I was in there, just me and a thousand bubbles gushing from my nose and mouth, filled with all the horror and the pain and rage of Marta being strangled, the terror of not knowing if she lived, the guilt that I'd abandoned her. The nauseating memory of that poor girl's arm nearly being pulled out of its socket. But that had been an accident, hadn't it? What Pedro had done—what he had *done*—that had been on purpose. I came up for air and screamed again, cursing him, calling him every foul name under the sun in every language I could think of—Latin, Spanish, Nahuatl—and slamming my palms onto the dock. When I emerged, hair soaking and cold, I felt drained.

Beyond me, to my right, a heron glided over the lake and landed by a grove of gangly ahuejote trees, the light reflected like a halo off its pure-white feathers. There were brown ducks too, swimming among the poised egrets and black coots, pecking algae from the grassy banks. Marta loved birds. She loved us. And I had left her alone, possibly to die.

My vision blurred at the memory of her terror-stricken eyes. Tears began pouring down my already wet face, and I slapped them away. It was all so wasteful, so sick and unnecessary, so much horror. Over what? My brother's image? His glory? His . . . his pathetic little prick? I bent over and screamed into the lake again.

When I emerged, someone behind me cleared their throat. I spun my head around and droplets streaked across the dock. Strands of my loose, wet hair got plastered across my cheeks and nose. I shivered as I stared at him.

The boy from last night—Juan Juanes.

He was a Moor, dark like the beautiful girl from the night before, and tall. His height was enhanced by a mop of curly black hair, which fell around his face and nearly obstructed his great, round eyes, which were tensed in an awkward mixture of compassion and fear. He was carrying a wooden tray with three steaming mugs.

"Real sorry to bother you, señorita. I've been waiting for you to . . . to finish . . . but if I keep this atole in the pot any longer, it'll burn the vanilla, and I really don't want to waste it. The prices . . . well, they're high at the moment, you see."

I didn't know what to say. If he'd been one of my brothers, I probably would've shrieked at him to leave me alone, but a pair of fluffy chickens scratched and pecked at the ground around his feet, completely at ease. I glanced up to study his lovely face again and was distracted by not one, not two, but *three* hummingbirds flying in a circle above his head.

He was completely oblivious. But I was not so ignorant of portents and symbols that I couldn't discern their meaning. They were a clear sign, from Nantzin or her gods, from whoever: a token of goodwill. The birds flew away, and I noticed the strong muscles of his bare arms, his lightly scarred, bronzed skin, darker than mine, and the atole he held in his hands. It smelled so wholesome, so inviting, so desperately good. My gaze flitted to the ceramic mugs.

Even if he'd missed the desperate way I looked at those mugs, he couldn't have been indifferent to the outrageous way my stomach squelched and grumbled.

He stepped forward onto the dock and lowered the tray. "Please, take one."

I reached out with a shaking hand and took one, murmuring thanks. The simmering warmth from the cup seeped through my cold fingertips, and the mixture of fragrances, milky cornmeal and delicate vanilla, sent the world into a slight spin.

I took a sip, and closed my eyes. When I opened them again, I gave Juan Juanes a tiny, tremulous smile.

He let out a breath and flashed a smile back, although he quickly became serious again. "Maybe we could take these inside. I—I didn't think your brother looked quite well last night, and I'm worried we might need to fetch a good doctor from town."

I nodded, not wanting to argue or divulge that even if that were true, the last thing I'd do now is announce our location to the gentry in town. Pedro, as our guardian, would certainly be told, and who knew what he'd do to us. I knew, deep in my bones, he'd meant to murder Nano and Marta. He'd set his dogs loose on us.

If he didn't kill us, at the very least, he'd throw us into the convent, and our plans to find Nantzin's story would be ruined. I wasn't going to let that happen. No, we needed to gather ourselves and some provisions, work out the third set of clues, and leave.

"I'd help you up, but . . ."

"No need." I straightened up and dusted my damp, heavy skirts. Either the thought of Marta's swelling red eyes or the sudden biting gust set my teeth chattering. I gripped the mug with both hands, and took another sip for strength. We walked back into the hut, and as he set the tray down on a rickety old table, I tapped my sister on the shoulder.

Catina woke with a start and sat up straight. After a moment, she shuddered into stillness, turned around, and began checking Nano's temperature.

He groaned and shifted to his back. "It's fine. I'm all right. Just sore."

"Your face looks like a cut of tenderized beef," I said, and it made me feel better, to insult him.

"Delicious as always, then."

Behind me, the boy let out a snort.

Nano tried to open one of his swollen eyes. "Who's that—our great rescuer?"

"Juan Juanes, at your service, Don Cano," he said, "although I cannot take credit for your sister's actions last night."

Nano groaned again. "Don Cano is my father, and Señor Cano is that bastard I'll never again call my brother. So please, Juan Juanes, call me Nano. I guess you've already met Isabel, and this is Catalina, though we call her Catina for short. She's deaf."

"Oh." He waved at Catina and pointed at the atole. A knot of worry eased, for he wasn't one of those morons who thought being deaf meant my sister was stupid. He didn't ignore her either, or treat her with crushing, patronizing pity.

My respect for him increased tenfold. Catina gave me a shy look, and I nodded, signing, "No need to ask for permission."

She shuffled toward Juan Juanes, who handed her a mug with a kind smile. To my surprise, she took a sip and said loudly, "Oh my goodness, this is lovely."

Juan Juanes broke into another radiant smile, which I caught myself staring at for just a moment too long before I blinked and said to Nano, "Well, seeing as you're not suffering from any life-threatening conditions, we should get moving. Thank you for your hospitality and your assistance, Juan Juanes. You have my word that you shall be rewarded—as soon as I receive the sums from my inheritance."

Our eyes met. He seemed to struggle with what to say next, then mumbled, "I wondered what might happen with my position, señorita, for it was mighty difficult to find one in the first place. No one wanted to pay a Moor to cook, you see."

My hands flew to my hips. "Fools! But of course you're still our cook! I've been meaning to come and pay my compliments to you! Anyway—I'm sure you can make up some story when you go back—say you were unwell. Our brother won't know you helped us, and we'd appreciate if you kept that to yourself."

Juan gave a firm nod, and for some reason, I felt he would be true.

"Thank you. Now, we have things to do." I waved at Catina to get her attention and signed only, "The three skulls was the third clue, correct?"

Nano interrupted. "Pardon me, I may not be actively dying, but I do not think we're in any shape to go anywhere, particularly on a mad, dangerous quest. We should send a messenger to Papa and inform him—and we need to see Marta, make sure she's not dead."

"And in the meantime, what—wait for Pedro to find us?" I signed and spoke at the same time, because I wasn't sure if he could actually see my hands properly through the slits between his swollen purple eyelids.

"Who knows how long it'll take the messenger to find Papa—they might not make it to Veracruz before he boards his ship." I shook my head. "No, we must assume he is gone, and we can't go home. We can't allow Pedro to find us, so we must keep moving. I'm doing this. Catina and I are doing this. You can stay here and hide, if Juan Juanes is willing to put up with you taking up his only mat, or you can come with us. Right, Catina?"

I glanced at her, somewhat unsure if she'd back me up, and while she did look her usual half-terrified self, she nodded. I looked at Juan Juanes, who stared at us as if he sat at the front row of a theater, watching a play go wrong.

"What did you say about the lady Marta?" he said hoarsely.

"Pedro tried to kill her and Nano last night," I said, voice hard and blunt. "Hence why I'm asking you, please, to keep our whereabouts secret from our brother. I fear he might murder us too."

Juan's features slackened with disbelief and horror. "Sh-should you not report him to the courts?"

"Indeed, we should," answered Nano.

"Sign, please," Catina murmured irritably.

I let out an exasperated sound. "Have you been asleep the last few years, Nano?" I signed and spoke. "What has Papa said *every single time* he's gone to the courts?"

"Nothing gets done without incentives." Nano spoke through his teeth.

I rubbed my index finger and thumb together and asked both my siblings, "Do you have a purse full of gold? Do you have favors to bestow, secrets to exchange? Do you have the ear of the viceroy or the archbishop?"

They shook their heads.

"Exactly. Without Nantzin and Papa, we're nobodies. *You* may be popular, but that's not the same as being powerful. Plus, you're a third son. I hate to say it, but the courts won't lift a quill for any of us."

"Good heavens, when did you turn into such a bitter old pear?" Nano raised himself to a sitting position and wavered on the spot. A flush of green bloomed behind his purple bruises, but the display of weakness did nothing to soften me, and I almost started ranting again. But whether it was the earthy scent of mud and chicken feathers permeating my nostrils, or Juan's worried voice in my ear, murmuring about his position and the price of vanilla, I figured I'd sound like a petulant princess.

So instead, I fixed him with a look and said, "Rest easy, brother, for this bitter old pear is going to make him pay."

And that's when we heard the shout. "*Pollo!* Pollito! Are you there?"

I looked behind me and saw Juan's features had darkened with embarrassment.

Nano's voice drawled with dry amusement in Nahuatl, "You're Pollo? Chicken?"

Juan whispered, "It's my cousin. He also works for you. I'll go see what he wants."

"Don't tell him about us," I hissed. Juan nodded.

A few moments later, he returned, mortification replaced with wide-eyed panic.

"What's happened?" I asked as I unsheathed my dagger.

"Esteban said your brothers are spreading some story about you being kidnapped. They are asking everywhere—for *me*!"

"Why you?" I asked and signed, trying to quickly update Catina on the situation. She squeaked in alarm and spilled her atole.

"The—the crayfish nets. We left them behind and someone said they were mine. What shall we do? I've asked my cousin to steer them away from here, but people know me from the markets and—and if your brothers pay enough, well, people are hungry. They will talk."

I nodded. "Well, you can't stay here, Juan. You're coming with us."

Juan Juanes hesitated for the fraction of time it took to read the severity of the situation in my eyes, and perhaps something more: a request, an appeal. Something I could not quite comprehend at the time. But with what seemed like a copper flush on his bronze skin, he began tearing around the hut, grabbing things.

"You've got to be joking!" Nano huffed.

"Shut up and make yourself useful!" I rounded on him. "Get your milksop bottom into the canoe. Catina—help him, go!" I signed.

His face reddened, but he allowed himself to be pulled up by our sister.

I stayed behind for a moment to help Juan. We rushed outside and went to the other, smaller hut, the kitchen. I grabbed two guajes—dried hollow calabashes—to hold water. Juan grabbed two paddles, and we ran to the canoe and pushed it off, following the sun as it set on the horizon.

I wasn't sure if I imagined it amid the lapping rhythm caused by our dripping paddles, but I could've sworn I heard a pair of hounds barking in the wind.

CHAPTER 11

Isabel Cano

3 March 1551

A dark, moonless night settled in fast, punctuated only by weak, flickering starlight and the flashing pinpricks of a thousand fireflies, their gleaming, bumbling flight paths reflected on the still surface of the lake. Juan was sitting at the back of the canoe again, and I was at the front, with my siblings between us. We must've been rowing for nearly an hour, and my arms were on fire.

I could feel a dreary exhaustion settling in, a ravenous hunger. At present the fresh air was soothing on my warm cheeks, but soon it would be too cold. Catina had stopped a while ago and placed her head on Nano's lap, unable to go on. I swallowed the urge to shake her awake and put her lazy arms to work. But it would only upset her, and the movement would probably make us topple over into the pitch-black water. I shivered in fear—I could not see a single point of land.

Wordlessly, Juan and I stopped paddling, and I gazed at the insects. "Did we bring anything to eat?" I asked. Nano scoffed from behind me and Juan said no. I bit my bottom lip, silently cursing my own stupidity.

"I don't mean to bother you, señorita, but where are we actually going?"

Nano mock laughed, but he kept his voice low as he said, "Yes, do explain to our new friend Pollo how you think you have found some secret book written by our dear illiterate mother. Somehow, in the middle of the worst agony of her life, on her deathbed, she found the strength not only to write these so-called chapters but to hide them in various secret, dangerous locations across Mexico. And she's left behind some clues and a map for us to find them, although I, for one, don't understand why she would bother. We're going to search for one now, even though I've been nearly beaten to death and we have no food."

"Well done, brother," I responded with an equally quiet yet derisive note. "I couldn't have summarized it better myself."

"Of course, Pollo, you ought to know my sister's only really doing all this because she wishes to escape the convent she's meant to be moving into in a few short weeks. Remember, sister? How you gave your word to our mother to become a nun, right before she died?"

I splashed him with water.

"Hey!" he shouted. The canoe wobbled dangerously. Catina woke up.

"What's happening?" she asked.

I felt grateful that it was dark enough that no one could see my face. I swallowed the knot in my throat and growled back. "He doesn't like to be called Pollo, skunk, and I've told you before—you're free to go! Be my guest, jump off the canoe and swim home. Good riddance if you drown."

Juan Juanes whistled low.

"What?" I snapped.

"Don't wish such things, señorita," he whispered. "Drowning . . . it is far too common a fate in these parts. I—I pray you'll never know the misery. Not only of losing a loved one but knowing their souls are trapped in the murky waters. They stare forever at the light, but can never again feel its warmth."

We all fell silent again, unsure of what to say, but I recognized the timbre of sorrow in his voice, stroking my own grief like a pebble thrown into a fathomless well. I wondered whom he had lost, to make him sound so miserable. More than one person, perhaps? It was clear he had been living on his own for who knows how long.

Where were his parents, his kin?

After a moment, I said in a small voice, "I didn't—I . . . I do want you to come with us, Nano, even though you don't believe it's Nantzin. I do. I really do."

Several waves smacked the hull of the canoe before he said, "I want to believe, but . . . why wait until now? Why not tell us in person, when she was alive? Why not give us the entire book—why break it up into pieces and hide it? And why would she want us to know half of these stories when, when they're horrible, excruciating . . ." His voice broke.

I bit my bottom lip and thought for a long time before whispering, "Perhaps she wanted us to have a choice. Perhaps she wanted us to earn her story. Show that we are worthy of every chapter. Go on a pilgrimage in her honor."

Everyone was quiet for a while. Then Nano cleared his throat and said, "Maybe. But look, if I'm to continue on this journey, you must learn to listen too. You can't make all the decisions by yourself. Pollo—Juan Juanes—too, Catina and I, we all get a say."

I rolled my eyes. "Fine."

"So, where *are* we going?" Nano asked.

I began to pull out the parchment scroll from within my satchel but realized it was pointless without any light, so I described the design on the cushion and said, "There were seven numbered eagles on the cushions, and seven locations marked with a cross on the tapestry map—Tacuba, the viceroy's palace, Xochimilco, Chapultepec, Guadalupe, Teotihuacan, and Iztaccihuatl. The third clue was Xochimilco, and I think it's an island, because an island can only be on a lake, right?"

"So, we're looking for an island in Xochimilco," said Nano, "with a small white house and three skulls drawn around it? Could be anywhere on the lake. Were there more clues?"

"There were flowers, many flowers. Cempohualxochitl, but white."

Juan gasped. "Oh no. No. We can't go there."

"To Xochimilco?" I said.

"No—to the island you speak of. The one with the white flowers of the dead. It is cursed, evil," he shuddered. "Even as a child, my grandmother told me of this place, and warned me never to set foot there."

"Why? What's so evil about it?" Nano asked.

"It's where . . . it's the home of . . ." He paused, trembling. "La Llorona."

Nano and I responded at the same time. "Who?"

Juan spluttered and said, "You don't know La Llorona? The Weeping Woman?"

"What are you all *saying*?" Catina cried out, unable to hold back any longer. She reached back and placed her fingertips on Nano's lips, and he gave her a short summary.

"Oh yes, Nantzin told me the story of La Llorona," she replied, and her voice became dry as sand. "She said she was first called Cihuacoatl, snake woman, brave one, goddess of childbirth, and she heard her wailing for all her children the night before Cortés arrived."

"Goddess of childbirth?" Juan scoffed. "She's a witch who killed her own children!"

I'd had enough. "Goddess, witch, evil, killer—she's probably just a woman who followed her own path instead of the one men set down for her. We're going to her island, Juan. You can stay in the canoe if you're scared."

He didn't move, didn't speak a word. A fluttering warmth spread from my gut to my cheeks, and I gulped and looked down, embarrassed at myself.

"I . . . shouldn't have spoken to you so rudely."

"Santa Maria, did I hear an apology?" Nano whistled. "No, not quite, but by God, that must be the first time in her life she's come close. You must've made quite an impression."

"Shut up," I muttered. "Please, Juan, will you help us?" I said again, and it was a little like earlier in the day, when I'd asked him to come with us for his safety, when I think I'd really wanted him to come for me.

After a moment, he sighed and said, "Very well, señorita. We'll have to row in turns, for it is a long way yet, several hours."

I swallowed, feeling a rush of warm gratitude toward him.

"Th-thank you," I managed to say.

We followed the coastline, rowing underneath the built-in bridges along two of the main causeways leading to the city, past the towns of Mixcoac and Coyoacan. We climbed out and dragged the canoe over the top of the dike built by my ancestors along the strait of Culhuacan, which separated the salt waters of Lake Texcoco from fresh waters of Lake Xochimilco.

There, we had to maneuver through the narrow channels flowing between the thousands of fertile chinampas, the manmade islands created by the ancient Xochimilca, whose crops still nourished the entire city to this day. We all rowed, even Nano, but Juan most of all. Even when he rested—unlike me, he did not sleep—he was our guide and seemed to know his way even in the dark, simply by looking at the sky, or at a particular tree.

There was a hint of dawn in the horizon when we rowed by a low-lying calabash plant loaded with green, overripe gourds and dew-kissed yellow flowers. We were so hungry that we picked them all and ate them, both flowers and fruits, though they were bitter.

Juan and I had a wistful discussion about the best way to eat calabash, and agreed we both liked it best in soup. Juan made a silly joke about dipping the fruit in the lake like a biscuit, and I found myself laughing hard. I glanced back at him, sitting at the rear, and he grinned. My stomach fluttered, until I caught the suspicious scowl on my brother's face and turned away. I bit the inside of my cheek and wondered and wondered what this bright new feeling could mean.

By the time we reached the place, a cold, white mist had begun to settle over the lake, and over us. We were all cold and exhausted, but

Juan most of all. It was no surprise that his words were slurred and hushed when he finally said, "That's it. That's her chinampa."

Songbirds were beginning to chirp and whistle. I took it as a good sign, the fact there were birds there, nestled inside the lanky ahuejote trees towering all around the edge of the water, their trunks blurred by the thickening fog.

As we drew near, a breeze picked up, swirling the mist around our canoe, and I felt a deep melancholy. It was as if every hurt I'd suffered, all the losses and heartbreaks of my short life, were happening again, all at once. Every fight with my siblings, every time my father had overlooked or scolded me, every slight I'd received from the New World gentry, Catina's deafness, Nantzin's terrible childhood and her drawn-out death, Pedro attacking Marta. The knot in my throat threatened to choke me. I thought if I began to weep, I would never be able to stop.

"Is it me, or is this place sucking the joy from the air?" Nano said with a shiver. "Not that there was much to begin with, but still."

"I feel so very sad," whispered Catina at the same time, wiping a tear from her cheek.

"I told you—this is a cursed place. We should turn back," said Juan, who'd sat upright and was rubbing his arms. "It's so cold."

I wished I had a rebozo to offer him, but I only had my hooded cape, and it was still damp. It probably would never be dry again, and why would he accept a gift from me anyway? Every boy I'd ever heard speak on the subject wanted a beautiful wife. Every man, every priest droned on about the importance of women being sweet and yielding and obliging. Someone just like Catina, I thought, with a wild pull of resentment.

I studied them quickly, as Juan stared with wide eyes at the island and Catina's flawless skin crumpled with worry. They were quite alike in temperament, and she had taken to him, I could tell. She was comfortable around him in a way she rarely was with anyone except Nano and me. How could she not be?

He was kind and steady, and his smile was a radiant comet. And I . . . I was a short, bony soon-to-be nun. My skin wasn't light enough to be considered beautiful, and my temper was as meek and gracious as a heavy sack of Toño's spiciest chilli.

"Isabel? Are you all right?" Catina asked, frown deepening.

I shook my head to clear it of these strange, spiraling thoughts, reminding myself that never before had I cared about being a wife, and that I would not start now. I said and signed, "Let's find a good place to tie the canoe."

We turned a bend in the island. The tall bulrushes nearby undulated with the waves we created, until we found a small floating dock between two trees. Juan threw out a rope and tied it around one of the planks, then held the canoe steady as we stepped out.

"Señorita—are you sure this is the right place?" Juan asked.

That same sense of intuition flitted within me, like when I'd first gazed at Nantzin's tapestry or the hummingbirds dancing around Juan's head. A certainty that felt soft, fluid, clear. Like the wind shifting the fog before us, revealing strange shapes: an owl, a serpent, a skull.

Three skulls. Portents of death, floating above an endless field of white cempohualxochitl, which was impossible. It was too early in the season, and the petals were the wrong color. Cempohualxochitl were orange—red, even. Sometimes light yellow, but never white. It was eerie, unnatural. Yet the flowers shone, waved in the perfumed breeze, white as polished bone, pristine. This was the right place.

I nodded my head back at Juan at the same time as a hazy orb of light appeared through the fog, hovering over the flowers, and drew brighter, clearer.

"Someone's coming," Nano whispered.

"Greetings," said a deep yet distinctly female voice, speaking in Nahuatl.

Her features twisted and blurred as she placed the lantern she carried by her bare feet. The fog swirled and gathered around her, until all I could see were her toes, muddy underneath the hem of her spotless white robe.

"Declare yourself and your purpose to the one who guards this holy island."

Her words struck me in their utter fearlessness. For she was a woman, alone and seemingly unarmed, in the middle of nowhere. We could've been ruthless, degenerate brigands. We could've been my brothers, intent on the type of sport that left women like her, women on the fringes of society, with their arms twisted and their larynges crushed. The image of Marta on the floor set my jaw, filled me with tearful courage.

"Greetings, holy guardian," I said, wanting to set her at ease, just in case her mind had drifted to the same place as mine. "Peace be with you. I am Isabel Cano de Moctezuma, and I come with my brother and sister, to seek your counsel regarding our mother."

"And the boy?" she asked.

"He is our . . . friend. He does not wish to trespass on your hospitality."

"He is wise, then. Follow me."

She picked up her lantern and walked away.

"What did they say?" Catina whispered and rubbed her arms.

Nano signed, "Utter madness. Surely you're not serious about going after her?"

I jumped up from the dock onto the island and extended my hand. Nano groaned but clasped it, then helped Catina up.

"Whoa," Nano whispered. I shot him an inquiring look, and he shrugged, saying, "I just feel . . . better suddenly, in my body. The terrible ache in my ribs is gone."

"How strange," I said. I felt the same as before, except perhaps the niggle in my throat from screaming into the water had eased. We walked on.

Sunlight began to penetrate the fog more forcefully, illuminating the island around us, as well as the back of its mysterious guardian, who we could now see was diminutive, a full two heads shorter than us. If it hadn't been for her voice, I would've mistaken her for a child. She wore a plain long-sleeved huipil and skirt, her long black hair undone and fluttering behind her. We walked toward a cluster of oaks covered in long strands of billowing silver moss, beside which stood a rounded, sturdy-looking white lodge. The mist finally dissipated as she stepped up and opened her tiny door.

She turned to look at us, and I sucked in a breath.

Catina clasped my arm, and Nano flinched and dropped his gaze.

It wasn't the first time I'd seen scarred skin like hers, as though it had bubbled and pinched until it resembled the tangled roots of a tree gripping on to a jagged cliff. But I'd never seen burns like that, across someone's entire face. Her nose was small, too small, as though it, too, had nearly melted away, and she had no eyebrows or eyelashes, though her pitch-black eyes remained unharmed. Looking into them felt as though I were looking beyond the stars. Tears welled and tumbled down her ruined cheeks, thick and fast.

I stammered, "Sorry, I—"

"Three children of noble blood," she interrupted, voice firm and unwavering. She did not sound like she was weeping, although the tears continued to fall.

Catina's grip hardened. Her voice was half a gasp. "I can hear her!"

"One death, three souls," she went on. "It was foretold. Come—we have much to discuss." She disappeared inside.

"Wait!" Without a second glance, Catina released me and ran after her. She had to bend to enter through the small opening. Nano and I glanced at each other, wide eyed, and followed, dropping to our knees.

The lodge was warm but dark, without a single window, illuminated by one small clay brazier. In the middle of the space was a circular woven mat. I helped Nano up. His jaw loosened, and I followed his gaze. The entire wall was covered in shadowy paintings of women in all stages of pregnancy and childbirth. Their faces were drawn in agony, fury, and despair as they squatted and released new life into the world.

There were some who appeared to be crying, rejoicing. They held their babies close to their bare breasts and kissed their foreheads. There were some, however, who had been drawn with closed eyes and loose limbs. I tore my gaze away from them and stared at the iron crucifix on top of a small table covered with a white cloth and dozens of pots, some empty, some with the strange white flowers and ears of maize. There was nothing else, not even a sleeping mat.

I wondered at the altar, at the presence of Christ in this strange place, with this strange woman, who had nothing of Spain from her looks or her speech. Was the cross there just in case the wrong people turned up? Had she incorporated his power into her armory, as so many other healers had done? Was she a true convert? I did not think so, but I had no time to wonder for long, because Catina had run up to the woman, who was placing a necklace with a heavy-looking jade medallion over her head.

"How is it possible that I can hear your voice?" asked my sister, who then turned to me when she received no answer. "Say something!"

"Uh . . ." I responded. "Um . . ."

"Are you speaking?" I nodded, and Catina's face crumpled. "What's happening?"

"The island is a sanctuary," the woman answered. "As long as your feet touch her shores, you shall suffer no pain. You shall see, and be seen, wholly, by her inhabitants."

Catina's lower lip wobbled. "So I can only hear *you*? While I stay *here*?"

My heart squeezed for her, but when we locked eyes she signed to me, her gestures blunt and swift, "Don't ever look at me like that again."

She may as well have shouted at me. I was so stunned, so taken by the way she was staring at me, as though daring me to challenge her back, that I could not think of a single response. I hardly recognized her.

At the same time, Nano said and signed at the woman, "I'm sorry, but who are you?" He had clearly not seen Catina's silent outburst.

The woman turned to look at him, and he took a step back. "I am the one who sees and suffers for all. The unborn, the living, and the spirits of the dead."

She shifted her gaze to me, and I noticed the jade pendant on her chest, a curling snake. "I deal in blood and secret sorrows. In exchange for what you seek, you must choose."

"Wait—so you mean you *do* have our mother's story?" I said and signed, feeling a strange mixture of trepidation and elation.

"Part of it was left for me to safeguard." She nodded.

"Who left it for you, and when?" Nano demanded.

"How did you know our mother?" whispered Catina.

The woman ignored them. "You must choose . . . give up your sorrows, your secrets, or your blood."

"What does that even mean!" Nano ran a hand through his hair and glared at me as if I was the bane of his life. "Thoughts?"

I clicked my tongue. "I'm sure it's not that complicated, brother. We either tell her a secret, or something that makes us feel sorrowful, or give her some of our blood somehow." I unsheathed my dagger and smiled. "I'm an open book. Will pricking my finger work? How much blood do you need?"

Nano shook his head and swore under his breath.

The woman cocked her head, her face pinched in pain. "Your smile is brave, though your heart is wounded. Ten drops will suffice," she said. I had no time to reflect on which specific wound of my heart she meant, because she had reached for one of the jars.

She elevated her snake pendant and balanced the jar on top of it, bringing it to me like an offering. I pressed my index finger to the tip of my dagger, expecting a sharp, echoing sting, but none came. She carefully collected my blood.

"No bodily pain, huh?" I said, and she nodded.

Catina slowly stepped closer to the woman. "I have a secret, but I am afraid to share it."

"Yes, we will take your secret—whisper it to the iron Christ."

My sister walked to the crucifix with the lady right behind her. I craned my neck to hear what Catina would say, what she could possibly be hiding from me, but I couldn't hear a word. For a moment, nothing happened.

Then the Christ began to weep. Catina gasped. The woman stuck out the same jar she'd used with me, and collected his teardrops, and then her own, once they began to fall.

"Madness," muttered Nano. His eyes were glazed over, wide with fear.

The woman turned to him at last. Fresh tears pooled in her mournful eyes. "Son, your grief is powerful enough to break you, as it has done your brothers already."

A myriad of emotions flashed across his features. His lips parted; his breath quickened. He narrowed his eyes, looking outraged. "You presume too much, madam!"

"I sense it. Tell the Christ of your sorrow, and release your pain."

"I'll not speak to that—that thing," he spat. "Give me that blasted dagger so we may get out of here." I shook my head but handed my blade over, and he pricked his finger. The woman sighed and collected a single drop.

She walked back to the altar and grabbed a long jar. From within, she took out a rolled-up leather diary. "What you seek," she said. I ran over and grabbed it, then hopped back toward the brazier, opened it, and read the first line.

"It's hers! It's the same handwriting as the others, see?" I waved the diary in the air.

"Hallelujah," said Nano. He signed, "Can we go now?"

"Wait—what will you do with our . . . with the liquid in the jar?" Catina asked.

Once again, the woman turned and walked past us, opened the door, and left, leaving us to bend over and crawl out after her. The day had brightened, and it took a moment for our eyes to adjust to the light. We blinked and I spotted her, marching purposefully back to the dock. We ran to catch up to her.

Beyond the trees, I was relieved to see Juan's canoe still floating. He had fallen asleep but woke with a start when he heard our footsteps swishing through the grass. He took one look at the woman and let out a garbled scream, nearly falling off the canoe.

"Juan! Juan!" I waved. "She won't harm you!"

He seemed to calm down at the sight of us, although he still pushed the canoe away with the paddle. The lady stopped in front of the dock.

"Tonight, before you fall asleep, pray for your loved ones," she said to Juan. "The three who drowned. Whisper their names, and they shall be free."

Juan's lips opened. "Wh-what?"

She turned to us and said, "When my three sons died in the battle of the causeway, I found a way to release their souls from the water. I shall do the same for your friend's family." She paused for a moment and gestured to the canoe. "I bid you farewell."

"It's been a pleasure." Nano gave her a sharp nod and grabbed hold of Catina's arm. She hesitated for a moment, looking at the weeping lady as though reluctant to step away from the one source of sound in her world, but the woman was staring at the lake, lost in thought. She clearly had no more to say to her, or any of us.

Juan brought the canoe back, although he angled it in such a way that he was as far away from the woman as possible. We stumbled back on, and had not pushed more than half a foot away when the woman jumped onto the dock, landing firmly on her two bare feet.

Juan and Nano shouted in alarm.

The woman began to chant, to wail in a strange language I'd never heard. A powerful lament that plucked the strings of my grief even more powerfully than Juan's voice had done in the night. Then, the flowers on the island turned their faces toward her, as though she were the sun, and indeed, all was suddenly warm around us. A streak of light fell from the sky and penetrated the surface of the lake, illuminating a harem of axolotl, dozens of them, circling underneath, flapping their feathery gills, blinking their glossy fish eyes.

"What's happening?" Juan shouted.

"Row, for the love of God, row!" Nano answered, grabbing an oar and shoving it in the water, scrambling to get away.

The woman raised the jar and poured our blood and tears from a height. They swirled and dissipated among the spiraling salamanders, which swam back into the depths. She kept singing, louder. Hundreds of birds, egrets, pelicans, sparrows, ducks, and ibises fluttered out from the trees and water, chirping and squawking. I watched them circling the island until they became specks as small as dragonflies, until I remembered I finally held Nantzin's words in my hands again.

I didn't ask for permission. I didn't care to hear any arguments or exclamations. I simply handed the manuscript to my sister and commanded her to read, then closed my eyes and listened to her voice, so like my mother's it was as though she were here.

Floating beside me. Alive again.

CHAPTER 12

Tecuichpoch

1520

My second husband was my uncle Cuitlahuac, who was elected and crowned the tenth huey tlatoani of the city of Tenochtitlan after my father was killed.

He was past forty. I had just turned twelve.

He could've wed my mother instead, who was daughter of the revered king Ahuitzotl, whose marriage to my father had brought the two rival branches of our royal family together. But *I* was the product of that union.

It was me, not my mother or sisters, who had an absolute claim to the seat of the ancient Toltec kings. I had a greater right than my own mother, even, to be wed to the new huey tlatoani and take over as his primary wife. And now that Malintzin had marked me in front of the Spaniards and they had named me in honor of their most beloved dead queen, I had become a symbol of power and unity to both sides—a chess piece to maneuver as they saw fit. This I was taught. This, I believed, was right and proper for a noble girl like me. And though I sometimes pictured Malintzin, the strength of her courage and what she would've otherwise done or said in my place, I kept my head low and did as I was told.

The marriage was performed in ritual only, for I was still too young and unbled. But it served my uncle anyway, who needed unity above all. The people rallied around him, around us, and he ordered a celebration, for we had dealt the Spaniards and their Tlaxcalteca dogs a great blow. We had killed thousands of them and sent them cowering back to their miserly hills, and even to this day, they do not forget how we humbled them that night, that Noche Triste. The Night of Sorrow. I hope they dream of it every night, as I did for years.

But I will tell you, gladly, how we made the survivors pay. It was a beautiful day. Before me, rising like a mountain, was the white-washed Great Temple, glimmering so brightly that my eyes watered. Thousands upon thousands of our people gathered in the vast sacred precinct. They surrounded the high platform where we, the royal family, stood in our finest regalia, our lustrous mantles and crowns of opalescent feathers and jewels and pelts made from our animal souls, our nahualli. The people cheered for us, and the clamor of their voices and drums and flutes and conchs was deafening.

Behind us was the great skull rack, rattling in the breeze, and in front of us, right at the foot of the temple steps, tied around the sacred oak tree, were the prisoners. Some trembled; some prayed or cried. They could no longer strut through our streets, demanding food and gold and women. They had been humbled, their clothes and armor torn off, replaced with rough maguey robes. Heavy wooden collars clamped around their sunburned, chafed necks marked them as newly enslaved.

One by one, they were given a drowsing draft to drink and forced up the steps, and then the priests cut out their hearts to great cheers, and our guards quartered their legs and arms and fed them to the gods. And though this spectacle, the heart sacrifice, was nothing new, though I had seen it a hundred times before, it was the first time I did not close my eyes or feel even a sliver of remorse or pity or disgust. My heart did not squeeze when their comrades screamed at the loss of their friends, or shouted the names of their mothers and children, for I could understand the Castilian tongue now, and this is what they said.

But this is how much I despised these men for how they had throttled my father and butchered my friends and cousins and half brothers in such a cowardly way, when they were unarmed, while they prayed and danced at the festival in the temple. This much I had learned by then. I had been told by my mother, who had covered my brother with her own body and pretended to be dead in order for them both to survive.

Indeed, you may be appalled at what the Catholic priests would call my sinful wrath and mercilessness, at the bloodlust I felt rivaled Huitzilopochtli's own. You may judge me, but I will tell you anyway, that I listened to their cries and useless pleading and watched their Spanish blood, as red as any of our own, spraying and drenching the priests from head to toe before flowing like a torrent down the hundred stone steps of the pyramid temple.

And I praised them, our lords of rain and war. I said their names aloud, Tlaloc and Huitzilopochtli, and thanked them for my freedom. For the feel of the warm sun on my face, painted bright yellow and patterned with stripes of blue in honor of the occasion, of my mother standing solidly behind me once more when so many of my family were gone.

I grasped my brother Axayacatzin's small, soft hand and smiled. He squeezed my fingers and wiggled the new nose plug of emerald and gold hanging underneath his nostrils, making me laugh.

I remember laughing, truly I do. Because later on, many months and perhaps even years, I remembered thinking to myself, trying to recall the last time I had smiled. And this memory came to mind. So it came to be that, after this ceremony of vengeance at the tender age of twelve, I would not smile again for so long that I became almost afraid of my own face. I would push up at my own cheeks and eyebrows, trying to reignite the sensation, the ease of smiling I'd lost, and I would fail time and time again.

But one thing that always makes me smile now, laugh even, is the notion that the Spaniards conquered us. Oh, they say, it only took five hundred men to conquer the Mexica, as if their thousands of Indigenous allies had been as useful as clouds of dust. It only took a year, they say. And I laugh, even now, I laugh at their bold-faced stupidity.

For it was not those men who conquered us.

No, it was the hueyzahuatl, the great pestilence they brought. The Spaniards simply came back for the remains of our carcasses, like tzohpilotl diving from the sky. And it happened so quickly after this ceremony of vengeance that it seemed almost as though I blinked, and one moment I was smiling, triumphant, and the next I was almost dead.

Indeed, in a matter of days, the fever built like a swirling storm in the back of my throat, my skull, which thrummed and ached until I groaned aloud, and it was so unusual a sound that my mother stood up. I remember we were sat around the weaving room, which was a marvelous room, so brilliant it made the murals come alive, the red-ocher background and green of the leaves of the bountiful fruit trees of the paradise underworld of Tlalocan.

And perhaps it was an omen, perhaps I ought to have seen it then, how a ray of light was shining on our lord Tlaloc in his paradise home of Tlalocan, where those who die from lightning strikes go to rest, and those who drown, like Citlalin, or those who are struck with plague. Perhaps it would've brought me some comfort in the next few weeks and months of despair, some of the darkest I can recall. To this day, I flinch to recall it. The pestilence, which crested like a wave, bringing misery and death to every corner of our city.

You cannot imagine the torment, my dear.

But as it was, we were all sat weaving, all the noblewomen together, my father's widows and daughters, except Citlalin, for whom we still mourned, and I nearly fainted from the pain in my head. And my mother, whose silken hair and doe eyes were considered to be the most beautiful at court, though she rarely raised her gaze, stood up and came to kneel by my side. She looked at me, and I saw how surprised she was, just from that one groan. Because I never complained, I never groaned. She had taught me well, although she no longer reprimanded me.

Indeed, she had grown soft in the year of my absence, and since the massacre at the temple, where she had thrown her body on top of my brother's and saved his life. She had missed me, and I her. And since I had been rescued, we had rarely left each other's side.

My mother placed her dry, cool hand on my forehead and sucked in a breath. And even today I think perhaps if she had not touched me, perhaps she might have lived. Or perhaps not. For the pestilence was like a rising fog of death, taking our spirits with it.

Everyone fell weary; everyone had bursting sores on the insides of their cheeks, which tasted of rust and infection. And our skin flushed an angry, vivid red within days, from our faces to our toes. Our skin swelled and blistered into fat pustules, which hardened like scales, until we looked like the lizards Axayacatzin and I had once caught for the mere pleasure of being children.

I would never feel lightness like that again. And I tell you, that is a terrible, sad death in and of itself, to lose one's childlike spirit so soon in life, to never again feel buoyant and at ease with the world.

My body, too, aged decades in a matter of weeks, and I forgot that I was destined to live, that my survival was foretold. I forgot because my mind was embroiled in nightmares and awful visions: a forest of fungi sprouting from human skin; the charge of a hundred fire-breathing horses; heads and skulls bouncing like rubber balls down blood-drenched steps; tiny cockroaches worming in and out of red and blond and brown wiry beards, scraping my cheeks, my neck, my exposed belly. The reek of mutton grease, of tobacco, horse dung, and pulque.

And we were so weak that we could not even lift our hands to scratch ourselves, and that is how so many of us died, because we were too weary to sit and eat and drink. And there was no one to bring anyone else food and water, for everyone was sick. But because we were the highest of all nobles, and we had so many servants, so many slaves, it did not matter. When one fell ill, another came to take their place.

This is the reason why I survived, though I know not how many people gave their lives for me, and it makes me tremble with shame and sorrow even now, because I did not know a single one of their names.

Yet I do recall the moment my fever broke, for I looked around our colorful chamber, our azure walls encrusted with glimmering precious stones, and hardly recognized my two sisters' swollen, crusted faces. I touched their chests and felt them rising and falling, and I sagged with ease until I spotted my own hands and arms. I felt the rough, brittle surface of my skin, the way a pile of dried leaves feel and look when they've been trampled underfoot, and knew I looked as gruesome as my sisters did, and smelled as bad—worse than the conquistadores did. For we had been sleeping next to each other, and we were covered in each other's filth. But even above the reek of our bodies, I tasted the blinding stench of decay.

I looked around and spotted the source: one of our enslaved girls, slumped over a dry incense burner in the corner, covered in pustules. A great, black fly crawled into one of her nostrils and flew out the other, and I knew she was dead.

I dry heaved and stumbled out, searching for help, calling out for my mother, but I was too weak, and I did not get very far. I thought someone would come, for there were always servants walking the hallways, but the time passed and no one came.

The palace was so quiet and empty, I thought for a moment I was the only one who had survived, and my heart seized, and I thought, *Well, if everyone is dead, then it doesn't matter anymore what I do or say.* And so I screamed and screamed as though my lungs were on fire, and finally, someone came running.

It was my young cousin, Cuauhtemoc, the warrior who had rescued me from the Spaniards when we had jumped into the lake. To my utter surprise, he held me to his chest and helped me up and half carried me to the banquet room. He sat me down, found a servant to fetch me food and water, and told me, to my undying relief, that my brother Axayacatzin and another seven of my half brothers were still alive. My mother too, though she was gravely ill. But my second husband, our uncle Cuitlahuac, was dead. He said I was widowed once more, that he had been elected the new huey tlatoani and I was to be his bride.

I stared stupidly at his face, for I had forgotten my manners completely. It was one of the only times I ever studied him so. I took in his marvelous lip plug, golden, shaped like an eagle's head and beak. The dark-brown shade of his eyes, rich like the chinampa soil that nurtured our crops. He was strong, his copper skin perfectly smooth except for a battle scar near his wrist, and he smelled like a mixture of copal incense and chocolatl.

My hungry stomach rumbled, and he called out for food again.

Then, also to my amazement, he begged me to help him save our beautiful Tenochtitlan. He said the Spanish would return and asked me to help him rouse our people and prepare them for war. He said he needed me to convince my brothers to be on his side, as one. He made me swear to help him, and I did. Because I was too weary to think, and he was huey tlatoani, my lord and soon-to-be third husband, and it was my sole purpose and duty in life to serve him and our people.

And because he had asked.

For once, someone had asked, rather than told me what to do.

I wish I'd known then I was being sent on a fool's errand. But that is a tale for another day.

My hope is that you will find it.

CHAPTER 13

Isabel Cano

4 March 1551

I paddled on without thinking, without seeing. A memory kept playing in my mind, of my mother's hand holding mine as I writhed in bed, sweating with the same fever that had robbed my sister of hearing. But I had known, always known, she had been there by my side.

I'd guessed, from the slight scarring on her face and hands, that my mother had survived the great plague, but I never realized she'd done it all on her own. Yes, of course, her sisters had been there too. But there is nothing quite so healing, quite so soothing, as having a mother who loves you sitting by your bedside when you are sick. I had simply assumed her mother, my grandmother, had been able to do the same.

I swallowed a surge of pain, for their suffering, and for my own. For this living ache of love and tenderness in my heart which no longer had a vessel to receive it. Not that either of us had been effusive in our affection for each other, but there had always been an understanding of its depth: a small smile, a warm look that spoke all the words we could not say. Now, the only thing I had left of her was this quest, which was turning out to be more difficult than I'd expected. But I pushed that thought away, because I had faith. I had trust, in Nantzin, in her plan for us, her intentions, whatever they might have been.

Vaguely, I became aware of the sounds around me—Catina's shaky, uneven breath, the chirping of insects. Eventually, Juan let out a low whistle and whispered, "Your mother wrote that?"

"Apparently," Nano murmured.

There was a long silence, broken only by sloshing waves rustling through a carpet of spotted algae and grassy shoots prickling out from the canal walls. A bright-red cardinal bounced from the branches of one ahuejote tree to another. An ibis scratched the black mud and picked out a juicy worm to eat. Dragonflies skidded past the hull of our canoe. I breathed in the thick, humid air, and was lulled for a brief moment into a sense of calm.

"There is power in that story," Juan replied in a reverent tone.

Nano swatted a fly and said nothing. I continued paddling, entranced. Juan guided us around the canals, lush with vegetation and wildlife, but as the sun rose high and more canoes were launched, it became trickier to maneuver. People emerged from their thatched cottages to chop wood and collect water, and we drew our hoods to hide ourselves. Even though we were far enough from the capital that we felt a little safer, we did not wish to draw too much attention, although no one seemed too interested in us anyway. They were busy going about their day.

I studied their worn, serious faces. The elders had pockmarked skin and various scars which marked them as survivors just like my mother. Men scrutinized their crops and tended the land, though I doubted it was theirs now. Half of whatever they managed to grow would likely be sold to pay tribute to a Spaniard. Still, they had to eat.

Children threw fishing nets into the lake, hoping for an early-morning catch. Women built fires to warm tortillas and tamalli for breakfast, the earthy smell of which made my mouth water and my stomach growl. I desperately wished to buy some, but we had nothing of value. We agreed it was best to go back to Juan's or the dovecote and gather provisions.

We passed around the guajes filled with water and drained them. At some point, after climbing over the dike again and reaching the open lake, I fell asleep, though it felt like three breaths later when Nano shook me and said, "We're here."

I let out a groan of pain. My entire bottom half was numb, my arms were on fire, my neck crackled and itched, and I was covered in mosquito bites. "Where are we?" I mumbled.

Nano pointed at the towering wall in front of us, stretching from the pebbled, grassy shore to beyond our line of sight into a thick forest of pines and oaks.

"Elvira's hacienda in Coyoacan."

"Are you serious?" I scratched my neck and the backs of my hands.

Nano's jaw clenched. "We need somewhere to rest. We're utterly filthy. Catina's been sobbing for an hour, Pollo has barely uttered a word. We have no food, no water."

"We have a lake," I mumbled lamely as I glanced at my sister, who was standing at the edge of the water, gazing back at the islands far in the distance, tears streaming down her face. Juan was standing beside her, his face contorted with concern.

He put an arm around her shoulder, and I was struck by a spike of envy, a sinking, nauseating feeling in my stomach, made worse by the grateful smile she returned.

Nano kicked the edge of the canoe, snapping me back to reality. "Our sister will turn into the new Llorona if we don't get her into a warm bath soon, so get out of this bloody canoe right now. Elvira will help us. I know she will."

"Fine." I got up and stretched my deadened legs before hopping out with a crunch onto the shingle. "Let's go and pretend we're here because we're hungry and thirsty, and not because you're desperate to see your sweetheart again."

"Why don't you wipe the slobber from your lips and shut them."

I growled at him, then stomped up to my sister and grabbed her hand a little more roughly than I'd intended, breaking her out of Juan's embrace and ignoring his cough of surprise, and the slightly bewildered, hurt look on his face when I added, "Keep up, Pollo."

We followed the edge of the wall for long enough that my temper eased and I began to suspect my brother's motives, remembering Gonzalo's words that he needed to marry a girl with a substantial fortune. "How rich are these people?" I asked and signed.

Nano's face darkened. "I forget you're impervious to gossip," he signed.

"Why? What's happened?" Catina piped up.

"Elvira's father rather enjoys placing a wager or two at the cock- and bullfights." Nano's laugh was mirthless. "The ranch is in shambles. It's only a matter of time before the Crown takes the encomienda back. He owes everyone money. He's wasted his entire fortune, and that of Elvira's. Everything her mother set aside to ensure a good marriage for her is gone."

"He bet his only daughter's dowry?" said Catina, aghast.

"Shameful, that," Juan said, chancing a tentative, questioning look in my direction. Our eyes met, sending a flutter through my chest. I looked away before he could catch the treasonous tug at the corner of my lips.

"Don't mention anything." Nano pleaded with his eyes. "I am only telling you because . . . well, you'll see."

We finally reached a huge wooden door by the side of a long, empty cobbled road overrun with weeds. Nano banged the brass knocker, and we waited, much longer than usual, until we heard the echo of hurried footsteps.

A breathless voice answered, "Pray forgive us, Don Toledo is not here at present. Please come back another day."

"Elvira—it's Juan."

There was a squeak and a pause, then a jangling of keys. "Damnation, why are there so many! Just—give me a moment."

I signed to my siblings, "She must answer her own door?"

Nano nodded and shushed me, as if I'd spoken out loud.

Finally, Elvira managed to unlock the door, and we all helped to push it open.

For a moment, she stood staring at us, jaw slack in disbelief. She wore the same gown as the night of the ball but looked well groomed, as though she were headed to another dance that evening. Only her red, puffy eyes betrayed her. And after taking another look at Nano, she began to cry. Nano stepped forward, and she melted into his chest.

"Thank God! I heard the news and have been praying all day for you. Is this the boy they speak of? But he is too young and sweet looking to be a kidnapper?"

Nano puffed out his chest. "You thought I could be taken by a little boy?"

"Pfft—you could be taken by a little girl. No—Juan here saved us." I punched his arm awkwardly and immediately grimaced, feeling like a dunce.

Juan's brows mirrored Nano's bemused expression.

Nano blinked and said, "May we come inside?"

"Of course, of course—please do." Elvira gestured to Catina to follow her, and we closed the door behind us. The reception room, usually one of the most opulent rooms in Spanish homes, was bare. Even the Moorish tiles had been picked off the stucco. Only one or two remained in the high corners. In fact, the one object left undisturbed was a single small crucifix hanging on the wall. Perhaps whoever had come to settle their debt had felt it would be sinful to take that holy item as well.

I glanced at our group and could tell my siblings were trying to keep their faces as carefully blank as I was trying to keep mine, but Elvira's cheeks still radiated heat as she led us through into the open central courtyard. "We're a little short on . . . many things . . . but at least we still have a little bit of food and a warm hearth."

"You are most gracious, my dear—señorita," said my brother, who also colored and immediately avoided my eye.

I did not wish to embarrass him, however, and truth be told, I found his slip endearing. The reality of the situation was beginning to sink in. My brother was enamored with Elvira, who, by the longing look on her face, more than reciprocated his feelings.

We had not fully crossed the courtyard, however, when there was a crash of a door opening, and in stumbled a barefoot man wearing only breeches and an unbuttoned, stained shirt. He held two necks in each hand: a bottle of dripping wine in one, and a swinging dead turkey in the other.

"Caught the bastard!" the man slurred. "Supper, darling!"

Elvira stood still, trembling. The look of adoration on her face was replaced by one of utter mortification. The man stopped and swayed on the spot when he saw us.

"Ah, back again, Moctezuma!" He smacked his lips and smiled broadly. "Have you good news? Has your father agreed to my terms?"

Nano shook his head. "I haven't had the chance to speak to him, Don Toledo."

Don Toledo's smile vanished. "Well, he can't be *that* keen on you then, girl!" he shot at Elvira. "He hasn't even *tried* to convince his father to buy you out!"

"Father, please," she begged.

Don Toledo threw the turkey in our direction and spat on the floor. "You gave up the prize, didn't you! You opened your fat legs! I told you he'd get bored of you!"

Nano strode up to him, snatched his bottle away, and smashed it on the floor, then grabbed him by the shoulders and pushed his back into the pillar of an arch.

Don Toledo was taller than my brother. He looked twice as strong. But his eyes widened, and if he tried to move, he gave no indication that he was able to.

I couldn't see my brother's face, but I heard his voice, hard and rough. "Sir, you disgrace yourself and your daughter, who is virtuous, kind, and loving to everyone she meets. She loves you and cares for you, even though you shame her. Go, please, and wash yourself, sleep it off, before you break her heart for good."

Don Toledo glanced back at his child, who had tears rolling down her cheeks again. A flush of shame marred his features. His shoulders slumped, and he looked at the floor.

Nano let go of him.

"I'm going out," Don Toledo said, and walked away.

"Papa, please don't!" Elvira said, but he ignored her.

We all shifted on our feet for a moment, unsure of how to proceed, avoiding Elvira's anguished face following her father's footsteps as he left the house. Nano had his back to us, his expression a mystery, but his fists were tight, and his breath loud and ragged as he, too, watched the man's exit.

Finally, Juan picked up the turkey and mumbled, "I could make some mulli to cheer everyone up?"

That balm of gratitude I was beginning to associate with Juan eased my tight chest, and I felt even more ashamed of my earlier outburst. I gave him a sheepish, appreciative look, but frowned when I spotted the shadows under his eyes.

"You need a rest. Shall we take it in turns?"

"I didn't know you could cook," Juan said with a shy smile.

"She doesn't, but she sure knows how to eat," said Nano as he turned back to face us. Our eyes met, and I knew we had forgiven each other for our little spat, that we were both on the same team once again.

I stuck out my tongue in jest. "I'm sure I'll be a much better help than you."

We bantered some more. Elvira cheered up marginally. She led Juan and Nano to the kitchen, and Catina and I to her chambers, which were as bare as the rest of the house. There was a rack with some worn old gowns where a wardrobe should've been, a small pallet with a simple wool blanket for a bed, and a wooden basin near the fireplace.

In spite of this, she gave us each a clean white chemise, although we had to keep our filthy skirts and hoods, since Elvira was several sizes larger and had none to spare. She also filled up the basin with tepid water, gave us some linen to dry ourselves with, and threw a log into her fire so we wouldn't be too cold. We thanked her, and she left to attend the boys while we placed our skirts near the fire to dry, and washed ourselves.

We wrapped the linen around our wet bodies, and I filled my sister in with everything that Elvira's father had said, and afterward braided her hair, making sure it was neatly and modestly tucked inside her hair cap, as Marta had taught us. Thinking of her sent a sickening pang of shame and guilt through my gut. I wondered if the doctor had managed to see her in time, and made a mental note to ask Elvira for news.

"I really do feel for Elvira," said Catina as she braided and tucked my own hair in a cap, "having to do everything by herself in this big, empty house. And poor Nano—he is quite taken with her, isn't he? Why hasn't he asked Papa for her hand yet? I'm sure he would pay, if he knew how much he liked her."

A memory flashed in my mind. I turned so she could see my hands. "I think he *has* asked, actually!" I signed, and told her what I'd overheard Papa saying the day Pedro had nearly struck my face. "Papa refused!"

"Oh no! Isabel, what will Nano do?" She sat down on the edge of the basin.

I shrugged, feeling torn for my brother, wondering why Nantzin had left so little to him.

"Even those two savages got enough to never have to worry!" I signed, then threw the clean chemise over my body.

I had just finished dressing myself when Catina exclaimed, "Santa Maria!"

"What is it?" I mouthed.

She held up her linen cloth, which was stained with blood.

CHAPTER 14

Isabel Cano

4 March 1551

"Are you hurt?" I ran to Catina and spun her around, checking her body for wounds, but there were none. She was also looking at her arms and torso when I noticed the droplets of blood falling to the floor from in between her legs. I turned away and cursed my luck, knowing she would not hear, schooled my face into calmness, and turned her around.

"It's your first moon," I signed.

Her eyes went round. "Is that why my stomach was hurting earlier? I thought I was just hungry, or maybe the calabash had done me ill."

"No, no," I signed, trying to remember everything Nantzin had said to me when I'd first bled. My chest constricted, and I fretted around the room in a panic, looking for something, thinking I shouldn't be the one having this conversation. My sister needed her mother, and all she had was me: a meager substitute, an utter farce. I was so flustered that I did not notice Catina had begun to strip her old chemise.

"Nantzin said to use little rags to stanch the flow," she said.

"She spoke to you about this?" I signed.

"Yes," she whispered, and continued tearing strips of cotton. "She called me to her room, and it was one of the last conversations we had."

My shoulders eased, though I sensed the subject was a tender one. I tapped her shoulder to grab her attention and signed, "You'll need to wash those really well with soaproot before and after you use them. And tie them like this, like a loincloth." I tied two strips together, one to go around her waist like a belt, and one between her legs.

"I suppose there will be no staying in repose for five days," she said with a sigh.

"Nantzin hated repose—she said it was for lazy Spanish women," I signed.

Catina nodded and turned away, then whispered so low that I thought I'd imagined it. "She always did share more with you than she did with me. Because she knew."

I frowned, then tapped her shoulder and signed, "What did you say?"

She shook her head, but looked on the verge of tears.

"Oh no—don't," I signed. I couldn't take her crying over Nantzin, not now.

The tears began to flow. "Isabel, I—I have something to tell you. I'm really sorry."

"What!" I was utterly bewildered now.

"It's my fault that Pedro hates you."

For a moment, I just blinked, confused. "I don't understand."

"*I* broke Pedro's bow!" she wailed. "That's the secret I told La Llorona."

My brows rose, and I shook my head in disbelief. I was too stunned to speak.

"It was an accident, and I should've said something. I'm so sorry. I was so scared, and then everyone was yelling. I didn't want them to be angry with me, or you!"

The truth of her declaration felt like a kick to my stomach.

My movements were rough and angry as I signed, "Why didn't you speak up? You have no idea of the damage you caused! And not just between Pedro and me!"

It was amazing, how something so small could become so destructive, a summer drizzle that ends in a ripping hailstorm. It almost seemed insignificant now, especially after hearing Nantzin's story. But it had been life altering to our family, what had happened after Pedro found his priceless bow in the garden and accused me of breaking it. Every member of our household had drawn battle lines over this stupid object and taken a side, Pedro's or mine. It had been like that ever since.

Now Catina was crying and nodding. "I know—I'm sorry. Nantzin, I think she always knew. I think she wanted me to tell you, but I've been too afraid."

For once, I refused to comfort her. Even though perhaps I did not feel as angry as I might've done before we began this journey, I was sick and tired of her sugarcoated cowardice. She needed to feel her shame. She needed to be alone with it, and grow up.

"I can't look at you right now," I signed. I grabbed my hooded cape and walked away.

Somehow I found my way through the echoing empty hallways back to the huge kitchen, one of the only rooms with anything inside. The earthen-red and wheat-colored walls were dotted with hanging comales of various sizes, ready to be heated for cooking tortillas or meat. Ceramic mugs and shelves with apertures held tens of ladles and wooden utensils of various sizes.

In the middle of the red-tiled floor was a huge stone petate for grinding corn. Beside it stood a large chopping table where the dead turkey and other ingredients had been laid out. I entered and found Juan all alone, his back to me, bent over and feeding wood into a fire he'd lit underneath the massive brick stove. He stood up, placed a heavy-looking pot on the grilled stovetop, and grabbed a knife.

"I thought Nano was meant to be helping you?" I asked, and he dropped the knife with a loud clatter. "Sorry!" I said.

"I didn't hear you," he said. "But then again, I always lose myself when preparing food," he replied, and picked up the knife, then wiped it clean with a nearby cloth.

"May I help?" I asked, and he nodded.

"Can you chop three onions? Here." He handed me the knife.

I hesitated slightly before I took it, and turned to the chopping table, feeling lost. Hadn't I seen the kitchen hands do this a thousand times? It couldn't possibly be that difficult. I grabbed an onion and cut it in half. There—that had been easy enough. I was about to quarter it, when Juan cleared his throat.

"Are you going to peel it?" he asked, and I glanced at him. His dark-brown eyes were twinkling with amusement, but there was a kindness there, an understanding. "I can tell you've never chopped an onion before . . ."

I stammered, feeling torn between a desire to pretend like I knew what I was doing, a long-standing impulse to defend myself and lash out, and a desire to join in delighting with him, even if it was at my own expense. The corners of my lips perked, and he laughed.

"You can be on water duty instead. I won't have you losing a finger under my watch." He gestured for me to put the knife down, and I grudgingly did.

"Can you at least teach me how?" I said.

"Firstly, you don't hold a knife like you might stab someone. You hold it like this." He peeled the onion and showed me, then gave it back to me to try, which I did.

"That's better, but make sure your index finger steadies and guides the top of the blade." He reached out and touched my hand, and we both stopped and stared at each other. Heat rose up my chest and into my cheeks.

"My apologies, señorita," he said, and backed away.

"No, I am sorry," I whispered, "for my rudeness earlier on. I'm not used to . . . My brothers, the people at court, they have always been rough with me, and I don't know how else to behave sometimes."

He was silent for a beat, then asked, "What of your mother—was she rough?"

I crossed the kitchen to a large open barrel filled with clear water and a huge ladle. I scooped some and poured it into the pot, where it sizzled into steam.

"No, she was not," I mumbled, hesitating only for a moment before continuing. "She never shouted at us, or spoke a harsh word. But we knew if she was displeased. A sadness would overtake her, a melancholy, and the silence was worse than any sermon."

Juan sighed. "My mother was the opposite. She was fire and spice, like all the best meals are." I turned and we locked eyes again, and even though there was a sorrow behind them, and behind mine, there was a new sensation there, a pull, a closeness. It felt good to talk to him, to listen to him. It felt easy. I moved back next to where he stood in front of the table, and began to peel the next onion. The space between us felt alive, warm and buzzing. I wished to lean closer, but I held my place.

"Did she teach you to cook?" I asked.

"Yes," he said. He paused for a moment before he began to furiously pluck feathers from the turkey. "She was born here, and bought as a gift for Viceroy Mendoza's wife. She wanted a beautiful doll to dress up and display, but he soon took a liking to her. So his wife banished her to the kitchens, not that it helped. When I was born, the viceroy did not wish his bastard son to be a slave, so he kindly freed us both after I was baptized."

My hands stopped moving as I reeled from the knowledge that this kind, gentle, easygoing boy was the son of the most powerful man in New Spain. I studied his features, comparing them to the old viceroy, who'd had a long face, dangling nose, and a rather protuberant forehead. But apart from the large eyes, Juan seemed to have inherited his mother's good looks. Softened, round cheeks and face, and of course, the luxuriant curls and the rich, dark tone of his flesh, gleaming bronze in the fading light. Thankfully, he didn't notice me staring. He seemed lost in his memories, and the words poured out as though he'd been waiting for just the right moment, the right person, to release them.

"Mendoza offered to have me educated, if she stayed. That's how I learned to read and write, and that's how I know a little of what you speak. The ruthlessness of the viceroyal court—I lived it every day. The vicereine made our lives miserable, and my mother was unhappy, very unhappy, there. Until she met the man who truly raised me, Tenoch. He was a coartado, a slave who'd bought his freedom. There was never a better, kinder man who walked this earth." His breath shook.

I gulped at the raw emotion in his voice and stared at his dexterous hands as they finished with the turkey, then lifted up to tie back his curls so they wouldn't get in his line of vision. A bit of down got stuck to his hair, and I resisted the urge to reach up and pull it away. He rolled his sleeves up and deboned the bird. Meanwhile, I still had not finished peeling my onion.

"What happened?" I breathed, and he smiled, seemingly pleased with my attentions.

"They married and left the palace, settled in the chinampa I took you to. I lived with them, though Mendoza kept paying for my education until he was sent to Peru."

"Does he know?" I asked breathlessly.

"What, that they drowned?"

I flinched. "And you've been all alone . . ."

"No, he does not. We never spoke, and I never wanted anything from him, not before, and certainly not now. Tenoch was my real father. He taught me how to raise chickens, and my mother taught me how to cook. I'd rather live off my hands and the land than be indebted to him in any way." In a stone molcajete, he began to grind ingredients, a tantalizing mixture of herbs and spices, xitomatl, fresh and dried chilli, and roasted achiote seeds that smelled divine and mellowed the pulsating ache in my core brought on by hearing his story.

"What was her name?" I asked, remembering Nantzin's words, how she felt about leaving behind a world that had forgotten my grandmother's real name. How she felt about not knowing the names of any of the slaves who had been forced to give up their lives for her.

He paused for a moment and closed his eyes, then whispered, "Abina. Because she was born on a Tuesday. Tenoch said they should also name my baby sister that, regardless of the day she was born. It was the only word my mother knew in the language of my grandmother. I don't even know what language that is. Only that it comes from the Gold Coast of Africa. That's where my grandmother was stolen from. I never got to meet her."

My heart pinched, and I gulped, not knowing what to say. There were plenty of dark-skinned people like him throughout the empire: Africans, Moors, and their descendants, some who were free, some who were not. The Spanish had brought free and enslaved Moors with them from the very first caravel, and continued bringing them to this day. They were such a part and parcel of our society that I had never really stopped to question it. The thought sickened me; a surge of hot, viscous shame made me reel. I had questioned plenty in my life, but I had never considered why my own mother had kept hundreds, if not thousands, of slaves until the day she died.

He continued grinding the ingredients. "Please, I can do that," I murmured, and he handed the molcajete over.

"That's not too bad." He nodded, and my breath hitched.

He looked older somehow, not the tentative boy who'd held a steaming mug of atole only yesterday. His sweetness was tempered by a loss I, too, felt keenly. Though it must've been worse for him, multiplied by three. His face was so close to mine that I could see specks of amber in his soulful, red-rimmed eyes.

He hesitated for just one blink before he whispered, "I understand, you know. If my mother had left me something of hers, the way your mother has, I would look through the whole of New Spain. I would cross the ocean and go back to the jungles of Africa, and I would face all the lions and tigers in the world, just to be close to her again."

My eyes swam with tears, and I felt that pull again, deep in my navel, drawing me to him. But we heard footsteps and edged away again, he to slather the turkey in the mixture of spices, and me to begin peeling the third onion.

Catina walked into the kitchen followed by my brother and Elvira, who were holding hands. Their faces were flushed, their lips swollen, and their hair disheveled, with bits of grass sticking out. Catina made a noise when she spotted us, and Nano cleared his throat awkwardly.

"There—there you are!"

I gave my brother a pointed look and raised my brow. "Yes, here we are, indeed. Where we said we would be."

Nano's eyes narrowed as he looked from me to Juan, who had gone back to the meal preparations. He signed at me only, "You've been by yourself, alone, with him?"

At the same time, Elvira said in an all-too-high-pitched voice, "It smells divine!"

"It is," I said, ignoring my brother.

Juan looked up at Elvira and smiled. "Thank you, but there's still much to do, señorita. Mulli takes time."

"Put us to work, then." I held his gaze.

Juan's eyes were brilliant, shining stars, and I thought if I were to look long enough, I might read my future in them.

Later that evening, after we had filled our bellies with mulli and tortillas, we sat by the kitchen fire to discuss our next steps.

"We'll have a sleep and then keep going," I said, sharpening my dagger with one of the kitchen whetstones. "Elvira, you're welcome to come, though I must warn you, there may be dangers ahead, and my brothers are on our trail."

Elvira hesitated, looking apologetic. "My father . . . I don't think I should—"

"Absolutely not," said Nano. "It is much too dangerous. There's no space in the canoe anyway." He turned to her and held her hands. "I shall need to accompany my sisters, of course, but as soon as they are done, I shall return to you, and we shall be married."

Catina and I gasped as he sank to his knees and offered her his golden signet ring, the one we all had, with Nantzin's eagle-and-snake crest.

"Fortune or no fortune," he said, placing it onto her finger, "I will not be kept from you. If you'll have me."

Elvira bent down and threw her arms around my brother, saying, "Oh, my love! Yes!"

Catina looked from him to me and said, "Did she say yes?"

I nodded, and beamed. Nano looked at me and, seeing the look on my face, broke into his best, most joyous smile. We all stood up to congratulate them. After a few moments, they made some excuse to leave the kitchen and failed to return.

We quietly packed our things and stocked up on food. Juan went off to find a place to sleep, and Catina and I went back to Elvira's room, avoiding each other's gaze. It wasn't long before Catina was overcome with fatigue and curled up on Elvira's bed to sleep.

I tried to sleep too, but my sister twitched and mewled the way she did when she was having one of her bad dreams and woke me up. I shushed her and tried to rest again, but I couldn't. I thought of Juan instead, and was filled with a desperate longing to search for him so I could speak to him once more, to hold him close, like Elvira had done with Nano. To comfort him for his losses . . . and be comforted by him in return. I thought of Nantzin and Marta, and silent tears slipped down my cheeks.

I turned away, just in case Catina woke up and saw me. I could not bear the thought of it. At some point, I fell asleep.

But after a few restless hours, there was a knock on the doors. The echo rang across the empty house. My heart drummed inside my chest.

There was a grumble underground, beneath the tiled floors. I swayed and thought perhaps it had been a small earthquake, but a blink later there was another knock, and Juan ran into our room, looking frightened.

"Maybe it's more debt collectors," he whispered. "Hopefully they'll go away."

They began to pound the door instead, followed by two sets of barks.

CHAPTER 15

Isabel Cano

5 March 1551

"Elvira, your drunkard father told us you're in there with our brother and sisters! Open the door! We just want to talk!" echoed a harsh voice that sent a shiver of dread down my spine. I scrambled to my feet and shook Catina awake.

"What is it?" she mumbled. I jammed her boots onto her chest and grabbed our things.

Almost immediately, Nano and Elvira ran into the room, carrying a torch.

"It's Pedro and Gonzalo, armed to the teeth. We've seen them from the window down the hall," said and signed my brother, eyes wide with fear.

"Quick, quick, follow me!" Elvira squeaked.

We ran behind her, downstairs and out the back of the house, past the empty cattle ring and into the unkempt field where, I assumed, animals had once grazed on the tall grass. The half moon was bright, but I still tripped on a gopher hole and fell. Juan helped me up, and without thinking, I held on to his hand until we reached a small canal near the opposite wall of the property. We paused, and I let go, whispering an awkward thanks, feeling the heat from my palm spreading to my ears, my chest, beyond my toes.

"It's shallow," said Elvira in between hard breaths, bringing me back to reality. "Take off your boots—jump in and follow it down to the river. The hounds won't be able to follow your scent." Juan, Catina, and I removed our boots.

Nano grabbed her arm. "You don't mean to stay?"

"It's not the first time awful people have come to search my home, but I know where to hide. Even with hunting dogs, they'll never find me." They looked deeply at each other for one tender, anguished moment, then Nano pulled her in and kissed her.

Catina and I blinked at each other, wide eyed, until the air was ripped by gunshot, making us all jump.

"Go, go!" Elvira said, plunging her torch into the water.

We all thanked her, then splashed into the canal and trudged forward, slipping and sinking into the silt. When I looked back, Elvira had disappeared into the shadows.

By the time we reached the place where the stream reached the outer wall, we could hear barking out in the fields, punctuated by my brothers' shouts, although no more shots were fired. Panting and huffing, we reached a circular iron grate that had been built around the dark, cold channel, which appeared to go all the way down into the ground.

"Are we trapped?" I said and signed, edging forward and feeling under the water. "Aha—there's a small space we can slip through, but we'll be soaked."

"I'll go," said Catina, surprising me again. She took off her satchel and handed it to me along with her boots, grabbed onto the rail, and swung herself in, feet first. When she came through, I passed her things and mine through the gaps in the grate and went next. Juan followed me, then Nano. We wedged forward as fast as we could into the lake.

"Where's our canoe?" I hissed. We looked around for a moment.

"Stolen," sighed Juan, and Nano swore. Juan shrugged. "It happens. Follow me."

We slipped into the marsh and traversed through the shallow, pitch-black waters as quickly as we could, following the shoreline north. Catina and I breathed hard, for our skirts were heavy and our feet kept sinking into the clay below us. Despite the bright moon, I was terrified of disturbing the reeds, or the creatures my brothers had spent countless hours tormenting us about: venomous snakes, leeches, spiders, and blood criers, those horned lizards that could shoot poisonous blood from their eyes. And I had to admit, the child inside me also worried about the mythical lake guardians. The ahuitzotl water dogs, who sank boats and snatched people from the shallows so they could feast on their nails and teeth.

I shuddered, and wished for a stallion, a warm, dry carriage. I desperately missed Juan's rickety old canoe. Something cold and slippery grazed my knee, and I fought back a squeal because I thought I could still hear faint barks in the distance. I strained to listen over our splashing steps, while at the same time wishing not to. Finally, we came across a small sailing skiff that had been tied to a dead pine near the shore.

"Let's take it," I said.

"We can't steal someone's boat!" Nano growled.

"Yes we can!" I barked. Juan climbed on board, and both he and Nano had to pull Catina and me on deck like a pair of half-drowned cats, leaving us splayed and trembling atop an expanding puddle on the wooden boards.

"There are only two paddles, and I have no idea how to sail," said Juan.

"I know how," grumbled Nano, who proceeded to hoist the sail, hissing commands none of us understood until he groaned in frustration and told us to just row and be quiet. We did as he told us, and we managed to get the boat moving, slowly at first, though soon the sail picked up the light breeze and we slipped out of gunshot range.

"The barking seems far away now—maybe we've lost them," Juan said.

"I'm worried for Elvira," I whispered as I tried to rub some warmth through my cold, wet sleeves. "We should've insisted she come along."

"She will be fine," Nano spat, and we all went quiet. After a while, he said more gently, "Where to next?"

"Ch-chapultepec. But we need to make a quick pit stop at home first," I said and signed.

"Why's that?" asked my sister and Juan at the same time.

I stood up and walked to the back of the boat, trembling with a mixture of cold and fear. I could no longer see the wall of Elvira's hacienda, or hear Nero's and Caligula's frantic barks, but I knew in my heart this wasn't over. We weren't safe.

I turned and signed, "Because next time we meet them, I will be ready."

We stayed close enough to land to be able to find our way back north. It was easy enough to navigate with the stars and the silver light of the moon, illuminating well-known landmarks and churches. Soon enough, we spotted the outline of our home towering above the rest of the forest in the near distance. We moored farther along than the place we'd initially run into Juan, two nights ago, and I was pleasantly surprised to find my weapons and gear had remained fully intact and untouched within the dovecote, as well as the bag filled with food that I'd prepared and the purse with the precious few coins I'd saved over the years. I ran back to the skiff, undetected, and handed my brother my rapier, sheathed inside its leather scabbard, then slung my bow and arrow over my shoulder.

Dawn brought with it a beaming, golden mist that filtered through the stark outline of the forest, sinking further into our wet clothes and making us shiver. Catina had curled into a ball near the mast. Seeing her tiny shaking figure moved me to pity, and I sat by her and put my arm around her shoulder. She leaned her wet hood against mine, and I knew she understood, implicitly, that I would forgive her.

I probably already had, but I could not yet bring myself to say it.

I took out and studied the scroll with the copies I'd made of Nantzin's cushions as we sailed back south toward Chapultepec. There were no giant grasshoppers leaping from its top, and we could not yet see the steps that had been carved into its face, or the remains of the ancient aqueduct my mother's ancestors had built to supply Tenochtitlan with fresh water from its many springs. But although it was still dwarfed by the snowcapped mountains and volcanoes far behind it, the hill was easily spotted, even from a distance.

As we drew near, we came across some Mexica ladies washing their clothes by the lake. Some items were already hanging to dry over the branches of an oak tree. Nano veered the skiff at my insistence, and we managed to trade one of our precious silver reales and five oranges for three cotton shirts, one huipil, as well as a skirt and three pairs of trousers made of rough maguey fiber. Juan thought we might've been taken advantage of, but I was too cold and soaked through to care.

Nano and Juan faced resolutely away from us as we changed behind the sail, but they certainly stared when we came out, fully dressed and mercifully dry.

"What?" I said.

Nano burst out laughing. "You're dressed like a man, and Catina's skirt is so large I'm surprised it's not fallen to her ankles. You're both still wearing hair caps—the whole look is ridiculous."

"Fine." I tore my cap off and loosened my braid, letting my long, damp hair fall free, feeling the breeze swirling through each thick onyx strand. It was so immodest that Nano glared at Juan, who immediately looked down at the toes poking out from his old leather sandals. He didn't have to look away for long.

Before either one of my siblings could do more than yelp, I unsheathed my dagger, pulled my hair together at my nape, and sliced it all off.

"Isabel, no!" Catina shouted.

"Estas loca?" Nano spluttered.

Juan looked up. For a moment, he simply blinked. Then he smiled.

I smiled back at him and then at Nano. "Don't you want me to look the part?" I said and signed. "It's genius, don't deny it. If people are looking for two Mestizas, a Spanish-looking boy, and a Moorish kidnapper, now they'll see three boys of various skin tones, and their . . . frumpy little sister. They won't pay us heed."

Nano rubbed his face and gestured between himself and Juan, then said and signed, "No offense, but we look nothing like brothers."

"We all thank the Lord for that," I said, and felt my cheeks warm.

"You also look nothing like a kidnapper, Juan," said Catina with a kind smile, as she pulled her skirt up from under her huipil shirt, trying to keep it from falling. "Although now we can't say the same about you, sister."

"Ha!" Nano pointed his finger at me as though he'd won the jest himself, and I snorted too, astonished yet delighted at my sister's unusual display of humor, even if it came at my expense. I walked up to her, and she flinched slightly as I picked her hair loose, then cut one of the ribbons off her discarded cap, pulled the excess cloth from her skirt into a bun, and wrapped the ribbon around it.

"There. The skirt should stay on," I said and signed. "Let's get a move on and try not to draw any attention to ourselves. Remember, we're looking for a small village near the southeastern base of the hill, not far, it seems, from some kind of pool."

"The Franciscans have built a small hermitage at the hilltop," said Juan, with an edge to his voice I had never heard before. "They were my teachers, and I know how nosey they can be. Let's empty our guajes. If they ask, we're here to collect water like everyone else."

"Good idea. Let's go."

◆ ◆ ◆

We failed to draw more than a few uninterested glances from fellow travelers as we wound our way underneath the shadows of thick and ancient ahuehuete cypresses. I shot a rabbit to eat later, earning a begrudging look of respect from Nano. Our feet crunched on pine cones and needles and small pebbles until we came across a trickling stream. We followed it, and before long, around midmorning, we reached a small clearing by the foot of Chapultepec Hill. A group of children were chasing each other around, close to a large pool of indigo water.

Juan drew close to me and said, "They're so tiny, they look like chaneques." Guardians of nature, ancient spirits that could either help you or lead you astray if you angered them.

"Their faces don't look wrinkled and old, though," I replied.

We drew our guajes and were preparing to walk to the pool to fill them and study the surroundings when one of the children, the smallest, tripped and fell in, and as if he were a boulder, disappeared with a splash. A girl began to scream, "My brother!"

The others looked around with panicked eyes and spotted us. "Help him! We can't swim!" But Nano and Juan were already halfway there. Nano dived into the spot where the child had fallen through and pulled him up to the surface after a few breathless moments. The children screamed again at the sight of his limp little body.

"Here!" Juan demanded. With ease, he pulled the child out and, to my surprise, placed him on the floor and sealed his mouth over the boy's own. The boy's chest rose. He did it again, and then once more, pushing on his lungs in between. Not three breaths later, the boy coughed, sprung into a seated position, and vomited all over himself and Juan.

It was mostly water, but the other children still made noises of great disgust, apart from the girl. She threw herself around her brother, crying, shouting her thanks in Nahuatl at Juan, who was trembling all over, nodding, his eyes glazed with tears. I doubted he even noticed the small chunks of tamalli sliding down his front.

"Who are you?" the girl demanded. "What are your names?"

We looked at each other, unsure of whether to answer.

Just as I was opening my mouth to say that it was best if we left, she said to Juan matter-of-factly, “I always wished to meet a Moor, and now one has saved my brother’s life. Are you their slave? I hope not.” Her thick brows stitched together as she shot us all, and Nano in particular, a very nasty look.

“I am no slave,” Juan said, so low that it made the hairs on the back of my neck stand on end. But the girl’s stare brought me back to my senses. She was studying me with a cocked head. Her serious eyes were like the color of the dark pool her brother had nearly drowned in. She was the oldest of them all, still younger than Catina. Yet something about her commanded respect.

She turned her gaze to Nano. “Good. You don’t seem like most coyotl Spaniards, or like those monks up there either. Are you the Moctezuma children?”

“Wh—” I spluttered. “What?”

Nano blinked. “What makes you say that?”

The girl shrugged. “A stranger came through here, three or four moons ago, riding a horse. No one saw their face, because they were all covered up in a hood, but they gave something to my grandmother, who is a famous healer around here. She received a message a few days ago again, telling her that the Moctezumas were on their way. That’s why we were here. We were waiting for you. They didn’t mention a Moor, though.”

My lips parted. Juan and I locked eyes, and he nodded.

“Would you take us to her?” I asked, and the girl smiled wide.

It was only a short walk from the clearing with the pool to the small village at the foot of the hill where the children lived. Our footsteps were muffled by a carpet of clovers. The snore-like croaking of frogs and fluttering of birds filtered in between the shrieks and laughter of the children guiding us.

Nano ran up next to me and whispered in Castilian, “Nantzin almost never rode horses, and she couldn’t have ridden by herself four months ago. And how could she have sent a message only a few days ago, from her grave?"

"Well, someone helped her. So what?" I hissed back, wondering briefly who it could've been, though it really did not matter to me. Perhaps a maid, or Marta? A quiver of arrows struck my heart at the image of Pedro's fingers crushing her windpipe. My throat knotted with guilt and rage, and I had to swallow it down, to keep walking.

A small yellow bird swooped down on a horned beetle. The gurgle of the stream dimmed away. I breathed in the scent of honeydew and pine to calm myself, but Nano bumped his arm into mine, disrupting my efforts.

"Think, Isabel! What if this isn't her at all? What if it's some kind of trap? Haven't you wondered why it's been so difficult, so perilous?"

I clenched my jaw and swallowed my retort, that what he really wanted was to get back to the comfort of Elvira's ample bosom. I would not allow his fretting to make me doubt my convictions, so I took another breath and said, "Look, I cannot claim to know her reasons, but I *know* it's Nantzin. I cannot explain it, but I just know."

"She was a powerful woman," he insisted, for he was just as stubborn as I. "She had enemies. People who wanted to . . . I don't know, discredit her. Tarnish her legacy. Take her lands away again. She walked a fine line between our father's people and her own. Some Spaniards hated that she'd been exalted by Cortés and Emperor Carlos over their own women, and some Mexica saw her as a turncoat for uniting with the Spanish."

I was quiet for a moment. "That's all the more reason for her to want to have a final say. For her to explain why she made the choices she made."

"You're not thinking straight."

The people out in the village stopped and stared as the children ran toward them, shouting the story of what had happened in the clearing. I marched ahead, wishing to put some distance between me and my brother, but it didn't work—I still heard the heartbreak in his voice when he said, "You just can't accept she's gone."

CHAPTER 16

Isabel Cano

5 March 1551

Tepahtih Nayeli, the girl's grandmother, insisted on feeding us, and I had never been one to turn down food, especially the type that smelled this good. After cleaning our hands with amolli soaproot in a large ceramic basin outside, we were invited to sit on a large straw mat on the floor of a big hut that looked like Juan's but neater, with flowers and herbs hanging from the ceiling, dozens of ceramic jars of all sizes placed in neat shelves against the adobe walls, and incense burners smoking with copal.

Tepahtih Nayeli cleaned and grilled my rabbit and offered us a huge bowl of popped corn, and steaming maize tortillas filled with calabash flowers; black, juicy frijoles; and succulent huitlacoche, the delicious fungus that grew on maize kernels.

Even Nano ate some, carefully wiping the black juice running down his chin. Catina had several, and Juan and I gorged ourselves as we discussed the merits of each filling and which type of chilli was better suited to the different flavors.

Something seemed to have shifted inside of Juan, and he seemed lighter, bolder, more willing to laugh. Every time his gaze fell on

Tepahtih Nayeli's grandson, he sat up straighter, prouder. I thought it was right for him to be proud. To have saved that little boy's life.

We were so enjoying our time with the children, who were learning Hand Talk from Catina herself, that we did not realize the sun had set. Tepahtih Nayeli began to usher the children to another hut to sleep, and we apologized profusely for trespassing, but she shook her head and told us to wait.

When she returned, she was dressed differently, in a long blue huipil embroidered with stars and moons. Her youthful face was painted yellow and her mouth and chin black, with a black spot on her cheek. "I have been expecting you," she said to all of us in Nahuatl, although her light-brown eyes lingered on me.

This time, however, it was Nano who answered first. "How? Your granddaughter said someone paid you a visit, gave you something that may belong to us. But who was it? My sister believes it was our mother . . ."

"I met the huey cihuatlatoani, the great queen," she responded, using a term that might have gotten her killed in front of the wrong people, "many years before you were born." She looked at me. "I helped her, and never saw her again, but I do have that which belonged to her, which she wished to share with you. But first, you must be cleansed."

Catina nudged me, and I quickly signed to explain what was being said.

Nano pinched the bridge of his nose. "Wait—you deny that you saw her recently, so who was it who gave you her . . . the thing you have of hers?"

Tepahtih Nayeli smiled kindly and shrugged. "A messenger, bearing her eagle-and-snake crest. I never saw their face."

Nano and I looked at each other.

"How will we be cleansed?" Catina asked.

"Come with me," the healer answered.

We followed her back out into the dark forest, silent except for the chirping of crickets and the whisper of leaves. Tepahtih Nayeli carried no torch but walked resolutely, without hesitation, without tripping on a single tree root or walking face first into a spiderweb, like poor Catina, who only just managed to not let out a shriek.

We could hardly see the healer or each other. Only her gentle, reassuring voice guided us through the scent of cedar and musk. At some point, a strong, warm, steadying hand found mine. Juan's hand, which sent a flurry of heat from my speeding heart to my weakened legs. My breath quickened, and not from the exertion.

Finally, when it was so dark we could no longer see our palms in front of our faces, Tepahtih Nayeli stopped and said, "We are in a very deep part of the forest now."

There was the quick, sharp sound of a flint being struck, and a few sparks, and then a torch was lit. After squeezing Juan's hand gently, I unwillingly let go.

It's not that I was embarrassed. In fact, I felt thrilled, set alight. His arm next to mine was like a warm beacon, and I couldn't help brushing it lightly against my own, sending a shiver of gooseflesh down my back.

But I didn't want Nano or Catina to see us holding hands, not yet. For now, whatever this was—this new, delightful, glowing feeling, both sweet and delicate—was something that belonged only to me and him.

In front of us, painted in dark colors and barely visible in our torchlight, was a circular stone structure with a domed roof. It looked like La Llorona's hut, except much bigger. A set of small deer antlers hung from a nail driven into the front door. A small heap of volcanic rocks was piled in a straw basket in front of it. Somewhere in the distance, an owl hooted.

"Help me build the fire for your temazcalli, your steam bath," Tepahtih Nayeli said, pointing to a pile of wood and a small opening. "Mind the well over here."

We did as she said, even Nano, who kept shooting annoyed glances in my direction.

The healer lit the fire and placed the volcanic stones close enough that they began to heat up and glow red. She said a number of prayers in

Nahuatl, welcoming the stones, the cihtli—*grandmothers*, as she called them. Then she gave us girls two plain cotton robes to change into, and the boys long skirtlike loincloths in the old Nahua style.

From the shadows where I changed, I heard Nano scoff. "You're not serious."

Tepahtih Nayeli's smile was plain on her voice. "You will thank me later."

"I cannot wear it." I turned back to see Nano pushing the cloth back into the healer's hands, who nodded, still wearing her calm, easy smile.

"As you wish," she responded.

Juan, on the other hand, had gone and changed, and was now standing by the door of the building, arms crossed over his bare chest, which, even in the poor light, I could see were chiseled, same as his stomach and legs: lean, but strong.

I shivered, though not from the cold air.

Catina bumped me lightly, and we shared a wide-eyed look. We covered our lips to keep ourselves from giggling and embarrassing our friend. We walked back to them, and Juan and I averted our eyes. I glanced at my brother, who had remained as he was, wearing his trousers and shirt, a thunderous look on his face as he stared at Tepahtih Nayeli leaning over the spitting fire. The healer burned the ends of a fistful of long, dry herbs or flowers—it was difficult to tell. They gave off smoke and a sweet, musky fragrance.

She walked back to us and began to chant, blew the smoke into our faces, waved the flowers around our bodies and between our legs. She looked into each of our eyes, and even though I had no idea what she meant by all this, I felt a comforting sense that she had been sent to help us, guide us, on our journey.

"Now, we will welcome you into the temazcalli," she said as she guided us into the building and around the edge of the walls, indicating where we should sit on the cold stone ground. She then walked back out of the hut, leaving the torch inside.

"Isabel, what do you think she's going to do?" Catina whispered.

"Yes, do please explain what the devil is going on," Nano hissed under his breath.

"We're cleansing, brother," I said and signed, but Nano shook his head. "Come now, it's a steam bath," I said. "We've had them before. How bad can it be?"

Nano's retort was interrupted by Tepahtih Nayeli returning again, this time carrying one of the glowing volcanic rocks in between the deer antlers. She placed it carefully in the middle of the floor in front of us. The inside of the hut immediately warmed up, the smell of smoke and earth hit the back of my throat, the skin above my lips began to prickle with sweat.

She went out again, and each time she brought back another stone, warming up the hut until my skin was soaked through. Finally, after she had placed half a dozen stones inside, she came back with a large jug and a white cloth, put out the torch, and shut the door. The room went pitch black, except for the grandmother stones, sparkling red like burning stars. Catalina shifted next to me, held my slippery hand with hers. She was breathing hard and fast.

"You forgot to leave the door open," Nano asked, the pitch of his voice half an octave too high. "I don't know if you've noticed, but it's a tad warm in here."

Juan snorted. It was more than a little warm. It was the pit of hell. It was like flying face first into Tonatiuh, the sun. My heart was racing; even my ears prickled. My throat was burning, my skin was on fire, the robe I wore was soaked through, and all I wanted was to tear it off. But I didn't. I didn't groan or complain, because I'd gotten us into this mess.

Tepahtih Nayeli dipped the cloth into the jug, spun it around in the air, and slammed it onto the stones. Droplets sizzled, filling the room with suffocating steam. She threw something perfumed onto the stones—copal, and something else, an essence I did not recognize. Slowly, I began to feel at ease again. My muscles melted, my breath slowed.

Then, from somewhere, the healer picked up a drum and began to play. She sang a song of ancient wisdom in Nahuatl. Her voice seemed far away, like an echo.

"What is *in* that water?" Nano's voice was still high, but it sounded slurred.

Tepahtih Nayeli's drum beat steady. "Come and be guided by our grandmother stones, and our grandfather, Huehueteotl Xiuhtecuhtli, god of warmth, god of fire, of light in darkness."

She threw another pinch of resin and the other substance on the sizzling stones, and I felt myself floating. Into a pitch-black hole I slowly fell, though I was not afraid.

I recognized I was held, cocooned in something soft, a warm, liquid thing. I swam in it, simply because it felt good and right and tranquil. But after some time, I felt myself becoming big, too big, for the liquid. The cocoon tightened around me, and I began to kick and thrash, until a crack appeared.

Light, endless warm light, poured in. I kicked some more, pecked the membrane around me, and emerged into the world. A courtyard and a mighty white pyramid rose before my eyes, bright and gleaming in the sun.

And there was my mother, high, up high at the top of the pyramid.

Nantzin's voice was too far away. She was telling me her story. I had to listen to it, quick, before I missed it.

I looked down at my slimy, wet arms and realized . . . they were wings.

CHAPTER 17

Tecuichpoch

1520–1525

My mother lived for another week. Long enough, I think, for her to be told that her children had survived the great pestilence, for her to see us alive and together one last time. Axayacatzin and I tried our best to nurse her, though we had not yet recovered our strength, but we could not dissuade death from stealing her away to Tlalocan, to the beautiful paradise where the people who die from plague are made whole again.

My brother and I cried our bitter tears alone in my chamber, and held each other so tight it felt as though we would be forged into one, that we would melt into each other like I had seen the Spaniards melt our grandfather's treasures into crude bullion, all those thousands of fine pieces that had taken our master jewelers years to craft. And now, even that bullion was gone. The gold had fallen into the lake during their mad retreat on the causeway, when they had trampled on top of each other's bodies to get away from our furious shower of arrows and darts. The treasure was lost, just like my brother and I were also lost, and there was no one to hold us except each other.

Everyone was grieving someone: a spouse, a friend, thousands of little children and babies who had succumbed to the great pestilence.

Each night, the wails of a hundred mothers echoed in the wind, drowning out coyotes and owls alike, and even the everlasting trickle of the tide rocking against our island city. Everyone was drowning in the depths of their grief, except Cuauhtemoc.

He had the spirit of our great gods inside him, he had Huitzilopochtli and Tlaloc both. He was the fire of war and the cool rain that precedes the sowing season. And he was planting the seeds for the destruction of the Spaniards, or so he hoped. I cannot fault him in this, which he saw as his divine duty. He was as his name suggests, the Eagle Descending, claws honed and ready to strike his prey dead from the sky.

He said I would be like the wind to him, the warm current that carries the wings of birds onto the sky. He spoke sweet words to set me at ease, for I had finally bled, my moon had finally begun, and it was time to become a wife not just in name but in deed.

My sister Mariana, who was two years older than me and of a more suitable age for marriage, tried to intervene, to point out that I was too young, barely twelve, or perhaps it was thirteen, I cannot recall precisely.

But it was a brave thing, for she risked the wrath of the huey tlatoani. She risked her very life in speaking out for me the way my mother would have done if she'd been alive—the way she had done with my father before he'd given me to Cortés.

But Cuauhtemoc said simply that we were at war, and that was the end of the matter.

And I will admit, I was relieved that Cuauhtemoc would be my proper husband, and not my father's brother, or a man with grandchildren older than me. Though I was still young, much too young. Only a babe, only a fool.

Indeed, I made the mistake of trusting in his pretty words, of forgetting what it meant to be loved and favored by the huey tlatoani. I forgot my father's greatest lesson because I was softened by Cuauhtemoc's gentleness and by the pestilence, just as my mother had been softened by my captivity and by the massacre at the temple. That is what losing someone dear to you does, what coming close to death does to the heart sometimes: it makes you forget to stay sharp. I would never forget again. But I am getting ahead of myself.

Cuauhtemoc needed to win over my older half brothers, because they had the support of the Tenochca, the people of Tenochtitlan. You must understand, Cuauhtemoc's mother was from Tlatelolco. He was considered Tlatelolca, and thus his influence on our city was incomplete. He needed to bring my Tenochca brothers to his side, to his way of thinking, so very different to our father, who had ordered caution and circumspection. Wisdom, in short, to prevent an unwinnable war and more pointless suffering and death.

But Cuauhtemoc was a general—the head of the Eagle Knights—the bravest, boldest, most feared warriors in all of Anahuac. He had been taught to fight to the death to defend the honor of our city and our people, many of whom thought like him. He was young—decades younger than my father had been, or any of my husbands—so he had that fire of youth, the desire to prove himself, to make his mark. And I wished to do my duty by him, as I had been taught to do, and because I was growing to care for him, although I had seen enough of death already. It was agony to listen to the laments of all those childless mothers and motherless children, cries that Axayacatzin echoed into my arms every night before he fell asleep and I was summoned to Cuauhtemoc's chambers to fulfill my wifely role.

After one particular night he commanded me and said, "Go to them tomorrow. Ask your two older brothers once and for all to endorse me publicly, for the young ones will follow, and so will all the Tenochca, the people of Tenochtitlan."

I went as soon as dawn crested over the horizon, but my brothers would not listen to me, though I begged on my knees and my voice trembled.

"It is pure madness," they said to me. "Even if Cortés is defeated, we know more ships are coming from across the seas, with more weapons and armories that we cannot beat. Only a week ago we received word that another huge ship was sighted on the eastern shores. Even some of our allies, even some branches of the Texcoca, are suing for peace."

So they did not outright oppose Cuauhtemoc, but they did not endorse him either, and in so doing they sealed our family's fate.

My sisters, Metztonalli, Yolloxochitl—who became Mariana—and I were summoned on some errand I cannot recall, that day when Cuauhtemoc struck.

It is a mercy, I suppose, that we did not see it with our own eyes or hear it with our own ears, though in the months of siege that came only a few short weeks later, I would witness enough battles to be able to picture death a thousand ways and more, and be driven nearly as mad as Mariana was. For she loved her full brother as dearly as I did Axayacatzin.

But Cuauhtemoc ended both their lives with his own blade. I know this, I know he killed Axayacatzin, because he brought my sisters and me to the throne room and, after we had greeted him the formal way, by removing our sandals and falling to our knees, and placing our middle fingers on the floor and bringing them to our lips, he said to us, "Your brothers were weak like your father, and in this greatest of wars against the white demons who would take everything from us, there can be no room for weakness or hesitancy."

I heard him say it as if from afar, that it gave him no satisfaction to order their deaths, especially the young ones. He said, "I struck the little ones myself, quick and true. I used my own blade, for only I am strong enough to shoulder the burden of their untimely, noble deaths. But take comfort in knowing that they all died like true warriors, by the hand of the huey tlatoani, who ensured they would not suffer."

And this is when I knew my mother's training had changed me for good, just as our dyes transform the color of white cotton forever, for I did not look up from the floor, I did not cry out like Mariana and Metztonalli did, though it felt as though my heart was seized by Cuauhtemoc's talons and pierced by his obsidian blade, and my body shook so violently that I felt my teeth clattering inside my skull. I did not make a noise. I could not.

But my soul, my yolia, blackened and shrank that day, I tell you. I tortured myself for many years, thinking if I had tried harder, if I had been more persuasive, if I'd had Malintzin's silver tongue, my brothers would have thrown their support behind my husband and Axayacatzin would've been spared. My little brother, my little boy.

And the devastation I felt from his loss was like a cold, heavy gray fog every day from then on. Even during the three months of siege, when the Spanish came back with their floating brigantines and they cut off our food and destroyed the aqueducts so we had no fresh water and our tongues swelled for thirst. Even after we nearly died again from starvation and the flux from eating adobe and straw, and after they burned and flattened our great city with their cannons, and on the roads lay the shattered bones and scattered hair of our valiant warriors, and the walls of our homes were slippery with brains and worms, I could feel nothing at all but my baby brother's shadow, the absence of his warmth between my arms.

My sweet Axayacatzin, who had not yet started studying with the priests at the calmecac. Who had only just mastered the bow and killed only one turkey.

Why, I asked myself. Why? He was only ten years old, still mourning his mother, still searching for pretty rocks.

I see him to this day, in the bright, inquisitive gazes of children running around the plaza. I hear him in their delighted shrieks, and my heart shrivels, my arms tingle, wishing I could hold him again.

I suppose the only small grace in that time was that Cuauhtemoc no longer touched me. I knew he felt the weight of my little brothers' deaths, the hunger on the faces of our people, the clear failure of his campaign, despite the ferocity and courage of our warriors, despite their best efforts to challenge every inch of land the Spanish gained . . . it all depleted his manhood. I would be summoned to his chambers at night for nothing.

Perhaps he simply wanted company, even though I would not speak to him, let alone look at him. But he would speak to me during those nights.

One time, he said, "The Spanish thought we would be paralyzed with fear at the sight of their weapons, that we would be like the tlacuache opossums that freeze with their jaws open at the sight of a mere tapir. But we are not cowed, though they are covered from head to toe in iron. That's the heart of the matter, for they are not better warriors than us, they do not possess greater intellect than us, and they are certainly no gods. The only difference between us and them is iron."

That was the night before he gave his last decree to his ministers.

I was there, and I remember it clearly, because it was the only time I felt a stirring of some other feeling in all those terrible months after my husband killed my brother. A sense that the eclipse the Spanish had brought was complete. There was nothing more we could do.

We could not shift the moon.

And that is what Cuauhtemoc told his counselors to tell his people, to say to them: "The Sun has set," though he meant our soul, our essence, for we were the People of the Sun. He meant our time as lords of this great land, of our beloved Anahuac, had come to an end. Our sorrow was such that we felt we were losing the sun in the sky, like we were losing the light in our lives. A great gaping maw of darkness and emptiness was enveloping our whole world. Even our gods were falling into this ruin, this death. Myself too. I felt myself sinking. For I was truly, wholly bereft. And my tears finally fell, and there was almost an ache of relief in that, because I had not been able to cry since Axayacatzin had been killed. So I cried for him too, that his death had been in vain and my beautiful Anahuac was lost.

Please, dear, hand me that handkerchief. This is too much for me, even now.

No, we must not stop. I shall not be able to speak of it again. Time is running out, and you must know. Everyone should know. Yes, I shall go on. I shall tell you what Cuauhtemoc said next, for it was a wise thing.

He said that while the sun was gone, and while everything lay in darkness, we had to join together, embrace one another, and keep everything we loved, everything we knew to be true—we had to keep it alive in our secret hearts. That was his command. And he beseeched the honorable fathers and mothers of our people to guide their children, to teach them the love for our land, to tell them how good our land had been until now. Because one day, our children would rise up again, and gain strength, and the sun would return, and our children would fulfill the great destiny of our beloved Anahuac.

And when I heard Cuauhtemoc's wisp of a voice and saw the tears falling down his own face, I understood his love for Anahuac, and Tenochtitlan, and her people. Against my own wishes, a kernel of respect grew in me for him, that he would strive to keep our fading hopes alive even in this great hour of woe. There was a power in his words, a promise. And I saw how our people and land were as dear to him as his own mother. More so, perhaps. I knew everything he had ever done was in their service. Because he hoped he would protect them—his people, his Tenochtitlan, his Anahuac.

And after this last decree, we tried to escape in a canoe. But as you know, we were caught. And that is how my reign ended, my dear. Two huey tlatoanis gone in a little over a year, and I could not tell you how I spent it, really, except in a haze of sorrow.

Although I do recall sweeping.

I was never good at weaving like my mother and my sister Metztonalli, who could make a loom weep with the beauty of her creations. I never had the fingers for it, or the patience, or the head for color and remembering which string to put my rod through. I would sit with the women and listen to their stories instead, back when they told them.

But there were no stories during the war, no way to go outside safely to the gardens, no brother to catch lizards with. So I would take a broom and walk through the palace, and the motion—to and fro, to and fro—would place me in a sort of trance where the deafening blasts of cannons softened, as did the never-ending drumming and shouting and the sounding of flutes and whistles and the agonies of men dying outside.

I would also look at the beautiful murals on the walls, and find myself lost in the images of the animals and the gods, of Tlaloc bashing a snake against a holy jug to let out the rain, of miraculous trees reaching the underworld with their roots, of Huitzilopochtli in eagle form, landing on a cactus and showing us, his chosen people, where to establish and build our city, surrounded by our grassy marsh and lake. And I studied every single detail on the walls, and swept until the whole room was left without a speck of dirt.

Cuauhtemoc and his priests praised me, saying I was keeping chaos at bay. That I was helping to maintain order and centrality and balance, for sweeping was a deed even Quetzalcoatl found worthy, the wind god, who swept the path for Tlaloc and his rains. Coatlicue herself had birthed her son Huitzilopochtli, the god of war, while holding a broom. They said I was an honorable lady, a worthy wife to our huey tlatoani. They told tales in the city of my noble bearing and my strength in these times of sorrow.

I am glad to have been of service to our people. To have brought them some semblance of comfort. But I tell you honestly, I did it all to keep myself from losing my mind. For these were far too many blows for even a grown man to handle, and there was no reprieve, not one single day of peace or rest from the horror and the grief.

The broom kept me upright, kept me going, somehow, during the siege and after.

I swept every day for the three years I was held captive by Cortés, with only Cuauhtemoc and sometimes Mariana and Metztonalli for company, when they brought us together to teach us more about the Christian God. When they decreed which aspects of ourselves and our culture to tone down, to forget and destroy. When they forced us at sword point to give speech after speech to the people who had survived the pestilence and the siege only to be enslaved. We kept our people from revolting even as they were humiliated further, made to dismantle the remains of our ancient temples, and use the same stones to build palaces and churches in the style of their new lords.

I swept when Metztonalli disappeared without a trace after Pedro de Alvarado took a liking to her. I think perhaps she hanged herself, or tied stones to her feet and threw herself in the lake, for I know with my whole heart she would not have gone with him willingly. I swept when Cortés tortured Cuauhtemoc by burning the soles of his feet, after his men failed to find their sunken gold. I swept after I cleaned and bound my husband's charred and disfigured toes and helped him learn how to walk again.

I swept after Cuauhtemoc and I embraced goodbye.

Though I never forgave him for killing my brother, I tell you faithfully, it was his one and only transgression. He never raised his hand or his voice to me. He never forced himself on me, though most would have seen it as his right as a husband, and I soon learned what a real virtue this was in a man. During our many hours alone together, he would sometimes play the flute, or recite his sad poems and songs and ask for my thoughts.

It pained me to see him go, hobbling away, using a cane. Cortés marched him and our great and loyal friends, Coanacoch of Texcoco and Tetlepanquetzal of Tlacopan, all the way to Honduras and, in his paranoia over a small joke they had made at his expense, hanged them all from the branches of a ceiba tree. The last three Mexica lords to rule over the Triple Alliance, the last remaining light spilling from a vanishing sun.

He extinguished them all.

As for me, I knew, even as I grieved the terrible news, that I was too valuable to remain a widow for long. I knew I would be forced to marry a Spaniard next.

Though that is a tale for another day.

My hope is that you will find it.

CHAPTER 18

Isabel Cano

6 March 1551

Light streamed through the open door when I woke the next morning feeling wounded and small. Or perhaps the world felt too large and wicked, too terrifying to face without Nantzin. But she herself had done it, somehow. She had held on to the one innocuous thing that had brought her any comfort, a broom, and had kept placing one foot in front of the other.

How simple, and yet how difficult that must've been.

How I wished, then and there, that she had never had to live through any of that horror, that betrayal, first from her father, then her husband. I had not known that Emperor Cuauhtemoc had killed my uncle. I had always respected the man; my own father and even the gentry of New Spain held him in high esteem for his courage. The Mexica venerated his name and memory. But what is courageous about murdering one child and bedding another? My vision blurred at the surge of love and sorrow and rage engulfing me like a rising tide. Perhaps I ought not to judge the man, but I could not help it. I wish he'd left Nantzin alone.

I scratched the insect bites on my hands and neck, stretched my fingertips and felt the comforting shapes of my sister and brother curled up next to me, facing the wall. I breathed in to calm myself, then turned to my side and saw Juan, on the other side of the hut and behind the extinguished volcanic rocks. He was awake too, lying on his side, studying me.

A warm glow radiated inside my core. He indicated to the door with his eyebrows, and I nodded. We rose without making a sound, and went outside. The sun was high—it must've been nearing midday.

Tepahtih Nayeli was nowhere to be found, but she had left all our gear, our weapons and bags, a bowl filled with an entire papaya, a bushel of bright-green guavas and pink prickly pears, and a half dozen tamalli on top of a small wooden table by the hut. There, too, underneath a small altar containing a jar of burning copal incense and strewn petals, was a small leather-bound book, written in Nantzin's hand.

"It's here," I whispered.

"At last." Juan smiled. "Well done. Let's fetch some water before we read it." We refilled our guajes with the water from the well, found a decomposing log by the edge of the forest to sit on, drank deeply, and ate some fruit. There was a trickle of a stream nearby, underneath the beat of a woodpecker drumming its beak on the trunk of an elm. Other trees surrounded us, tall ashes, leafy ahuacatl, and colorines with their coral-red flowers and scarlet beans sticking out of knobbly pods.

"It's beautiful out here," Juan said, and I nodded, feeling oddly shy around him, remembering how he'd held my hand last night, the way his body had looked in the firelight. Luckily, he was now fully dressed in a pristine white cotton shirt and trousers. In fact, we were both surprisingly clean, without a trace of sweat on our bodies. Our brand-new garments were freshly laundered and smelled of orange blossom.

"I don't remember getting dressed, do you?" Juan asked, as though reading my thoughts. I shook my head. There was a little bit of wind, and the temperature was cooler in the shadows. Juan edged closer, sealing the gap between us, and I allowed myself to lean into him, to feel comforted by his warmth, his strength.

"I heard my mother last night, telling her story. Did you hear anything?" I murmured, and because he was gazing out into the forest, I steeled myself to study him, to anchor myself to the specks of amber in his brown eyes, his curling eyelashes, his thick brows, those full lips. Something in me awakened, and I yearned, suddenly, to touch them. But I did not dare.

Juan sighed, looked up to the sky. "I saw my family. They were glowing, all three of them." His voice shook. "They said La Llorona freed them from the water."

"They did?" I whispered.

He nodded and whispered, "They were proud of me."

"Of course they are." I grasped his hand, and our eyes locked for the space of four, five warm breaths. He held my gaze as he inched his face closer to mine. I couldn't look away, I couldn't move. My heart raced, my vision swam, my lips parted in anticipation.

"Oh no, you don't!" Nano shouted.

Juan and I jolted away from each other so quickly, I fell off the log.

"Are you all right?" Juan tried to help me up, but Nano slapped his arm away.

"That's quite enough of you trying to get your hands on my sister!"

I sprung to my feet, burning with embarrassment. "Shut it, Nano!"

Juan spluttered, "I wasn't trying to get my hands—"

Nano laughed. "My friend, I spend my life at court. I know how your mind works."

"Because you're exactly the same?" I jabbed at his chest.

"You're about—to become—a—nun!" He enunciated his words by jamming the knife-edge of one hand into his other palm. "And it's my duty to protect your virtue!"

"What about Elvira's virtue, huh? Were you this scrupulous with her? When you were sneaking around her hacienda and we didn't see you for hours?" I shouted.

Nano's face burned carmine. "That is—completely different. Elvira and I love each oth—I am going to marry her!"

"Aha, and how will you keep her?" My tone was ugly, my embarrassment turning to rage. How dare he allow himself to have dreams, and yet crush my own? "You would condemn the woman you love to a life of poverty?"

"Isabel—" Juan attempted, but I would not listen.

"No, answer me, brother. How will you provide for her the way a noblewoman deserves to be provided for? When you don't have a single coin to your name, no trade, no skill, no land, no proper inheritance, nothing! You promised her the world, but it's empty, like the miserable house she lives in!"

Nano's face drained of color. He bit his white lips to keep the tears at bay. I gulped and trembled, froze as a sudden surge of shame waded over me, making me wish I could take back my words. But it was too late.

After several moments, Nano whispered, voice thick with emotion. "Before she died, Nantzin spoke to me, alone. She told me . . . to trust in her choices. To trust in you and stay by your side. Protect you and Catina. Well, I've tried. I really have. But it's impossible. Throw away your life, your security, your virtue. Break your word. Go on your mad quest, if you wish. But I'm leaving, and I'm taking Catina with me."

He turned on his heel, marched back into the hut, and soon emerged again, dragging a bewildered, half-asleep Catina by the arm.

I was still too mortified to think, to act. I could only watch as Catina struggled against him, tried to prize his fingers open and said, "I don't want to go home! You're hurting me! Isabel, what have you done?"

Nano let go and signed at her, "I shall not force you. But know this—Nantzin wanted us to be safe, above everything. She never put us in danger. And there is danger here, I can feel it. Not only from our brothers. Whoever delivered these journals, they do not mean us well. I do not wish to see you hurt."

He did not include me in that last statement. He did not even look in my direction. Catina's chin wobbled, her eyes swam, but her back straightened, her fists clenched. She had that look of defiance again, the same as she had given me in La Llorona's hut. She did not need to speak for us to know her answer.

Nano shook his head. "So be it," he said, and quick as a panther he stalked back into the forest.

"Wait!" Juan called from beside me, and I came back to my senses.

"Nano, wait!" I ran after him, but he had already disappeared into the shadows of the thick forest canopy. I called after him again, but he didn't answer my desperate summons.

And so I let my brother go.

We spent the rest of the day trying to find our way out of the forest and back to the skiff. It was both a relief and a worry that it had been left untouched. I bit my nails and gazed back at the line of trees one last time, hoping Nano hadn't gotten lost, hoping he was safe, that I might see him again and beg his forgiveness.

Catina was inconsolable as we gathered our paddles and launched the boat back into the lake as the sun was setting beneath an overcast, gray sky. For the fifth time that day, she fixed me with a furious look of disappointment and said, "Did you have to be so hard on him? Why can't you ever hold your tongue!"

I hung my head, feeling like my own mother were here, reproaching my actions. Worst of all, Juan had barely said a word to me since we'd left the temazcalli, though he had signed to Catina plenty of times, asking if she wanted water or if she was hungry. His silence told me all I needed to know. He also felt I'd gone too far, struck too hard, broken my brother's heart in a way my sister never would've. The thought filled me with a maddening, swirling blend of sadness and shame and jealousy that I could hardly contain. But I had already caused enough damage. I had earned this pain, and would serve my penance in silence.

We made sure to stay close enough to the shoreline so we would not get lost and rowed north until it was too dark to see, taking turns and not saying much. It was hard work, for a bleak wind stirred up the surface of the lake, pounding small, silent waves onto the hull, sprinkling our faces with brine. We ate the remainder of Nayeli's food in silence.

All I could hope for, as we tied the skiff to a tree overhanging an island past the marshes of Azcapotzalco, was that we might find some solace in the hills of Tepeyac, in the arms of the Virgin of Guadalupe and Nantzin's next clue.

It took a long time to fall asleep. Every creak of the mast, the light scratching of reeds against the hull, the chirping of bats and hooting of owls flying overhead kept waking me. Catina and I slept back to back to one side of the mast, too stubborn to turn around and hold each other for additional warmth. Juan slept curled up against the bow of the ship, and his light snoring also broke through my dreams, which were filled with images of Nantzin jumping through flames, running from wolves, screaming in terror.

I gave up trying to sleep early the next morning, before dawn, and sat with my back against the mast. Once again, a heavy mist gathered around the lake, carrying the marshy smell of peat and light decay, making it hard to see and chilling the exposed flesh of my neck and ankles, which I gathered under my robes. I threw my hood over my head and blew on my fingertips before rubbing my swollen eyes.

Nano should've been here too, next to me. Guilt and sorrow gnawed at my chest and my throat as I thought of my mother's story and the awful way I had treated my favorite brother, when she had lost her own. Where was Nano? Would he be safe from Pedro and Gonzalo? How would we find each other again?

"Isabel," Juan murmured in his sleep, startling me. I studied him for a long time, feeling a whirling mess of feelings, mostly disappointment in myself. I had upset him with my show of temper, I knew it, just like it had always upset my brothers and my father to see me in a rage. It was unbecoming, hideous, that's what they said. There was no stopping Juan from thinking the same way about me.

No matter that he had made a point to say that the best food had spice and fire, which I thought, with a flash of warmth, perhaps meant he liked the fire he saw in me. But he'd not seen then how I could wield it, the damage I could do with my words. Even if he did not yet see me the way my brothers saw me, it was only a matter of time. And just like Nano had done, he would leave. He was too good anyway, too kind and beautiful and honest. He deserved someone who could offer that back to him. Someone like Catina, though it made my stomach turn to acid, especially when I thought of the smile she had bestowed on him after the visit to La Llorona. Was there more than gratitude and friendship there, for her?

"Isabel," he sighed once more, and my heart leapt with sudden, possessive joy. He wasn't saying my sister's name, he was saying *mine*. He was dreaming of *me*. And he was so close that if I only reached out, I would be able to touch his loose curls strewn near my feet.

A sudden heat spread all through my body at the thought of waking him and sitting close to him like we'd done yesterday morning, when he'd nearly pressed his lips over mine. The thought caught my breath, almost as if it were truly happening, as if more than just cloth and mist were caressing my body, transcending it, and pooling into a heavy warmth between my legs. But all I could do was sit, entranced by this new feeling.

It was too much for me to comprehend, I could not even think to act on it. And when Juan finally woke up a few hours later, I felt too flustered and embarrassed by the memory of those sensations to even greet him properly, though perhaps it was for the best.

These feelings of mine, those dreams of his, they couldn't possibly last.

Our temperaments were far too different. I would only end up disappointing him even more, hurting him, and the mere thought of it was too painful. I would not, could not, bear to see him struck, the way I'd struck Nano.

Juan had already gone through so much, and he was so alone in this world.

I gave him a wordless half smile and picked up a paddle.

"The mist is clearing. Let's set out while Catina's still asleep," I whispered.

Juan's shoulders dropped, and he turned away to begin rowing east, toward the causeway stretching across from us in the near distance.

There were so many canoes near the causeway linking Tepeyac to Tenochtitlan that it took us a while to find a place to anchor our skiff. In among the cacophony of sloshing waves, paddles slapping the surface, and people shouting greetings and warnings at one another, we managed to secure the boat. We gave three boys who were fishing nearby one of our last maravedi coins to keep an eye on it until our return, although we still took everything else of value with us.

We must've looked a strange sight, three silent youths wearing spotless white garments with no armor yet armed to the teeth, heading toward the hill where the shrine of Guadalupe stood. But no one gave us more than a passing glance.

There were too many people everywhere, weaving around boulders covered in lichen and blossoming trees, carrying flowers and fruits as an offering. Indígenas and Spaniards called her our lady, our mother, tonantzin. Unlike the sober atmosphere in the city, here they sang and prayed, they banged drums and sounded rattles. Some dragged themselves forth on their knees, crying out in pain as an offering.

As we walked, I studied the drawing I'd made of Nantzin's clue.

"The only image is of the Virgin and the eagle upon her shoulder, so I suppose that means we need to go see the tilmahtli and hope for the best," I said out loud.

"What?" Catina asked.

I said and signed, "The only clue is the robe of Juan Diego."

Nantzin used to love telling us the legend, of how only a year after my brother Andrade was born, the beautiful Virgin Mary appeared to the Indigenous convert Juan Diego Cuauhtlatoatzin and spoke to him in Nahuatl.

"She came to console us," Nantzin would say. If my father was out of earshot, she would add, "She came to show us the path forward, the middle path, between the old world and the new. We must worship Christ, of course, but we must not forget our ways. That is why she appeared on the same hill where Centeotl, the goddess of corn, and Coatlicue, the mother earth, had been venerated even before my great-grandfather's time."

"Have you been before?" asked Juan, the first words he'd spoken to me in hours.

I shook my head no, and wondered why. Both of my parents had been devoted to Our Lady, and yet we'd never come to pay homage, to see Juan Diego's miraculous tilmahtli where the Virgin's image had materialized in front of the old bishop as proof of her sanctity.

"Me neither," he said, and fell silent again.

We climbed up the steep grassy slope, where the atmosphere had turned almost festive. The winds had cleared the mist and the overcast skies and revealed a beautiful, clear morning. A group of musicians sitting on large grayish rocks near a flat part of the hill strummed guitars and played their flutes. People sat to break their fasts and watch them.

We carried on for a little while longer. I kept my eyes lowered to watch my footing, until Juan said, "Oh," and I looked up.

The tilmahtli was not yet in view, only the small shrine, but what it lacked in size, it more than made up in magnificence. There were flowers everywhere, forming a cape, a fragrant, vivid mantle spreading to the sides and the back of the temple, rising like a small pyramid and obscuring the roof. A golden cross was barely visible over the top of them.

Here and there were slivers of copal smoke, rising and curling into the wind, carried out into the majestic hills and volcanoes beyond. We stopped to take in the views of the brilliant lake below, reflecting the light-blue color of the sky, the snowcapped volcanoes and lush green mountains in the far distance, and the long causeways anchoring the sprawling, floating city at its center. The city that had once belonged to my mother.

We followed the crowds, waiting for our turn to get close to the shrine. It was a slow progression, and we were jostled around and squeezed into a line. Catina walked in front, me in the middle, and Juan behind me. He kept uttering awkward apologies whenever he bumped his front against my back, and I responded in kind, pretending that it did not send a fresh chill down my spine each time he did so.

Everyone wished to get as close as possible, the worshippers to place their offerings and whisper their prayers to the Virgin, and we to see if there were any other clues. Finally, we arrived at the front of the shrine, and both Catina and I froze.

Then Catina cried, "It's her! Isabel, oh my goodness, it's her!"

"Who? What?" Juan asked.

For several heartbeats, I could not speak. I merely stood, lips parted, eyes gleaming, swelling with joy and grief and confusion. Because there, right in front of my eyes . . . was my mother. She was young and healthy, her cheeks full, her body supple and round with child, but it was unmistakable. The almond eyes, the light-brown skin and raven hair, her delicate nose and brows. Catina fell to her knees. She reached out to touch the mantle, crying, "Nantzin!"

Juan crossed himself and knelt too, yet no one seemed to pay them any mind. They could've been any one of a thousand other devotees who also moved around us, crying out to her in the same exact way, aching for their heavenly mother, their Guadalupe . . . tonantzin.

I had to look away and back several times to make sure I was not imagining it. But it was true. The beautiful woman in front of me, the one whom everyone was praying to now, was my own Nantzin, Tecuichpoch, who had been baptized Isabel.

Tears swelled and threatened to spill, for everything and everyone she'd lost, for myself, for the way I longed for her. It was an echo in my chest, a long, suspended note. Would it ever hurt less, saying goodbye to her? I had to force myself to stay in place and not leap into the shrine and wrap the tilmahtli around my shoulders.

But then, as I looked at the image again, I hiccuped into an incredulous laugh instead . . . at her daring, her genius. Because here she was, here she would always be, here she would reign over and be venerated by a nation that was rightfully hers.

The last empress of the Mexica had immortalized herself, melded her image into the second-holiest Spanish deity, and become a mixture of both. An eternal, glorious queen.

I wished I'd brought something to place by her feet, and silently promised I would return. The horde of people had started to push me along. I quickly scanned the shrine and the image for any signs that could lead us to her next chapter, but there was nothing.

"We'd better go," I said and tapped my sister on the shoulder, tried to help her to stand. But someone cut in front of me. An older Nahua gentleman offered Catina his hand and pulled her up. He looked between her face and the face of the tilmahtli, and let out a yelp.

"It's her! It's her! Our Lady of Guadalupe!" He shouted in Nahuatl, and grabbed Catina's hands. "Help my daughter, please, she is sick with fever!"

Catina shot me a look of terror. "Isabel?"

"She's only a girl! She's not the Holy Virgin!" I shouted, but people had turned around and began to cry out, seeing the resemblance between my sister and the image. They wanted to touch her feet, her skirts, her hair. They pleaded in Nahuatl for her to heal them and their families. Mexica who had fought against the Spanish, and those who had joined them too, people from Tlaxcala and Huexotzinco, shouted their sorrows: They had helped the Spanish, and now they were hungry and tired. They were made to work and still had no food to feed their children; the coyotl Spaniards had taken everything from them. They demanded exorbitant tribute, defiled their women, stole their boys and men and forced them to work far away on the silver mines.

"Bring them back, bring our children back," they demanded as they crowded around us. The air became hot and difficult to breathe. "Help us," they begged.

So many voices, pleading, crying out, drowning my sister's own cries. Juan and I tried to reach her, but we were pushed aside. Juan had to hold me to keep me from being trampled. My heart was hammering. I could no longer see her.

"Leave her alone!" I screamed, but no one listened.

"We need to get help," Juan said, looking around for anyone who might be able to stop the mob. But who?

"I don't want to get courtiers involved!"

"Or monks," Juan said, shooting a couple of Franciscan friars in the distance a dubious look. We were just about to run toward a group of nuns when I heard singing.

"Wait, listen!" I said, looking around.

Catina had begun to sing, and slowly, one by one, others joined in, falling to their knees, until only my sister was left standing, the multitude around her easing to a quiet hum, as the words to an ancient Mexica song spread down the hill.

Who am I to soar, to sing like a flower.
A butterfly of music.
Sweet and fragrant is my song.

Let our pain disperse. Let our hearts rejoice.
I have descended, a swan from green waters.
I have arrived, my wings unfurled beside the petal drum.

Sweet and fragrant is my song.

My songs, born of fertile soil, are lifted.
I cultivate them, beside those who till the soil.
I am your humble servant.
Sweet and fragrant is my song.

I herald the ancestors, plumed in golden glory.
I guard the flower fields, rejoice in bright jewels.
I am a hummingbird, delighting in a hundred colors.
Sweet and fragrant is my song.

She sang for what seemed like hours, in Nahuatl and Castilian both. She sang until the sun was high in the sky and people felt hot and hungry. Only then did they seem to realize that she was only a young girl and let her walk away, back toward Juan and me, who rose from the grass. We spread our arms, and she embraced us.

"You were incredible," I signed. "I can't believe you did that."

Catina's face was streaked with tears and flushed from either the sun or her feelings, but she smiled. "I can't believe I did that too. I was so scared," she answered, voice hoarse.

"Tell her she sang well," Juan said to me, and I signed.

"Thank you." Catina smiled.

"Pardon me," said a soft feminine voice behind us in Nahuatl. We spun around.

The woman was only slightly taller than us, but bone thin. She was wearing a black veil that fell at the sides of her face and covered most of her faintly pockmarked, tanned skin. Her long, fine huipil, also black, was trimmed with gray rabbit fur at the neck and sleeves and embroidered with feathers and flowers, a royal design. The kind my mother had favored. Her eyes were lined with age and held a deep sadness within. She did not smile, looking at my sister intently, then at me. Her gaze lingered on my short hair. She extended her hand.

"Catalina and Isabel, we've not met before. I am Mariana Moctezuma."

◆ ◆ ◆

We followed Mariana to a copse of trees higher up on the hill, where she had set up a beautiful woolen mat with some food inside a wicker basket: a mixture of puffy, freshly baked rolls in the Spanish style that made me think of Nano with a squeeze of the heart; sweet, thick maize cakes flavored with vanilla and sprinkled with chia seeds; and more fruits, juicy, earthy guanabana and sour pitahaya, pink on the outside and white with black seeds on the inside. Mariana indicated that we should eat, so we sat and ate in silence as she watched us, seemingly studying our every feature until it became too unnerving for me.

"I believe you're our aunt," I said in Nahuatl.

"Half aunt," she responded.

I nodded. "How come we never met you before?"

She looked away, back down toward the altar. "It's too difficult to explain." After a long while, she whispered, "I'm sorry."

"Oh, I didn't mean—"

"I am here now, aren't I?" She continued whispering, looking away from us, toward the altar. "I know I should've been there before, but you can't blame me."

"We're not blaming—"

"They look just like you, yes. I see it now. Just like you said. It's hard, it's so hard. They look just like you." She continued whispering to herself.

Juan and I shared a wide-eyed look. I signed to my sister, trying not to move too much. "She's talking to Nantzin, out loud."

"What's she saying?" Catina signed back. I quickly told her.

"Well, I'm not surprised. Now we know what she lived through," Catina signed.

War, plague, conquest, betrayal, violation, death, loss, marriage, childbirth . . . What *hadn't* she and Nantzin lived through? It was a miracle that Nantzin hadn't ended up talking to herself, to all the ghosts in her head. Although . . . it was no coincidence, I felt, that Nantzin's body had ravaged itself, that she had ended up a twisted mess of skin and bone at too young an age. She had never spoken about any of this, as far as I knew, and perhaps it had taken its toll in a different way—not on her mind, but on her body and spirit.

"Tía Mariana?" I said, placing a gentle hand on Mariana's elbow.

She immediately stopped whispering, then turned toward us slowly. "I was entrusted to give you this." From inside the basket, she took out a diary.

"Thank you kindly," I said, and she nodded. I hesitated before asking her, "Did my mother give this to you in person?"

Mariana blinked at me, then shook her head. "I went to see her the week before she died, but I received this a month after, from a veiled messenger bearing our Moctezuma crest. They also wrote a note saying you would come here after her death, and begged me to wait for you, to help you if you came. I have come every day since she died, to make up for my absence in her life."

"Do you know if she wrote this herself? Or did someone else write it for her?"

Mariana trembled. "I don't know, child. I know not how to read and write myself. I thought she could not either, but your mother was always very clever, though she barely spoke aloud, and we barely spoke to each other for many years. She might've learned at some point."

I wanted to ask her more: If she knew the identity of Nantzin's secret servant. If she had a guess at who her messenger could've been. I strongly doubted it was the woman in front of me. She seemed so fragile, I couldn't imagine her riding around the Valley of Mexico when it seemed a breeze might topple her to the ground. But perhaps I was being unfair. This aunt of mine had survived the conquest, after all.

She was still here, when my own mother was not.

Almost as if she had read my mind, she looked into my eyes and whispered, “She couldn’t speak much by the time I saw her. Every word was a struggle. I don’t know anything more than what I’ve told you.”

After a pause, Mariana looked away again, back at the altar, and murmured so low I almost missed it. “Yes, I am also glad. I shall listen, I will. Yes, I must. Let’s hear it then. Dear ones, read the story.”

I moved close to Catina so she could read along with me, opened the chapter, and began to speak Nantzin’s words softly aloud.

CHAPTER 19

Tecuichpoch

1526–1528

The wealthy encomienda of Tacuba, all the servants and slaves I had owned as empress of Tenochtitlan, along with my royal hand, were given as a bride prize to Captain Alonso de Grado, for his long, bloody, and dedicated service to Hernán Cortés.

It was Malintzin who told me, after she had returned from the pointless, long, and deadly expedition to Honduras, that the old captain was to be my fourth husband.

"How old is old?" I asked, and she replied, "Around thirty-seven."

Only twenty years of difference, I thought. It could be worse, and perhaps he will die soon enough. I did not know then that this thought would quickly grow into a prayer, a hope, a feverish, single-minded obsession. But first, let me tell you of that morning with Malintzin.

We had taken a seat next to each other on a bench underneath the shade of an ahuacatl tree growing within the gardens of Cortés's newly built fortress in Cuernavaca. I recognized, with a flare of blinding-hot rage, some of the carved and painted stones around us, taken from my father's own palaces and rebuilt haphazardly into high arches and impenetrable walls. I turned away and studied Malintzin as a way to calm myself.

She, too, had been reshaped. Cortés had married her off to another of his captains, Juan Jaramillo, and she was no longer a slave but a free noblewoman.

This is what she had desired most in the whole world. Freedom for herself and her children—the young son she'd had with Cortés and Jaramillo's newborn girl in her arms, who were now peers of the New World aristocracy.

Her little boy ran around the garden, playing with sticks. A light breeze carried her clean, floral scent and flickered the down feathers lining the geometric embroidery of her beautiful huipil. She had played her hand well, though she did not crow, nor look down at me for having lost it all, just like she had warned my father we would. I wondered, for a moment, if she thought it had been worth all that bloodshed. But it was too late to go back. There was no point in dwelling in sorrow or rage. I had to focus on what lay ahead, and on her, for she was speaking to me in grave counsel.

"De Grado is an hidalgo, a nobleman by birth, shrewd and cruel," she said. "I will not frighten you by recounting the things I've seen him do in battle, except to say he enjoyed the pain he dealt. He loved a brawl, even with his own company."

She hesitated, then said, "He was always chosen to assist during torture, including that time with your husband, the Lord Cuauhtemoc." A tremor ran through her body, for she had been there, she had seen the Spanish deal the burns I had cleaned with my own hands.

Then she said with an unusually bitter scoff, "Of course Cortés is naming him Protector of the Indians." She looked around the empty garden and lowered her voice to a mere whisper, though we spoke in high Nahuatl, a language only nobility used.

She said, "I do not believe him capable of upholding the Laws of Burgos, let alone being the man in charge of policing them."

When I looked back at her blankly, she explained patiently that the Laws of Burgos prevented the illegal enslavement of Indígenas, and described how the Spaniards ought to treat their workers, how they should pay them and nurture their newly baptized Christian souls.

"It would do you good to become well acquainted with the Spanish system of law," she murmured, "as a landowner, and in case you find evidence that de Grado is at fault. It might be a way to put him aside . . . if you find the marriage lacking."

I chewed my lip, for a thread of anguish had unspooled from my chest at the thought of what I was about to face. Whatever my sisters had endured with Cortés, Malintzin too, and thousands upon thousands of our women. And for Malintzin to warn me, she must've been deeply concerned. Her brow was pinched, her lips pressed tightly.

This warning was coming from a woman who had commanded a legion of Spaniards. I swayed on the spot and nearly fainted, but Malintzin grabbed my arm with a strength I could never have guessed from her slight form, looked into my eyes with a fire burning in her soul, and hissed, "There is no shame in survival. Do *whatever* you must do, remember who you are, and survive without shame."

Her tongue seemed to become a serpent, green and yellow; her words slithered through the holes in my ears and burrowed into my memory, hardened like scales and became a shield that I would raise over and over in the next year of my marriage to that despicable man, de Grado.

Everything about him was an insult, an affront to my person, my culture, my people, my body. His loud, booming voice, his sycophantic laughter at any of Cortés's dreadful puns, his small weasel eyes, always narrowed in suspicion, skewering me like a piece of meat. I hated them, and his broad, calloused hands. How they groped and pinched and grabbed at me.

I made it a point to immediately learn the Laws of Burgos by heart, and was fortunate, through de Grado's entourage, to make an acquaintance with a devout follower of the honorable Dominican friar

Bartolomé de las Casas, the famed abolitionist, and one of the only worthy men to ever cross the Atlantic. And this follower of de las Casas, a novitiate whom I believed was called Pedro Gallego, taught me the Laws of Burgos and encouraged me to think further on those flutterings of guilt I'd begun to have regarding the treatment of slaves who had been forced to die during the great pestilence so that I could live.

And I quietly spoke some of my thoughts to Pedro, whom I somehow felt I could trust because he was gentle and patient and almost reverent of me. And we pondered aloud the reasons why so many who'd lived under my father's rule had turned against him. Why Malintzin had gambled her life so resolutely on those people capable of restoring her freedom, those strangers to us people here, those whom we called teteoh at first, not because we thought them gods but because their presence was inexplicable to us, and because they wielded weapons the like of which we'd never seen.

He suggested my father had been cruel—that he had sacrificed too many people to our gods. But I could not agree, and most of our people would not have either. I told Pedro that he did not understand what we were raised to understand, that those people had died like Christian martyrs, that they had gained honor and privilege in their deaths.

I could not say more, though, because I was afraid that he would think I still believed in our old myths, that a flowered death by the obsidian knife was a way to repay an ancient debt to our gods. It had not been evil, it had been necessary, and it had aggrieved us greatly.

We had mourned the need for sacrifice, though not as much as we mourned now, when we were all being slaughtered and enslaved for lesser reasons, for greed and power and lust. The invaders acted like loosed beasts, and I was married to the vilest one of all.

I felt myself a prisoner inside my own body, humiliated in a way I'd never been before. Indeed, I finally understood my sisters' despair, for every time de Grado spilled his seed inside me, I felt as though I were being filled with the eggs of a thousand insects, hatching and crawling all beneath my skin, and after a year, I could no longer wait to gather enough evidence to denounce my husband. I did not have the patience or the fortitude to play as long a game as Malintzin could play.

Instead, I headed to the forest of Chapultepec, not far from my new home.

I had long heard whisperings of a medicine woman who lived in the shadows, who was known for her gifts in herbs and remedies. She was a healer, a protector, a priestess in all but name. When I implored her to help me, she gave me a powder.

"Mix it with his drink before he falls asleep," the healer said, "and he will not rise again. But be warned. The power in this drink comes from Earth Lady, from Tlaltecuhtli herself. You shall whet her keen appetite if you use it, and she will not let you take from her without demanding twice the bounty. A loss that will bring your own heart to her mighty lips."

"Speak plainly, kind lady," I responded. "For I am weary and cannot bear a riddle."

She gave me a look full of pity and said, "If you use the powder, two souls will perish. The first will be your victim. The second, someone dear to your heart, for Tlaltecuhtli relishes in eating hearts, and this is the only way she will be sated."

I thanked her and immediately forgot her warning, because there was no one left alive who was dear to me. Not even Mariana, for we had become strangers since she and her new husband had raised a lawsuit against me, claiming she was the primary daughter to our father and therefore entitled to my encomienda, when she had one of her own. There was no one else to consider. I did not think I would ever allow anyone near my mangled heart again, so I gave a silent prayer of apology to Tlaltecuhtli, and doubled my resolve.

That very night, after de Grado had mounted me again like the tame little broodmare he took me for, I fixed him his nightly aguardiente. The powder was clear and odorless, not that any scent could've broken through the stench of that liquor. He fell asleep almost immediately, and I watched, my heart racing in my throat, as the gentle rise and fall of his broad, hairy chest slowed down until it stopped. After almost an hour, I poked him, then slapped him hard across the face. If he'd been alive, I would've been whipped or thrown across the room, as he sometimes enjoyed doing.

But he did not wake up.

It was the first time in years that I'd smiled, though I'm sure if I'd seen my reflection in the looking glass it would've been a wild, twisted thing to behold. I did no other harm to his body, for I did not wish to raise suspicions against me. Instead, I went to lie beside him, my dead husband, and fell into a deep, peaceful, dreamless sleep.

And you can see, perhaps, why this is a story I have never revealed to anyone before. Why it has remained a secret between me and the woman in the forest, who in her great mercy gave me the gift of death, a gift I do not regret—though later I would, indeed, pay double the price.

Still, I wish de Grado had suffered more for his great crimes against my people, and against me. Though I had vowed to obey him in my Christian rites, though I had been raised to submit, and though de Grado had tried to break me with his cruelty, I never forgot Malintzin's counsel.

I never forgot who I was.

Not some whore to be bought and bent and prodded. I was Tecuichpoch, daughter of Moctezuma Xocoyotzin and Chimalexochitl, the last empress of the Mexica.

No one would, nor could, take that away from me. Not now, or ever.

But . . . ah yes, you groan, and you would be right to. Because my triumph and freedom were short-lived, as everything seemed to be in those days. And you may think, just like I thought so often, How is it possible? How could one person bear so much suffering and ill luck? And I have no answer, except perhaps to say that I knew who I was, I knew I would survive, and there were people around me in worse conditions than mine who looked to me for comfort and fortitude. All these thoughts kept me stepping one foot in front of the other. Even when the path led back to Cortés.

He came to my home just one day after Alonso de Grado died, after the doctors and the priests had proclaimed it a natural death and I was widowed once more at eighteen. I wore a black huipil trimmed with fur, for it was a cold, humid winter. Cortés wore an armored breastplate, wrought red and black for blood and sorrow, with a thick quilted cloth underneath made in the Mexica warrior style. Many conquistadores wore them, for our climates were much too warm for chainmail and they always expected an attack.

I gave him a stiff bow, and stilled with a breath the tendrils of dread that rose and encircled my chest and neck.

He threw his arms in the air and exclaimed, "My poor girl! How you have grown, and what great sadness befalls us all. My great true friend is gone, your beloved husband. We must bear this grief together. Though I must say, you are lovely even in grief, a rose blooming in frost. It pains me to leave you in this great home, all on your own. No, I cannot. I must remember, your father placed you in my care, as my ward. He beseeched me to ensure your safety. Indeed, I cannot, in good conscience, leave you here all on your own with the threat of riots and uprisings and at risk of being taken by that viper Nuño de Guzmán, who would certainly use you most dreadfully against me.

"No, you must come with me at once to Cuernavaca."

He went on and on, as he loved to do, and never let me say a single word. I stopped trying to respond and simply stared down at his butchered hand, the one missing two fingers. They had been amputated after his retreat from Tenochtitlan, and it brought me a tiny, twisted sense of joy that he was maimed so. I was even more pleased when he hid his hand behind his back, for I realized his enormous vanity had been wounded.

I gazed out of the window at the beautiful forest and the dark, glimmering surface of my beloved lake, and let his droning voice wash over me, remembering that to this hollow wolf of a man, only he himself existed, and sometimes the emperor and his father, whom he was forever trying to impress. Even the Lord Jesus was but a tertiary figure in Cortés's mind, though he would've taken great pains to deny it.

Before the fortnight was over, I was transferred to Cortés's palace in Cuernavaca, which was several days' carriage ride away. I had no say, and would've been a fool to speak against him anyway. I would have been a fool to deny, even now, that I was terrified of the man who had overthrown my father and killed my husband. Even his own Spanish wife had not escaped the clutches of his greed. Rumors were rampant that he had murdered her, for she had not been noble enough for his liking, nor capable of bearing his heir. It had caused such a scandal that he had been investigated by the Crown, though nothing had come of it.

Indeed, I was afraid. Not a single person I knew had ever outmaneuvered him, except Malintzin, and she had done it by being as malleable as clay, by handing him the Mexica Empire on a gold platter.

But what could I offer Cortés, when he had already taken everything from me?

Even his coat of arms screamed my defeat. The new emblem bestowed upon him with such honor by Emperor Carlos was a shield divided into four quadrants: the double-headed black eagle of the Spanish empire in one; the golden lion of conquest in the second; the three crowns he had usurped, those of Moctezuma my father, Cuitlahuac my uncle, and Cuauhtemoc my husband. And the last icon was of the island city he now governed—my own beloved Tenochtitlan.

Cortés adored his monstrous coat of arms so much that he'd commissioned the best sculptors in New Spain to delicately carve it into every door, and he'd invited the best artists to handsomely draw it as the centerpiece in every room, so that everywhere I looked in his house, my new prison, I was reminded with a sick blow to the stomach of the demise of my kin and country and reign.

He gave me but a week to somewhat settle before he found his way into my bed, and I would be lying if I said I tried to fight him off, that I screamed or did anything other than close my eyes and clench my jaw and bear it like the warrior I had been raised to be.

For there was no fighting a man who had killed thousands, and for whom the violation of women came as easily as breathing. Whatever or whomever he saw, he felt he owned, and he took without regard. Though he convinced himself otherwise, of course, of my willingness, of his own prowess in pleasuring me, in being an honorable man, in doing the right thing by promising to find me a good husband. He would say I was the only India he could've ever married, that he almost regretted his wishes to marry a Spanish noblewoman instead, as though this slight was the greatest honor of my life.

He talked in low murmurs for hours on end, like a buzzing insect, and the only way I could withstand this new form of torture, the only way I could bring my face to smile, was to recite the Legend of the Sun in my mind. I reminded myself of Tezcatlipoca the trickster, Quetzalcoatl the feathered serpent, Tlaloc of the rains, and Chalchiuhtlicue, his wife of jade, all of whom had sacrificed themselves to bring forth a new age, a new sun. Tonatiuh had been next, and he had demanded the heart sacrifice to begin each day anew.

I would try to remember every word of the song, and it would help me escape, drift away from even my own body when I needed to.

And whenever that failed, I pictured his death a hundred different ways, by stabbing him through the eyes, strangling him like he'd done with my father, hanging him off the branches of a tree like he'd done with Cuauhtemoc, poisoning him like I'd done with de Grado.

But the healer from Chapultepec was now too far away. I was alone, with only his guards for company. I had no means to escape.

Only his little son, Malintzin's boy, was any sort of comfort to me, for he was bright eyed and quick witted and sweet, like I imagined his mother might've been before her enslavement, and he loved tamalli so much he reminded me ofttimes of my brother Axayacatzin. I tried to teach him some Nahuatl, so he might know his mother's tongue, but I was quickly rebuked.

Though I will say this for Cortés: He loved his child dearly. No one who knew him doubted how much the man cherished having children, even if raising them was another matter. But he treasured his boy so much, in fact, that I realized the one thing I had in my power to give him . . . was another child.

And as soon as I discovered this weakness of his, I began to encourage him. I stroked his insufferable pride and swallowed my own until I finally, quickly, mercifully became pregnant. Only then did I begin bargaining for my freedom.

Though that is a tale for another day.

My hope is that you will find it.

CHAPTER 20

Isabel Cano

7 March 1551

I tried in vain to gulp down the knot choking my throat. It seemed like even the wind had died down to nothing, even the trees around us were leaning in, trying to listen to Nantzin's tale. The violations she'd endured. Her confession.

My mother, the woman who now stood below us, being praised by the people as the image of the immaculate Holy Virgin . . . had committed murder.

And could anyone blame her? Would I not have done the same, or worse?

Much worse, without a doubt. In fact, a part of me wanted to set off right away, fly off down this hill on the back of a giant eagle, and set fire to the traza, the center of the city in the middle of the lake. The city square that they had taken from Nantzin and given to full-blooded Spaniards—I would burn it, and all those people, in her name.

Beyond the farthest shore of the lake, the Popocatepetl volcano let out a plume of white, cloudy smoke. From behind me, Juan likewise let out a long exhalation, filled with all the sadness I would never dare express.

I looked to my left and studied Mariana's blank, pale expression. She sat rigid, back straight, unblinking. There were no tears, so she was truly a Moctezuma in her blood. She had lived through this as much as Nantzin had.

"I'm so sorry," I said. Catina nodded beside me. She must've read my lips.

"It is what it is," Mariana whispered. "As your mother wrote, our world had already ended four times before. We thought the Fifth Sun would come amid the shattering of the earth and a blackening sky. That we would be devoured by the fearsome tzitzimimeh demons who live among the stars. But, of course, this was not the case."

I had nothing to say to that. No, their world, the Fifth Sun of Tonatiuh, had ended in the chaos of smallpox and the clamor of gunfire. The demons had sailed from across the seas, not the stars. My own father had followed Cortés on this quest, and destroyed the island city glimmering like a jewel in the low distance.

The sun peeked from behind a cloud, hot in the sky, turning the lake a shade of red, as it must've looked during the conquest, saturated with blood.

I flinched inwardly, feeling suddenly sick, picturing my father raising his favorite weapon, *my* favorite weapon, the bow, again and again, a thousand times and more. How many arrowheads had he let loose? How much blood had he wiped from the sharpened end of his sword? How had my mother been able to put all his crimes aside and marry him? How could she bring herself to have *us*, with *him*?

A terrible doubt entered my mind, a thought that made me feel nauseated enough that I tasted bile in my mouth. Had my father . . . forced himself on Nantzin, like de Grado and Cortés had? I squeezed my eyes shut and put my head between my legs.

"Isabel, are you unwell?" Juan asked, but I could not answer, for I was battling with myself, sifting through every image, every memory of my parents throughout my life.

They had fought, sometimes, many times, mainly over the best way to raise us all and make us stop fighting with each other. But they had been loving too, in the way only we Canos could love. Playful, teasing, aloof one moment, intense the next. They had stood next to each other in church, my father a step behind, giving her the place of honor. He had fought for her lands in court, for decades. My mother had been at ease with him. She had leaned into his touch whenever he'd come home.

And my father had cried over her body, truly sobbed like a child. I had seen it with my own eyes. He had gently kissed her cold hand a dozen times and more, her cheeks, her forehead. He had revered her. He would not have hurt her, like them.

And if this story was anything to go by, my mother would not have stood for it. She would've killed him, like she had de Grado, or tricked him like Cortés.

I breathed a little easier then, once, twice, three times, until Juan and Catina's worried voices permeated my consciousness.

"I'm fine, I'm just a little dizzy, that's all."

"It is the height," Mariana said. "Indeed, I used to feel this way whenever we climbed the steps of the temple as children, and the people looked as tiny as ants. But it will pass, like everything does. Good or bad, nothing lasts forever."

She looked down the hill at the hordes of people surrounding the tilmahtli of Guadalupe and tilted her head. "But perhaps you will, sister."

We were quiet for a few breaths, lost in somber thought, until she nodded again and said, "Now, if you would help me rise."

Juan and I stood and helped Mariana stand, then all three of us escorted her back down the holy hill to the Tepeyacac causeway. Juan offered his arm, and she took it without question, guiding us and whispering indecipherably down a cobbled pathway leading to a stable that was reserved for nobility. A servant waited for her in front of her own finely wrought carriage.

"I thought perhaps you might be accompanied by your brothers," she said, as she set foot on the carriage step. "I would've liked to meet them."

"We were traveling with Nano," I said, feeling a sharp barb of pain in my chest, "but he's gone . . . home."

Juan glanced sideways at me, and I could sense his disappointment again at how poorly I'd behaved. That it was my doing that Nano was not with us any longer.

"I see," Mariana said. Before we said farewell, she gave us a silver coin each and said, "I wish you luck in your onward journey. And do come see me when you return."

We made our way westward through busy crowds mingling around the base of the hill, which was more jagged this way, with fewer trees and more boulders. The tension from yesterday had returned. Both Juan and Catina kept shooting furtive glances at me, and I felt wretched. Even when Juan and I locked eyes and he asked me again whether I was well, and I felt that pull in my navel to open myself up to him, I could not. I was too afraid, too cowardly, too ashamed of myself. I wished to make it up to them somehow.

That was why, when we finally spotted the skiff a few yards away, the sweet scent of grilled maize from a stall nearby made me pause.

"You go on," I said to Juan and Catina. "I'll get us some to take on the journey."

I ordered three cobs and watched as the vendor grilled them to perfection, my mouth filling with moisture, my stomach growling impatiently. I'd just given the man some money and taken a bite when someone shouted Catina's name. I whirled around to look toward the causeway. The hairs at the back of my neck stood on end, and my heart plummeted to my stomach.

It was Pedro and Gonzalo.

"It *is* her! Grab her!" shouted Gonzalo, but of course she could not hear.

I stood on my tiptoes, trying to spot them among the crowd, but I was too short. I swore and scrambled back up the rocky face of the hill, throwing the beautiful cobs to the ground, just as Nero and Caligula began to howl.

My heartbeat sped to a frenzy. The crowd began to scream. I pulled myself up onto a smooth, even rock protruding from the hillside. Down to my left were my brothers, barely holding on to the hounds' leashes. The creatures were beside themselves, snapping at heels, leaping at people's arms.

Pedro and Gonzalo struggled to rein the dogs back in and shouted at people to get out of the way, but the terrified horde had nowhere to go. Some ran into the water, tripping on the slippery rocks and patches of reeds and grass. Others clambered up to the side of the wall, pushing vendors aside, sending their goods scattering on the dirt road.

My brothers quickly made their way to my sister, far down on my right side.

Catina had waded into the lake and was washing her arms and face, unaware of the chaos behind her. Juan stood on the unmoored boat, trying to catch her attention, waving and shouting, but it was all in vain.

I heard a cry and looked back as Pedro fell flat on his back. The leash around Nero's neck had snapped. The beast leapt into a sprint, chilling my bones. This was the offspring of war dogs trained to maul people's entrails out . . . and it was running straight to Catina.

In a blink, I had my bow and arrow in position. I took aim, but my face was slick with sweat. My bow slipped from my chin, and the arrow struck the hull of a canoe instead. Catina jolted, and I cursed. My hands shook, and blood rushed to my head, nearly blinding me. But Nero was closing in on my sister, who had finally realized the danger she was in. She turned and slipped on a rock and fell on her backside, her belly and throat completely exposed.

I wiped my face with my sleeve, breathed once, nocked my arrow, and let it fly with an unspoken prayer just as Nero leapt in the air, jowls open wide.

Catina kicked at him, but Nero's teeth sank into her calf. She let out a scream just as my arrow plunged into the dog's ear and the side of its skull, an instant too late. Nero released her and flopped to his side, his dying body twitching and sloshing with the lapping waves. Blood poured from both their wounds and dispersed like a red cloud around them. The last thing I saw was Juan jumping into the water, holding on to a rope. I scrambled down the hill, scratching and scraping my skin in my haste to reach Catina.

"Seize that boy!" Pedro shouted, but even though I felt a mass of people moving with me, behind me, no one grabbed me. I plunged into the water and reached a wailing Catina at the same moment Juan did. I didn't want to look at the mess of skin and bone that was her leg. All I knew was that I was grateful that other people had crowded around us and were shouting suggestions, for I had none. My arrows were useless now, and all I could do was cry as I held her upright in the water. Someone lifted her out of my arms, and another person wrapped a bandage around her mangled wound. I nearly fainted at the sight.

"Back to the shore! She needs a doctor!" one of the people shouted in Nahuatl.

"No!" I said. "Onto the boat, please, hurry!" I'd lost sight of Pedro and Gonzalo, but surely they were closing in on us. Only this crowd prevented them from reaching us. What if they let the other hound loose?

Somehow we made it back into the boat. The people carried and jostled us onboard and pushed us away. Juan and I grabbed our oars and began to row, and then Pedro shouted, "You killed my dog! Pendejo—you killed my dog!"

I was engulfed in a rage so powerful I thought the boat would burst into flames. How could he care more for his dog than his sister? This was his fault, all his fault. I placed the paddles neatly down and stood up with my legs wide for support.

"What are you doing?" said Juan.

"Stop moving," I snarled, and forced myself to subdue the frantic beating in my heart and ignore my sister's shrill sobs of pain.

Pedro and I locked eyes, and he finally saw me, saw who I was.

"Isabel?"

Once again, I drew my bow and arrow. Pedro's face drained of color.

"No!" He turned back and began to splash through the water to the shore where Gonzalo stood, holding Caligula, who was whining, pacing back and forth, distressed at the sight of his dead brother swinging on his master's arms.

But I was too angry at all of them to care. I was going to rid us of that evil creature once and for all. I stilled my breath and pulled the string, but the boat rocked just as I let my arrow loose. It sank into the mud a mere inch away from Caligula.

Pedro let out a cry of relief, and I rounded on Juan. "You did that on purpose!"

But he was already rowing us away.

"Why did you do that?" I raised my voice at Juan, and felt a release from the pressure of rage and helplessness, followed by immediate self-loathing. How could I be shouting at my one friend? The one person who was helping me when I needed it most?

For his part, Juan rowed on silently, brows knotted and gleaming with beads of sweat. He did not reply. I glared back at the shrinking shoreline, at the figures of my brothers and the dogs blending into the crowd. This was not over. Next time, I would not miss.

Juan's labored breath and my sister's mewling cries tore my mind away from revenge and into action. By some miracle, I managed to open the sail. The wind was blowing in our favor, and we began to make our way quickly toward the marshes west of Tepeyac, near the town of Azcapotzalco, where my half brother, Andrade, had his main residence. I could see it in the distance: the wall of his hacienda not far from the shore, growing larger.

"If he's anything like those other brothers of yours, I'd rather we not go there," said Juan as he tore a strip of cloth from his shirt and handed it to me.

"No, Andrade's not like them. He will help us, I'm sure." I didn't say I didn't know who else to turn to. That I felt more scared than ever before in my entire life.

"Tie that cloth tightly around Catina's thigh, above the knee," Juan said. He was sitting in front of me, at the bow. "It might help to stanch the flow of blood."

Catina whimpered. I had been avoiding looking at her and the blood-soaked bandage around her calf, dripping onto the floor of the skiff. I bit my bottom lip and forced myself to turn around and do as Juan suggested.

"It's going to be fine," I whispered to her pointlessly. "We're going to get you some help. Just hold on." She couldn't hear what I was saying, and her eyes were shut tightly, her body taut and shaking in pain. I doubted she had even noticed my trembling touch. When I turned back around, Juan was looking at me with brown eyes full of compassion.

"What!" I said, trying to sound fierce, but my voice cracked and tears fell down my face. I smacked them away and swore, furious at my body for betraying me.

A look of hurt marred his tender features.

"No—wait," I blurted, before he could turn around. "I didn't mean to be horrible. You've been nothing but kind to me."

The rest of my words choked and died in my throat. How much it meant that he was with me. That he had faith in me. How relieved I was to not be completely alone right now. How much I wished for him to hold me. That we'd bridged that tiny gap between our lips, back at the forest in Chapultepec.

It seemed he was thinking of the same day, for he stared at me for a breath, then whispered, "Did you mean what you said to Nano? In Chapultepec?"

I flinched at the memory of the look on my brother's face. I hated myself, the venom that had poured out my mouth, the fact that Juan had seen it all.

"I—I wish I'd been kinder in the way I spoke to him," I responded.

"I see," Juan sighed and turned away, and I felt worse somehow. He'd wanted me to say something else, something different, but I didn't know what. My brain was a jumble, my heart a wreck. The only way I knew how to relate to boys was to fight with them, stir up trouble, make their lives as hard as they made mine, or worse.

I thought of how Nantzin had been with my brothers, with my father. She'd never been hostile, but she hadn't been overly warm either. Not cold precisely, but distant. Reserved. She'd hardly ever touched them, though with Catina and me, she'd been more at ease. Perhaps it had been unfair on her part, to treat us so differently. Perhaps my brothers had longed for her touch as much as we had, and they'd resented us for having more of it. But of course, they did not really know . . . as boys, they couldn't imagine what she had lived through. What I now knew other men had put her through.

Perhaps I'd been born to pour out the rage she'd been forced to suppress. Certainly she'd never chastised me for it, not seriously enough for me to stop.

Juan cleared his throat, breaking me out of my thoughts. "The water is getting too shallow for the boat, and the marsh is too thick. We must get out and walk the rest of the way. Are you strong enough to lift her to my arms?"

I nodded, although I felt weaker than ever as he splashed down onto a patch of green sedges, sending a pair of dragonflies buzzing past his head. I turned around. Catina's skin was pale, her eyes pinched and her breathing shallow and quick. Juan held the boat steady as I reached under her neck and knees.

Her eyes opened in panic, and I mouthed, "It's all right—we're getting help." Tears streamed down her cheeks and she moaned in pain even though I lifted her as gently as I could, though my legs were unsteady from both the waves and the bloodied bandage in the corner of my vision that I could not quite ignore. She began to cry again as I lowered her onto Juan's arms, and my whole body twisted into itself, as though it were a wet cloth being beaten and wrung to dry.

Before jumping off to follow him, I grabbed the satchel containing all my mother's stories but left everything else behind.

The mudflats lying in between mounds of spiky vegetation were slimy and slippery, the air hot and humid, and the warm, shallow water stank of rot. We both kept sinking into the sediment, once even up to our knees, so much that it felt like the lake did not wish to let us go. I felt as if I were living out one of my many nightmares, where my heavy limbs dragged when I desperately wished to run.

Thankfully, Juan managed to keep hold of Catina, even though his breath was ragged and labored. I felt in equal parts grateful and helpless and distressed that I had pulled him into this mess. Finally, after the longest quarter of an hour of my life, we crossed through to dry ground.

From there it was only a short walk to Andrade's main entrance, which I recognized from our visits with Nantzin in the year after he had married, before she had fallen ill. I ran ahead as fast as my muddied legs allowed and banged on the huge brass knocker, shouting at the top of my lungs for help. A guard opened the heavy wooden door just as Juan arrived, panting from the effort of carrying Catina, his dark skin glistening with sweat.

"Quick! Help us inside. I need to see my brother, Don Andrade! We need help!"

"No beggars allowed!" The guard nearly pushed the gate back on my face, but I let out an almighty shriek and shoved him out of the way, running up the large patio. He gave chase, but I was already past the stables and up the steps leading to the main door, which was open.

"Andrade! Andrade! Mari! Ayuda!" I screamed, surprised that my voice could make it past the knot of desperation clasped around my throat. Where were they? Would Catina bleed out before we could get help? The guard caught up and grabbed me by the waist, threw me over his shoulder like a sack of flour. His grip was strong, unyielding.

I twisted and bent, making myself heavy, trying to throw him off balance, all the while shouting, "Let go! Juan Andrade is my brother! Help! No!"

"Isabel!" My brother's voice boomed from above. "Put her down! Dios santo—what's happened?"

The guard dropped me, and I ran halfway up the steps, sobbing. "It's Catina, she needs a doctor, quick! Pedro's dog attacked her. She's outside."

Andrade flew down the steps like a vision, cape billowing out his back, sword by his side, his full, dark eyebrows narrowed in utter focus. The tight knot in my belly loosened somewhat. My big brother was here, the man my mother swore would've made a fine king.

He shouted out commands that I could no longer hear. The guard ran back out grumbling apologies and only moments later ran past me up the steps, Catina in his arms.

I looked back at the door. Andrade was rushing back in, Juan by his side.

"The doctor is here already, attending Mari."

"Oh no, is she unwell? Is the baby?"

"She's fine. I like him to visit regularly. He will see Catina immediately."

A surge of relief washed over me. My knees buckled and I fell back on the steps. Both men rushed forward. Juan got to me first. He knelt in front of me. "Are you all right?"

I nodded, and we locked eyes. I felt so overcome with emotion that for a moment I forgot myself completely and reached out to brush one of his curls away from his damp forehead. Juan leaned his face into my touch, only slightly, and his eyes closed for just one breath. Then I caught the outraged look in Andrade's eyes.

"What are you doing?" my brother snapped, and Juan jerked away from me.

"Please help me up," I groaned. Juan reached out his hand, but Andrade pulled him back by the elbow.

"Allow me," Andrade said. I accepted his offer of help with a roll of my eyes, which made his widen in fury.

He pointed his finger straight into my face and said, "How dare you look at me so! Rumors have been rampant, and we've been worried half to death. Mari and I haven't slept in nearly a week because Pedro and Gonzalo claimed a Moor kidnapped you!"

He looked sideways at Juan. "I assume this is not the case, but still—none of my messengers have reached your negligent father. Nano is nowhere to be found. You come back dressed as a boy and Catina's been mauled by a dog. Marta is dead under very suspicious circumstances. Explain yourself!"

The air rushed out of my lungs as if I'd been kicked in the chest.

"Marta is dead?"

Andrade's expression pinched and immediately softened. "Agh, teicuh." Little sister.

His arms opened, and I fell into them, wailing at the newly opened gash in my heart.

CHAPTER 21

Isabel Cano

7 March 1551

In a haze, I was led upstairs into one of the guest chambers. It was several hours later, after Andrade's maids had washed and dressed and fed me in between embarrassing yet uncontrollable bouts of crying, after Andrade had come to sit by my bedside and reassured me the doctor had sutured and bandaged Catina's wounds, and that she was asleep and would heal, that I finally remembered to ask about Juan.

Andrade tensed and frowned. "He's been given bread and board for the night in the servants' quarters but will be leaving first thing in the morning."

"What—why?!"

"Don't look at me like that—he's asked to leave!" He threw his hands up. "I convinced him to stay the night, but his manners are atrocious, Isabel. He's declined to speak on the matter of your acquaintance or his services to you, which I cannot imagine were insignificant. I have offered to reward him for his troubles, but he's refused."

"I must speak to him." I made to rise from the bed.

"You'll do no such thing." Andrade put his arm out to block me.

My eyebrows rose. "You're right. He *has* done a great service to us. He saved our lives, mine and Catina's and Nano's!"

"Saved your lives? What happened that nigh—"

"He gave *us* board and what little bread he had. He's given us his friendship and arm at every turn." My voice broke. "I'll not shame myself by rewarding his kindness without so much as a proper goodbye."

"You've been shaming yourself every day you've been by his side, alone and unchaperoned!"

"Oh please." I jumped and skirted around him, but he grabbed my wrist. He'd never used such a rough gesture with me before. It reminded me of the way Pedro was always trying to force me to bend to his will. The thought burned hot and angry in my mind, and I snarled, "Release me."

He did not. "Why didn't you come to me at once, if things at home were so dire?"

"I had no time to think—now, let me go!"

"You're wearing nothing but a shift! It is unseemly," he said through gritted teeth.

"Oh, brother," a bored feminine voice drawled from the dark corridor, "hand her a robe and let her say goodbye. I'll chaperone her myself if it'll shut your whining."

Andrade let go of me, pinched the bridge of his nose, opened the door wide, and said, "Leonor . . . back so soon?"

"I know, you miss the days when I hardly remembered we were related."

Leonor Cortés's feminine figure emerged from the dark corridor. The glow of firelight made her seem taller than ever. She crossed her arms and cocked her head at me. "I heard a happy rumor that the girls had been found, and decided to delay my journey to Zacatecas to ensure myself of their well-being."

"They've only been here a few hours—how could you possibly know?" Andrade said, but she merely shrugged and gave him a half smile.

Her presence was such a surprise that I could not help but pause and stare. There was nothing in her haughty, wry expression that betrayed any depth of warm feelings toward me. She looked down at me the way she always had, eyebrows slightly raised and nostrils widened as though she were being offered a platter of sugarcoated entrails.

Regardless, she was offering to help, so I smiled sweetly and said, “Sister, you are generous. I shall robe myself and Andrade can take us down to the servants’ quarters.”

As I turned and put my robe over my shoulders, my gaze fell on my satchel, the one still holding all my mother’s journals. My fingers itched and tingled, and I felt a sudden urge to hold them close. It seemed to me a warning, which I chose to heed.

I wrapped the strap across my body. “Take me to Juan . . . please,” I added.

Andrade took us to his study instead and ordered a servant to fetch Juan. While we waited, Andrade lit some candles and poured himself a shot of reeking aguardiente.

He offered a glass to Leonor, who shook her head elegantly, pointed at his selection of bottles and jars instead, and said, “I’ll take some pulque.”

Andrade scoffed but poured a milky white liquid out from a ceramic jar, which she swallowed with a single fluid motion. She caught me staring, and her lip curled, whether defiant or mocking I could not tell, but she offered no explanation.

Our half brother did not seem at all surprised. He paced the dark room up and down, making gruff, pained exclamations about the strength of the liquor between each sip. Finally, just as I was about to tell him to do us a favor and down his drink for good, we heard a pair of quick footsteps coming from the hall.

I stood to greet my friend, suddenly conscious of the plush, elaborate velvet robe enveloping the finely woven shift I wore underneath and my chopped, loose hair and bare feet.

Even though Juan had seen me running for my life, dressed as a boy, soaking wet and filthy with mud, this particular facade of mine seemed like the worst so far, especially under Andrade's scrutiny and the mocking glimmer in Leonor's gaze.

My shame was tripled when he walked in, took one look at me, and averted his eyes. He seemed embarrassed. I suddenly wished I'd listened to Andrade, or that Leonor had insisted I put on a gown, at least for his sake if not mine.

Wasn't that what sisters were supposed to do? To be honest with each other? Protect each other? But what kind of sister had she ever been, when I could count on my two hands the number of times she'd come to see us, let alone spoken to us.

Andrade cleared his throat, but I couldn't let him set the tone for our parting, so I said, "My brother says you wish to leave tomorrow, but I would have you stay. I've explained how indebted we are to you."

"There is no debt," he said, and the rough tone of his voice startled me. "It's my own choice to leave."

"But why? Surely you need to rest, and here you'll be looked after—"

"I can look after myself, Isabel, thank you." He still did not meet my eyes. Andrade hissed, probably at the overfamiliar use of my name.

I ignored my brother, took a step forward, and whispered, "Juan, what's happened?"

From behind me, Andrade clicked his tongue to show his annoyance.

Juan glanced at him, then back down at me. "Your brother has kindly reminded me of my place in society, and yours."

"Indeed," Andrade said. "You seem to have forgotten you are the child of an empress! A princess in blood, if not in name."

I turned to glare at him. "I know more about being our mother's daughter than you—"

"Then you'll know that nothing is more important than our lineage, Isabel. Whatever happened between you two ends right now," Andrade said and gestured between Juan and me.

"You have no right to tell me what to do!" I shouted.

"Isabel, please," Juan said softly. I turned and our eyes locked, and there was regret there, sorrow. "Your brother has a point. You are a noblewoman, and I am—"

"A son of slaves," Andrade spat.

I sucked in a breath, stunned to silence by my brother's venom. Juan bristled and seemed to grow in stature until he was taller even than Leonor. I thought he would bring up the fact that the old viceroy was his father, that he had been educated in the same manner, probably by the same monks Andrade had been taught by.

Instead he said, "I am the proud child of two people who were *born enslaved* and who sacrificed everything to secure their freedom and mine."

He did not need to raise his voice, but we all shrank back at the hard look in his eye. "I'll not spend a moment longer than I have to in a place that condemns others to a fate I despise. I refuse to be served by those who have no say in the matter, and that's why I shall leave, immediately. I thought I'd remain until sunrise, but I see now that's too long a wait."

I covered my lips, astounded by my stupidity and callousness. How could I have been so foolish and careless to bring him here? In the chaos of everything, I'd forgotten Andrade still kept his own enslaved people. I felt a sick, twisted feeling in my stomach, a nauseating shame at having a brother, a mother, who'd kept people's lives in chains. Tears stung my eyes at the thought of what Juan must've been feeling since his arrival. What he must think of me.

I spluttered. "Juan, I'm so sorry. You're right—I forgot that Andrade, I didn't think—"

"No . . . you didn't." His voice was hoarse, dull and wounded.

With those three words, the unbridgeable chasm that ought to have been apparent to both of us when I woke up in his tiny hut became visible. The conditions of our utterly different births, which we had been able to ignore in the thrill of adventure, in the rocking of a canoe and the light of a bonfire. But if I could overlook this monumental part of his essence, of his life, what chance did we have of truly understanding one another? I would always be blinded in some way to the tens of thousands of privileges I'd taken for granted, which had been completely denied to him throughout his life.

I shook my head. I had thought my rage was going to be the instrument of his heartbreak, but instead my ignorance had dealt the mortal blow.

As though reading my mind, he took a gentle step forward and whispered, "It's no use. You said it yourself, to Nano. When you reminded him of his duties to Elvira."

I flinched at the memory. "I didn't mean—"

"No, you were right to do so, and I, too, must listen to your good sense. You see, I may be free to keep my hens in their coops, but I could never keep you—and I'd not want to, even if the cage was solid gold and encrusted with rubies." He studied my face, as though wishing to commit every part of it to memory. His beautiful, kind eyes shone, and the tears I was holding back fell thick and fast.

"I'll take my leave now," he said, and bowed his head to me before stepping back.

"One moment." Leonor spoke quietly from behind me. Both Juan and I turned to stare at her. She rose, walked two steps toward him, and handed him her entire jingling purse.

"For your services to my mother's daughters."

I noted her failure to call us sisters, but there was a strange shuttered expression on her face that made me wonder if this was a painful thing for her to admit.

"No, I cannot." Juan pushed the purse back, but I grabbed it, noting its significant weight, stuffed it inside the satchel, and pressed the lot to his chest.

"Please, take it," I said. "For me." His eyes widened as he took it into his hands and felt the weight of my mother's journals.

Keep them safe, I mouthed, and he nodded. His hand grazed mine, warm and firm and calloused. I nearly pressed my lips to it, but before that thought was fully formed, he walked away, leaving me standing in the cold breeze of his absence.

There was a long silence, and no one moved. Until Leonor's droll notes rose from behind me. "Well, that scene was certainly worth a full purse of gold."

"Shameless, the way he spoke to me—does he not know at one point in time he would've lost his head for even looking at my face?" Andrade grumbled.

Leonor made a tiny sound at the back of her throat. "That time is long gone, Juan Andrade."

"Yes, your father made sure of that, Leonor Cortés!" Andrade rounded on her.

This time, Leonor did laugh, a dry, mirthless thing, which made me turn around to look at her again. The smile on her face was dangerous and did not reach all the way to her glinting eyes. They reminded me of a pair of beetles, the beautiful, iridescent types that fed on rotten wood. She got up and poured herself another drink.

"All of our fathers made sure of that." She drank the liquor again, all in one gulp, and turned to usher me out. "Now, I'm sure this little lady wants nothing more than to return to the privacy of her chambers and shut the door on both our faces."

"You're not wrong," I said, glaring at Andrade, "and as soon as Catina can walk, we'll leave."

"You'll do no such thing," Andrade said, and then his eyes widened, as though a thought had suddenly struck him. "In fact, all three of you are staying—indefinitely."

Leonor laughed again, a clipped snip of a sound. "Oh, you do amuse me. How I wish I'd come to pester you more often before."

"I jest not," he answered, though he smiled, seemingly pleased with himself. "I must write to dear stepfather Cano immediately and, Leonor, to your new husband."

"And pray, what will you say, dear brother, to my husband, whom we both hardly know, and to the stepfather who cares not for you?" Leonor narrowed her eyes, reminding me of a predator stalking her prey.

Andrade poured himself another drink, and my brows knotted.

"True. True. Cano cares not a lick for me but adores his two little girls, as do I! Let us be clear on that. And everyone knows that that husband of yours is utterly besotted with his young bride, and who can blame him, for he's won himself the crown jewel of New Spain!"

Andrade raised his glass to both of us in turn, took a sip, spluttered a cough, and continued, "But unless our dear Gonzalo agrees to sign over the deeds to the towns that are rightfully mine, and unless your husband agrees to make me an equal partner of his mine in Zacatecas, I swear on our mother's soul . . . they shall never see you again."

CHAPTER 22

Isabel Cano

8 March 1551

In the morning, I tiptoed pointlessly into Catina's dark, stifling room. I carried a tray with two empty mugs and a steaming jug full to the brim with chocolatl sweetened with honey, the way she loved it best. To my surprise, she was already awake.

"Isabel?" she whimpered. I placed the tray on what I thought was a vanity, and drew the curtains back slightly so we could sign.

When I turned to look at her, however, I let out a cry and ran to her bedside. She was half sitting, leaning back stiffly on her pillows, as pale as a skull and gleaming with sweat.

"My leg is aching." She indicated with her chin. Her bottom lip wobbled. I lifted the bedsheets and was relieved to see the clean bandage around her swollen calf, with no foul odor or other signs that her sutures had come undone.

"Have you moved it at all?" I signed, and she gave a minuscule head shake—no. "It's probably just numb from being in one position," I signed, glancing around the handsome room.

I grabbed a nearby cushion, gently lifted her ankle, and placed the pillow underneath, then placed another under her knee.

She groaned her thanks, and I signed, "Have some chocolatl now, it'll help."

I brought her the frothy, fragrant drink and blew on it before holding it up to her lips. She took a few sips but declined to finish the cup.

"I'll get Andrade to call the doctor," I signed, brows knotted with worry.

She leaned her head back and stared at me for the space of two breaths, before whispering, "I hate being at your mercy."

I blinked in surprise and signed, "You are not at my mercy."

The corner of Catina's lip twitched. A spot of color appeared on her cheeks. "Yours and Nano's, though you are both kind about it."

"Don't be ridiculous," I signed. "We are not nearly kind enough. *I* don't do nearly enough, especially when it ought to have been me who lost her hearing, not you."

A weak huff escaped her, and it was difficult to tell whether it was an attempt at laughter, a mark of frustration, or simply pain, but she murmured, "No more guilt, Isabel. No more . . . pity." She reached out a hand and I took it. Her grip was firmer than I would've thought possible in her state. She fixed me with a look and said, "There's nothing wrong with being deaf. Apart from hearing, there is nothing else I cannot do."

I nodded, then took my hand back and signed, "I know that. I've always known that. You are better than me at practically everything except eating and fighting." She clicked her tongue in amusement, but I continued. "I just want to make things . . . easier for you. Better."

Catina's eyes shone. "You have, and I am so grateful. But I must fight my own battles now . . . stand on my own two feet."

Both of us glanced at her bandaged calf and let out a small chuckle.

"Right after my leg heals," she said.

I spent the majority of the next few weeks tending to Catina, bringing her meals, feeding her, changing her bandages, helping her up, and trying to get her to walk again.

When she seemed stronger, I broke the news about Marta and held her as she cried. Her body shuddered in near-perfect silence as I tried to stave off the flood of horrible images threatening to drown me, of Nantzin holding her little brother the same way, of the look on Marta's face when Pedro had his hands around her neck, the gnawing pit of guilt at the thought that I could've done more to save her.

Andrade and I had a shouting match every day, whenever he caught me bringing something to Catina. I had taken Juan's refusal to accept help from Andrade's servants to heart, and it bothered him to see his own noble sister doing such low, menial tasks.

"I can make it so only the *free* servants attend to you," he argued each day. "This madness must stop."

"I'll stop when you set them *all* free—and us too, for that matter!" I snapped. "We're not cattle to be bartered and traded. You're keeping us prisoner, your own sisters, do you realize that? Nantzin would be ashamed of you!"

His brown skin flushed a shade darker. "Nantzin promised me those towns, and I'll not let that greed-addled father of yours take them from me." It went on and on in circles.

We were forbidden from leaving the house and had guards posted outside our chambers, following us wherever we went. Leonor suffered the same treatment, yet she seemed unaffected by the situation, bored even. The only thing she'd requested was a loom to do her weaving, which Andrade had agreed to. She spent countless hours alone in her room with her loom, only emerging at unexpected hours throughout the day to call on Andrade and poor Mari, who was near Leonor in age and had grown up worshipping her.

Leonor seemed to relish the opportunity to return Mari's attentions and inquiries about the comfort of her stay with quiet, backhanded compliments on the decoration of their home, the food, the way the servants behaved, and everything she could see out the window from the garden. It drove my sister-in-law mad.

On the few evenings I joined them at dinner out of sheer boredom, Mari would look at me and begin to cry. "Husband, you cannot keep holding your sisters hostage like this. What are you doing to them . . . to us? We have plenty now. We do not need more land. Is this really worth the love of your family?"

But Andrade was adamant. "We are finalizing matters, my dearest, don't worry yourself. The Cano boys are falling in line. We've agreed to meet here in a few days, to sign over the deeds. Leonor's husband shall send a representative too."

We were not told when the meeting would take place but decided to prepare in advance nonetheless. Catina's leg had not healed completely, but she could walk on it and even run for short distances. We'd been practicing in her room.

We knew the day had come when we were told to dress in our best clothes—Andrade had paid for a new gown each for Catina and me. As usual, she wore hers better than I. There was something fetching about the way she stood, exactly like Nantzin, with her back erect and her hands clasped in front of her, shy gaze facing down. A picture of regal modesty I could never hope to emulate, though I was much less envious than I had ever been, knowing what it had cost my mother to learn. Still, I had no need of a looking glass to see the brutish stance of my shoulders and the deep-set frown marring whatever handsome features I might've shared with either of my sisters.

Leonor walked downstairs with us, and as usual was as poised and relaxed as a cat who is used to lapping up its fair share of cream.

Andrade sat behind his desk, flanked by armed guards wearing his green-and-white livery and one of the same clerks from the day my mother's will had been read. Mari had excused herself, pleading ill health, but I think she could not bear to see her husband stooping any lower. And she could hardly bear to be in the same room as Leonor anymore.

We were ushered into the seats beside Andrade's desk.

"I'm surprised you're not tying our wrists to the chairs," I said.

Leonor gave me an appreciative nod for once, although Andrade rolled his eyes.

"Here's paper and writing charcoal, as requested," he said. I took them and tested them out. I had agreed to write down key words so Catina could follow what was happening.

There was a knock at the door, and the guard introduced the imposing Spanish-looking gentleman who walked through as "Luis Cortés, here to represent his sister Leonor."

Leonor rushed to him and stood on her tiptoes to kiss both his cheeks.

"Everything is ready," Luis said, holding her hands, and Leonor blinked slowly, lazily. She linked her arm through her brother's and stood beside him, a ghost of a smile on her face. She did not bother to introduce us, though I no longer cared about her petty games. Luis, for his part, did not even glance at us. He gave Andrade an inscrutable, curious look. My brother ignored him and sorted through some of the papers in front of him.

Another knock sounded, and the guard's voice was drowned out by the hammering in my chest as all my other brothers, Pedro, Gonzalo, and Nano, walked into the room side by side. Catina stiffened beside me, and I, too, sat up and studied them quickly. They were unarmed, and I took a deep, settling breath.

Pedro and Gonzalo spared us only a severe side-eyed glance before turning their attention on the Cortés siblings and Andrade. Nano and I stared evenly at each other for the space of several silent beats, though my mind felt like it was buzzing with the pressure of a thousand angry thoughts. What was he doing with them? Had he changed his allegiance? Had he told them about Nantzin's book? What had they promised him? Land for him and Elvira in exchange for what—his silence on Pedro's guilt? Had he forgotten the way Pedro had attacked him? Or had my words wounded him more than the heel of Pedro's boots ever could?

I raised a querying brow, hoping he could somehow hear the questions flaring in my mind, but could not keep the stinging flush of guilt from settling on my trembling lower lip and jaw. He looked away from me, his face a mask, and I could not discern an answer.

"Let's get started, shall we?" Andrade said. "The clerks are here to bear witness to these transactions, which should be quite straightforward if we all agree to play nice."

"God, you're insufferable," hissed Gonzalo, and I almost snorted in spite of myself. But the only sound in the room was my charcoal and the clerk's quills scratching against our respective pieces of paper. Catina glanced down to read mine, then we looked back up.

Andrade ignored him and looked at Luis and Leonor. "It'll be easier to start with you, sister. I've come to an agreement already with your husband. A representative of mine will join you on the journey back to Zacatecas, and ensure my interests are protected."

"Lovely," said Leonor, voice dripping with sarcasm.

"Indeed. You are free to go." Andrade smiled.

"Oh, but I shall be sorry to miss the rest of this meeting. You are all so entertaining, it makes me feel so very sad that I was never allowed to spend time with you growing up."

Her brother Luis leaned his head down on hers. "Tragic, querida. Alas, your immeasurably rich husband awaits."

Nano scoffed; Catina waved goodbye. Leonor bowed low to all of us and walked through the doorway with Luis, closing the door without a backward glance.

Andrade shook his head and looked back at Gonzalo. "Now, brother . . . all you need to do is sign here, here, and here. And you will effectively transfer the deeds of Ocoyoacac, Chapulmaloyan, Coatepec, and Tepexoyuca over to my name."

"Fuck you!" Pedro shouted. Catina flinched. She had easily read his lips. "That's all we came here to say. You think we're going to hand

Gonzalo's lands over to you in exchange for two runts?" He pointed at me, and there was hatred burning in his eyes. "That bitch killed my best dog—you think I care what happens to her? I'm here to make sure she rots in that convent for the rest of her life."

I ground my teeth as I wrote that down, and Catina shook her head.

Andrade chuckled. "Pedro—genio y figura hasta la sepultura, eh? It seems you'll take that nasty temper to the grave. Or prison, which will come first if you fail to heed me."

"That's your problem, isn't it, cabrón?" Gonzalo shot at him. "Just because our mother heeded your every whim, doesn't mean we will."

"You would have a third of these lands without our father, without all the years he spent at court on Nantzin's behalf," said Pedro. "And yet you can't spare a few shitty pueblos for his son, your own blood. Then again, you've always been a greedy prick."

Andrade's smile was dangerous, his voice even and low as he said, "Well, I'd rather be a prick than a murderer."

Everyone sucked in a breath.

"Did he say murderer?" asked Catina, who had probably meant to whisper, but it came out almost as a shout.

"Tread carefully, Andrade," warned Nano.

"Oh, I always do. Indeed, I am so careful . . . that I have collected several pages' worth of eyewitness accounts detailing Pedro's involvement in the death of our dear aunt Marta."

Nano's head swiveled to look at Pedro, whose eyes narrowed again, but sweat had broken out on his forehead and upper lip. "Marta died from a bad fever."

Gonzalo nodded emphatically, and I shook my head in disgust. "Liar," I swore under my breath as I wrote what they'd said. Catina glared at Pedro like never before.

"Marta contracted a death humor from a ruptured larynx, according to the coroner who assessed her. Of course, the story spread by you around town was that the newly hired cook—the Moor—had throttled her and taken my sisters and brother hostage. But after meeting the young man, I began my own private investigations into the matter. It seems that several ladies of ill repute"—he glanced in apology at my sister and me, then continued—"along with a few of your father's guards were under the distinct impression that *you* had something to do with it. That they had been threatened and bribed to shift the blame to the new cook. But their new accounts are eerily similar—it will be difficult to convince a judge to take your word over all seven of theirs. And one of the guards who gave an account . . . is a full-blooded Spaniard."

He let the meaning of his words hang over all of us. As Mestizos, we understood implicitly that the word of a Spaniard was akin to law. Even a guard without a shred of noble blood, unlike us, would be seen as more trustworthy than my own mixed-race brother, who was not so stupid as to fail to see that Andrade had him cornered.

"What do you want," Pedro whispered.

Andrade stood slowly. "Nantzin promised me the *entirety* of Tacuba. Every town, and every tribute payer working in every field. Your meddling father must've convinced her otherwise at the last moment, when she was too weak to think clearly, but I do not forget." He glared at Gonzalo. "Those towns do not belong to you, and if you don't sign them over, I will ensure that your most beloved brother Pedro never sees the light of day ever again."

Gonzalo and Pedro fell still as twin statues. Only Pedro's clenched fists and whitened knuckles showed his true feelings. I scribbled furiously for Catina, unable to distinguish these emotions swirling inside me: part elation, part dread. I wished for Pedro to be brought to justice for killing Marta, even though the shame and scrutiny toward our family would be unbearable, but I also did not want Andrade to win.

Nano was the one to break the silence.

He pointed at the men sitting beside Andrade, flanked by guards. "What are the clerks and guards for, then? It seems you've already made up your mind. Why would Gonzalo hand over his towns to you if you're going to arrest him anyway?"

Pedro glanced at Gonzalo and then at the door.

"Don't even think about it," said Andrade. "You must've seen how many guards I hired for today's happy purpose. But of course, Nano asks some excellent questions. As always, he's the most astute of you."

"Make your point, carajo!" said Nano.

Andrade nodded his head in an empty, regal gesture. "If Gonzalo signs, my friends here have agreed to nullify the witness statements and authenticate your claims instead. You will, of course, be expected to pay their very reasonable fees. Pedro shall walk away a free man, and I shall send guards to apprehend the young cook to be brought to justice instead."

I jumped to my feet. The guard beside me clamped his large hand on my shoulder.

"What is it?" Catina stood and grabbed the guard's arm. "Let her go!"

"Juan has done nothing wrong!" I shouted at Andrade at the same time as I tried to wrench away from the guard's hands.

"It's a shame you've been no use to me in the end, sisters. Take them to the convent," Andrade said to the guards, who pounced on us. "But be gentle with them!" he added.

"Fuck your gentle!" I screamed at the top of my lungs even as the guard threw me over his shoulder and carried me away. "No! Pinches cobardes! Juan saved your life, Nano, you coward! No!"

The guard shut the door, but I kept cursing and punching and biting like a crazed cat, trying to get away even as the two guards carried an equally furious Catina and me all the way into a windowless carriage. They threw us in and bolted the door from the outside.

CHAPTER 23

Isabel Cano

29 March 1551

Catina and I threw ourselves against the carriage doors to no avail. It was not the convent that had us in such a frenzy, but the fate of Juan. It would be so easy for the courts to frame him, a poor, dark-skinned boy without family, without any known friends of consequence who lived close enough to intervene.

And it was all my fault, all my stupid fault, for involving him in this nightmare in the first place. I felt feverish with guilt. I wanted to throw up from the rage and the panic. I tore the sleeves off my dress and the frill collar constricting my throat, which was raw from screaming and sobbing. My shoulders hurt from how many times I'd slammed them into the door. Eventually, we could no longer go on, and we both fell back into our seats, facing each other, sweating and panting.

"How could Nano do this?" I signed, my movements slow and exhausted.

Catina shook her head, her face pinched in pain. She began to cry, not in her usual soundless way but with loud, keening, startling wails that made the hairs on the back of my neck stand on end.

"Is it your foot? Let me see!" I signed.

Catina kept on howling. She waved me away and managed to say, in between shuddering gasps, "I wish Nantzin was here."

And if there had been a window, I would have looked out and tried to distract myself in some way. But there was nothing for either of us to do in this rattling, stifling dark box except sit and wait and think, and for me to listen to the depths of my sister's grief. Those cries that amplified the cavernous loss I *also* felt, the wish I *also* whispered every night before I fell asleep. The same words Catina had spoken.

I wish Nantzin was here.

And before I knew it, my hands were covering my face, my palms and cheeks were slippery with tears and snot and spit, and I was sobbing so hard I thought my ribs would crack. And I shed all the tears I had not allowed myself to shed, from some unfounded belief that somehow they would make me less worthy of being my mother's daughter, less of a Moctezuma.

But Nantzin had cried, now I knew—she had also cried, many times over. She had also loved deeply and lost. And the thought of all the losses she had lived through made me cry anew, like a wounded animal being struck by one poisoned arrow after another. I cried until, somehow, I fell asleep.

But I couldn't have been down for too long, I thought, because when I woke up, lying awkwardly on my side of the bench, the carriage was still thundering down the road. Catina slept opposite me. It dawned on me that it might've been several hours since we'd left.

We had possibly gone past the center of Tenochtitlan, where the convent was.

I bolted up and began to search again for any gaps I could look out from. I found a tiny peephole in the front of the box, to the side. I couldn't make out much except the back of the guard's thick neck, the trotting horses, and some flashing scenery on the sidelines, plains of tall grass and endless fields of squash and maize. No landmarks I could recognize, and barely any people.

I sat back down and looked around the box, trying pointlessly to find another way out. My heart pounded in my chest; my stomach clenched, hard and hot as one of the grandmother stones from the temazcalli. I felt an inexplicable sense of awareness, of dread, deep in my bones. We were in danger—and for once in my life, I was completely unarmed. No dagger, no bow, no atlatl . . . not even a sharp enough hairpin to cause damage.

The carriage made a turn, and I looked out the peephole again. We had left the main road, and our new path was much rockier and uneven. The carriage bounced and juddered too hard for me to keep looking out from it.

After about half an hour we slowed down to a stop. One of the men said, "Didn't they say to drop them closer to the back of the ruins?"

"It's close enough," the other replied. "I'm bursting for a piss, and they've stopped screaming." He lowered his voice. "You know, I reckon they're asleep." There was a short silence, meaningful enough to raise the hairs on the back of my neck.

"We can't—they're ladies," the first man whispered, confirming my worst fears. My palms began to sweat. My shoulders felt like they were coiling into themselves.

"Have you ever heard a lady cursing like that savage little prieta? Look at the scratches she left on my arms. It's because they're Mestizas, not proper Spanish."

"What if the doña finds out?" the first man murmured.

"We'll make sure she doesn't." The carriage shook as the men jumped off. I only had a fraction of an instant to shake Catina awake and pull her behind my body.

"Don't make a noise. Try to stay inside the carriage," I signed, ignoring the sudden look of terror in her eyes. "Go for the eyes and groin, like Papa taught us."

The doorstopper was pulled off with a scrape. I bent my knees, preparing to launch at the guard's face and gouge his eyes out. Hopefully I would be able to grab the horses' reins and steal the carriage before they caught me. Instead, there was a whooshing sound and a crack. An arrowhead jutted out from the middle of the door. I jolted and hit my head on the ceiling. Catina shrieked. The guards shouted, but their voices were cut short by the sounds of thundering hooves and another voice booming, "Stand back! Isabel, Catina, are you in there?"

"Nano!" I screamed. "Nano! Yes!" I gasped and turned to my sister, signing, "It's Nano!" She nodded but didn't move, looking petrified.

"Hey—hey, I said don't move! Stand back! Stand back!"

There was a sound like steel blades being drawn followed immediately by the whoosh of a pair of arrows loosened in succession, and twin thuds like heavy sacks of flour being dropped on the ground.

"What was that?" I shouted, and pounded on the door, fighting the hysteria rising like a lance through my stomach. "Nano, Nano! Are you hurt?"

"I'm here," he said, and opened the door. I gasped at the mess of splattered and dripping blood, so bright it would've been mesmerizing if it hadn't been for the guards sprawled over the ground, limbs splayed in awkward angles.

Both their left eyes had the shaft of an arrow sticking out of them, a grotesque display of perfect bowmanship that almost made me forget what those men had been planning to do to us. But at the thought, my eyes swam with tears. I looked up and could see nothing else but the furious look on my brother's face.

I jumped off the carriage and into his arms, sobbing. "They were talking about us—they were planning—they wanted to—"

Nano shushed me. "I know, I know."

I fought the urge to slam my fists into his chest and asked, "How could you know? Don't tell me you've ever done anything like it!"

"No! Never!" He looked scandalized. "I swear!"

Then another voice whispered, "They were loosening their breeches."

My gaze snapped toward the sound, and my lips parted.

Juan, who was wearing a hood that nearly covered his whole face, was gripping the pommel of the horse's saddle as though his life depended on it. Clustered behind him was a tower of nohpalli and a dry-looking tree leaning on a pair of large boulders. He let out a yelp as the horse puffed and leaned down to nibble on some weeds protruding from the rocky ground.

Nano and I rushed to his side as I spluttered, "How did this happen? How did you two get together? How did you find us?"

"Juan came straight to me after he left Andrade's house," Nano replied, his voice hoarse and his stare oddly vacant. "I've been hiding him—but it's too long a story. We can wait for tonight."

I wished to push him more, but Juan nodded in agreement and said, "We must deal with those . . . men. Can one of you, *please*, help me get off this beast?"

We helped Juan leap off onto the dry ground. Nano kept shooting furtive glances at the guards splayed behind us. The horse huffed, and Nano put his face against its neck, stroking it silently, though it was unclear whether his intention was to calm the animal or himself. Then his back began to shudder. He let out a choked sob, and I turned to Juan with a panicked look.

My older brother was crying. This had never happened in my entire life.

Juan sighed, placed an arm around Nano's shoulders, and squeezed them. "You gave them a choice," he whispered. "You warned them. It was more than they deserved."

I agreed. In fact, there was an ugly wish in my heart that I'd been the one to pull the bowstring, but I held my tongue and studied Juan instead. The way his eyes focused with concern, the gentle, patient tone he used on Nano, on all of us.

We didn't deserve him. I certainly didn't. I gave a silent prayer of thanks that he was safe, and waited until Nano's tears had dried and his breath was even once again before I said, "We should hide them behind those rocks. Juan and I can do it—you should wait in the carriage."

Nano shook his head and started walking back to the carriage. His boots scratched on the gravel and kicked up plumes of dust.

"I'll not leave you to clean up my dirty work. And I cannot leave these arrows here. Someone may recognize them as mine." He leaned down and yanked the arrowheads free from the guards' eyes with a liquid sound that made my stomach turn. More blood flowed, and soft pink tissue dripped down onto his dusty boots, leaving a smearing trail as it slid back to the bloody ground.

"Let me see to Catina, and I'll come help you after," he murmured.

Juan and I followed Nano, who climbed into the carriage at the same time as we took hold of the bigger guard's boots. We huffed and grunted as we pulled him behind the boulders and the tall nohpalli bush, away from the view of the road.

"We should take his sword," I said, "He won't need it." Juan shot me an uncomfortable look but didn't stop me as I took the guard's weapons and everything else of value.

"Uh, before we forget, here." He removed the satchel from around his chest and gave it to me. "Your mother's words."

I hugged the satchel to my chest and murmured my thanks, but I couldn't bring myself to look at him, to see the kindness emanating from him—I couldn't trust myself to not cry again when he'd already been forced to console my brother. We had burdened him enough, placed him in enough danger, me and my broken, twisted family. He had to leave before they caught him. I couldn't understand why he was still here. If I were him, I would have been on a ship out of Veracruz by now.

"Thank you for trusting me with them," he said. I glanced up at him, and the words slipped out before I could stop them.

"I would trust you with my life."

He blinked, and his features darkened slightly. I thought perhaps he was blushing, and for a moment we stared at each other. My heart sped up, but he nodded in acknowledgment of my words before clearing his throat and asking, "Sh-should we bury him?"

Of course he wished to change the subject. He had made his feelings clear at Andrade's house. We were too different—our backgrounds, our families, our positions in society were too far apart. Not to mention our tempers.

It was agony to think so, but perhaps we could still be friends.

"What—and deny the coyotes and zopilotes a well-deserved meal?" I raised an eyebrow and Juan pouted, which made me laugh, then ache.

But I could not let him see that. I could not hold on to him. It would be pure selfishness. I had to respect his wishes, and I had to make sure he was safe. So I gave him my best, friendliest smile and forced myself to say, "It's a perfect opportunity now, for you. You have enough gold, you should take Nano's horse and leave."

He blinked, then said, "Oh yes? And go where, exactly?"

"Somewhere safe, away from Pedro and Andrade. Veracruz . . . find a ship." My voice was too high, too bright, my smile felt like a stony grimace. "Go to Peru or Africa . . . where—where did you say your grandmother was from?"

"Somewhere in the east," he said. "But I don't want to go there, not yet."

"Oh no?" My brows knotted.

Juan stepped closer and lightly caressed my cheek with the back of his hand before I could even blink, let alone think. My mind went as blank as an empty canvas. My blood rushed hot through my ears, my eyes, which swam with blinding spots as if I'd stared too long at the sun.

"No. I'd like to stay with you if . . . if you'll have me," he said, before dropping his hand behind his back, as if he had done as much as he dared. But there was a whole world of longing in his gaze that I could not tear my eyes away from.

And even though there was a dead body between us and a quickly darkening sky, my limbs and brains felt as loose and unhelpful as moistened clay. Every argument and logical retort faded to mist as I bit my smiling lip and replied, "Yes, I would."

The earth was too dry and compact to dig but a shallow grave. We did the best we could to cover the guards' bodies with rocks and gravel and spread dust and more gravel over the trail of blood on the ground, then bridled Nano's horse to the carriage along with the two others and set off.

Juan and I steered the horses, while Nano and Catina sat inside the carriage. I asked Juan again to tell me what had happened since he'd left Andrade's house, but he said he'd rather wait to tell the story with Nano. For once I did not argue, as steering the carriage and finding our way demanded our utmost concentration.

There were road signs here and there, pointing north to Lakes Xaltocan and Zumpango, west to Cuauhtitlan, south to Tenochtitlan, and east toward Teotihuacan, one of the last locations which had been marked on the tapestry map. The ruins were well known and lay somewhere east of Lake Xaltocan. We followed the northeastern road, keeping in view the collection of marshes to our right. There were very few people, mostly shepherd boys following their flock around the rocky hills surrounding the greenish waters.

After a few hours, the sun set behind our backs, and we decided to make camp. We found a suitable place underneath the canopy of a wide cypress and built a fire. Nano and Juan had been clever enough to pack some food: a small sack of doughballs made with a paste of ground amaranth seeds and mezcal honey, several tamalli that we warmed over a flat stone near the fire, and a few xicama turnips that could be eaten raw. We sat down, and Catina fell asleep immediately next to my right leg. As I took a bite of tamalli, Nano finally filled me in on what had happened since we'd separated.

"After our disagreement, I thought of going back to Elvira, but I couldn't face her. I knew she would be disappointed to think that I'd abandoned you—"

"It was all my fault," I said through a mouth full of dough. "I shouldn't have said those things to you. I didn't mean any of it." I swallowed. "I was angry and it was wrong."

Nano looked down, and I glanced at Juan, sitting opposite me, next to Nano. The firelight shifted, wafting shadows over his features and making them impossible to read.

"Thank you, but I needed to hear it," Nano murmured. "I had nowhere else to go but home. I had to convince Pedro and Gonzalo to take me back in. It was difficult—they had lots of questions about what you'd been up to and . . . about the tapestry and the cushions they discovered in your chambers."

I looked sharply at him. "What did you tell them?"

He ran a hand through his hair. "I told them Nantzin had left a map of Grandfather Moctezuma's treasure and that I was helping you find it."

Juan shook his head. "And they figured out some of the clues."

I covered my mouth. "No . . ."

"Yes, but they're an almighty mess, so I don't think they will do anything about it. Everything Pedro said earlier—it was a ruse to get Andrade to release you. We planned it together, thinking if Andrade believed that we didn't care about you, he wouldn't hold you hostage anymore. In truth, Pedro has not been sleeping or eating. For all his bravado, he walks around the house at night muttering prayers."

"Oh please, he's praying over his dead dog, not me." I flicked a fallen leaf off my knee with my nail.

Nano sighed. "I heard him saying your name. Plus, he got the priest to come bless the house and sprinkle holy water over the landing where Marta died."

"Where he strangled her," I said through my teeth. "Let's not forget that detail. If you heard my name upon his lips it was probably said in curse, not prayer. No—there is no pity left in my heart for any of them. As of today, I have no other brothers but you."

Nano looked at the horses, tethered to the cypress, but he offered no response. I didn't want to upset him again—I didn't want him to think about the dead men who'd owned two of those horses—so I decided to change the subject.

"So how did you two come to be together?" A breeze sparked the embers of the fire. Warm, acrid smoke drifted over my face, making my eyes water.

Juan's gaze flicked from Nano to me. "Well, the night after I left Andrade's house, I went to your place, hoping to find *him*"—he gestured to Nano with his thumb—"to tell him where you were. I had to be very careful to not get caught, but you remember my cousin Esteban?"

"The one who called him Pollo," mumbled Nano distractedly.

I rolled my eyes and took another bite of tamalli.

"Well, he helped me get a message to your brother," said Juan. "They hid me in the dovecote while all the negotiations between your brothers were going on."

Nano huffed, alert again. "I couldn't believe Andrade was using you two as bait . . . Then again, he's shown his true colors to us Cano men, many times before."

I frowned, but before I could ask what he meant by that, Nano continued, "When the date was set to meet, Juan agreed to help me rescue you. I never dreamt we'd be rescuing him instead." He looked to his side and reached out to hold Juan around the shoulders. "I'm sorry about my brothers. I swear I will help you any way I can."

"Thank you," Juan said. I froze mid-bite as they looked at each other evenly, intimately, as though they were sealing something important. An understanding, perhaps, of what they meant to each other now, after everything they had been through together.

Nano squeezed him once before releasing him and saying, "So, what's our plan?"

I swallowed both my mouthful and the knot in my throat and rummaged in the satchel beside me. "There's only two clues left, Teotihuacan and Iztaccihuatl. Catina thinks the next one refers to the Pyramid of the Moon. It's pretty self-explanatory. There's her eagle flying over a pyramid under a half moon. Some kind of curl, and some words I don't know." The flickering glow made it difficult to study the image. "And there's lines under the pyramid. They look like roots to me. What do you think?"

I shared the scroll with Nano, who nodded his thanks. "Why put a chapter in Teotihuacan, though? The ruins have been abandoned for hundreds of years."

"I'm sure Catina will have some ideas."

"I just wish I knew who the messenger is, the one helping Nantzin," Nano said.

I sat up. "It's definitely a woman. Those guards mentioned something about not letting a doña know about—about what they were planning to do to us. She must've paid them to take us away, not to the convent but toward the ruins. I heard them say so!"

Nano's eyebrows shot up. Juan said, "All of the people involved—the cook, Tepahtih Nayeli, your aunt Mariana, La Llorona"—he shuddered—"they were prepared for your arrival. Whoever the messenger is, they've been tracking your movements."

"But does this person mean to help or hurt us?" Nano asked.

"Well, clearly they made a mistake in hiring those brutes," I spat.

Juan nodded. "I don't believe that was part of the plan . . . When your mother wrote this, I doubt she expected your older brothers to be chasing you with hounds and keeping you hostage in exchange for land. She probably wanted this journey to be more . . . gentle. You said it in the canoe, and I think you're right. It's somehow like she wanted this to be a pilgrimage in honor of her life."

Nano and I shared a look, and I saw my own grief reflected in his gaze. Nantzin would've never imagined what had happened since she'd passed. I certainly couldn't have. Even though Pedro had always been rough and prone to bursts of rage, like me, I never would've pinned him as a killer.

"She was the only one holding us together, wasn't she?" Nano whispered. "As people, as a family. We all just wanted to make her proud."

My eyes swelled, and I nodded.

He sighed. "Perhaps we still can."

It was Juan's turn to slap Nano's back. "And I will help you in any way I can."

CHAPTER 24

Isabel Cano

30 March 1551

We took turns keeping watch throughout the quiet night. In the morning, we decided the carriage would draw too much attention and set off again on horseback. The terrain sloped upward, toward the hills surrounding the liquid basin of Mexico. Away from the lakes, the air was dry and crisp, the grass a faded yellow, the spiky, shrubby vegetation dull green and dusty. I missed the constant trickle of water, the patter of waves, the singing sparrows and quacking ducks scavenging for food. Out here, the only animal we spotted was a brown rabbit our horses startled out from underneath a low-lying cactus.

Catina and I shared a horse, and the boys sat on the backs of the other two. There was only one saddle between us, so we gave it to Juan, who was a terrible mount. Nano had to keep a hold of both horses' reins, and Juan looked sick with worry. His bronze skin had a greenish tinge to it, and he kept closing his eyes and murmuring prayers. The horse huffed and flicked its head in annoyance at having to carry such a fussy rider, but Nano managed to keep it trotting at a steady pace between his horse and ours.

A few hours later, we came across a small hamlet and asked for directions. An old couple we crossed paths with pointed east toward a green hill they said was the famous hill of Coatepec, and we followed an ancient, arid road toward it. Magueys with towering yellow flowers and spiky yucca trees speckled the rocky, uneven terrain. A weak mid-spring sun flickered from behind the clouds every now and then, though it brought little joy since there was a constant wind that stirred up specks of soot into our nostrils and made our eyes water.

Catina kept our spirits up with stories and legends. "They say Coatlicue of the serpent skirt conceived Huitzilopochtli while she was sweeping. Her daughter, Coyolxauhqui, and her army of four hundred stars were outraged by their mother's indecency, and decided to kill her while she rested right on that hill of Coatepec. But Huitzilopochtli, the sun, leapt from his mother's womb armed for battle and defeated his siblings. He tossed Coyolxauhqui's head into the sky, and it became the moon."

She finished the story as we drew to the foot of the hill. The wind died down, and we decided to stretch our legs and give the horses a break.

"You know, you are really good at telling stories," I said and signed, and Catina beamed. "I just wish they weren't all so . . . bloody."

"True," murmured Nano. "I've had enough of blood to last me a lifetime."

My heart twisted for him. I handed the reins to Catina and walked to Nano's side. Almost as if he knew my intentions, Juan sped up and walked off with Catina. They began to practice hand signs, as he wanted to learn more.

I cleared the knot tightening around my throat and whispered, "I am grateful to you. For coming back. For saving us from those guards."

He bumped me with his elbow, which I took to mean "You're welcome." But it was not enough. He had killed two people, and I could see how much it was costing him.

"I was so frightened," I said in the smallest voice, the loudest I could muster.

Nano stopped and looked at me, his expression raw and furious, his eyes swelling. Then he threw his arms around my neck and squeezed. I squeezed him back, as tight as I could, and felt my warm tears vanishing into his shirt.

"I was almost too late," his gruff voice cracked. "I couldn't have forgiven myself if . . . if they'd laid a hand on either of you. I was stupid to leave you. I'm so sorry."

I nodded into his chest, feeling a strange sense of ease settling over my shoulders and back. Like a part of me was becoming tethered to something again. I could've been a spider, weaving my torn web anew. Nantzin and Marta were gone, my father had left, Pedro and Gonzalo and Andrade might as well have died. But Nano was still here, and Catina, and Juan.

"And you were right," he whispered. "To search for Nantzin's testimony. I've not been able to stop thinking about it. I read all the journals again in the dovecote with Juan. I know now, I can feel, they are meant to guide us, help us. Regardless of who the mystery messenger is, or their intentions, we must find them all. We must learn the full truth of what she endured and honor her."

"Yes, and we must never fight again," I answered softly, and Nano laughed and pulled me gently away, keeping hold of my shoulders.

He looked older now, on the cusp of manhood. He smiled that crooked smile of his—the one that drove the ladies at court half mad but which to me was just a special dollop of light—and said, "Now, now, let's not make promises we cannot hope to keep."

I laughed back, and we walked in step with each other around the edge of the sacred hill of Coatepec. Down into the distance, we could finally see the abandoned ruins of Teotihuacan, the grand ancient city of my mother's forebears. The city that our own Tenochtitlan had been modeled on, an ode to masonry and order.

"We had a map of this city in our library! That's the Avenue of the Dead," said Catina, pointing to a huge dirt road in the middle of the city.

Two pyramids, brown and speckled with shrubs, sat at each end of the road, and one towered in the middle, a huge thing the size of the mound behind us.

"The Pyramid of the Moon is the one down there, closest to us. The Pyramid of the Sun is that large one in the middle. The Pyramid of Quetzalcoatl is at the end."

"They're . . . enormous," I said. I had never seen anything like it, but I easily pictured my ancestors walking along a similar long, wide avenue, wide enough for twenty horses. I imagined the imprint the Teotihuacan priests would've made as they climbed the countless steps to the temples to cut out living hearts.

"There's a *lot* of vegetation," Nano said and signed.

"Are those nohpalli?" I asked and signed, and Catina nodded.

"They're everywhere!" Nano said, clearly dismayed. The Pyramids of the Sun and Moon especially had rows upon rows of nohpalli growing around their bases, thousands of green sentries, some twice as tall as Juan, covered in sharp thorns longer than my fingers.

"We'll lose half our flesh trying to get through," said Nano, who seemed to be thinking along the same lines as me.

"How does one get into a pyramid anyway?" added Juan.

"Perhaps if we get closer we might find a way inside," I answered.

We quietly circled the outer rim of the city for hours and never set eyes on a single soul, though we agreed it felt like we were being watched. At first, I thought it might be someone sent to guide us. It made my heart throb, to think that Nantzin had placed guardians at nearly every stage of this journey, to make it easier for us to find her words. But this time, no one greeted us, no one showed us the way.

We would have to find her next chapter all on our own.

"Perhaps someone has made a way through the nohpalli already," Juan said, and though we looked and looked for signs that someone had taken a sword or a machete to the great, thorny forest, we could find none.

We picked, peeled, and ate some of the pink pear fruits from the nohpalli, and cut many of the younger, tender paddles, the vibrant-green ones, to cook and eat later, stuffing our dwindling sack of food with as many as we could carry. It seemed as if the cacti were trying to bribe us. As if they were saying, *Here, take this offering of food and leave our temples in peace,* and it reminded me with an awkward tug of the stomach of my grandfather Moctezuma, trying to ward off the Spaniards.

We reached a shallow river crossing through the middle of the Avenue of the Dead, but again, the nohpalli made a wall lining the edge of the water and there was no clear way in. Soon after, the sun began to set, so we decided to make camp near one of the abandoned, smaller structures on the outskirts behind the Pyramid of Quetzalcoatl.

They appeared to be a collection of stone buildings, homes perhaps, three in all. They formed a natural barrier against the breeze, facing a small but elaborate shrine about the size of two of our horses. The small temple had been decorated with the head of a feathered serpent, and it stood in the middle of what could've been the central courtyard.

The roofs of the buildings around the small temple had caved generations before, but the entry steps were still intact, as well as some of the colonnades.

We led the three horses into one of the homes to the right of the complex and tied the reins around a central colonnade. It made for a nice stable, and there was plenty of grass for them to graze on. As for ourselves, we settled on the structure facing the opening to the complex. Nano sat on the steps to keep watch, and Juan began to clean the nohpalli paddles with a knife as Catina and I gathered kindling to build a fire.

Once the fire was hot enough, we speared the nohpalli through with the dead guards' swords, grilled them over the flames, and gorged ourselves. Even Nano ate at least five, though they were slimier and stickier than usual as we'd not been able to boil them beforehand.

"They're missing salt, of course, and the best way to prepare them is chopped in a salad with tomatl," murmured Juan apologetically.

I laughed. "They're delicious, tangy and crisp with the smoked flavor from the fire, just the way I love them."

Nano nodded. "I could definitely eat more, but I won't be able to walk."

"What are you all saying?" Catina asked, frowning. "You're being rude."

"Sorry," I said and signed. "Just commenting on how good the nohpalli are."

"Oh." She took another bite and nodded. "They're the best I've ever had."

"Right, well—we must have a better plan for tomorrow," I said and signed. "We have two swords we could use as machetes."

"There's too many cacti, too densely packed. It would kill us," Nano said and signed.

Catina took out the scroll and studied it for several moments before exclaiming, "What about under the ground?" But before we could answer, we heard a rustling close by, and all of us except for Catina whirled around.

Juan shouted, "Chaneque spirits! They're setting the horses loose!"

Nano and I bolted into the dark toward the stable.

"What's happening?!" Catina squealed from inside the temple.

"Juan—stay with Catina!" I shouted without looking back.

Nano and I spread ourselves across the entryway, blocking it to keep the horses in. The animals neighed and kicked the ground. Two small creatures scrambled away from them toward the shadows, and then one of them made a mad dash toward us, screaming in a way that raised the hairs on the back of my neck.

For a blink, I truly believed it was a chaneque and fell back, until I saw her very human eyes glimmering with terror. I tackled the girl around the waist into the dirt, and she screamed, trying to claw at my face.

We wrestled, and I shouted in Nahuatl, "Peace! Peace! I won't hurt you!"

The other girl charged us, but Nano grabbed her by the arm and managed to restrain her. It took several moments before they stopped struggling and screaming. Nano and I kept repeating the same words, "Peace. Peace," until they settled.

Only then did I back away from the girl lying underneath me and said, in between panting breaths, "See? You're safe to go. But if you're hungry, we can offer you food."

"You have nohpalli," she said boldly, still breathing hard. "We do too."

"And you are sick of it—is that why you're rummaging through our supplies?" Nano said, very gently, but the girls still flinched.

"We won't hurt you," he reassured them, and let his girl go. She ran toward me and the other girl and helped pull her up. I couldn't make out their features in the dark, but something about the way they stood, with the same stubborn set of their shoulders, told me they were probably sisters.

I stood up as well and dusted my skirts, looking down. "Well, if you're tired of nohpalli, we have some tamalli and xicama. Come and share in our meal."

The girls looked at each other, then back at us and nodded. They followed a few steps behind as we neared the fire and paused as they spotted Catina first and then Juan. I quickly introduced them to try to set them at ease.

"This is my sister Catina and our friend Juan. Catina is deaf."

"I am Tlaco, and this is my little sister, Xoco," said the girl who had attacked me. She did not take her eyes off Juan, but continued to speak. "Xocotzin is also deaf in one ear, and a little in the other from a cannon attack on our village after we rebelled. It was years ago."

We sat around the fire and continued to swap stories as Nano and Juan warmed some tamalli for the girls, who said they had been on their own for a while. They'd settled in Teotihuacan three or four moons ago.

I translated what they said to Catina, and they were fascinated by Hand Talk. They excitedly showed us some of their own signs: *look*, *hawk*, *snake*, *soldier*, *maize*, *coyotl*, and more.

"We try not to speak, if we can help it," Tlaco said. "We hide during the day too. Many people travel through here, many men. We don't want to get caught by them—nothing good happens to girls who get caught by men. We watched you today."

"We thought you were chaneques," Juan said in Nahuatl, startling the girls.

"No, but we have seen strange sights in this city, and heard strange sounds, whispers and hisses, coming from underneath the ground," Tlaco whispered, a strange sparkle in her eye. She was obviously keen to tell her ghost stories, and it seemed like Juan could sense it. He asked her to go on, and she did, leaning into the fire so that her features danced.

But an idea was forming in my head, so instead of translating to Catina, I signed, "Do you still want to go to the convent, after we finish . . . doing this?"

Catina's brows knotted and she signed back, "I hadn't thought about it, truly. It felt like a good idea, but only if you were there."

"I don't want to live in a convent," I signed back.

She was silent for a moment, then glanced at Juan and signed, "I can see why."

Nano had begun to pay attention to our conversation. He watched me intently as I ignored the flush creeping up my neck and signed back, "Well, what would you wish to do instead?"

"I want to help other deaf children," signed Catina immediately, eyes gleaming with purpose. "I want to teach them Hand Talk."

I beamed, feeling a surge of warm affection and pride. "You'd be a great teacher."

"We could start a school!" Nano signed, surprising me. "But that would require funds."

"We would start small, one or two pupils at first," I signed, feeling more and more excited, and it went on like that for some time, the three of us picturing Catina's school and how she might set it up in secret so that our father could not find out, for we all agreed he would be aghast at the thought.

We spoke deep into the night. Catina fell asleep first, as usual, but Tlaco and Xoco were full of questions about who we were and why we were here. We were still unsure how much we could trust them, and held back, though they were not deterred.

"Are you grave robbers?" asked Xoco, but Tlaco clicked her tongue.

"Fool—they are much too refined for that. Look how they hold their nohpalli, with their little fingers in the air," teased Tlaco, holding her own pinkie up high, making us laugh.

"You have run away from home, then," said Xoco, narrowing her eyes.

I coughed a laugh and said, "Something like that."

Tlaco shook her head. "Of course—is it bad men? It always comes down to bad men, doesn't it. I hope they're not following you."

I tried not to share a look with Nano, but Tlaco noticed even that and sighed.

"They're following you," Xoco whispered, matter of fact.

"Not currently, we don't think," Nano said. "There was a fight before we left. I don't know if . . . I don't think they would've made it out of there all in one piece."

He looked at me, and I read the worry in his gaze. I shrugged, for there was nothing we could do, and in any case, they deserved it. The fire crackled and spat luminous freckles of ash that scattered around us as the conversation died away.

Soon enough, we began to yawn in spite of ourselves.

"We can keep watch for you," Tlaco said.

"We're used to being awake at night," Xoco added.

We said there was no need, that we would take turns with them, but none of us did.

Every single one of us fell asleep.

CHAPTER 25

Isabel Cano

31 March 1551

The next morning revealed a glorious, cloudless, piercing sky. Everything was as it had been the night before. Tlaco and Xoco were awake, the fire was still roaring, and the horses were all happily grazing in their stables. I felt a rush of gratitude toward the girls, that they had stayed up all night so that we might sleep in relative safety and comfort.

I made signs for them to take my place, and they nodded sleepily.

Juan and Nano woke up a few hours later and went out to scout the surroundings again. They came back just as Tlaco, Xoco, and Catina were rousing.

"Any luck?" I asked. The boys shook their heads and sat to drink from the guajes.

I sighed and looked up at the moon, floating full and round and silver gray amid the blue horizon. It was the only object for miles, it and the pyramids in the distance that we could not find a way into.

Tlaco came to stand beside me. She followed my line of vision and grunted. "That Juan of yours said you need to get in there . . . for some reason."

Xoco came and stood beside her sister. She looked up at me, and there was something in her open, querying gaze that made me decide to trust them.

"Before my mother died, she left something for us in there . . . inside the Pyramid of the Moon. But we can't get through the nohpalli, we can't find the entrance."

Xoco snorted, and Tlaco shook her head as if I'd said something foolish. "There's no entrance from the outside. The only way into the pyramids is through the tunnels."

"And you know where they are?" I asked, astounded.

"We do," said Tlaco, with a shrug that turned to a shiver. "But we must wait until after dark."

We built up the fire again and waited until the deep hours of the night, because the girls said the entrance into the tunnels would only open then. We did not even have to leave camp, although we each took a satchel with a few supplies and my mother's writings. The moment the moon was at its highest point, Tlaco pointed to the small temple in the center of the complex courtyard. We lit a torch, walked the few steps to the shrine, and circled to the side facing away from our camp, the one with the effigy of a serpent's head that was now glimmering and shining with a mixture of silver moon and golden torchlight.

"The head . . . it's a doorway," Tlaco whispered. "It leads to the tunnels underneath the city. You must place your arm between its fangs, and it will open. That's how we found out. I dared Xocotzin to do it, about a moon ago." Both sisters visibly shook. They looked as terrified as the night before, when we'd wrestled each other on the ground.

"Perhaps you and Xocotzin ought to stay with the horses," I ventured, and Tlaco nodded, shoulders sagging with relief.

The sisters took a step back, and the rest of us turned to face the large sculpture, the head of a snake festooned with a mane of turquoise feathers. Between its two glistening fangs was a dark, circular opening. I had thought perhaps it had been a fountain spout, but now we knew the truth. Juan and I looked at each other and then at Nano and Catina.

"I guess . . . I'll do it," I said flatly.

Nano crossed his arms protectively across his chest. "By all means, ladies first."

"My arms are too thick for that hole," Juan mumbled, avoiding my gaze.

I snorted. "Right." Then I gulped and outstretched my arm, plunging it deep into the hole of the snake's mouth. My fist pushed against something slippery and rodlike at the back.

"Xocotzin? What must I do now?" I hissed, breaking into a cold sweat.

"Turn the stick thing on its side!" Xoco called back from the shadows.

I turned the rod, and there was an echoing groan of stone. I yelped and quickly pulled my arm back right as the serpent's head slowly swung outward like a door, revealing a narrow opening with steep, carved stairs going down into the pitch-black earth.

Catina patted my shoulder and whispered, "That was very brave."

"Indeed. You've put us all to shame. I—I'll go first this time," said Nano, and stepped inside the opening, carrying the torch. Catina went after him, followed by Juan.

"Good luck!" called Tlaco and Xoco in unison, as I stepped in behind them.

The first thing I wished was that I'd run back for another torch. Some of the steps weren't wide enough for even my small feet, and I had the petrifying thought of missing one and slipping and knocking everyone down to their early deaths. I stilled my savage mind by breathing and counting, a dozen, fifty, one hundred steps, two hundred, going down, down, until they began to elongate and we reached a smaller tunnel carved with effigies of owls, bats, xolotl dogs, and other creatures of the night. The still air tasted cool and damp, and reminded me faintly of moss and mildew.

"I guess we keep going," whispered Nano, though it sounded like a wild hiss in the absolute silence of the place. We walked on in a single file. I kept my eyes down, to keep from treading on Juan's feet.

"I don't like this," Juan mumbled in front of me.

I suppressed a shiver and the sudden, overpowering need to hold his hand. Especially when Nano let out a yelp and stopped suddenly, causing us all to bump into each other.

"What is it?" I whispered. Juan was so tall and his back so broad that I could only see the shifting of Nano's torch this way and that.

Was he studying the walls? I looked closely at them too, and my breath hitched.

"These are human skulls!" Nano's voice was hoarse. "Madre Santísima, the whole wall is lined with them. There must be thousands."

"Oh . . . I really don't like this," Juan repeated. Catina began praying in Latin under her shivering breath.

I touched Juan's trembling, surprisingly warm back in what I hoped he knew was a reassuring gesture and not a push to keep going, and whispered as we walked on. "Don't worry. Look, this is Anican, she used to be a weaver, a really good one—it was a shame she had a lazy eye. And this was Ilhuicamina . . ."

"Isabel, you mustn't speak ill of the dead!" Nano said through his teeth.

"I'm not! I was about to say Ilhuicamina here, he was a renowned deer hunter, and this is his brother Cipac, who was terribly jealous of him. They were both in love with Xoxopanxoco. Look, she's here too. Even her skull is pretty. Simply admire those cheekbones. You'd never guess she was the most powerful soothsayer of her generation. Very sad story, really—she knew her marriage to Ilhuicamina was doomed from the start."

Juan's back shuddered again, this time with silent laughter. I kept my fabrications going for as long as I could. Until we reached a point where there was a fork in the tunnel path, with a turn to the right. We grouped together to study the new opening, which had a thick frame with carvings depicting the sun, tongues of fire and flaming serpents carrying it across the sky.

"Where do we go now?" Nano said. I shrugged and tapped Catina's shoulder and signed the question, hoping she'd have some ideas.

"I think this tunnel was built underneath the Avenue of the Dead." Her voice was too loud and echoed through the passageway in a way that seemed unholy. "This path surely leads to the Pyramid of the Sun, judging from these carvings. So, I believe we should keep going along the main path, toward the Pyramid of the Moon."

"There haven't been any other turns, so hopefully we'll not get lost," I whispered and signed. "We can always return if this path is a dead end."

Dead end, dead end, dead end. My voice mocked me as it carried down the tunnel. Juan and I shared a look before we turned to follow Nano.

The temperature dropped quickly. My teeth clattered and the sound drilled into my skull, until I thought that all I would ever see again were skulls with teeth, inside me and around me. The light from Nano's torch flickered and played tricks with my vision, and I thought for certain the teeth from the skulls on the wall were clattering along with mine. I thought I heard a whispering too, and attributed it to Catina's ongoing prayers, though I could not be sure. Behind me was a maw of pure darkness, and I could not help the haunting feeling that a skeletal hand would soon reach out and pull me down into black depths.

Finally, I could not bear it. I reached out and grabbed Juan's hand. His firm grip was reassuring, needy too. As if he had been waiting and hoping for me to rescue him instead.

Soon, the formation of the skulls changed. They were no longer on straight rows but undulating, like waves, and in between each row of skulls was a line with carvings and colorful paintings, glyphs that appeared to depict a naked moon goddess, surrounded by turquoise rabbits, conchs, spiders, and interwoven snakes.

The tunnel went on and on, and I wished that I'd listened more intently to Nantzin's nighttime stories of the gods and their symbols so I at least knew what I was looking at. I finally couldn't take the cold and clattering of my teeth and the whispering, whistling sound anymore and said, "Nano, can you ask Catina what she thinks these symbols mean? For if this is the city of the gods, and the Pyramid of the Moon is the feminine pyramid, is this supposed to honor the mother of the gods? But I thought that was Coatlicue."

"And I thought the goddess of the moon was Coyolxauhqui," whispered Juan.

Nano stopped in front of us and turned to sign to Catina, who sighed.

"I don't really know. Teotihuacan was built thousands of years before Tenochtitlan, before the Mexica had even left our ancestral home of Aztlan . . . the Teotihuacans must've called this goddess something different. But a goddess as powerful as this would have many names. There are many water features here on the wall, like the waves the skulls are making, and this greenish stone. Jade stone, so she could have been succeeded by Chalchiuhtlicue."

I shivered, and we walked on for another quarter of an hour or so until Nano stopped and said, "You were right, we've reached a dead end."

"What? No . . ." I whispered.

"Come see for yourself," my brother said.

I squeezed past Juan and Catina and stared at the wall at the end of the tunnel. It was painted with a magnificent mural: the image of a huge green goddess with wide-open arms, adorned with a stunning feathered headdress from which the head of a bird protruded—an eagle or owl, it was impossible to tell. She wore jewels befitting her divine nature, a long turquoise necklace and jade nose pendant with spider fangs. There appeared to be a spiral-shaped symbol near her mouth, like a curling breath.

"Can anyone else hear that whistling sound?" I said, and touched the wall all over. At the joints, I felt it, a cool sensation caressing my fingers.

"There's a breeze!" As soon as I spoke, a faint snarl sounded from behind the wall.

"Did you hear that?" I turned and looked at my siblings and Juan, who shook their heads. "I swear I heard a growl, like an animal."

Juan shuddered. "Tlaco said Xoco heard all sorts of things that she could not, when they were coming down those steps."

"Now, now, let's keep our heads on tight," said Nano. "This has to be some kind of door, if you say there is a breeze. Ah, yes, I feel it here on the edges."

"I think, perhaps, that this is the same symbol sewn on the cushion," Catina said. "But the words on the cushion—I didn't know them. Not Nahuatl . . . perhaps Teotihuacan?"

Catina tried saying the words once, twice. She emphasized them differently each time. We all took a turn, but nothing happened. Meanwhile, the whispering and growling grew louder in my ears, and I even heard the cry of a hawk. It was so cold, I was trembling from head to toe. The others seemed completely unbothered by the noise. I covered my ears, but the whispers kept rising.

"Maybe we need to say them at the same time!" I shouted, and the ruckus stopped.

Everyone turned to look at me. Nano did a count down from three, and we all said the words at the same time. There was a sudden freezing gale, and Catina and I screamed as our torch blew out. We huddled together as the stone mural slowly lifted up with a rumble and a circular chamber was revealed beyond.

The chamber glowed with the faint silver of moonlight, illuminating the surroundings: three bejeweled skeletons sitting on a stone dais upon a pitch-black floor, which was shifting strangely, like lustrous silk undulating in dark shadows.

"Why is the floor moving like that?" Juan's voice sounded like ash.

Nano murmured, "Saints, are those . . ."

"Scorpions!" Catina screamed and clambered back behind us. My mouth dried up and I fought the urge to run. There must've been hundreds of thousands of crawling spiders and scorpions, layers upon layers of black, glimmering insects, clambering over each other and back up the walls, trying to escape from something. The light, perhaps.

"Wait—they're leaving through those little holes on the walls," I squeaked.

In the space of a few frantic heartbeats, the insects were gone, revealing the rest of the contents of the chamber and several sets of pure-white bones strewed around the stone floor. I recognized the fanged skull of a jaguar and the beaked skull of an eagle. Ceramic bowls and extinct incense burners surrounded the dead, as well as thousands of obsidian and jade figurines, beautiful shells, and other offerings.

I studied these treasures until I spotted it—Nantzin's journal. It lay in between the bony hands of the middle skeleton sitting in the highest place upon the stone dais, no longer dressed but still lavishly adorned with a matching gold headpiece and necklace encrusted with tiny turquoise mosaics. Bright golden bangles surrounded its wrists and ankles.

"Shall we just . . . go in and grab it?" I asked.

No one made a move. We all huddled together in the cold tunnel, our breaths misting in front of our faces until we took a step forward in unison, then another, trying not to disturb any bones or offerings. When we were close enough to the dais, I reached out above my head and tried to gently lift the journal down, but the skeleton's grip was firm. I pulled harder, to no avail. The wind whistled through the cave, carrying the echoing sound of a woman's laugh. No one mentioned it, and I broke into a cold sweat.

"What is taking you so bloody long?" Nano hissed.

"She's not letting go," I snarled. A loud groan split the silence, and we all shouted.

The stone mural was coming down again.

"Run!" Nano shouted, grabbing Catina by the waist. "Come on!"

I pulled again to a chorus of laughter ringing in my ears. "Just—give it to me!" I shouted at the skeleton.

Juan grabbed my arm. "Isabel, it's a trap!"

"We can't leave it!" I screamed and glanced back. Nano and Catina were trying to hold the stone mural up, but it was halfway down already and showing no signs of stopping.

Catina screamed, "Hurry!" at the same time Juan took a jingling something out from his pocket and threw it at the skeleton, which immediately released its grip on the journal. I clutched the book, and we ran back to the opening, which was three-quarters of the way down. We rolled and squeezed through right before it shut with a resounding boom.

We were panting, and I felt feverishly warm, despite the cold.

"Did you get it?" asked Nano.

"Yes," I gasped. Juan whistled and Nano burst into laughter, a manic sound that tore through the darkness and somehow soothed my frenetic heart. I laughed too, in relief. There were a few clicks like flint being struck, and soon the torch was lit once again.

We walked as fast as we could away from the mural.

"Did you get it, Isabel?" Catina asked again, and I nodded. She let out a breath.

"Thank goodness that worked," Juan said, and took off his cloak. His shirt was drenched through.

"How did you get it to let go?" I asked, trying not to stare at the linen clinging to his broad, chiseled back, feeling the knowing stares of the thousands of skeletons on the wall.

"I paid for it," Juan answered.

Nano guffawed again from the front. "What do you mean, paid for it?"

"I figured these dead nobles were probably more or less the same as our new ones. You saw the treasure in there. Remember? Nothing gets done without incentives." He rubbed his index finger and thumb together, exactly as I had done all those weeks ago in his hut.

The meaning of his words snapped my legs to a halt. "You didn't!"

Juan turned and shrugged. "I did not want to be stuck in there when those spiders and scorpions came back—hey!"

I turned and ran back into the dark, feeling my way through the skeleton tunnel with my hands. My siblings and Juan yelled and chased after me. I got to the mural and banged on it, saying the Teotihuacan words again before they arrived, but the mural stayed shut.

"Say the words with me!" I yelled and signed, but everyone refused. "Nano, Catina—Juan gave all his gold for this! We must get it back."

Juan shook his head. "Isabel, we can't—"

"Juan, that gold was for you! To—to start over, and be safe, and not have to worry about the price of vanilla." Tears fell down my cheeks.

Nano's jaw slackened. He looked as panicked as I had probably looked the other day when he'd cried after killing those guards. He gulped and said, "You're crying?"

"She's crying!" Catina shouted, looking as struck and worried as my brother. She turned to him and said, "Do something!"

Nano looked around helplessly, then handed Catina the torch and began to rummage in his bag with his back to us. "I think I have a tamalli left in my pouch."

"I'm fine!" I rubbed my cheeks, but the tears would not stop flowing. "Agh—Juan, I can't believe—your gold."

Juan stepped forward and wrapped me in his arms. I clutched him to me and let his body envelop my own. I breathed his warm, welcoming musk, which reminded me of smoke and earth and something sweet, like tree sap or honey.

"I value my life. I value your life," he said, and I felt him smiling. "A simple thank-you will suffice."

I shook my head and mumbled into his chest. "No, no, it will never be enough."

"Here's the tamalli." Nano turned a mere moment after Juan and I let go of each other. Catina said nothing, but she wouldn't meet my eye.

I thanked my brother and accepted his offering. Then we all turned and walked back through the tunnel in silence.

Juan and I held each other's hands the whole way. The contact felt like a torch in and of itself, the only point of light and warmth and focus. But I had to let go when we reached the stairs, when Nano said with a trembling voice, "Actually, before we leave I'd like us to read Nantzin's story all together, if you don't mind."

I passed the book to Catina, and Nano gestured for her to do the honors.

The steps were so narrow that we could only sit one person per step. I leaned my back against Juan's knees and waited with painful anticipation as Nano held the torch over Catina's head. She took a deep breath and began.

CHAPTER 26

Tecuichpoch

1528–1531

Cortés agreed with my assessment that no self-respecting Spanish noblewoman would ever consent to marrying him if he insisted on keeping his pregnant mistress at home. He had to get rid of me, and soon. A dozen suitors of his choosing wrote back to his missive, eagerly seeking my hand. For even though I carried his child, I was still one of the wealthiest landowners in New Spain. I was the Lady of Tacuba, and my noble blood and lineage were recognized across the oceans by the Holy Emperor and his pope too.

And clearly, I was fertile. The next child, their legitimate child, would inherit it all.

"Whomever shall I honor with such distinction?" Cortés murmured, staring at the letters strewn across his horse-size wooden desk.

And I replied, bold as never before, "I think I ought to have a say in the matter, especially as your last choice was not at all to my liking."

He turned and gazed fondly at my growing belly and agreed that I could choose the man from his list. I begged him to write a quick letter to Malintzin, requesting her impressions of each of them, for they were all conquistadores, all men of his company, all older by at least a decade. I couldn't picture the faces of half of them. They had always looked the same to me: tall, bearded, shielded, murderous. I hoped she would counsel me like she had done with de Grado, and to my endless gratitude, she did.

Andrade and Cano, she wrote back, *are the only men of quality from that list. The rest are as bad as de Grado or worse.*

Cortés laughed at her response, which made me want to throttle him. He read on, saying that she sent compliments and begged us to give her son a warm embrace, and that was the extent of our correspondence.

In fact, it was the last time I would hear from her, for she succumbed to a resurgence of the great pestilence a few years later. I still think of her when I see a comet in the dark sky, a shooting star, burning bright and precious for a brief moment. Though I know her name will outshine my own, I cannot begrudge her. I thank her, even now, for her small kindnesses during the most unbearable of all wars.

So it came to be I picked Andrade, thanks to Malintzin, for his name came first. And I cannot describe my utter surprise when the man who rode into Cortés's fortress turned out to be the same novitiate from whom I had spent countless hours learning the Laws of Burgos, whose full name I had not known was Pedro Gallego de Andrade.

We were married that evening in Cortés's own chapel, and I further warmed to him when he knelt in front of me that night of our wedding and said, in a trembling voice, that he had prayed most fervently to God to bring me to his side. That the moment de Grado had died, he had realized he could never become a monk as long as the possibility existed that I could be his wife, that I could learn to love him.

And he said he would make it his life's work to earn my love and trust and show his gratitude to God for this great miracle. That my choosing him, accepting him as my husband, was the greatest honor of his life. For he knew the kind of men de Grado and Cortés were, and he had lain many nights awake in anguish, thinking of my suffering. And he would never bring me pain, he swore. He would never bring me more pain, he corrected, than he had by taking arms against my people, which was the greatest regret of his life.

He said he knew I could not forgive, but he offered his promise—that he would never touch me unless I wished it. He would never speak an unkind word. He would lay down his life for mine. Whatever it took, he would prove his worth to me.

I see him now, with those wide blue eyes looking up at me, pooling with tears, desperately wishing I believed him. Knowing, after everything I'd been through, that I never would. And still, he tried. He did not touch me on our wedding night, for I did not wish it. Not then, and not for a long time. Even after he carried me away from that monster Cortés and we moved back to my estate in Tacuba, we were caught in a dance of hesitation.

It helped that he was very handsome, same as my oldest son is now. He carried himself with pride, but he was not conceited. He was strong and lean, perceptive to any changes in my mood. Intelligent too, and kind. Children ran to him, for they knew he always carried fruits and seeds and cacao beans to give them. Dogs trailed him, pressing their snouts to his palm. Horses whinnied when he came to the stables.

As for me, he indulged my every fancy as I threw out and burned everything de Grado had ever touched and rebuilt our new home and filled it with infinite murals and paintings of birds and forests and waterfalls so that I might always feel like I was outdoors. He bought me all manner of glimmering trinkets, jewels, sweets, and cakes, and when in passing I mentioned how much I missed the food from my father's table, he went and found an old palace cook, to my lasting delight.

He still works for me even now: our Toño, who is as dear to me as my own blood.

We spoke often on whether we should release him and the rest of my slaves. Pedro urged me to do it. But I always hesitated. For how would they fare outside the confines of my encomienda? I knew how Indígenas were treated by most Spaniards, worse than cattle, worse than beasts of burden. No one cared for the Laws of Burgos, no one enforced them. Good men like Friar de las Casas who preached in the name of dignity and human decency were publicly mocked. The only limits were people's own conscience, which conquistadores and encomenderos sorely lacked.

So I kept my servants, though each day their enslavement weighed on my soul, and Pedro's gentle admonishment became more difficult to ignore. He spoke the truth, that it was the gravest of sins, the most abhorrent thing, to take away the freedom of another human being.

And though I knew some of what that felt like, in those days I snapped back, saying that these people would've been free had it not been for him and his coyotl Spaniards. And even though it was not completely true, for we Mexica had enslaved thousands before the Spaniards had ever set foot in Anahuac, he would fall silent except to say that he repented for the pain he had caused us and all he could do was to show me his everlasting remorse.

He really *was* lovely to me, looking back. His dearest, most heartfelt wish was to bring me back some of the ease and comfort which I'd lost at the hands of so many of his friends and comrades, and of himself. There was nothing he would not do, if I asked.

He rubbed my feet when they swelled and I could hardly walk. He agreed to bring the weeping sorceress of Xochimilco to our home so that I could have as painless a birth as possible. And after my Leonor was born and she was taken from me by her father's kin, he held me in his arms as I rocked with sorrow. For although I had pledged to give the child back to Cortés, I did not count on how it would hurt me, how it would gut me. Even though she was the spitting image of her father, I would have happily kept her, my firstborn, my girl.

Giving Leonor away was the worst mistake of my life, and Pedro was the only reason I did not tie stones to my feet and throw myself into the deepest part of the lake.

Each morning he brought breakfast into my chamber and coaxed and fed me, and we walked together through the forest. Every afternoon we watched the sunset painting the dark waters in front of our new home in shades of pink and blue. Though at first it was colorless to me. I could not relish any of it, this newfound freedom to walk through nature again, and hear the sounds of birds, and feel the soft, cool moss underneath my bare feet.

But after many months, this fresh new wound sutured and joined all the others, those thousands of cuts and lesions that had turned my heart into a living, weeping tapestry of pain. I wonder, sometimes, how it has managed to beat for so long, and if perhaps this is why I am dying now, though I am not so greatly advanced in age and I have children who are young. Indeed, my grandmothers lived far longer than I did, and my mother would've too, had it not been for the pestilence. But here I am, dying, and soon, when there is still much more to tell.

I want it to be known, I want to make it clear, that Pedro helped me. Though it terrified me that I should care for him. That I should begin to look upon his face and swell with nothing but affection and a deep yearning. There were times I hated my body for betraying me so, betraying me to this conquistador who had helped to bring me and my family so low. But he instinctively knew this, and if ever I stilled or froze at his touch, he would let go and murmur, beg forgiveness, remind me of his undying love, until I softened once more. Then he would start anew the careful kisses and reverent caresses that I had begun to relish.

And after a time I learned to care not that he was Spanish, or that he had sailed from across the seas to follow Cortés.

For, I argued with myself, had it not been a Mexica, my own husband, who had lacerated my soul when he murdered my most beloved brother, an innocent boy of ten? Had it not been a Mexica, my own father, who had gifted me as a concubine to his worst enemies?

Therefore, I reasoned, perhaps it did not matter where they came from. Perhaps all men in this great, big, unforgiving world were worse than wolves, and I ought to be glad to have found a rare exception. A man who worked each day to cherish me, who delighted in me, worshipped me, who brought me the only pleasure I'd felt in years.

One who never wavered from his candlelit vows made only to me in the presence of his single, precious God.

Indeed, after a time I let myself be loved by him, and I rejoiced, I truly did, when I realized that I was bringing Pedro's child into the world. And when my son was born, it felt like I was bringing forth a light, a boy unlike others, made from sweet matter, from love and gladness and trust. My first baby boy. Juan Andrade, my heir, my little tlatoani. How much hope he brought me! Hope that I had not survived in vain, that I would have another child to keep my bloodline alive, a boy to hold Tacuba for the Moctezumas forevermore.

We held a great banquet in his honor, and the newly appointed bishop of New Spain, Bishop Zumárraga, gave him his rites of baptism, and Pedro beamed with pride and joy. And I, too, was so swept up in my love for my son that for once I did not mind so much the stares from everyone around me—the newly arrived Spanish ladies gawking at my beautiful huipil and long, unveiled hair; the careful glances from the surviving Mexica noblewomen who had been bartered into marriages with the conquistadores holding on to them, who leered at me as though I were a dish they'd love to savor. I ignored them, held on to the crook of Pedro's arm, tightened my hold on my beautiful boy, and eased my lips into the demure smile my mother had taught me. A smile that revealed nothing at all.

A smile very unlike the one I gave Pedro that night, when he told me again, for the thousandth time, how much he loved me. When I finally gave in and opened my heart to his tender love. Despite my best efforts to crush my feelings, to keep my heart safe, it gave way just as stone eventually does to the constant trickle of pure, sparkling water.

And I will tell you, dear one, that I am not ashamed to admit that I fell in love with him, a conqueror who had thought to become a priest. I had been among the like my whole life, those holy warriors, so he was nothing new to me in that regard. My father and grandfathers had been the same; my first four husbands too. Men who thought themselves gods, who had taken land and men and women because they believed it was their birthright.

But this man, this Spanish man, I believe truly regretted the harm he had caused us in his youthful greed and lust. He had been the first man to see me as more than a pretty thing to own and use and trade. And he had loved me, oh yes, he had loved me like I was the fabled treasure he had crossed the entire ocean for.

In a way, I am glad I did not believe him sooner. I am glad I held off opening my heart to him for those first few years. For that night of Juan's baptism, after we had fallen asleep, the Earth Lady Tlaltecuhtli came to claim her prize, just as the healer in the forest had forewarned when I used the poison that killed de Grado, though I had long forgotten her.

But I know it was the goddess who shortened his life, because I had never allowed myself to truly feel the buoyant, warm brightness he coaxed from me, and because there was nothing wrong with Pedro's health. But his heart simply stopped beating while he slept.

The goddess Tlaltecuhtli swallowed it whole, and left my baby and me in desolation.

And I swore in my grief that I would never again marry. I swore I would never love another man, that I would only ever love my son, and the daughter I had foolishly given away and whom I would've given anything to hold again in that moment.

All these vows I would not keep.

But that is a tale for another day.

My hope is that you will find it.

CHAPTER 27

Isabel Cano

1 April 1551

I bent over on my knees and wept. Openly, unashamedly, in front of my sister and brother and dearest friend. And my racking sobs echoed into the dark tunnel and were soon joined by the hiccuping cries of Catina, and the shuddering, sharp breaths of Nano, and the low, choked murmur of Juan, who rubbed my shoulders.

"She suffered too much," I wailed. "And she never deserved any of it. Not any of it!"

"Of course she didn't," said Juan, and something raw in his voice made me think he felt the same for his own mother, another woman whose life had been marked and stolen by the voracious greed of men. I straightened up and clasped his hand with my own again.

After a pause, Nano said in a quiet voice, "Nantzin never spoke of Andrade's father." In the flickering torchlight, his eyes looked swollen. He absentmindedly patted Catina's shoulder, who was sitting on the step below him, still crying.

"Not to us anyway. But perhaps to Andrade," I said.

"He turned out very different from his father," Nano said, voice thick with bitterness.

"It's true, she spoiled him," I mused. "He could've been sweet. Remember how he used to be sweet to us girls? And he still is with Mari. He is good to her. But . . . she always gives him what he wants. Just like Nantzin did. Perhaps she felt guilty that his father died."

"It sounds like she thought it was her fault," Juan added. "For using that death potion."

"She had to!" I said a little defensively. "She couldn't stay with de Grado."

"Or with Cortés." Nano nodded. "I wonder if that's also why Nantzin left so much gold to Leonor."

"Maybe," I said, then sighed. "We ought to have been kinder to Leonor. She didn't even grow up with her father, though perhaps that was for the best."

"We can always write to her and offer an olive branch," Nano said, and groaned as he tapped Catina on the shoulder and lifted himself to stand. "But for now, I am cold and weary and in desperate need of a piss."

Juan and I spluttered a laugh.

"You are revolting," I said, though my lips twitched into a grin.

We climbed the rest of the way up in silence and found Tlaco and Xoco waiting for us in camp. They had let the fire die, but the sky was beginning to lighten and birds were beginning to stir and sing.

"Did you find what you were searching for?" Tlaco said, and I nodded.

"Good. I'm relieved you're back in one piece," she murmured before laying on her side to rest. I volunteered to finish the dawn watch, but after a few moments, I found it too difficult to stay awake, so I rose and walked a few steps away, toward the stable.

I looked up at the moon and thought of Nantzin again, of how much she had kept hidden from us, though I could not find it in my heart to blame her.

I simply felt . . . robbed . . . of the mother I could've known.

Memories of her flittered in front of my vision, like pages turning in a book I had not understood until now. The far-off, shuttered look in her eyes, her half smile at church, how we sometimes had to call her three, four times before she would answer. How it always took her a moment to catch on, and how she blinked as if she were waking from a dream.

Don't disturb your mother was what we often heard, from servants, from Marta, from Papa. It was the first, most important rule in our family, though she never said it herself. As far as I can remember, we trod carefully around her, our own, wounded creature of myth, who would disappear for hours into the forest if we could not rein ourselves in and be good.

I realized with a pang that I had spent my whole life missing her, grieving her. The parts she had never been able to show us, until now. And there was only one chapter left, though this did not strike me with as much sorrow as it might have a few weeks ago.

I finally felt a wind of hope now, for what my future might hold, with Catina and our school, with Nano and Elvira . . . and with Juan.

I looked back down at the camp, and it was almost as if he could hear my thoughts, because Juan shifted and rose from where I thought he was sleeping. He sidestepped my brother who was snoring and walked quietly toward me.

The gloom in my heart immediately lifted, and I turned away, toward the gentle horses, as if they might help me fix the mess that was my face and cropped hair. There was no point even trying to wipe my tear-streaked cheeks clear of dirt and pinch them for color, for my fingertips were almost black with a layer of grime. I tried to wipe some of it off on my filthy skirts before I felt, rather than heard, Juan's presence behind me, warm and beckoning.

"Can you not sleep?" I whispered as I rubbed the horse's mane.

"No," he murmured. "I keep thinking about—well, about your mother."

I whirled to look at him. He hesitated by the entrance, giving the horses a wary look.

I walked closer to him, and wordlessly we sat beside each other on the steps. He took my hand in his, and I felt a blossoming warmth rising up from my gut to the tip of my ears. I stared at our intertwined fingers, at the lovely tanned and brown pattern they made, no longer worried about dirt.

Juan lifted our joined hands and kissed them, a gesture so tender that it made me ache with a blend of longing and gratitude. Then he said, tentatively, "I keep thinking . . . and, and wondering, whether your mother . . . if she would've liked me."

I lifted my eyes to meet his and saw there was an ocean of depth behind his question. I nodded, trying to think of the right words to reassure him, but he looked away and rushed to say, "If she had met me, and known who . . . who my parents were, and how poor I am. How little I can offer you. A life of hardship, of working your hands raw just to survive. Even this perilous journey has been a welcome reprieve from the endless worries. How could any mother want that for her child? You would live a life of dignity and safety in the convent, of comfort. I want you to know, I would never begrudge you that life."

I squeezed his fingers tight and used my other hand to tilt his cheek so he would look down at me again. His quick puffs of breath warmed my face lightly, bringing to mind the pleasant bitterness of chocolatl.

My throat burned with emotion as I whispered, "If Nantzin had known you, she would've seen how . . . how kind and brave you are. How gentle and patient and noble you are. You have never needed a title for that. And she would've loved you. I know in my soul, she would have. She wanted me to be safe, yes, but I have never felt more safe than when I'm by your side. If I had known then, and told her what I truly wanted, she would've understood."

Juan swallowed hard and leaned his face on my hand. His curls fell over my fingertips, and I tucked them back behind his ear. They were as soft as I'd imagined them to be, and for some reason, that knowledge made me feel desperately sad. My face pinched. My thoughts careened past my vision, the image of me snapping at him on the canoe, at my brother in the forest. Hurting him over and over and eventually pushing him away.

But Juan caught my falling hand and asked, "What's the matter?"

I didn't want to say it, but because he had been truthful with me, and because his face looked as open and willing as the cloudless sky above us, I felt I ought to be open with him too. I ought to return this gift of trust he had given me, even though it made me feel as frightened as if I were running back into the nest of scorpions crawling in the tunnels underneath our feet.

I opened my mouth twice before I steeled myself and managed to choke out, "I don't think I . . . I fear . . . *you* might never be happy with me." Juan's brows knotted with confusion and something akin to hurt, and I rushed to clarify. "Because I'm not . . . like you. I'm not kind. I'm rough, and mean, and quick to strike in anger. I'm not gentle, or sweet."

Juan's face shone with relief, and he let out a soft chuckle before saying, "Whoever said I wanted sweet?" That drew a huff of soft laughter from my lips, but before I could respond, his expression grew serious again. He drew closer to me, so close I could make out every island of gold in the brown sea of his irises.

"Isabel, you are passionate, yes." His expression softened into a shy smile that matched mine. "But everyone who truly knows you knows there is no one more caring than you. The way you protect Catina, the way you challenge Nano—it comes from a good and loving place. They love you for it, and I do . . . I love you too."

My lips parted and my breathing stopped, but I could not quite believe what I'd heard. I stammered, somewhat stupidly, "You—you love me?"

Juan nodded, and smiled with a hint of pity at the look on my face. "Indeed, I do."

I chuckled and murmured, "And I . . . I love you too."

And I could not tell if it was he who moved first or me, or whether we moved together to bridge the tiny space that remained between our lips. And our touch was feather soft at first, but no less miraculous, for it seemed like the compass of my world shifted and the only true north in existence was this kiss, here and now.

And then Juan tilted his head and caught my lower lip with more force, and a more delicious feeling I could not have dreamt of. Everything swam with a light so potent that I was gloriously blinded, and I felt like those portraits at church, of saints pierced by a halo of infinite brightness, lifted into the heavens.

Only when the horses behind us huffed and snorted did we break away from each other. We were still holding hands. Days might have passed, and I would not have known. He, too, was swaying, and looked as dazed and astonished as I felt. We leaned in once more, but someone in the campsite stirred and coughed.

Juan sighed. "It's probably best if we get some rest."

I rolled my eyes, and he smirked, then rose and pulled me up to my feet, wordlessly, and we ambled back to the campsite together. He kissed my hand again before settling down next to me, and I ran my hands through his curls and over his forehead and watched him fall asleep.

And I felt a fierce protectiveness of him then, more powerful than I had ever felt in my life for anyone else, including Catina. A feral feeling at the thought of him suffering. I wanted to be able to soothe him like this always, to burn the people who had given him cause to doubt himself—idiots like Andrade.

Because I knew he was another gift from Nantzin. That she had seen through my ruse and sent him to me: In my hour of greatest need, he had been there. I closed my eyes and thanked her for him, and in the warm breeze I thought I felt her smile.

◆ ◆ ◆

It was past midday by the time I woke after swapping a watch with Nano, and we decided our next move. We studied the drawing I'd made of the next clue, of the eagle flying over a long, smoking mountain, and agreed it was the volcano of Iztaccihuatl, as it had been marked on the tapestry map with a cross, like every other place we'd been to before.

"But the volcano is enormous—how will we know where to look?" Nano said.

"Let's get there and make sense of what we're dealing with," I said.

Tlaco and Xoco shared a worried look, and I laughed. "Oh, you don't think we'd simply abandon you, after everything you've done for us? No, I have a . . . proposition for you."

"What's that?" Tlaco said with narrowed eyes.

Nano turned, too, and tapped Catina's shoulder to grab her attention.

I said and signed, "What if I told you there was a safe place for you to live together for the rest of your lives, where you'd never have to worry about food, or being cold—where you'd never have to worry about men."

Nano's lips parted, but he stayed silent. Catina beamed and nodded for me to go on.

Xoco smiled sadly and whispered, "There is no such place."

Tlaco's eyes were slits. "And even if there was, I would say, 'Why are *you* not there now?'"

The corner of my lips twitched, and I involuntarily glanced at Juan, thinking of the way he'd kissed me this very morning. Tlaco did not miss this and fixed me with a shrewd look that heated my neck and face.

I cleared my throat, then said and signed, "It is a real place, called a convent, where women live. They take vows of chastity, poverty, and obedience in honor of Christ."

"These women are like monks? We had monks come to our village," Tlaco said, placing her fists over her hips. "They professed to be chaste, but our older sister said some of them were not."

Juan's face darkened at this. I did not know what else to say, so I answered, "They are like monks, indeed. They are called nuns."

"Only Spaniards can be monks. We are not Spaniards," Tlaco said, matter of fact.

"No, indeed. Most nuns are Spanish women, or born to two Spanish parents. We are Mestizas, but we have lifelong places secured in the convent. Everything is paid for."

"And you do not wish to take these places?" Tlaco repeated, as though we might be more stupid than she had originally thought. Which was probably true.

"I . . . I am not . . . prepared to take their vows," I said, avoiding eye contact with everyone, especially my brother and Juan, for it was a coarse thing for a lady to admit that she did not wish to be chaste forever.

"What about her?" Xoco bent her head toward Catina. I signed the question to her, relieved to have everyone's attention diverted away from me.

Catina answered, "In truth, I would be happy in the convent. I could teach deaf children there, I am sure. The vows do not faze me." She paused, then looked at me, eyes shining. "But I would miss my sister too much. I may not wish to live in her shadow, or be at her mercy, but I do wish . . . to have her always in my life."

My throat caught, and my lip trembled. I nodded back at her, not trusting myself to speak, but she understood. Our love had never needed words.

"Well," Tlaco said, kicking a rock by her feet, "if neither of you want to live in this warm, safe, man-free space with endless food, we'll take it off your hands."

Xoco cackled. "Where is this refuge, and when can we leave?"

We gathered our things and began the journey south. Neither Tlaco nor Xoco nor Juan knew how to ride, so we split them up between us Canos.

Nano took Tlaco, who was keen to learn and was soon cantering several lengths before us. Xoco went happily with Catina, who eagerly responded to her entreaties to hear more tales of the old gods. Juan sat behind me, holding my waist so tight that it would've made me reel had he not been so petrified of falling. I laughed and spurred the horse to a trot, and he shrieked, a shrill, high sound. I guffawed and did it again.

"Please! I paid a skeleton a fortune for our lives!" He hugged me tighter, but after a while, his body eased into rhythm with mine.

The hours and scenery passed in a luscious blur as I leaned back against Juan's chest and enjoyed the warm comfort of his arms around my core. We hardly even spoke. We did not need to. I had never in my life felt happier, and I knew he felt the same.

As we rode, the girls asked more questions: how we had earned a place of honor at the convent, and how they could possibly pass as well-bred ladies when they could not even read or write or speak Castilian fluently.

At least they had both been baptized. Thus, we spent most of the ride teaching the sisters basic manners and other facts about our family and the court. There was not much we could do about their Castilian, but at least they understood the basics of the Catholic religion.

"Really, I think all you have to do is take a vow of silence and never meet our father or brothers, even if they come to visit. Just send them away. Keep to yourselves. Wear a veil over your faces. No one else will know you're not us. I've lost count of how many times I've heard the coyotl Spaniards say that they cannot tell Indígenas apart."

Tlaco's eyes glinted. "If I weren't so tired of being hungry and, well, tired, I would be worried about spending a lifetime surrounded by Spanish women."

"Perhaps it is a small consolation, but most women who end up in convents do tend to be of a more un-*convent*-ional nature," Nano joked from behind her. When they didn't respond, he sighed. "I mean, they might not be so bad."

Tlaco and I shrugged at the same time.

"And if they are," I said, "you can always escape."

Tlaco shook her head. "If the food is good, I will bear this new life with good cheer."

I had a fluttering of doubt then, of what I was giving up. Those basic things Nantzin had been without more times than she would've cared for: a full belly, security, peace. The future she had offered us, her beloved daughters. Was I spurning my mother's last blessing? But it did not feel that way. I was giving it to someone who truly wanted it.

And perhaps it would grate Tlaco and Xoco eventually, to be surrounded by the unwanted women of New Spain. Or perhaps they would flourish. Whatever lay ahead, I felt in my bones that the convent was not for me; it had never been for me. And if this quest was Nantzin's way of showing me a different path, a different future, of giving me a choice, however uncertain it might be—I would take it.

We crossed two shallow rivers before reaching the old city of Texcoco, flush with spiraling ferns and sweet-smelling pines, alive with the song of birds readying themselves for the night, a sound I'd sorely missed. Huddles of small lime-coated stone buildings and newly cobbled streets lined the edge of a third river flowing onto the eastern shore of the grand lake, which was glimmering in brilliant hues of purple and pink, mirroring the sun setting beyond the distant mountain range.

We dismounted and found our way to the busy embankment, as we'd agreed it would be best to get Tlaco and Xoco to the convent as soon as possible, before too many people started asking questions—or sent a search party for us, if they hadn't already.

I inhaled the perfume of the water. Unlike the grassy mildew of the western marshes, or the humid earthiness of the southern chinampas, the eastern shore smelled like fresh brine, clean and beckoning. I fought the urge to dip in for a swim and instead joined the search among the canoes and skiffs gathered along the shore.

There was a passenger barge leaving for Tenochtitlan within the hour, so we sold one of the horses to pay for fresh clothing and passage for Tlaco and Xoco.

"Just ask for directions to the Convento—there's only one, so you cannot possibly get lost. They were expecting us days ago. Tell them the guards abducted you, but you got away—get upset and they'll probably leave you alone for weeks!"

We practiced them saying the words in Castilian, and their performances were so convincing that I would've thought them blue-blooded damsels had I not known better. Then, Catina took off her signet ring and gave it to Tlaco.

Her voice wavered as she whispered, "This should help if anything goes wrong. No one shall question that you are a Moctezuma while you're wearing this. You're going to be safe, fed, and warm for the rest of your lives."

Tlaco gave us both a piercing look and a sharp nod. "I will return this to you one day."

"When you no longer have need of it," I said, voice thick with emotion.

We said our goodbyes and watched the girls as they shrank into tiny shadows with the trailing barge and melded into the blurry island in the far distance.

We spent some of the silver from the horse sale on two rooms inside a neat, pleasant tavern by the shores of Texcoco. I was overjoyed to be able to clean myself and sleep in a fresh straw bed next to Catina, and we spoke for hours of all the plans and dreams for the school we would open together, until we fell asleep.

And that night, I dreamt I was an eagle again.

I perched on the tip of a flowering cactus, the only object on a tiny island surrounded by an endless, peaceful lake. The hot sun warmed my beautiful brown feathers; the light gleamed over the bend of my golden beak. A breath of air cascaded over the surface of the water, making it ripple. It flowed upward, carrying a song of sorrow, which disturbed my plumage. The wind stirred an urge in me, impossible to suppress. I dug my powerful talons into the supple flesh of the cactus and launched myself high, opening the length of my wingspan and gliding on the current of warm air up into the azure endlessness above. The song intensified until I found the source. A dying woman, covered in a mantle of snow. She beckoned to me, and I landed on her right breast.

This is where you find me, she said.

The next morning, I woke up with my vision as clear and sharp as the eagle's. We would find Nantzin's journal on the peak of Iztaccihuatl.

How we would climb it, however, was another matter.

We continued on horseback along the road toward the small lakeside pueblo of Chalco, a journey that took most of the day and brought us closer to the famed volcanoes, the Popocatepetl and Iztaccihuatl, revered as star-crossed lovers since the dawn of memory. Puffs of white smoke unfurled from the Popocatepetl, while the many peaks of the Iztaccihuatl made us fall into a thoughtful silence. Climbing her would not be an easy task.

As night approached and the sun faded behind thickening gray clouds, we decided to find a room somewhere in Chalco. A quiet, bleak place, hardened as only places that dare to exist at the foot of fiery mountains can be. Townsfolk hurried to clear their wares from the central market, wary of the quickly approaching storm, but they pointed to a house in the distance when we asked if there was anywhere to stay. A clap of thunder unleashed a downpour as we turned the horses and rode to the house. I knocked, and a towering figure opened the wooden door to us, letting out a waft of the most delicious, familiar smells.

I looked up at his face, and let out a strangled cry of astonishment—for the man standing in front of me was our old cook, Toño.

CHAPTER 28

Isabel Cano

2 April 1551

Toño's eyes widened for a fraction of a heartbeat before he frowned at the sheet of rain pounding into the mud around us and on top of our trembling bodies.

He grumbled in Nahuatl, "I guess you're staying the night." Then he flicked his chin and added, "You can tie the horses out on the back post."

Nano and Juan hurried off, and Toño showed Catina and me inside his home, an adobe structure with a pair of cone-like thatched roofs built like a figure of eight. It was made up of two large round rooms separated by a small opening to what must've been the kitchen, if the warmth and flickering firelight and heavenly scents were anything to go by.

This room was dimly lit by a single clay brazier, revealing several reed mats neatly rolled and stacked against the wall, which was painted a faded shade of yellow. A broom hung on a nail by the door, clearly one of the more used items, for the spotless stone floor appeared to have recently been swept. I warmed with embarrassment at the muddy trail of footprints left behind by my boots, but Toño did not seem any more bothered than usual. He pointed to a trio of stools positioned next to a flat wooden chest that clearly doubled as a table and said, "Take a seat. I will bring your dinner."

"I can help!" I offered, but Toño shook his head. "You are my guests. Sit and rest."

I signed to Catina, who obeyed, but as soon as Nano and Juan entered, carrying our soaking supplies, I made them take off their boots and began to sweep, which was a stupid move, as it only brushed the muck around the floor, leaving ugly, elongated stains.

"Sweep *after* the mud dries," whispered Juan, with a dazzling smile that made my breath hitch, before he carefully laid down the rest of the gear and hung his dripping cloak on another makeshift hook by the door. Nano followed, then clapped his hands as Toño returned with a pair of steaming ceramic bowls.

"What have you made, dear man?" Nano said. "It's so unbelievably good to see you. Did you know, I've taken a liking to food recently?"

"This is frog-leg stew," Toño grunted. "With ahuacatl and chilacayote."

"My . . . favorite." Nano blinked, but he sat on the stool opposite Catina with good grace. Juan offered me the last seat, but I wanted to stretch my legs after riding all day. Toño unrolled a mat, disappeared, and then reappeared several times with two more bowls, a basket lined with a cotton cloth containing a small tower of delicate tortillas, and an additional plate.

"For the bones," he said.

I immediately sat on the mat next to the wooden table and dipped a tortilla into the broth. I scooped a chunk of smooth green ahuacatl, filling my mouth with its nutty, creamy flavor, followed by the earthiness of the maize tortilla cooked over the wood fire.

Toño hovered nearby, underneath the kitchen opening, blocking it with his massive build. His tanned fists, crisscrossed with scars from dozens of burns over the years, were curled on top of his hips. He watched me with a look of thunder, just as he had done a thousand times before. I said nothing, waiting for his impatience to boil over.

This had always been one of our favorite games.

He finally burst. "Well?" I hummed and nodded in pleasure. He huffed, which I knew to mean he was satisfied. I looked up and caught his eye. There was a gleam there that made me smile, for I knew then he was as glad to see me as I was to see him.

"This meat is so tender. My goodness!" Juan exclaimed, in between nibbles of a frog leg. "What is that *flavor*?"

Toño eyed him with a hint of curiosity and muttered, "I seared the meat in butter before adding it into the stew. It works nicely with charal fish as well, that butter. It's the only good thing these coyotl Spaniards have brought over with them." He flicked his chin at Nano, as if he was somehow more of a Spaniard than myself or my sister, though a lot of people treated him that way because of his lighter skin and eyes.

I frowned, but Nano winked at the cook. His charm was on full display as he said, "Now, now—I've seen you enjoying a bite of pork every so often. And chicken, and beef, and lamb."

"I would rather never have had cause to taste them," Toño hissed, and Nano sighed.

"Fair point," he murmured before grabbing a frog leg and tearing off the flesh.

Toño stared for a moment longer, then turned back to me and said, "And perhaps one of you could explain why your brothers came charging through town yesterday, demanding directions to the top of the White Woman?"

Juan, Nano, and I whirled to look at him.

Catina choked on some broth and said, "What's happening?"

I put my bowl down and signed to explain, then said, "Pedro and Gonzalo came here?"

"They came through Chalco on horseback with one of them blasted dogs," Toño said. "I watched them, but they did not see me. They loaded their horses with ropes and food and rode off after the townsfolk drew them a map."

Nano swore and Juan shook his head. I spluttered and signed and said, "They were here . . . yesterday?"

Toño nodded. "More than a full day ago."

Catina read his lips and said, "But . . . they'll be miles away by now."

"We'll have to run to catch them," I whispered.

"Neither you nor they will get far in this storm," Toño said.

"But we must get to the top of Iztaccihuatl before them!" I said. "It's . . . important."

He huffed and looked away for a moment before saying, "If you stay the night and rest, I shall tell you how."

"My mother's people were snow runners back in the old days," said Toño that night after we had all finished our meals. "They were strong and fast and would use an ancient trail to climb up and down the mountain to collect snow for the huey tlatoani and his family. It was a delicacy, you see, to flavor the frozen crystals with fruit juice or vanilla or honey and chia and amaranth seeds. Your grandfather was mad for it. I myself climbed the mountain many times, when I was a boy."

He explained the trek would not be easy, and that we would need to leave our horses at some point. "And you must spend the night at one of the refuges higher up the volcano. Otherwise, you will get sick from the climb and die."

On the stone floor, using a piece of charcoal, he drew us a map of the many peaks along the Iztaccihuatl. "She is like a sleeping woman. Camp the night before you attempt the summit. You will need to carry water, for there is only snow in the volcano, and building a fire to melt it is much too difficult. I will give you extra rations, because it might take a day or even two to return to Chalco."

We uncurled the reed mats, and I slept fitfully that night beside Catina, who mumbled gibberish in her dreams. Juan and Nano settled back to back in the same room as us, while Toño made himself comfortable in his kitchen, although at one point I wondered if his snores would knock the entire structure down.

He woke us at dawn, as promised, and we realized he'd gone off and gathered even more provisions for us: rabbit furs to cover our hands and ears, and woolen tights and capes. He refused to accept our silver, but I went ahead and hid it underneath the clay brazier anyway.

We dressed as warmly as we could, for even down here it was chilly and damp with dew. At least the clouds had parted and the day was clear. Nano donned his sword and gave me his bow and quiver to strap over my cloak. Toño had told us there were many travelers who frequented the pass between the volcanoes, not all of whom were friendly.

Toño pointed to the long volcano in the near distance and said, "Remember, you will scramble at first, for it is rocky as you make your way up the wall of the Woman's feet. Then there are more steep rocks to the knees. The trek goes up and down, up and down many times as you walk along the legs and thighs and torso. And then you tread down, down onto her stomach, which is covered with ice. Be careful not to slip—go slowly, slowly. Then head back up toward the spiral rock that marks her belly button, and you will finally see the breasts. The right one is the higher peak. When you get there, don't forget to give thanks to Iztaccihuatl for providing you with safe passage, or you may never return."

As the others loaded the horses, I approached him, daring for once to touch him on the arm. He froze and did not look at me as I whispered, "Twice you helped me now, Toño. When you gave me that book so many weeks ago, and now. Even though my mother—even though she kept you from this life . . . all those years."

An apology seemed so insufficient, so empty a gesture, that the words stuck on the bolus of shame gliding up my throat, blocking it.

Toño studied my face and sighed. "There is no excusing your mother, child. However noble her reasons were. It took her too long to make good on her promises to set us free. But her choices no longer determine mine. I finally do as I please, and it pleases me to help you in this matter, which we both know you will not give up on."

I sniffed. "She trusted you."

"I fed you, and her, and all her children, did I not?"

"All my life," I replied hoarsely. "You made us the best food in all Tenochtitlan."

He nodded and murmured, "Food never lies."

I threw my arms around his torso and squeezed before walking away with tears in my eyes. For I understood his meaning—that he had cooked for us, cooked the best meals, because he cared. He helped us now because he cared. It had always been his choice to care. Even though we were the children of the woman who had kept him enslaved.

I would never understand. I would never master that kind of mercy.

He did not wave goodbye, but I hoped we would see him again on our return.

I mounted my horse, and Juan once again settled behind me, much more at ease. Catina took the reins this time, and Nano sat behind her. If either of them noticed the way Juan hugged me to his chest and kissed my cheek from behind, they did not say, though I grinned like a fool and felt a bubbling rush of mirth, which nearly made me giggle like those blushing women at court. I stole a glance at my siblings, but they both seemed distracted, awestruck by the mountains towering in front of us.

A steady column of gray steam was rising from the top of the Popocatepetl. The Smoking Mountain always made his presence known, but this felt a little foreboding somehow. Nano frowned, looking determined. He patted Catina's arm and said, "Let's move."

They took the lead, and we trotted into the forest surrounding the volcanoes. Tree roots stitched the soft, leaf-strewn path, cleared by heavy traffic of the brambles and ferns encasing the feet of towering ocotes and thick moss-covered oaks. Monarch butterflies and a multitude of other flying insects flitted between tufts of pine needles and angled shafts of weakened sunlight. Tiny birds hopped from branch to fallen trunk, trilling a song that echoed far beyond our line of sight.

As for us, apart from the horses' hooves rustling the dead leaves along the trail, we were silent, alert for any signs of our brothers. A squirrel sprung out in the path in front of us, and I tried to shoot it, but I could not get my arrow out in time and missed. Nano saw this and chuckled quietly, a smug look on his face.

"There goes breakfast," he said, and I stuck my tongue out at him.

The sun was high up by the time we reached a gushing stream. The horses were unsettled. We thought they might be thirsty, so we hopped off to give them a break, let them drink, and also to refill our guajes. The wind cascaded through the trees, jostling as many leaves in the canopy above us as there were stars in the heavens. The clamor was deafening, but we mounted and rode on.

The forest thinned, and we reached the wide-open pass between the two mountains, which Hernán Cortés had modestly named after himself.

We continued trotting endlessly upward on a rough, slightly muddy road, framed by miles of bushes and tall, swaying grasses and solitary pines, gleaming after yesterday's rain. Their fresh perfume mingled with the sweet notes of leather from the saddle and the warm, lively musk from our horses. I wished to go ever faster, to gallop with my cape billowing behind me, all the way up to the top of the mountain, but the horse would not cope long at that speed with both Juan and me on its back.

At the same time, I worried about my brothers—where they might be, whether they might find Nantzin's journal before us. What would they do with it? Would they burn it, like I'd been tempted to do the first time I read one? Would they try to use it as a bargaining piece? To get us to give up Juan, perhaps? So Pedro might get away with killing Marta?

Well, it would never happen. I would shoot them both first.

I pictured the grim scenario as if I were studying it from a vantage point, like a bird. I did not wish to kill them, no, but it would do them good to be maimed a little. If I shot their sword hands, it would tarnish their manliness as well. It would take them years to recover their grip strength. Perhaps they would finally learn their lesson.

Oh, how I wished to be the one to teach them.

I scanned the horizon, but there were no signs of other people around. Ladybugs and bees and grasshoppers chirped and buzzed alongside us. Zooming flies annoyed the horses, making their ears twitch and their tails flicker. But apart from the insects, it was only us, our horses, and the two volcanoes towering on either side of the pass. The storm and the menacing-looking steam rising from the Popocatepetl must've scared the usual travelers away.

Once again, I wondered *who* had journeyed this way on behalf of Nantzin.

Not Toño, for the two guards had spoken of a woman. Marta, perhaps? No, she could not have done all this, and she would not have done it on principle. I almost laughed aloud at the thought of her descending the steps to the tunnels beneath the pyramids in Teotihuacan, of seeing the rows upon rows of skulls. She would've fainted outright.

Then it struck me raw that she, too, was a skeleton now, as hard and white as any of those thousand others lining the walls of the tunnels. My lip wobbled, and I wished again I could've done more for her. I *would* do more, I vowed.

In my mind's eye, I once again drew targets around my brothers' hands.

After some hours, a hare skirted across the path, but I was too slow again.

This time, Nano snapped at me. "I'll take the bow back if you miss again!" which irked me to no end, but I kept my mouth shut. I did not wish to admit that I was finding it difficult to concentrate with Juan's hands on my hips.

"Sorry," Juan whispered in my ear, but my reply died in my throat when a sudden rumbling shook the earth and I was robbed of sense.

Catina screamed, expressing the terror I could not. Grass and bushes rustled violently, like peacock feathers in a courtship dance. The horses neighed and reared, throwing us all off. I landed with a thud on top of Juan, who groaned in pain. The impact winded me, and in between tiny quavering orbs of blinding light, I saw that the horses had bolted. By the time I regained my breath and vision, they were gone.

We continued juddering with the ground around us. Stones and rocks bounced around rippling brown puddles, until the earth stopped trembling as swiftly as it began.

Nano cried out as he struggled onto his feet and stumbled to Catina's side. She whimpered, "I'm fine, fine!"

"Are you hurt?" Juan said to my brother, who had bent over, hands on his knees.

Nano shook his head in response.

"I'm—sorry," I breathed, "for—crushing you—like that." A stream of sweat was dripping over my temples and nose. My fingertips were shaking, my whole body.

Juan sat up and pulled me to his chest. "Not your fault," he murmured.

He was trembling as well, as if the earthquake had burrowed deep into his body and was refusing to let go.

"Are *you* hurt?" I looked up at him, and he shook his head before kissing my forehead.

Then Catina gasped. "Look!"

I whirled to look in the direction of her gaze and saw the Popocatepetl had shot a puff of black smoke into the air.

"That is a *terrible* omen," she whispered.

"I swear—if that volcano erupts . . ." Nano's voice was hoarse.

"We'll be dead before we can squawk," I said, and Juan snorted a laugh into my ear.

Nano shook his head and said, "Please don't encourage her."

"Can't help it, brother," Juan said, and sighed. And the sound somehow made Nano straighten and take stock of how Juan and I were holding each other. The fact that I sat on his lap, with my arms around his torso.

He locked eyes with Juan. There was something searching in my brother's gaze. Juan's hold on me tightened. I stilled, holding my breath, only vaguely aware that Catina was now looking between Nano and Juan and me. But I dared not even blink.

The muscles in Nano's jaw and forehead softened. He looked at me then, as tenderly as he had ever looked at me before, and gave me the tiniest nod. And although I did not think I had cared for my brother's blessing, receiving it felt like a boon. A tear slipped down my cheek, mingling with the sweat, and I smiled back.

We stood and searched around for anything that might've fallen off the horses, which turned out to be a couple of guajes, a small parcel of tortillas, a rope, and a rabbit pelt. I had kept my bow and quiver strapped to me, as well as the satchel with Nantzin's journals. Catina had tied her mittens to her belt, but I had taken mine off and placed them on the saddlebag, and now they were gone. Nano had his sword and woolen cape. Juan hated the cold and had kept even his ear covers on the whole time we were riding.

There was no question, however, of whether to turn back. Not one of us mentioned it. We all dusted ourselves off and steeled ourselves.

"I think we should bow to him," said Catina, and so we knelt before the mountain, in the hopes that it would appease the Popocatepetl.

Then we carried forward with the intent of climbing over the body of his sleeping lover, for she held the treasure of my mother's last words hidden within her mighty chest.

CHAPTER 29

Isabel Cano

3 April 1551

The journey to the little camp felt endless, every breath a struggle. The path sloped at an angle that made my calves scream. The vegetation was dry. There were fewer pines and trees, and only grassy, spiky bushes as far as we could see. We were starving, but held off snacking on the few tortillas we had. There was no game anywhere, and I soon grew angry with myself for having missed the squirrel and hare earlier in the day.

"I have a pounding headache," Nano said. We thought it might be because of the fall, but soon, all of us had sore heads. The cold air seemed thin and insufficient to my lungs, even though I gulped it down until my throat was screaming.

The sky had darkened and was peppered with the glow of a million stars by the time we reached the tiny abandoned hamlet that Toño had described to us the night before.

"This must be the place where we are meant to camp," I wheezed.

We huddled inside a small hut. "Look at this," Nano said.

There was a blackened pile of kindling in the middle of the hut.

Juan said, "It's only recently been extinguished, maybe in the last day."

We shared a look. "Hopefully someone friendly," Nano said.

"Anyone have flint to light it?" I asked, but everyone shook their heads. Our stones had been inside a saddlebag too. We had been too intent on the climb to look for more, and now it was too dark, too late.

"I'll take first watch," said Catina between chattering teeth.

A relentless gale blew all night, sneaking through every crack and crevice, shaking the hut and boring like a slick knife through every layer of cloth and into my skin. Juan and I held each other, too cold and miserable for it to mean anything. Nano curled up next to my legs, too frozen to feel any sense of pride. Around midnight, Catina began to cry.

"My calf is aching," she whimpered. I left the little comfort of Juan's arms to rub it for her until she fell asleep, shivering, with Nano's arms and cloak around her.

Not an hour or so after that, the wind died down. We ate two frozen tortillas each and decided to carry on, as Toño had said it was best to leave before dawn and we weren't going to sleep anyway. It was difficult to follow the trail in the near darkness, with the bushels of straw-colored grass in the way, and we got lost twice before we found the path again.

After a while, the walk and climb warmed us, and even Catina said, "This is not so hard." Soon, however, the route climbed steeply and the ground became rockier, with sharp flint and obsidian rocks strewn about like pieces of broken glass.

"We ought to find some good flint for later," Juan said, but as soon as he stepped away from the path, he slipped and cut his knee open.

He swore, very unlike him. In the too-near distance, there was another rumble from the Popocatepetl, sending my heart aflutter, conjuring the image of another earthquake sliding the ground beneath our feet, burying us in stone.

As I stepped to help him, and almost as if she knew my thoughts, Catina mumbled to herself, "And the deceased are haunted by the fear of clashing mountains."

Nano said and signed, "What are you saying?"

Catina answered, "It's a line from an ancient poem describing the path to Mictlan. The journey the dead make as they find their way to the underworld."

"Sorry I asked," Nano muttered. We carried on in a line led by Nano. I followed, and Catina and Juan brought up the rear.

At some point Nano made a sound of disgust, stopped, and pointed. I rushed forward and could soon make out the curling pile of excrement left too close to the path.

"Is it fresh?" I asked.

"I would touch it to see if it's still warm, but I don't think it looks warm," Nano said. "It doesn't look dried up either, though. I'd say it's quite fresh."

"That's positively vile," groaned Catina.

"What are we looking at?" Juan said. "Oh."

"Caligula's for sure," I said, feeling a pang of dread. What if we were already too late? What if they had Nantzin's journal already? How would we ever get it back?

"Let's be on our guard," Nano said, and we kept walking in the same order as before.

Even as the sky lightened, the temperature dropped, like a quickly retreating tide, the higher we climbed onto the mountain. We followed a route of loose scree and dirt.

My nostrils dripped and dripped until they clogged over and I had to breathe through my parched mouth, and the tips of my ears throbbed as gusts of wind battered my ear canals, making them ring painfully. For hours I walked, alternating between covering my ears until my fingertips froze and sticking my hands underneath my armpits until they warmed. Catina began to limp, and she and Juan were soon trailing quite a way behind Nano and me. We stopped to let them catch up and took our first break when the sun rose in beautiful soft tones over the dark plain stretching below us, though the mellow light failed to bring any more warmth.

Juan passed one of the guajes around, and we drank and ate another tortilla each. "We've eaten half of them now. We must save the rest for later." His voice was a visible plume of steam, swirling like the Mexica symbol used to convey speech in a painting.

Nano looked around and swore under his breath.

We followed his gaze, which was facing the mountain, and my spirits sank. The exhaustion from not having slept last night slammed into my bones, nearly dragging me to the ground.

Because the path ended in just a few feet, and there was no clear trail rising over the volcano's body, only a mess of boulders and rocks that formed a solid, impenetrable wall.

"How are we ever going to get over that?" Nano said.

"I . . ." I had no answer. But then, I thought, we could not stop now.

We had come so far. And maybe, just maybe, I thought with a twist of raw, indescribable emotion, these were the same thoughts Nantzin had thought. This was how she had kept herself going, even as the cruelties of conquest continued to pummel her.

Terrors upon terrors, losses upon losses were hurled at her for years, and she was knocked down so many times. Yet she lifted herself back up again. Because she knew she owed it to herself, to her family, to her lineage to survive and keep going.

And now, I owed her too. I would not fail her.

"Isabel, are you unwell?" Juan asked, head tilted in concern.

I touched his arm, smiling to convey my gratitude, and said, "I . . . I'm just thinking—that wall must be Iztaccihuatl's feet, like Toño said. We'll help each other climb over them. One step at a time." I smiled to cheer them on. "And we have that bit of rope."

We scrambled on our hands and knees over the ridge wall. Juan took the lead and was surprisingly agile and flexible, a mountain lion, sure of his footing and strong. I followed, bleating like a newborn goat, much less confident. My arms and legs trembled as I pulled myself up the rock wall. My skirts billowed in the air. A single thought circled around my head: if I were to fall, I would surely break my skull or neck.

I stopped when I reached a large boulder to sit and rest and wipe my sweaty, dusty hands, and to help pull up Catina, who was clambering behind me, wheezing and groaning. We clasped hands, but somehow her foot missed a hold, and she slipped down with a bloodcurdling scream.

"Hold on!" I growled as Catina dangled and tried to find a perch for herself. Nano panted a string of colorful curses as he scrambled underneath her and pushed her up at the same time as I pulled her over with as much strength as I could muster. She landed on top of me, and I held her quivering body. Nano was soon beside us.

He held us both to his chest and snarled, "*Why*, God, did you burden me with a pair of headstrong fucking sisters? Jesus, I think I might vomit." But then we locked eyes and burst into a fit of hysterical laughter.

Catina looked between us and joined in, tears streaming down her face.

"Everyone safe?" Juan shouted from way above.

"Safe but not sound!" I shouted back. Our laughter gently died down to hiccuping breaths and then silence. We sat for a moment longer, looking at the beautiful ravine stretching down into the mountain pass we had traversed through yesterday. On the other side of the small dipping valley, the Popocatepetl rose like a mighty titan into the sky, half lit up by the rising sun, half in shadow, his peak surrounded by a ring of white clouds that contrasted with the straight gray column of smoke emanating from his crater.

"Do you think Nantzin is watching us right now?" Catina whispered hoarsely, looking into the distance. "Do you think she's proud?"

And the sound of her little voice asking the one question I dwelled on each day made my chest throb with that familiar longing again, that swelling ache of loss I had begun to recognize as a permanent feature of this new life without Nantzin. I sensed the tide of black grief that had pooled within my heart after she'd died, and which sometimes rose unexpectedly to remind me that she still lived inside me, that I still loved her. Tears clouded my vision, but I no longer cared to hide them. I nodded, because I could not speak.

Nano clutched us closer, then let go and signed, "She *is* proud of us. She was always proud. That, I do not doubt." He shook his head. "What I still don't understand is why she didn't just . . . sit us down and tell us these stories. Why would she test us this way?"

"She couldn't have told us," I signed. "She couldn't have said half of these things to us out loud, not really. Can you imagine what Marta would've done if she'd overheard any of it? Papa would've disapproved too. He didn't even like it when she told us stories of the gods at night—he said they were fairy tales. No . . . Nantzin had to show us instead. She wanted to show us these glimpses of the world as she knew it, before it was torn from her."

Nano breathed in the cold air. "Perhaps you're right. But you have to admit, asking your children to climb to the top of a volcano is a rather peculiar thing to do."

I looked up at the remaining wall and signed, "And there's still a long way to go."

We slowly climbed to the top of the feet and over the wall of boulders and stones, where Juan was waiting for us with a beaming smile.

"Look at all this snow!" He flapped his arms and cloak like an excited, oversize bat, and we laughed and exclaimed in delight, then bent over to scoop some snow. I squeezed the icy material in my fist, and it flattened into a small ball with a satisfying crunch.

"It's freezing, truly freezing!" Catina said before dropping it back and drying her hands on her skirts. "It pains my fingers, from how cold it is."

Nano put some in his mouth and swallowed, then immediately clutched his forehead and swore. "Ay, mierda! It's burning my brains!"

I roared with laughter, nearly folding in half at the look on his face.

"But . . . Toño said it was a delicacy!" Catina pouted. "I was looking forward to trying it."

Juan could hardly keep a straight face. He looked away so Nano and Catina wouldn't see, and pointed. "Come now, those must be the knees."

The path ahead was an undulating ridge covered in alternating patches of rock and bright, gleaming snow. We walked on, Juan in front this time, me behind him, then Catina and Nano. After some hours, blisters formed and burst on my heels, and I hobbled along in excruciating pain. But soon the snow blanketed the entire terrain, and my feet were so numb from the cold seeping through the soles of my frozen boots that I could no longer feel anything.

The sun rose higher, reflecting a piercing brightness that made my eyes water. But it was not bright enough to provide relief from the chill, especially when the wind began to blow, sending eddies of snow swirling around us. I suddenly missed my long hair and the protection it would've given me in this weather. I hugged the rabbit fur around my neck and crossed my arms over my body in a futile attempt to keep a little bit of warmth.

The ridgeline wound up and down, up and down for hours. There was no vegetation, no sign of life, only endless peaks and false summits, which we sometimes had to scramble over on our hands and knees. We were so unbelievably high now, we had a bird's view of the land, though the eastern side of the ridge, far down below, was a sea of clouds pierced here and there with the tips of other hills and mountains. To the west, the valley Nantzin had reigned over was mere patches of color: straw-colored earth, miles of green forest, and the enormous, glimmering blue-brown expanse made up of our five beloved lakes.

The snow built up thicker as we reached a white ravine, but Juan was sure footed, and he somehow found the path through. I stepped where he stepped, and so did my siblings, so it seemed as though only one person was walking, not four.

We were too hungry and tired and cold to speak. Except once, when the wind blew, carrying with it the sound of shrill voices. We stopped and looked around the mountain, but there was only snow, ice, and rocks as far as we could see ahead and behind us. A gust of wind burrowed under my hardened skirts and bit into my skin, and I flinched, burying my face in my arms.

Nano managed to speak through his convulsing jaw. "You—you know, now that I think of it, there were no footprints on the path when we started, were there?"

Juan shook his head and mumbled, "I haven't seen any on the journey."

We looked at each other. Perhaps Pedro and Gonzalo hadn't made it this far after all. It surprised me to feel a tinge of worry for them, mostly for Gonzalo, but there was nothing we could do. If we left the ridge, we might either fall to our deaths or lose our way and starve. We continued for what seemed like the entirety of my life until Juan stopped again and shouted, "Do you think that's the stomach? A round bowl of ice, like Toño said."

We slowly caught up to him and stared down below us.

"How on earth are we going to get down there?" Nano asked.

"You and your obvious goddamn questions!" I snapped, and placed a tentative foot on the ice, but as I lifted the other, the one on the ice slipped from underneath me. My stomach swooped to my throat and I screamed as I plunged down the bowl, my vision blurring as I slid ever faster on my back, even as I tried to find a grip on the ice. It was not too far down when I slowed to a stop at the opposite end, a bare, rocky hillside.

My hands were burning, thrumming to the imaginary beat of a thousand tiny pickaxes. I forced myself to look at them and half snarled, half shouted in rage.

Two of my fingernails had been ripped off. My palms had been grated raw and were bleeding down my wrists. I glared back up at the ridge. Through my tears, I saw the others were scrambling on their backsides toward me, slowly, occasionally sliding and letting out a startled shout. They kept asking if I was hurt.

"I'm fine! I'm all right! It's just a bit slippery!" I cried, voice cracking as I attempted to ignore the throbbing in my skin and fingers. But it felt like being singed by flame.

Juan reached me first. He hissed as he lifted my wrists to look at my quivering hands, handling them with as much gentleness as one would a wounded bird.

His thick, curly eyelashes had frost on them, his lips had split and cracked, but he looked at me apologetically and mumbled through chattering teeth, "My shirt is filthy, I don't think I should bandage them with it."

I winced at the thought of anything touching my hands, but then the wind blew and punctured my every cut with its sharp, frozen teeth. I whimpered, "God, it hurts."

Warm tears trailed down my frozen cheeks.

Catina reached me next. "Oh, Isabel," she whispered, and immediately took off her rabbit fur mittens. It was agony to put them on, and I flinched at the thought of having to peel them off later, but it seemed a better idea than leaving my hands exposed.

Nano and Juan helped me to get back on my feet again, and we clambered up the dirt hillside on the other side of the stomach bowl, back up to a rocky spiral.

Catina said, "That must be el ombligo, the belly button."

Beyond the spiral, on the other side of the bowl, was Iztaccihuatl's flat chest and the twin peaks of her breasts. The blinding sun was high, and something silver and pointed gleamed near the volcano's left bosom.

"Is that a pyramid?" Juan asked, excitement palpable in his voice.

"Only one way to find out," I said. My whole body seemed to be convulsing with a mixture of pain and cold and exhaustion.

"Madre de Dios, I'm tired," said Nano.

We all linked arms and limped and hobbled toward the strange, glimmering, small pyramid—so small that when we reached it, it barely came to our knees.

Nano tried to pick it up. "It's heavy! I think it's solid silver!"

He put it down, and we all hunched over to study it. Engraved all around it were symbols: a chapulin grasshopper, a small crescent moon, the Virgin of Guadalupe, all the places where Nantzin's story had been hidden. And on one of the four sides of the pyramid was a small impression, an eagle devouring a snake, the mirror image of the crest on all our rings.

Nano's face fell. "I gave my ring to Elvira!"

"And Catina to Tlaco," I said, holding out my hand to him. "But I still have mine."

I cringed as Nano peeled off my mitten and carefully took the ring off my bloody finger.

He handed the ring back to me, and I placed it in the matching indent.

It was a perfect fit.

I turned it, and the side of the pyramid opened downward.

Inside its plush, velvet stomach was Nantzin's last journal, and seven eagles the size of index fingers, carved from solid gold.

CHAPTER 30

Isabel Cano

4 April 1551

I reached in to pull out Nantzin's journal and tucked it safely inside my satchel next to the others. It would not do to read it now, with the wind gusting and the temperature dropping. Above us, wisps of clouds and moisture were beginning to swirl and grow in size.

"The weather is turning," whispered Catina, a worried look on her face.

I grabbed the golden eagles next, no longer caring about the pain in my hands. I gave two each to the others. "One for you and one for Elvira," I said to Nano. "One for you and one for your school," I said to Catina, who read my lips and grinned. "And one for you, and the other for the gold you paid the skeleton," I said to Juan.

"But that means there's only one left for you!" said Juan.

I shrugged as I gritted my teeth and put my ring and mitten back on.

Nano signed and said, "It doesn't seem fair. You're the one who convinced us all to come along. We would have nothing if not for you."

They all nodded and seemed to be about to argue with me when a roar split through the sky like a thousand cannons firing at once. We screamed and covered our heads and dropped to the ground, which shook for a moment beneath our feet again.

"No, no, no!" shouted Nano. We turned to look behind us.

The top of the Popocatepetl had blasted out a mighty plume of jet-black smoke high into the sky. A blink later, there was another deafening explosion, and a torrent of glowing, molten rock burst out from its crater like a gruesome fountain being siphoned from the deepest pit of hell. My mouth opened in a silent scream and I forgot how to breathe. Terror mingled with awe as the liquid fire crashed back down the Popocatepetl's summit, splattering it with a thousand glowing embers. A sudden warm gust slammed into our bodies, reeking of ash and sulfur.

"We forgot to thank Iztaccihuatl," gasped Catina.

"Let's get out of here!" Juan said, grabbing my hand. I winced but didn't pull away. Nano tried to carry the silver pyramid, but by the time we'd reached Iztaccihuatl's frozen belly, it was clear it would be impossible to scramble back up if he held it in his arms.

"Leave it!" I shouted, and he reluctantly put it down near the bare stone wall of the bowl, where we found several rocks to use as spikes to help us clamber back up the slippery glacier wall. Every step up was agony for my hands, and my face was encrusted with frozen tears by the time I emerged back up on the ridge.

Eddies of snow began to fall, first light and fluffy and then more heavily as we slowly trekked back up and down the winding ridgeline of Iztaccihuatl's torso and legs. The journey seemed to take five times as long because we were terrified of losing the path. We tied the rope to our wrists to make sure we did not lose each other either.

Soon, the sun began to set and the snow thickened, piercing our wet clothes, striking us like arrowheads, curling and twisting into horrifying shapes, a thousand frenzied beasts intent on clawing out our frozen hearts, wailing and screaming and raging a terrible song into the howling voice of the wind.

Juan slipped, yanking me down with him. Nano and Catina struggled to help us up.

"We'll never make it down the knees and feet!" shouted Nano. "I can hardly move my fingers, and it will be dark soon. We need to find cover!"

My skull and teeth were clattering with such fierceness I thought they would shatter. I looked around, but there was nothing, nowhere to take cover on this godforsaken ridge. A bubble of terror and panic threatened to swell up and blind me, a feeling white and feral as the sheet of snow mauling us. The certainty that we were moments away from death.

Then I heard the echo of a bark in the distance. No one else seemed to have heard it, and when I looked around to find its source, I could not see anything through the gusts of swirling snow. But then I heard it again.

I pointed with my rabbit mitten and pulled on the rope. The others followed, and I prayed. I prayed fervently to Nantzin, to Jesus Christ, and Huitzilopochtli and Tlaloc and Iztaccihuatl and Guadalupe as Coatlicue and the Virgin Mother both. I begged them to spare us. To spare the life of the people I loved most. I prayed to them at the same time as I raged and cursed at myself to go on, go on.

Don't you dare stop! Carajo! Don't you dare let Catina and Nano and Juan die, I said over and over as I followed the barking sound that only I seemed to be able to hear.

Then Catina pulled on the rope and pointed to a rock jutting ahead, in the shape of a terrifying yellow lizard. The spire of rock holding its body was also tinged yellow and somehow clear of snow. We trudged our way toward it and were hit by a gust of hot steam emanating from a crack on the wall, large enough for even Juan to squeeze through. We said nothing else, simply scrambled inside and into a pitch-black cave, which reeked of sulfur but was as mercifully warm as a temazcalli.

We slowly felt our way inside the narrow, damp, jagged tunnel, and stepped on several shallow puddles of scalding, steaming liquid that soon melted the ice on my boots and smarted the blisters in my feet. When we were far enough away from the screaming, biting wind, I pulled on the rope again.

"Let's not go too far," I said, voice low and hoarse, barely audible beneath the obscene growl of the storm raging outside. "We don't want to get lost and not be able to find our way out in the morning."

We untied our wrists from the rope and huddled next to one another on the hard, coarse floor, our backs to the wall. None of us spoke a word. We were too weary and frightened.

I could hardly sleep from the way my taut body was shuddering, and it felt like hours before the drifting steam eased into the spasming muscles of my arms and legs and softened them, before my fingertips prickled and stung and eased the worry in the back of my head of whether I had any feeling left in them. Eventually, my head relaxed on Juan's shoulder, and I fell into a deep, dreamless sleep.

It seemed but a moment later that I woke with a start and immediately groaned at the overwhelming ache pulsating from every sinew in my body. My lips and heels and the gashes where my nails had been were afire. I could hardly move. And I could not hear a sound. I thought, for a blink, perhaps I had grown deaf. Perhaps the deafness I was owed had finally come to claim me, and it was not such a bad thing after all.

None of it was bad at all, in fact. I was alive, gloriously so, as was Juan on my right and Nano and Catina on my left, closer to the entrance of the cave, though they were still fast asleep, curled on the ground. I glanced at the bright cave mouth and saw a piercing blue sky beyond, and realized that my deafness was simply a result of the stillness that had followed the dying storm.

Indeed, the wind had stopped screaming. The storm had passed. And soon enough, tiny, muted sounds began creasing into my awareness, droplets falling from the yellowing cave wall into the hot pools, Nano's gentle snores, and the scrape and echo of a pair of dragging footsteps.

This gave me pause.

It took some time for my mind to catch up because my thoughts were sluggish, battered down by a lack of food and the mad rush away from the summit and the gentle, mesmerizing curls of steam floating around our bodies.

But eventually, I turned and let out a cry of alarm.

The others woke too, grumbling and looking as worn as I felt, but their eyes widened when they followed my line of vision and saw that Pedro and Gonzalo had emerged from deep within the cave. Their clothes were ragged and torn, and Pedro had a filthy bandage wrapped around his left eye. Our brothers froze as they spotted us, and we stared at each other.

I stumbled onto my feet, ignoring a fresh spike of pain, and positioned myself in front of Juan and all the others, wobbling as I blocked their path.

"One wrong move, Pedro, and you'll be joining your dog," I whispered, for I could not speak properly. My throat was as hoarse as if I'd been screaming for days.

"Dogs, you mean," Pedro said with a mad, twisted smile. "Caligula ran away before we reached the cave. I cannot imagine he's alive."

So the barks I'd heard had been real. I felt a twinge of pity for the dog but still reached behind for an arrow, nocked it, and pointed it straight at my brother's leg. My arms screamed in agony, but I held the bowstring taut.

"Please don't," pleaded Catina from behind. "Pedro, it was me! I broke your bow two years ago, not Isabel. Please, can you two let it go?"

Pedro blinked between us, his two sisters, and a shadow passed over his face before he said, "Nano, can you tell Catina that this has nothing to do with a fucking bow?"

I felt Nano's movements as he signed to Catina, but she didn't respond.

"What's it about, then?" I croaked.

He hesitated, opened his mouth, and then closed it. I could not help myself. This war had gone on too long. I aimed at his heart and said, "Speak, carajo! Tell us the truth! Why are you so goddamn awful to us?"

"Because she loved me the least!" he blurted, and I flinched, nearly releasing my arrow. His shrill voice reverberated across the hollowed cave.

"She didn't even say goodbye! Can you imagine what that's like?" Pedro's voice cracked. "To be the only one she didn't say goodbye to? All of you had an audience with her. Every single one of you. Andrade and even that illegitimate cow Leonor saw her—more than once. Leonor came to visit Nantzin in the middle of the night to talk, for months. I knew because I could hardly sleep from worry, and I saw her coming and going. I knew our mother was dying, and everyone got to have a final word with her. She called every single one of you for a private audience, *except* for me!"

"She wanted to speak to you, she said so to me," whispered Gonzalo, but Pedro did not seem to hear him.

"And how is that our fault?" I shouted, though my voice hardly rose past a whisper. "You have chased us around the valley, threatened us, set your dog to maul Catina—all because you're sad you didn't say goodbye to Nantzin? We're *all* sad, pendejo!"

Pedro looked at Catina, gaze flickering to her leg, and said, "The bite was an accident."

I laughed. "Please. What else are you doing here, if not hunting for us? For Juan?"

"I want nothing to do with him." Pedro pointed his chin at Juan. "That was Andrade's ploy."

"I don't believe a word that comes out of your mouth. The fact that you're here, that you're free, means Gonzalo signed over the deeds of his towns to Andrade, which means you've let an innocent man take the blame for your crime." I glared at them both, at Gonzalo, who stared at me in awe, as if he'd never noticed me before.

I asked him in a singsong voice, "Were you hoping Nantzin had left you some gold at the top of the mountain?"

Gonzalo blushed and rasped, "You—you weren't at the convent. We got worried."

"Bullshit! Let's go," I hissed, out of patience. I took a step back.

"Wait! Gonzalo didn't sign anything," said Pedro. "When you were taken away by those guards and Nano ran after you, there was a huge fight. We held Andrade and the other guards back and barely got out alive. When we didn't find you at the convent, we figured maybe you'd come here because of those cushions Nantzin left you. We know there is no gold, that's just an old legend. We—I wanted to make good on my word to Papa, to take care of you." His voice trembled. "Because I know I failed. I broke my promise and I wanted to . . . to make amends."

"You liar! You're going to try to get away with the murder of Marta, who loved all of us, even you." I pointed at Pedro's face with my arrow, and my voice broke. "For some unfathomable reason, she loved you, and you strangled her to death!"

I might as well have slapped him, the way he looked at me.

Then his hands flew to his grief-stricken face, and a choked sound escaped his lips. He fell to his knees and began to sob, rocking back and forth, on and on, and I was so astounded that I could not move. None of us did.

Then after several painful moments he croaked, "I'm sorry."

His face was ugly, shining with tears, contorted in a mixture of madness and grief, and the bandage across his eye was soaked through. He pulled at his hair and screamed at the top of his lungs, "I'm sorry!" His cry echoed, on and on.

I slowly lowered my weapon as he mumbled in a trembling voice, "I can't stop seeing it in my head. My hands—what I did. In my dreams Marta is there, every night. So maybe you should shoot me. Spare me this agony. This shame. I can't live with myself."

From behind me, Catina quietly began to cry, and I admit, there was a part of me that felt a seed of pity. Until it was overshadowed by the hard stone of truth. By my promise to him—that I would never again let him get away with something he knew was wrong.

I squared my shoulders and pierced him with a look. "No. As much as I want to—and believe me, I want to—I'm not going to let you take the coward's way out. If you're truly sorry, cabrón, you'll come with us and turn yourself over to the Crown. You'll confess and face whatever sentence the judge sees fit for you. You'll serve your penance."

Pedro looked at the floor for a long time, then nodded, more to himself than anyone else. He wiped his nose on his sleeve.

"You're right," he said, surprising me again. "But first, let's get off this mountain."

◆ ◆ ◆

Without our horses, the journey back to Chalco lasted three long, painful, and uneventful days. Pedro did not try to run away or attack us, not even once. He walked on in front of me as if he were held in chains, though they were of his own making.

Once we had rested a night in Chalco, Toño helped us procure passage on a raft heading to the strait of Culhuacan. From there, it was less than an hour's walk to the causeway of Iztapalapa, which led straight to the city of Tenochtitlan.

We finally arrived, bruised, bleeding, filthy and exhausted, at the foot of the same courthouse where we had all gathered to listen to the judge reading Nantzin's will.

Gonzalo gave us some silver and a hug goodbye, even me, but Pedro and I only nodded at each other as he turned himself in to the royal guards and was escorted inside to face his fate. Gonzalo followed behind him, like a faithful dog. I knew he would be by Pedro's side every step of the way. He would defend him, whatever honor he had left, and even though I hesitated to admit it, there was beauty in that kind of fierce, devoted loyalty.

As for me, I vowed to not think of them again.

I only hoped Marta would be at peace. I prayed she would forgive me for not choosing her, my second mother. I hoped she would understand.

We used Gonzalo's silver to hire a carriage and immediately fell asleep inside, arriving in what seemed to be only a blink later to our eerily dark and quiet home. All the servants were new, though they recognized Nano, who told them we were his cousins. They drew us all baths and dressed our wounds and prepared a room for Juan.

Elvira arrived at some point while we were readying ourselves for dinner. She came in to greet us, surprised and delighted, saying that she'd recently heard gossip that the Moctezuma girls had arrived at the convent and taken vows of silence.

I knew then that Tlaco and Xoco had made it safely.

I sneaked away as Elvira and Catina attempted to converse in Hand Talk and rushed to Juan's chamber to tell him the happy news. I was surprised to find him leaning on his arms over the balcony railing, looking out at the lake, wearing our red livery.

"What on earth are you wearing that for?" I asked.

He started and laughed as he turned to face me. "Hello. It was the only thing that fit me that was clean."

I frowned. "We'll have to get you some new clothes at once."

"Oh, I thought I looked rather dashing," he said, and pranced toward me as if we were in the middle of a dance. His puffed-up breeches bounced along with the ruffles on his neck and wrists, and I snorted a laugh. He bowed and kissed my hand.

There was a gash on his cracked lips that was still healing, and he looked leaner, no longer boyish, yet somehow even more handsome.

A sly smile tugged at the corner of my lips. "You look dashing in anything."

He wiggled his eyebrows up and down. "Tepahtih Nayeli's outfit in particular?"

My whole face burned hot, and he chuckled again, ran his fingers across my knuckles, then turned my palm to study my bandaged fingertips. "How are they feeling now?"

"Better, thank you," I answered, relishing in the tender way he looked at me. My heart careened as he placed a hand on my back and gently pulled me close.

I stammered out, "And . . . and how is your knee?"

"Also better," he said, leaning toward me until his nose and forehead were touching mine. He closed his eyes, breathed deeply, and whispered, "Everything is better now."

"With you," I whispered, and pressed my lips to his.

That evening, after a mouthwatering feast of pickled nohpalli and chayote salad; roasted pork leg with salted, melt-in-the-mouth crackling; and turkey empanadas with saffron rice prepared by Juan's cousin Esteban, we gathered by the light of the fire in the living room and ate fruit and read Nantzin's last chapter together.

CHAPTER 31

Tecuichpoch

1532–My death, soon

How does one describe a marriage, a partnership, an affair of love and sadness, of joy and resentment that has lasted nearly twenty years? We have written my story so far in six of these pretty little leather diaries, but this tale is thrice as long as any of the others, and we don't have much time. I feel it. You can hear it in my voice, can you not? I can hardly draw enough breath into my lungs to speak. Today, I could barely eat, and I do hate to go hungry, for it reminds me of those terrible days of siege. My bones are in agony, but let us keep going. Bring me some water, please, my love. And hurry. You must write the end tonight. We must not delay, for this story is the most important of all.

Perhaps we ought to start at the beginning—because a sweeter time in my life I cannot recall, especially as I had been desperately lonely since Pedro's death. I had a young son who demanded every spare ounce of my attention and no family or real friends to speak to, only lawyers. I'd spent most of my twenty-second year of life mourning Pedro inside the hideous new courthouse at the newly rebuilt center of Tenochtitlan, submitting one petition after another to the Crown after its useless government took Tacuba away from me.

They had argued that the lands were given to Pedro as a bride prize, and that since he had left behind no will, they ought to revert back to the Crown. Already some other encomenderos had moved in, quick as rats to a new den. But thanks to the battles I'd fought against my sister Mariana, I had learned a few tricks about the Spanish system of law and immediately filed an opposing suit.

Emperor Carlos had since restored some of the towns to me, but more remained to fight over, and I was utterly exhausted by it.

So exhausted, in fact, that I ran straight into a man's chest as I turned a dark corner, and did not immediately pull away but stood instead with my hands covering my face. I was too weary, you see, to hide the sick mortification drawing tears to my eyes. I knew not what else to do. I could not let anyone see me cry, especially not a coyotl Spaniard.

As for him, the man simply stood with his arms frozen by his sides, as though afraid to touch me, though the back of my hands and my face were plastered on his chest, rising and falling along with his quick breath.

"My lady, are you unwell? Shall I fetch a doctor?" He whispered in perfect Nahuatl. And I was so stunned that I looked straight up into his eyes. Only then did he recognize me.

"My God, Doña Isabel, forgive me!" He sank into a low bow. "I ought not to have been walking so dastardly quick. The lighting in this building is simply atrocious. Please, allow me to introduce myself—Juan Cano, at your service. But pray, are you hurt? Do you need me to escort you to a doctor?"

I shook my head and thanked him, though I had barely listened to what he had actually said, for I had been focused on his accent. I could not comprehend how he spoke so well. It was not unusual for conquistadores and monks to learn Nahuatl—even some encomenderos did—but they normally struggled to pronounce words, or peppered their speech with Castilian. Yet this man spoke as though he had been born with a Mexica tongue. And I told him, "Your accent is very good, Señor Cano," which made him blush and grin.

"That is the highest compliment, Doña Isabel. I will treasure it always," he said. Then he bowed again and excused himself and his rudeness, looking genuinely torn as he begged pardon, for he was late for a very important hearing, though he would have rather stayed to converse with me, which, he said, had always been a dear wish of his heart.

Well, I thought, he was not unlike other Spanish courtiers, trained from birth to flatter and charm. I was immune to those tricks, and usually found them repellent.

I nodded goodbye and made my way back to my carriage and home to my little boy and thought nothing more of this Cano, except that his name sounded familiar, though I could not place where I'd heard it before. I also thought he'd had a lovely turn of expression, particularly when he had apologized to me. And he'd spoken Nahuatl so beautifully, as though he loved my language as his own, so I liked that about him. But nothing more.

Not long after, I forced myself to attend a special Mass held by Bishop Zumárraga to celebrate the consecration of yet another newly built church in the center of town. I had received word, through a servant I'd secretly placed in her care, that my daughter Leonor Cortés would be in attendance, and I wished to see her.

Unfortunately, Leonor had fallen ill and had to stay home. Thus, I had to withstand nearly three additional hours that week of standing and sitting and kneeling and listening to Latin, which I never managed to learn, while the peers of so-called New Spain scrutinized my every move. Worst of all, my sister Mariana sat only two places away from me and kept trying to catch my eye. She'd been trying to see me, to make amends, but I was still too angry with her to forgive.

It was for all these reasons that at the end of the service, I made my way through the throng into the empty confessional, at the side of the church, and stayed in there until it was quiet enough outside that

I thought everyone had gone. The priest never came, and I was glad, because all I ever did in those days was hold my baby, go to church, and attend hearings at the courthouse—I could not make up enough sins to keep me sitting there for long.

When I came out, however, I was startled to see Juan Cano leaning on a pillar in front of the wooden booth. He seemed surprised to see me but smiled warmly and sank into another low bow. I returned his greeting with the smile that meant nothing, the smile my mother had taught me, until he spoke.

"Doña Isabel, I cannot imagine what you could've possibly done to spend half the day in that box," he said in Nahuatl.

For once, I could not suppress the true smile, nor the words which came unbidden to my lips. "You have caught me, Señor Cano. I am but a coward, hiding from the crowds." I did catch myself before I said *coyotl* instead, though it seemed almost like he read my mind.

A look of pain flashed across his face, and he whispered, "We are the worst of wolves, señora. I do not blame you." I had nothing to respond, for I could not deny it, so I bid him good day and began to dawdle toward the church doors.

I moved slowly, because a part of me wished he would follow, and when he did not, I turned to see whatever could be the matter. It was then I saw how he covered his face with his palm and shook his head in frustration, and it was so endearing a gesture, to see a grown man struggling so, that it drew a bubble of laughter from my lips.

The sound echoed through the nave of the church. He looked up and turned the brightest shade of red. But instead of giving in to his shame, he laughed as well, and it was as pleasant a sound as I'd heard in months.

"Well, Doña Isabel, it seems you have caught me right back," he said, voice ringing.

"We are but a pair of cowards, then," I responded.

Juan Cano weaved quickly through the front row pews and into the center of the church toward me. He bowed again before looking intently into my face, and said, "Something tells me that is not truly the case."

Once again, my face betrayed the hint of a true smile. "No, it is not."

"May I call on you, please?" He beseeched me with a look.

And I responded, "Yes, you may."

Thus, it came to be that Juan Cano began to court me. He would come to my home for a cup of chocolatl and bring my son and me a gift: flowers, a wooden horse, sarapes or sweetcakes, and anything he felt we would love. We would talk about everything, except the war of conquest which had brought him to my lands, and he gave me excellent advice for the petitions I'd made to the Crown. He would play with my son and tell him stories, and they were so beautiful together that it made me ache with a meld of joy and sorrow, for I missed my husband Pedro and wished daily that he were here.

Juan sensed this too, for he never took liberties. He never called me by my first name, or even touched my hand. He would bow low and at times look at me with such intensity that if I'd had light skin like his, I would've burned crimson. But that was the extent of his pursuit.

Until one day, after about four months of daily visits, he hesitated at the doorstep.

He took off his feathered hat, and rushed to say, as if he did not wish to lose his nerve, "Doña Isabel, I hope, perhaps in vain, that you know why I come to see you and your son each day. Though I have wavered in the expression of these strongest of feelings, which I cannot deny myself when I am in your presence. I . . . firstly, I do not wish to presume that you feel anything for me at all. I am not worthy to be but a loyal and devoted servant and friend to you, which I pledge to be no matter your response."

His voice trembled, his olive eyes filled with tears as he gazed at me on the step above him and said, "But I should die a wretched death . . . if the cause of your hesitation was from my own omission. And I know you have but recently lost your dear husband Pedro, whom I knew personally as a good and honorable man. I cannot ever hope to replace such a man, such a father to your son, who is as precious to me now as if he were my own flesh and blood." And here his tears fell from the sheer love he felt for my boy.

I had never seen a man cry from love. Only from pain and death and humiliation and sorrow, and my own vision blurred in response. But he was not finished. He whispered in a hoarse voice, "It is . . . my greatest wish . . . to be a good, loving father to him. And above that—a good, loving husband to you. And you need not respond now. If you need more time, I am happy to wait. I have waited all my life for a woman such as yourself—for *you*, the most gentle and brilliant and most courageous person I've ever met. And if you will have me someday, I will count myself more blessed than the Holy Pope."

I smiled at this blatant heresy, and extended my hand to him, which he grasped as though it were a lifeline. He brought it to his lips and kissed it and then turned it over and kissed the center of my palm and my wrist, and his touch felt as luxurious as being wrapped in the finest furs. I swayed as a heady rush of pleasure and warmth traveled from my neck to my ankles, and it was this glorious feeling, more than any of the sweet, earnest words he'd spoken, that made up my mind.

I pulled Juan back up the steps and into my bedchamber, and except for those times when he has had to return to Spain to argue my case before the highest courts, we've never spent a night apart from each other since.

And yes, it was a hasty choice made in a haze of loneliness and hunger, but I do not regret it, though we have not been so well suited in other matters, such as the rearing of our five children, and other affairs dear to my heart, such as my desire to release my servants from slavery, which has grown ever more fervent through the years. We have argued on this matter, back and forth, back and forth until it has become a thorn in our marriage.

But at last, I have won. Or at least, my illness has.

For it is my dying wish to release those whom I've enslaved, and Juan has vowed to uphold this wish in my honor. The will has been signed, and there are many witnesses. And I cannot tell you the peace this knowledge brings me. Unlike the worry I feel when I think about leaving my children, and how they might fare.

For I know, in my bones, I have not been the best mother. There is no excuse, truly. Or perhaps there is. Perhaps you may one day understand, though it is difficult to describe what it is to become a mother and see yourself and those who came before you reflected in their very faces, their mannerisms, their speech.

Those very people who have caused you the worst of harm, who have perished in the most gruesome ways, who have betrayed you, come back to haunt you.

But you are meant to love them, these creatures you give life to. Even when you cannot stand another fight between them, the earsplitting noise and chaos and commotion that strains your body tighter than strings in a lute. The constant struggle to gain your favor, your attention, the relentless need for the touch that you find difficult to give—for what if you lost them, just like you have everyone else?

Surely it is best to hold back, to take a walk in the quiet forest instead of comforting them. The servants can hold them, their tutors or their aunt Marta. Because when you hold them, it feels just like holding your little brother when you both were grieving your mother, and it's too much to bear. You are terrified all the time, because you know deep in your marrow that losing any of them would be the *one* wound your heart and soul could never recover from. You have heard the keening cries of a thousand bereft mothers, and the mere thought of that kind of pain is enough to make you want to die.

You withdraw, even though you love them. And I do.

I love Juan Andrade, my tlatoani, who is *so* like his father and my own that I sometimes must blink twice when he speaks. I love my son Pedro, who storms and screams just like my cousin Cuauhtemoc used to before launching into battle. I love my son Gonzalo, who, when he thinks no one is looking, gazes at rocks and plants with as much curiosity and wonder as my brother Axayacatl used to. I love my son Juan Cano, as charming and savvy as his conquistador father. He is the one I worry about the least, for he is admired wherever he goes.

The girls, of course, are another matter.

They have been much easier to love and indulge, in a way I was never allowed to indulge myself—or you, my dear Leonor. How bittersweet, to have you here so close to me, at this late hour in life. I wish I could've spoiled you like I have spoiled your sisters. At least that's what their father and their aunt Marta always complained that I did.

And I admit I've utterly failed to rein them in like my mother did with me. I tried when they were little, but any resolve evaporated after they fell ill with fever. After that, I could not find the strength inside me to clip their wings. And for better or worse, in a way, it was the most healing thing—to watch them grow loud and unruly, even vicious at times. Like my darling Isabel, my little warrior.

Catalina would be the same, I believe, had she not been struck shy by her deafness, though she has strength in abundance. My youngest girl has the spirit of my mother at her softest, most loving moments, like she was in those few months we spent together before she died.

Through them and you, I see what I would've been like had I not been taught that my single purpose in life was to lower my eyes and yield. Through them and you, I recovered some of the sense of wonder and ease that had been ripped from me.

But I was never whole after the conquest, no matter how good my last two husbands were, no matter how beautifully, how softly, how dutifully they loved me, how much they fought for my lands and rights. It was not enough, and I am sorry that our children have paid the price.

Although I do hope that in reading this, they might come to forgive me. To understand how precious and fragile life is, a worthwhile gift that must be fought for and shared. I pray that they will not close their hearts to each other, to kindness and goodness and pleasure, even though it comes with the risk of grief and hurt. Truly, there are people on this earth who are worse than snakes. You must be wary, but persevere.

Because you are eagles like me, my children, you were born of my body. Your mother was the last Mexica empress. You are Moctezumas, and you belong to this magnificent land, Anahuac, and to the People of the Sun.

You shall carry forth the light, whatever that looks like for you. It pains me to not grow old to see it, but I know it shall be great, your own special tale for another day.

My hope is that you will be brave enough to find it.

POSTSCRIPT

15 December 1550

I, Leonor Moctezuma, natural daughter of Tecuichpoch, baptized Isabel, and the man known as Hernán Cortés, do hereby swear in the name of God our Heavenly Father and his Holy Son Jesus Christ that I have drawn this account as relayed to me by my mother between the dates of 10 July 1550 and 12 December 1550, two days before her death, and that it is a faithful rendering of her exact words to the best of my knowledge and ability.

It is her last wish that I share her testimony with all my half siblings upon her death. But, in the famous words of my father and his conquistador dogs, I must say, obedezco pero no cumplo.

I obey, but I do not comply.

It seems to me a folly to simply hand over the account of her extraordinary life to them on a silver dish.

These, the only words I ever truly shared with my mother.

I cannot, in good conscience, do it. For I have studied those petulant children of hers. Half of them do not wish to know her anyway.

Thus, I shall ensure that only those who are deserving of her truth receive it. I shall ensure that they suffer as I have suffered, for I wished my whole life to be close to our mother, as they were. To have her by my side each day, as they did. But I was kept from her. I was lied to. Though that is my own tale.

And perhaps it is petty revenge, but this is who I am.

Though if any of you survive and are reading this now, do write to me in Zacatecas. I dearly wish to know how you got on, and what you thought of the little tests I laid out for you.

Sincerely,

Leonor

EPILOGUE

1 May 1551

Querida Leonor,

I toyed with the idea of sending you this letter along with a poisonous snake in the hopes that it would bite you. Then I figured you are so full of venom it would probably have the opposite effect of killing the poor snake, and so I changed my mind.

We survived your "little tests," as you so charmingly described them. Nano, Catina, and I returned safe and sound from the summit of Iztaccihuatl about a month ago, along with Juan Juanes, the boy you met at Andrade's that night when you came to see us. The one you gave a full purse of gold to. Was that your way of assuaging a guilty conscience, by the way? And what about the seven golden eagles? That was also you, wasn't it, not Nantzin.

In any case, you may be pleased to know Juan and I are happily engaged, and we are putting the golden eagles and our dwindling inheritance to good use.

We are starting a school, Catina, Juan, and I—the Tecuichpochtzin School for the Deaf. And there is much to do. You cannot even imagine what it takes to run a school. Or perhaps you can, I would not know. Consider this an invitation, if you'd like, to write to me sometime, if you have any advice, and so I may get to know you better. You may address your letter to the Convento, as my counterpart there will be able to find me wherever I am.

I have also been instructed to tell you in this letter that Nano and Catina forgive you, whether you care for their forgiveness or not. They wish for you to know they bear you no ill will. I think it took them both a few weeks to come to that conclusion.

It came as a blow to all of us, truly, to read your postscript and realize you'd led us on a wild, dangerous chase around the valley. Nano was deeply upset with me for not listening to his repeated warnings that Nantzin had not arranged any of it. He did not speak to me for an entire week, thanks to you. But we're on good terms again. And I think perhaps he can see, as I can see, how much better off we all are because of this adventure. I hope it stings you, frankly, that I am grateful, for I do not think you meant it to be a good thing.

Sadly, Nano and his betrothed are leaving us to go back to Spain, to Cáceres, where Elvira's mother's family comes from. They will help finance the school from across the seas.

And this is the other reason I write to you, really, for I know you're much too rich for your own good, and if you wish to part with any more of your gold, we would be grateful to receive it.

All the best in your new home in Zacatecas.

Sincerely,

Isabel

ACKNOWLEDGMENTS

In the same way that Isabel and her siblings were guided throughout their quest, I, too, received an extraordinary amount of help from various people as I attempted to understand and recreate the five-hundred-year-old world of my people, and for that I am truly grateful and humbled.

Thank you to Paco Juárez Rodríguez and the Humedalia team for the most special day out canoeing around the chinampas of Xochimilco. Thank you for driving home the absolute necessity of preserving the two percent of what remains of our ancient lakes, which have been drained to the great detriment of our nation and of our native species, including the axolotl salamanders, which are now critically endangered in the wild.

If you are all inclined to help, you can "adopt" an axolotl via the National Autonomous University of Mexico program (visit https://www.ib.unam.mx/ib/adopta-axolotl/). This program aims to conserve the local wildlife in Xochimilco and strengthen the seven-hundred-year-old chinampa agricultural practices that are still alive today. If you do adopt an axolotl, I thank you in advance for your support.

Thank you also to Lucía de la Barra and Eva Vásquez Benítez for teaching me how to cook traditional mole and dulce de mamey, and especially for the priceless gift of books and conversation on pre-Hispanic dishes that formed the backbone of Isabel's love of food.

Thank you to all the staff at Monte de Piedad, for the personal tour of the old palace of Axayacatl and for all the resources. Thank you, Tía Maricarmen, for arranging that meeting.

Thank you to Marian González Hernández, our hiking guide and climbing expert on the volcanoes and mountains around the Valley of Mexico, for her endless cheer and descriptions of what it was like to summit the Iztaccihuatl, which unfortunately due to poor weather and atrocious levels of personal fitness, I did not manage to do.

Thank you to my sister, Ana Lucía Robleda, for accompanying me on that hiking journey to Iztaccihuatl, and for her rendition of what it was like to go through a warrior temazcal ceremony. And of course, thank you (*cough* you're welcome) for being my sister and inspiring all the simultaneous bickering and sibling love that is present throughout this story.

This novel would not have been possible without the many exhibits at the Museo Nacional de Antropología and the Museo del Templo Mayor in Mexico City, two of the best museums in the world, and the detailed and dedicated research from other authors. Muchas gracias.

I also want to thank the authors who contributed to the *Historia de la vida cotidiana en México*, edited by Pablo Escalante Gonzalbo; *Moctezuma's Children*, by Donald E. Chipman; *Visión de los Vencidos*, by Miguel León-Portilla; *Fifth Sun*, by Camilla Townsend; *Aztec Women and Goddesses*, by Miriam López Hernández; and *The Aztecs*, by Richard F. Townsend. This is not an exhaustive list of references, but these are the books I consulted most heavily, and which I consider must-reads in the subject.

Researching and writing a book is only part of the journey. Publishing it is another matter, and I want to thank my superhuman agent and her team, Johanna Castillo and Victoria Mallorga at Writer's House, and Alexandra Torrealba, my lovely acquisitions editor at Amazon Crossing, for your encouragement and excitement in bringing this second book of mine to life.

A thousand thanks to my entire Crossing team, for being absolute superstars and caring so much for my first two babies. Thank you, Taylor de Lano, for looking after all the authors at Crossing so well. To my publicists, Rachel Gul and Kelly Pike, thank you for your excitement and the many ways you've tried to get this book noticed. Thank you to my editors: Stephanie Gorton, for all your helpful and wise suggestions; Jenna Justice, for your brilliant copyedit! Thanks also to my production manager, Andrea Nauta—for bringing this book out in less than a year, which is light speed in publishing. Thanks massively to Laura Dailey, for your hawkeyed proofread. Thank you also to Emily Mahar for such a brilliant new cover and Rob McCaleb for my first ever book map! It is so beautiful.

Thank you also to the lovely Mariely Lares, author of *Sun of Blood and Ruin*, and Constance Black, for your excellent feedback in my early drafts and your friendship most importantly. To all my author friends—you know who you are—thank you for keeping me sane in this wild business. Your support means the absolute world.

Thank you to my comadre Colleen Ferries and my loveliest friend Laura Skilleter, for flying from Australia to the UK to support me in the launch of my debut novel, *Daughter of Fire*. And to every single one of my friends and family across the world who have cheered for me and put up with my constant reminders to please, *please* buy my books and share them and review them. I never take it for granted when you do.

I love you all so much.

Thank you to my parents, as always, for your unwavering support and enthusiasm for this writing passion of mine, and all my other projects. Thank you for flying to help me whenever I need an extra hand; thank you for being amazing grandparents to my boy. Thank you for keeping the pride and love of Mexico and our culture alive in our hearts and our homes as we moved across the world.

Thank you to my son, for expanding my heart in ways I never knew it could.

And to my husband, Craig, who has learned to make tortillas from scratch so I can eat them whenever I want, who cries when he listens to mariachi, who belts out every word to "México Lindo y Querido" after he's had a few tequilas, and who keeps trying to learn Spanish so we can teach our son together. Thank you for loving Mexico alongside me.

And finally, gracias . . . to one of the greatest loves of my life—to Mexico—and our good, courageous, resilient, hardworking, honorable, talented people across the globe. I wrote this story with you and for you, and I hope it makes you proud. I hope it brings you strength in these times when we are once again being vilified and scapegoated and mistreated.

I hope it reminds you that we are seeds.

AUTHOR'S NOTE

Not much is known about Tecuichpoch or her daughters, except the basic facts relayed in this story, such as that Tecuichpoch was the daughter of Moctezuma Xocoyotzin, that she was around eleven years of age when the Spanish arrived, and that she and at least three of her half sisters were given as a "gift" to Cortés upon his arrival in Tenochtitlan.

We also know that she was married six times and was the primary consort of the last huey tlatoani, Cuauhtemoc, who defended Tenochtitlan in the final, doomed siege against the Castilians. It is also true that Tecuichpoch, later known as Isabel Moctezuma, la Señora de Tacuba, was arguably the most important woman in New Spain at the time.

She left behind a will where she famously freed all her slaves, which was heavily remarked upon. And yes, she had seven children who fought for decades over her inheritance.

Her two legitimate daughters, Isabel and Catalina, were accepted into the Convento de la Concepción de la Madre de Dios, a prestigious nunnery that only admitted full-blooded Spanish girls. Their acceptance despite their status as Mestizas was a strong indication of their favored status as granddaughters of Moctezuma and daughters of la Señora de Tacuba. In May 1553, both girls renounced their rights of inheritance to Tacuba on behalf of their father and their Cano brothers. They specifically left out their brother Juan Andrade.

Regardless, all four of Tecuichpoch's sons married and had children. Juan Cano moved back to Cáceres and married Elvira de Toledo. They founded a great house that stands to this day. His progeny achieved the ranks of count and duke.

According to the internet, there are around two thousand descendants of Isabel Moctezuma still living today.

STAY IN TOUCH

Want to read Leonor's response to Isabel's letter (and a little something extra)?

To obtain this bonus material, all you have to do is join Sofia Robleda's monthly newsletter, *Author Antics*, which has updates on her writing, favorite books, and new projects.

Sign up here: https://geni.us/TOMG-bonus-content.

Don't forget to confirm your subscription and follow the link in your inbox to get the bonus content! Thank you so much!

ABOUT THE AUTHOR

Photo credit © 2025 Michael Oosthuizen

Sofia Robleda is a Mexican writer and the author of *Daughter of Fire*. She spent her childhood and adolescence in Mexico, Saudi Arabia, and Singapore, and completed her undergraduate and doctorate degrees in psychology at the University of Queensland, Australia. She currently lives in the UK with her husband and son, and splits her time between writing, raising her son, and working as a psychologist, supporting people with brain injuries and neurological conditions. For more information, visit sofiarobleda.com or follow @sofiarobleda on Instagram.